Enemy Series

THE
SACRIFICE

Books by Charlie Higson

THE
SACRIFICE

CHARLIE HIGSON

Hyperion
New York

Printed in the United States of America

First U.S. edition, 2013

10 9 8 7 6 5 4 3 2

G475-5664-5-13284

Library of Congress Cataloging-in-Publication Data
Higson, Charles, 1958–
The sacrifice/Charlie Higson.—First U.S. edition.
pages cm.—(The enemy; book 4)
Originally published in Great Britain by Puffin, 2012.
Summary: "Follows the dual storylines of Small Sam on his
search for Ella and of Shadowman's discoveries about Saint George
and the Disease itself"—Provided by publisher.
ISBN 978-1-4231-6565-1
[1. Horror stories. 2. Zombies—Fiction. 3. Survival—Fiction.
4. London (England)—Fiction. 5. England—Fiction.] I. Title.
PZ7.H5446Sac 2013
[Fic]—dc23   2012036699

Reinforced binding

Visit www.un-requiredreading.com

For Sam and Joe

I would like to thank David Cooper for showing me behind the scenes at the Tower of London, the place I would definitely run to at the first signs of a zombie uprising.

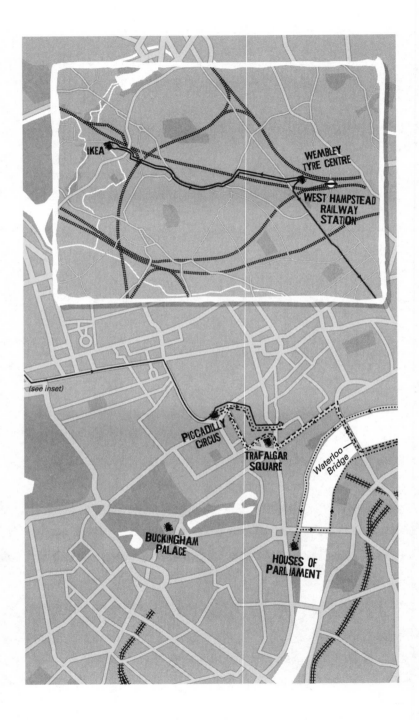

IKEA

WEMBLEY
TYRE CENTRE

WEST HAMPSTEAD
RAILWAY
STATION

(see inset)

PICCADILLY
CIRCUS

TRAFALGAR
SQUARE

Waterloo
Bridge

BUCKINGHAM
PALACE

HOUSES OF
PARLIAMENT

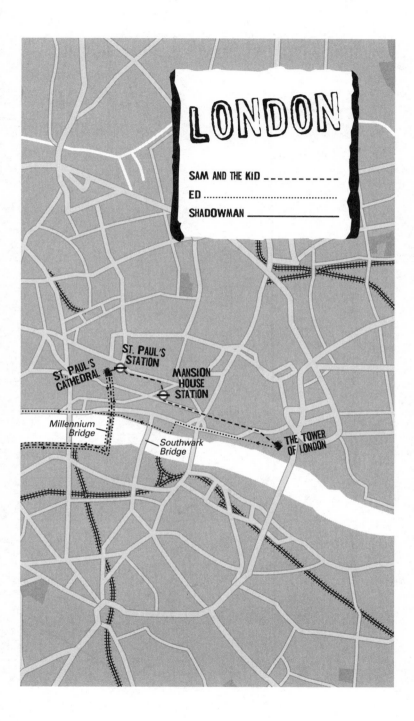

THE
SACRIFICE

PROLOGUE
THE GREEN MAN

Come closer. Don't make me shout. It hurts me just to talk. Don't get to talk much. Don't get many visitors. Come and sit with me. Come on. I'm not going to eat you. . . .

Ha, ha, ha, ha, ha, ha . . .

Sorry about that. Just my little joke. A typical dad joke. Why not? I *am* a father. I had two boys and a little girl. She came out wrong. My girl. Please. Don't hide over there in the darkness.

All right. Stay there, then.

Let me tell you about myself.

I am a fallen angel. Wormwood. I came down to earth with a bump. A bump so big the whole earth shook. Lay there for a long while, just dreaming. Not alone. Not then. Other angels had fallen from the stars with me. Some died— millions upon millions—never got to make friends with anyone. But enough of us lived.

Our first friends, they weren't much: small fry, hardly VIPs, just germs and microbes really. We lived among them. Long time ago that was. Back when everything was all just swamp and bog and butterflies. Then the crawling things made friends with us, took us in. That was swell. It was a bug's life. We could get about more, see something of the world, riding with the insects, praying with the mantises, battling with the beetles, eating crap with the flies. You know the sort of thing.

No?

Kids these days. They don't know anything.

God, I'm hungry.

Come closer so I can smell you better.

Where was I? Oh yes, back in the jungle—the big green. We were happy living inside the bugs, but we wanted more. We knew we were destined for greater things. It was the mosquitoes showed us how, the fleas and the ticks, the little blood-sucking vampires. They showed us how to move up in the world. How to make friends and influence people. As the bloodsuckers sucked, we moved on to bigger things. I did a bit of social climbing after that. Made friends with rats and bats and monkeys. But our best friends, the ones we really loved to get inside, were the human beans. Walking around on their two legs. Couldn't get enough of them. We got on like a house on fire. Though back then there weren't any houses, of course, not yet. Just trees and leaves and dirt and the big, big green.

Oh that *green*. How I miss it. We lived in a green world, my people and me. You should have heard the monkeys sing as they scratched their fleas. . . .

I've got you under my skin . . . That's what the human beans sang.

What's that you say? *I'm* a human bean. . . .

I guess I look like one. I guess a *part* of me is human. I'm a whole lot *more* than that, though, so stop interrupting and let me tell you my story. Because when I finish we're going to eat.

I was telling you about the big green.

Things went well. Year upon year. I couldn't have wished for more. I thought we were kings of the world. And the walking men did whatever we wanted. Still works. Haven't lost it. Even here the human beans bring me things. Mostly it's junk food. Rats and mice and cats and dead birds. When they get fired up, though, and the song is in them, when I sing to them so sweetly, they bring me what I really want.

You.

So sit still now while I tell you my story. There's no point running around like that, in the dark, you'll only hurt yourself. There is no way out. Do you think I haven't looked?

Come closer so I can smell you. We need to get ready for the feast. . . .

You probably can't see me too well; they keep it dark in here. They know the light hurts my eyes. But they must have told you all about me? Yes? I am Wormwood, the fallen star. Grew up in the green and the green got into me. Maybe you can see me glowing just a bit. My green skin. Wormwood, the star, the angel, the Green Man.

Now I was telling you about way back when we were kings of the jungle, me and the other fallen angels. Well, pretty soon. After only a few years, a few thousand years, maybe a few million, who's counting? But as I say, *pretty soon*—when you measure it against the stars up there, twinkling away like it was just a bit of fun—pretty soon there weren't any walking men left, only us angels. Making ready to birth our children into the green world.

What fools we were. Thinking we were kings. We weren't kings of anything. We were just dirt-eating monkeys. No better than the bats and rats and beetles who'd been our friends over time.

I was just a flea. That's all. A fallen flea. An angel, was I? Maybe once, too long ago to mean much. We'd been living inside the creatures too long. The walking men had been the best fit, but we were as foolish as they were. We'd spent too long with them. Their thoughts seeped into ours. We got muddled. Shouldn't ever have listened to them. Anyway, we asked them, "Is this the world?" And they answered us, "Yes. Yes, it is. It is all of it, the green, the muddy river, the trees, the dirt, the rats, the bats, and the monkeys."

This is the whole world.

And then one day we realized we'd been living in a closet. Ha, ha, ha, good one! Stuck there in the dark, thinking that the closet was the whole house. Because, you see, if you'd lived your whole life in a closet, that would be all you knew. You'd think there wasn't anything else.

There was a whole lot else, though, and it was big and bright and loud.

Sometimes I think we should have stayed there, dreaming that our little huts under the trees were the whole world. But one day, not so long ago, we opened the closet door and out we went, blinking into the sunlight. Too bright for us, got us all turned around at first, muddled and befuddled.

There was a lot to take in. Found we weren't alone, and we weren't kings at all. Soon saw there was a whole lot more to the world than green. There was blue and red, bright yellow, black and white, and gray.

So much gray where the walking men had made their homes, chewing up the green. I do still miss the green that was my home for so long. Here it's gray and black and dust and ashes.

Here? *Where is here?* Seems I've forgotten. I can remember the long ago better than the yesterday.

I'm hungry now. Been waiting a long time for them to bring me someone like you. You see, sometimes it feels like I'm the boss and they work for me, and sometimes it feels like they're in charge and I'm their slave.

Are you a boy or a girl? Not that I'm fussy. Your meat all tastes the same. Oh, come on now, don't be scared. I don't like that. Why do you think I'm talking to you? I want to be your friend. All I ever wanted was to make friends, just like I did with the germs and the fleas and the bats and the rats and the monkeys and the men and . . .

You know, sometimes I wonder if I remember any of it right. If I'm even who I think I am. Am I an angel or a flea or a walking man? That is the question. No, don't talk, don't make a sound, just listen, will you?

We'd made friends with walking men, you see, so that we could learn their language, walk in their shoes, think inside their boxes. And we grew to talk like them, and walk like them, and think like them. Maybe some of us even *became* men, no longer angels. As if the sucking flea could gulp down so much blood it might turn into the beast it was feeding on.

When the fear comes on me, when my memories flicker and die, I am scared that I am becoming just a man, just another walking man.

With a man's name.

Mark Wormold from Promithios.

Not Wormwood at all. Not an angel. Won't ever return home to the heavens where I was born.

Look at me. I was once the Starchild, the exterminating angel, the great flea, king of the world, the mighty Wormwood. I was born in the heavens, I fell to earth, I grew up in the great green, and then I crossed the blue and something went wrong.

I became a man.

Mark Wormold.

You see, the walking man, the human bean, *Mark Wormold*, was stronger than me. We fight over this castle, this body, every day, fight for the best seat in the house. Sometimes he wins and sometimes I win, but each fight makes me weaker, so that I fear that one day the walking man will kick me out or make me his slave.

Has that already happened?

Sometimes this place feels like a dungeon, sometimes a palace.

But I'm getting off the point. Which was . . .

God knows.

Never mind.

Never mind.

Let's get on with it. My stomach is turning somersaults.

Come over here, child. Sit a little closer. Soon neither of us will be hungry anymore. . . .

**THE ACTION IN THIS BOOK
BEGINS EIGHT DAYS AFTER
THE END OF *THE FEAR*.**

Unreal City,
Under the brown fog of a winter dawn,
A crowd flowed over London Bridge, so
    many,
I had not thought death had undone so many.
          —*The Waste Land*, T. S. Eliot

1

Small Sam wasn't dead. His sister and his friends all thought that he'd been killed, that the grown-ups who'd snatched him from the parking lot behind Waitrose had eaten him, but right now he was walking across the grounds of the Tower of London with the Kid and a load of other children. They were heading for the White Tower, a big square lump with smaller towers at each corner that sat bang in the middle of the castle on a small hill. Sam, who was something of an expert on castles, knew all about the White Tower. It was the keep, the first part of the castle to be built here. William the Conqueror had started the building work in the eleventh century, with stone specially brought over from France, and his son, William II, had finished it.

Sam felt like he was living in a dream. He'd always been obsessed with knights and castles and fantasy. He'd lost count of the number of times he'd seen the *Lord of the Rings* films. And now here he was, actually living in a real-life castle. Some of the other kids even wore armor and carried medieval weapons. Though they had to leave them at the door as they filed inside.

The boy in charge, General Jordan Hordern, had called a council of war, and everybody in the castle was expected to attend, even newcomers like Sam and the Kid.

Once inside, they climbed to an upper floor, where there was a big room with windows on all sides. They found places to sit on the wooden benches that were arranged around the edges. Sam, who had visited the Tower several times, tried to remember what this room used to look like. He couldn't picture it. The local kids had removed the exhibits and returned it to how it must have looked in the Middle Ages. There were banners and pennants hanging on the bare stone walls, and candles lit the dark interior. A long table had been set up across one end, and behind it stood four guards with halberds—double-handed weapons that looked like a cross between an ax and a spear. There was a smaller table to one side where two girls and a boy sat, writing on loose sheets of paper.

Ed came over to Sam and the Kid. It was Ed who'd found the two of them a few days ago, wandering, tired and wet, along the road that led to the Tower, and he'd taken it on himself to look after them. He still couldn't quite get his head around the fact that they'd survived for so long out there by themselves and had made it here alive. It was up to him now to make sure they stayed that way. By finding them, they had become his responsibility.

"You just sit here and listen, okay?" he said. "Just watch."

He glanced at the Kid. He was an odd boy, odd and unpredictable, and had his own way of talking. He was prone to speaking out, and Ed didn't want him to pipe up during the council.

"What's going on?" Sam whispered.

"To tell you the truth, I'm not sure," Ed replied. "But I have to be over at the council table with the other captains. I'll explain anything you don't understand afterward."

He looked at the Kid again, holding his gaze.

"Don't be tempted to join in. All right?"

"Aye, aye, Skippy. Message received and misunderstood."

"Seriously, Kid, zip it."

The Kid zipped it, miming the action.

"I'm as much in the dark as you are," Ed went on. "General Hordern called a special meeting of the council, so I guess he'll tell us what this is all about."

"That's him there, isn't it?" said Sam, and Ed turned to see a boy with thick glasses come into the room flanked by two more guards.

"That's him. I better go. Remember, zip it."

Sam watched Ed go and take his place with several other kids who were settling down at the long table. Sam suddenly felt nervous. Aside from Ed, he didn't really know anyone else here. He felt like a new boy starting in big school. Other kids were always whispering about him and pointing. He felt safe with Ed. He'd been a bit scared of him at first. Ed had an ugly scar down one side of his face that pulled it out of shape, but Sam had soon learned that he was kind and friendly and not frightening at all. Sometimes, though, Ed would go quiet and stare into the distance. Sam didn't say anything, but he knew that Ed was sad about something. He didn't need to ask what. They were all sad in their own ways. They'd all lost family and friends.

Sam and the Kid had been left alone for their first couple of days at the Tower. They'd been given food and allowed to sleep for most of the time. Now they were feeling more normal, and Ed had offered to show them around properly. They'd just been getting ready when they'd been told to come to the meeting.

Jordan Hordern sat down, flanked by four boys and three girls. He waited, blank-faced and unreadable behind glasses that were held together by Band-Aids around the bridge of the nose and one arm.

He waited for the room to fall silent. Didn't have to say anything. It was understood.

He looked around.

General Hordern couldn't tell anyone, but the truth was that he could hardly see anything at all anymore. It wasn't just that the lenses in his glasses were scratched and old. His eyesight was steadily getting worse. There were dark patches in the center of his vision. It was still clear around the edges, so he had to look sideways at things to see them properly. He'd never liked to look people in the eye before, and now it was nearly impossible.

He wouldn't let the idea enter his thoughts, but it was there, lurking in the back of his mind. He was going blind. What use would he be then? How could he keep his position in charge here at the Tower if he couldn't see anything?

It was important that nobody knew. For now he had unquestioned power over everyone at the Tower.

The kids sat in absolute silence. He was pleased. He'd

known teachers at school who could never get a class to shut up. Jordan had given them hell, and now here he was, just a boy, able to control more than a hundred kids.

Sam couldn't take his eyes off the general. Jordan scared him. There was a stillness and a coldness about him. He was like a statue or a big old crocodile at the zoo. Sitting there without moving. Who knew what weird thoughts were going on behind that calm exterior?

Sam could feel the tension in the room. As Ed had explained to them, nobody knew what this meeting was about, but by the look of Jordan it was something serious.

At last the general spoke.

"Okay," he said. "Let's get started."

Sam had been expecting something medieval, full of *verily*s and *thee*s and *thou*s, and *aye* instead of yes. It was a surprise to hear Jordan talking so normally. But why not? They weren't really in the Middle Ages, were they? They were in the middle of London in the twenty-first century.

"This is a special meeting of the war council. In fact, it's a military tribunal. Which means it's a trial."

The kids on the side table started writing furiously. A hum and murmur went around the room, but it was quickly silenced when Jordan raised his hand. Everyone was looking around, though, trying to figure out who wasn't there. Who might have been arrested.

"A boy has been caught trying to steal food from the storerooms. As you know, when I took control, I wrote up a list of rules, and stealing is one of the worst crimes on it, especially stealing food. You all know the rules. So there's no excuse for breaking them. Having said that, I want this trial to be fair. So I will give the suspect a hearing. Bring him in."

All heads twisted around now toward the doors as a boy was shoved through them, his hands tied behind his back, an armed guard on either side of him. He was tall and fair-haired and had a bruise on one cheek. His shirt was slightly torn. He looked like he'd been crying, his eyes all red and swollen. Mixed emotions—fear, anger, defiance, hatred, and embarrassment—flickered across his features.

The boy was made to stand in front of the big table, and his hands were untied. Everyone in the room was staring at him.

"What is your name?" Jordan asked.

"You know my name, Jordan, you asshole," said the boy, and a couple of the kids giggled. Jordan didn't react; his expression didn't change; he didn't even blink. He remained cold, blank, patient.

"Tell us your full name."

"No."

Jordan raised his head now and stared at the boy. He so rarely looked directly at anyone that the effect was quite powerful. The boy dropped his own gaze.

"Bren, *Brendan*, Eldridge."

"And what have you been charged with, Bren?"

"Oh, for God's sake, this is stupid. This isn't a proper court. We're all just kids. I know I did wrong. So give me a slap and let's get on with our lives."

"What have you been charged with, Bren?"

"Stealing! You know it's stealing, okay? I stole some canned fruit. Big deal, boo hoo. Naughty me."

Jordan looked over toward the side table.

"The charge is stealing food."

"Big deal," said Bren.

Jordan paused for a few seconds before going on. "Without food we die," he said.

"Tell me something I don't know." Brendan gave Jordan a dismissive look.

Jordan ignored him. "Stealing from other kids is one of the worst things you can do," he said. "If we don't look out for one another, we're all going to die. Therefore, Brendan, I reckon stealing food is as bad a crime as murder."

"Oh, come off it, Jordan. It was just some canned peaches."

"Was it?"

"Yes, it was. You know it was."

Again Jordan turned to the side table.

"Make a note of that. The suspect has admitted to stealing the peaches."

"Hey," said Bren. "No, I didn't. I was talking hypothetically."

"I'm going to call Captain Ford for evidence," said Jordan, and he nodded to the boy sitting on his right, who had long straight black hair and Japanese features. The boy stood up.

"For the record, can you state your full name and occupation, rank, and regiment?" said Jordan.

"Seriously?"

"Just do it, Tomoki."

"My name is Tomoki Ford. Captain of the Tower Watch."

"Can you tell us how you caught the thief?"

"*Alleged* thief," said Bren. "If we're going to have a proper trial, then I'm innocent until proven guilty, aren't I?"

"You've already made a confession," said Jordan.

"I wasn't under oath."

"We don't bother with that. You already said you stole the cans of fruit."

"Prove it."

"Okay," said Tomoki. "About ten days ago Captain Reynolds of the Service Corps came to see me. He told me that he thought someone was stealing from the Tower stores. He'd noticed some small things had gone missing, and when he checked he found out that other stuff was gone as well."

He took out a piece of paper from his pocket and showed it to General Hordern. "I've written it all down. Do you want me to read it out?"

"No, just give it to the clerks afterward."

"Okay, so anyway, Captain Reynolds got his team to check much more carefully every morning and evening. It was soon obvious that stuff was being nicked nearly every night. Just small amounts—the thief probably thought that it wouldn't be noticeable. I told you about it a week ago." This was addressed to Jordan, who nodded. "And you told me to put a special watch on the stores. We built a hiding place and took turns to stake them out. We saw Bren come in just after midnight last night—he had his own key—and we saw him take three cans of peaches away in a backpack. We followed him back to his room in the Casemates and arrested him."

"All right, all right. This is boring," said Bren. "Three cans of peaches. I admit it."

"Once we'd locked Bren up, we searched his room," Tomoki went on. "And we found all this."

Tomoki paused as three kids brought in boxes packed

with food. The murmuring started up again. Someone whistled. Bren's head drooped and he looked ashamed.

"Do you admit that you stole all this as well?" Jordan asked.

"Yes," said Bren quietly.

"Were you working alone?"

Bren nodded and Jordan asked Tomoki if he agreed.

"We don't think there was anyone else in on it. That's why we followed him, to make sure."

"Do you want to say anything else, Bren?" asked Jordan. "I can't really see the point, but if you want to."

"No. I don't want to say anything. Just . . . I'm sorry, I suppose. It was stupid."

"Saying you're sorry won't change what you done," said Jordan. "You're a coward, Brendan. Stealing off of other kids. You're a traitor. You don't care about anyone except yourself."

"Yeah, all right," said Brendan. "I said I'm sorry."

"Okay," said Jordan. "So if nobody has any objections, then I reckon you're guilty."

"Yeah, okay. I'm guilty."

Tomoki sat down. "So what's the sentence, then?" he asked.

"As I said"—Jordan stared at Brendan—"I think stealing food from other kids is as bad as murder. So the sentence is death."

2

Nooooo!" Brendan launched himself across the table at Jordan, and the whole place went crazy. Kids were jumping up out of their seats, all shouting at once. This had taken them totally by surprise. Brendan, who was screaming a torrent of filthy abuse at Jordan, tried to wrestle him to the ground. He wasn't getting anywhere. Jordan was immensely strong and managed to throw off his attacker, seemingly without any effort at all. He rolled Brendan onto his front and pinned him to the ground, pulling his arm up behind his back. He held him there, increasing the pressure on his arm until Brendan begged him to stop.

Dusty and bedraggled, with dirt clinging to the tears on his cheeks, Brendan stood up. There was snot streaming from his nose, and his eyes were so raw and swollen it looked like they'd been punched.

"Take him outside," said Jordan, no hint of emotion in his voice.

Jordan headed for the doors, and the guards who had brought Brendan in retied his hands and dragged him along behind. The other kids were still in turmoil, milling around, talking excitedly to each other, eyes wide, waving their hands, not quite believing that this was happening.

Sam sat there, a concerned expression on his face, too young to understand his feelings. He didn't know the boy, Brendan, but he was shocked by what had happened.

"Heavy-duty," said the Kid. "Nobody expected the Spanish Inquisition."

"Do you think they'll really do it?" said Sam.

"Don't ask me," said the Kid. "I'm a stranger here myself. But strangers have left on longer trains before."

Ed came over to them; he had a boy with him who Sam recognized. He was called Kyle and rarely left Ed's side. Kyle was big and loud, always telling dirty jokes, very different from Ed. He acted as a sort of bodyguard for Ed, who, it seemed, could do nothing to shake the big square-headed boy off.

"You okay?" Ed asked, squatting down so that he was at the same level as the younger kids.

"Does this happen a lot?" Sam asked, and Ed shook his head.

"Never before. A few kids have been punished for things, but never like this. We better go and see what's happening."

"Will Jordan really do it?"

"God knows. I have no idea how his brain works."

"I think it's cool," said Kyle, grinning like an idiot. "This is gonna be good."

"Kyle!"

"What?" Kyle gaped at Ed with an expression of wide-eyed innocence.

"Nothing."

As Sam stood up, Kyle winked at him and said, "Baaaaaa," making little horns with his fingers.

"Shut it, Kyle," Ed snapped. Kyle just laughed.

"Why did you do that?" Sam asked. "I heard someone else make a sheep noise yesterday."

"It doesn't matter." Ed put a hand on his shoulder. "I'll tell you about it some other time."

Sam wanted to know now, but it was clear that Ed wasn't going to talk about it. He and Kyle strode on ahead, and Sam and the Kid followed them out to where everyone was assembling on Tower Green. Sam was familiar with this corner of the castle. He'd been sleeping in a room in one of the medieval timber-framed houses that lined the green on two sides. If it wasn't for the fact that most of the grass had been dug up and replaced with vegetables, it did very much resemble a traditional village green. In addition to the houses, there was a small stone church, and you could imagine you were deep in the English countryside rather than in the heart of London.

Brendan had been dragged to a cobbled area in the center of the green, where a chopping block was set up. It was a replica, dragged out of an exhibition in one of the towers, but it was solid enough, and next to it was a large and very real ax. Jordan must have arranged for this to be done while everyone was inside.

"This is where they used to chop people's heads off in Henry the Eighth's time," Sam told the Kid. "I read about it. Anne Boleyn and Catherine Howard were both executed here."

Ed shook his head at the sight of the block and ax. "Jordan's gone nuts," he said. "This isn't right."

Brendan's friends were crowding around Jordan, all talking at once, like soccer players arguing about a penalty decision with a referee. Jordan ignored them and came over to say a few words to Kyle, who nodded. Then he stood on the block to address the crowd.

"You may think this is harsh," he shouted. "But if we don't take our laws seriously, there's no point in having them. Without laws we'd be just like animals. The punishment for murder is death, we all agreed on that—"

"Only because we thought it would never happen," a girl shouted from the crowd.

"That's irrelevant," said Jordan.

"Who said stealing food was as bad as murder anyway?" asked another girl. It was clear that Jordan's decision was not a popular one. The kids were scared and angry.

"I did," said Jordan. "And I stick to it. Food is very precious now. As I said, if we don't have food, we die."

Ed pushed his way to the front of the crowd and walked right up to Jordan. "No one wants this," he said. "Stop it now."

"He has to be punished."

"Yeah? Okay, so who the hell are you going to get to cut his bloody head off, huh? Or are you going to do it yourself?"

"Me," said Kyle, stepping forward. "I'm going to do it!" He picked up the ax and took a couple of practice swings, kids jumping out of the way.

"Don't be stupid, Kyle," Ed protested.

Kyle shrugged. "It's a difficult job, but someone's got to do it."

Jordan instructed his guards to hold Brendan down on the block, but now even *they* were having second thoughts. They refused and backed off, hands up in surrender.

Jordan took hold of Brendan himself, ripped the shirt from his back, and forced him to kneel over the block, his bare neck on the rough wood.

"Now be a man, Bren," he said, holding him firmly in place. "Don't struggle. Accept your punishment."

"This isn't fair," Brendan sobbed. "You can't do this."

"He's right." Ed stood between Kyle and Brendan. "You're not going to do this, Jordan. You go on about what would happen if the law breaks down, but as far as I can see, if we start killing each other, then law already has broken down. For God's sake, the world's dangerous enough as it is without you making it worse. I won't let this happen. And I reckon most people here will back me up."

"So what do we do with him?" asked Jordan calmly. "How do we punish him?"

"There's another punishment. We talked about it when we drew up the rules. It's still pretty heavy, but if you insist on making a point . . ."

"What punishment is that, Ed?"

"You know what it is. You made it up. If it's the only way, then do it. But it's still your decision, not mine. I'm just reminding you of the option. Personally I think Bren's been punished enough."

"What is it?" said one of the girls who had shouted out before. "What are you going to do to him?"

Jordan thought for a while, his strong hands gripping Brendan. "Okay," he said at last, and let Brendan go. "Ed's asked me to be soft, and this time I will be. But I want you all to remember this. The law's the law. We didn't make the rules for a joke. If you break them it's serious."

"What's the other punishment?" the girl repeated. "Tell us."

"Exile."

3

Sam, Ed, and the Kid were standing on top of Byward Tower, the inner gatehouse at the castle. They were leaning on the battlements, looking down as Brendan was led out of the gates and along the walkway toward the outer gatehouse, Middle Tower, which had been the main visitors' entrance to the castle. The walkway passed over the flooded moat, and once again, with the traffic of London stilled, the crowds gone, and the kids in their shining armor, Sam felt like he had slipped back in time to the Middle Ages.

There was a gang of kids working in the moat, standing up to their thighs in water the color of coffee. They were covered in mud and were working with shovels and buckets, slopping muck everywhere. They looked up and stared as Brendan went past, then returned to their work.

Brendan walked with his head and shoulders slumped. He'd been given a pack with some food in it—some of the same food he'd stolen—a sleeping bag, a bottle of water, a sword, and a knife. Four boys with halberds marched beside him. Kyle, Tomoki, and Jordan Hordern walked at the head of the little procession; a small group of Brendan's friends brought up the rear. Nobody else had come to see him leave. It was too unsettling. This was nearly as bad as cutting his head off. Everyone in the Tower feared being alone in the outside world.

"What'll happen to him, d'you think?" Sam asked.

Ed sighed. "I hope he finds some other kids, another settlement. There must be some out there."

"Like at Buckingham Palace," said Sam.

"What's at Buckingham Palace?" Ed asked.

"My sister, Ella. She went there with all my friends. Another boy told them it was safe."

"I hope he was right, for her sake." Ed smiled at Sam, the scar making it look like a snarl.

"She's still alive," said Sam. "I know she is."

"Yeah, I'm sure she is. But it's hard to get there from here. He'd have to go through the no-go zone."

"What's that?"

"Okay." Ed pointed westward, toward St. Paul's Cathedral, then swung his arm slowly round to the north.

"We don't ever go that way," he said. "It's the old City of London, the business district. Not many houses or shops, so not much food to be found. Plus, it's weird in there. The sickos are dangerous and unpredictable. How you two ever made it through alive I will never know."

"We was half stupid, a third lucky, and three-quarters ferocious," said the Kid. Ed nodded, frowning slightly. Sam hardly noticed the Kid's weird way of speaking anymore, but Ed was obviously still getting used to it.

"Well, that's the no-go zone. From Aldgate in the north,

down past the Bank of England to London Bridge. It cuts us off from central London. So, whatever you do, don't go back into the no-go zone, okay?"

"Okay."

"Roger wilco Johnson."

Ed continued sweeping his arm around, like the hand of a clock making a full circle.

"To the east is fine," he said. "And it's safe to cross over Tower Bridge. It's quiet that way."

Sam looked at the bridge. It was the famous one that could be raised up and down to let ships through, and it had tall spiky towers at either end.

There was a shout, and they returned their attention to what was happening below. Brendan had made it through Middle Tower and was being taken across the wide-open space that lay to the immediate west of the castle, where several cars were parked and the kids had collected piles of scrap. Ed watched the sad little group of children, the scarred side of his face twitching.

"Maybe he'll be fine," he said. "I mean, you two sprouts made it by yourselves. Brendan's a pretty big guy, knows how to fight. There haven't been a lot of sicko sightings lately. Yeah, he'll be fine."

"Do you really think that?" said Sam.

Ed laughed bitterly. "Not really, no. He hasn't got a hope in hell unless he finds a safe place before nighttime."

Sam shivered despite himself, felt a wash of prickly goose bumps skitter over his skin. Seeing Brendan kicked out was upsetting him. He remembered how Brendan had looked when he knew he wasn't going to be killed. How happy he'd been and then how he'd changed when he understood what he'd have to do. What exile meant. He'd pulled himself together and shouted at Jordan. "I'm not a coward! I'll show you I'm not."

But everyone could see just how scared he was.

It had all been really heavy and it had thrown Sam. He'd felt safe here. Something he never thought he'd feel again in the awful hours after being taken from the Waitrose parking lot. That night had been so extreme, so utterly terrifying, he'd already shut it away in some secret part of his brain. It was a film. It hadn't really happened. To even touch on those memories would make him crazy.

The Tower had been a magical place. Properly safe. It was a real castle, built to keep out armies of knights. The walls were high and thick, there were always guards patrolling the walls, there was even the moat full of water. Grown-ups didn't stand a chance of getting in. The thought of living like someone from the Middle Ages had thrilled him at first. . . .

But he'd read enough about the Middle Ages to know that they were a time of violence and uncertainty.

Out there, where Brendan was going, was the real world. The world Sam would have to go back into if he was ever going to see his sister again.

On the other side of the open ground stood the ticket offices. The group of kids stopped, and Brendan's hands were untied. A girl ran up to him and threw her arms around him. Sam remembered what it was like at elementary school when all the fifth-grade kids left, the hugs and tears in the playground, the weeping and wailing.

"She loves him dearly," said the Kid. The girl let go of

Brendan and returned to her friends. "But she don't love him enough to go with him. Poor show."

They watched as Brendan turned to shout something at Jordan. One of the guards leveled his halberd at him. Brendan spat on the ground and strode off past the ticket offices.

"Not that way, Brendan," Ed muttered to himself. "Not the no-go zone, you idiot."

"Well," said the Kid, "I guess that's the last we'll see of him. Tutty-bye, old fruit."

Ed shook his head. "I still think Jordan's gone too far. He's going to make himself some enemies if he keeps on like this."

They were distracted by a shout and laughter from the kids below who were working in the moat. A girl had slipped over and was covered from head to toe in filth, her hair over her face like strands of seaweed. When Sam looked back over toward the ticket offices, Brendan had disappeared. It was as if nothing had happened. Life went on as normal.

If only Ella was here, Sam thought. Instead of halfway across London.

4

"What are they doing down there playing silly buggers in the moat?" the Kid asked.

"Trying to get rid of the water," Ed explained. "We need to drain it so that we can grow food again. It's a good wide strip of land and well protected. We used to grow everything we needed there."

"Where did all the water come from, then?" Sam asked.

"The Thames." Ed nodded toward the flat gray water of the river that ran directly alongside the tower. "We can't do anything to stop it rising. There used to be a barrier—well, there still is one, but it's useless now."

"What?" said Sam. "You mean to stop the water from getting into the moat?"

"No. To stop the river from flooding everywhere."

"That's the Thames Barrier," said Sam. "I've heard of it, but I never knew what it did."

"It was lowered whenever there was a tidal surge from the North Sea, otherwise London would have always been flooding. It's not far downstream of here. There's no one to operate it now, of course, and no power even if there was. Every now and then we get a really high tide and the water overflows the banks. The last one flooded the moat. It had been dry for two hundred years before that. The level drops a little every day, and we're working to bail it out. It's only a matter of time before it happens again, though. And with the moat flooded we can't grow much food, so the scavenging parties have to go out more often and they have to go farther each time. It's getting dangerous. The Pathfinders are really busy."

"What's Pathfinders?" Sam asked.

"When we got here, Jordan Hordern arranged everyone into military units."

"Was there no one here before you came, then?" said Sam.

"There *were* some kids, but they weren't very well organized. Jordan took over from their guy—the one at the trial yesterday—half-Japanese guy? Tomoki?"

"Oh yeah, I remember him."

"It was Jordan who really got this place together," Ed went on. "He figured there was loads to be done but that most kids wouldn't want to do the crappy jobs like cooking and cleaning and washing up."

"Too true," said the Kid. "I would not want to join the royal washer-uppers. Not in any way, shape, or form. No sirree. That would not suit the Kid, thank you, madam."

"Exactly." Ed laughed. "But Jordan figured that if he made everything like in the army, people wouldn't mind so much. He put everybody into regiments. The idea was that each regiment would be proud of what they did and no regiment would be any more important than another. It works pretty well. Boys and girls are mixed up so that nothing's seen as being either girls' work or boys' work, either."

"Have you got officers and everything, then?" Sam asked.

"Sure. Each regiment has its own captain, and each captain is equal."

"Are you a captain?" asked Sam.

"Yeah, I'm captain of the Tower Guard." Ed said this casually, but Sam could tell he liked being an officer.

"I want to be in your regiment," said the Kid. "Don't want to be in the kitchen rattling them pots and pans, thanks all the same, don't mind if I don't. Not one time, for the money, not two times, not three times, not anytime. The Kid is not for cleaning."

Ed shook his head and chuckled. "Yeah, well, Jordan carefully chose the names of the regiments to sound more exciting than cooking or cleaning or, I don't know, maintenance. The kids down there—" He nodded toward the moat. "They're Sappers. Anything that needs to be built or demolished or repaired is up to them. Anything inside the buildings—furniture, weapons, clothes, books, tools, firewood, whatever—is the responsibility of the Armorers. The Engineers look after anything mechanical, and the Service Corps deals with all the food. Finding it, cooking it, and growing it. The only other nonfighting unit is the Medical Corps, who you've already met.

"Then we've got three combat regiments, each with its own captain. The Tower Watch, the Tower Guard, and the Pathfinders. The Tower Watch are a sort of police force; they deal with any problems inside the castle. That's Tomoki's regiment. As I say, I'm captain of the Tower Guard. Our job is to defend the castle and patrol the nearby streets." Ed pointed out a boy and girl standing on the walls below, scanning the area with binoculars.

"We've got troops on lookout duty on the walls, the towers, and the gatehouses all day and night." As Ed was speaking, the two lookouts waved up to him. The girl then nudged her friend and started talking excitedly to him, throwing glances back up at Sam and the Kid. Sam noticed a look of irritation on Ed's face, and when Ed continued speaking, he sounded distracted.

"We also organize all the training," he said. "So you'll be seeing quite a bit of me. Everyone has to do at least an hour of military training and exercise every day."

"Cool." Sam was excited. Maybe he'd get his own sword and armor. "So what do the Pathfinders do, then?" he asked.

"They go out on the streets, guarding the forage parties, and exploring." Ed rattled this off quickly, like he wanted to be done with it. Something was annoying him, and Sam wondered if it was his fault, if he was asking too many questions. Ed glanced back to the two lookouts, who were still staring up in their direction and discussing something, like two bystanders at the scene of a car crash.

"Keep your eyes looking outward!" Ed suddenly shouted, and they guiltily went back to what they were supposed to be doing. Ed muttered something under his breath.

"Come on," he said, walking across to the stairs. "I want to show you something."

He led the way down to ground level, and they emerged at the bottom of the tower.

"As you can see, we've got an inner wall and an outer

wall." Ed seemed more comfortable down here. "And they both have sort of houses built into them. This road runs between them, all the way around."

Sam and the Kid looked down the cobbled road that curved between high walls on either side.

"It's called Mint Street," Ed explained. "The buildings in the outer wall used to be where they had the Royal Mint. You know, where they made all our money in the olden days? Afterward they were converted into homes called Casemates for the people who worked here. You've been staying in the sick bay, but now that we're sure you're okay, you can move into one of the Casemates. Most of us live there. Except Jordan, who lives in the Queen's House on Tower Green where the governor used to live. You'll be okay here. If it was safe enough for the Royal Mint, it'll be safe enough for you two shrimps."

"Look after the pennies and the Kid will look after himself," said the Kid.

Ed didn't take them down Mint Street, however; instead he started walking along the road that joined it, Water Lane, which took them past the riverside wall of the castle.

"That's the Bloody Tower to your left and Traitor's Gate to your right," he said. "But we're going to the old pub."

They soon arrived at one of the buildings set into the outer wall, where a gas-driven generator was set up outside a window.

Ed gave it a friendly slap. "When we found this, it was the Engineers' job to get it up and running. They scrounge gas from abandoned cars. They're also collecting any usable cars they find, and we're starting to clear the nearby roads. The plan is that we might one day be able to drive around here."

Ed unlocked a large wooden door using a key from the ring that hung at his belt. He pushed the door open and the kids followed him inside.

On all the walls there were old regimental badges, flags, and photographs of previous occupants of the Tower. At one end was a bar, still well stocked with drinks.

"This used to be for all the people who lived and worked here," Ed explained. "We use it as *our* social center now. Once a week they fire up the generator and we get to chill out with electric lights, music, and DVDs. What do you think of that?"

There was a big flat-screen TV on one side of the room, with chairs lined up in front of it. Sam and the Kid grinned like greedy idiots in a candy store. They'd thought they'd never get to watch movies again.

"Sit down."

Ed got a couple of cans of Coke from behind the bar and gave them to the little kids. Even though the Coke was warm, they drank greedily. It tasted unbelievably sweet.

Ed sat next to them. He looked serious. "There's something I need to talk to you about," he said.

"What?" Sam's heart was racing, whether it was because of the Coke or because Ed was making him nervous, he couldn't tell.

"I wasn't sure whether to say anything about it." Ed's voice was quiet and calm, like an adult giving bad news. "But, well, people are talking, word's gotten around, and I'd rather you heard it from me than from someone else."

5

Ed stared at his sneakers. "I used to go to a boarding school down in Kent called Rowhurst," he said. "When it all kicked off, we were stuck there. One of us, a boy named Matt, was hiding out in the school chapel and got carbon-monoxide poisoning from burning a load of stuff to keep warm. He went weird. Started seeing visions and got God in a big way, a big weird way. He made up his own sort of crazy religion. Got obsessed by this kind of god he invented called the Lamb, said the Lamb was going to save us all, and he made this ridiculous banner, with two boys on it. The Lamb and the Goat, he called them. One was fair-haired, the other kinda dark. It was some sort of yin-and-yang thing, if you know what I mean, which you probably don't. Good and evil. Something like that. I never could make much sense of it. Nobody could, except Mad Matt. And the thing is, when you two first appeared here, strolling down the road in the rain, the thing is . . . well, you looked exactly like the picture on Matt's banner. And people have been joking that you're the Lamb and the Goat."

"Baaaaa," said Sam, copying Kyle.

"Yeah. Baa is right. I mean, you must have noticed kids talking, like those two up on the wall?"

"Yeah," said Sam. "I thought it was just because we were new."

"No. It's freaking some kids out, some of the ones who knew Matt. We all headed into town together, met up with Jordan Hordern and his crew at the Imperial War Museum. Then a load of us came here."

"So you're saying some people actually think we might be this lamb and goat?" said Sam.

"Baby goat," said the Kid.

"What?" Ed looked confused.

"I'm the Kid, ain't I? The baby goat."

"Yeah," said Sam, "but admit it, Kid, we're not gods, are we?"

"Speak for yourself, maggot."

"Well, I'm not gonna start worshipping you, you worm!"

"Okay, okay." Ed held up his hands. "I just thought I ought to let you know, all right? Because someone's bound to say something. Like Kyle did. So come on, then, we'll continue with the tour."

They left the bar. Ed locked up and they went through the inner wall and up toward the White Tower. There were kids busy tending to the makeshift raised beds with wooden sides that covered much of the paved areas. The famous Tower of London ravens were pecking around between them. Big and black and mangy.

"It might be cool to be a god," said Sam. "But I wouldn't

know where to start. I've always wanted magic powers . . . I don't have any, though."

"I do," said the Kid.

"No, you don't."

"I do."

"Oh yeah, like what?"

"I can talk to animals."

"Prove it."

"All right." The Kid shouted at a raven. "Hey, bird, get lost!"

The raven flapped noisily away, unable to fly on its clipped wings.

"See!"

"See what?"

"I talked to it, didn't I? Never said it would understand me."

"Idiot."

"Fool."

"Moron."

"Twitmonger."

"What's a twitmonger?"

"Okay," said Ed. "I'm glad you're not taking it too seriously."

"So what happened to Matt?" asked Sam. "Is he here?"

"No. We got split up on the way. Last I saw of him he was floating down the Thames on the wreckage of a boat. God knows what happened to him. I really hope he drowned. He was nuts and he was dangerous."

"I'm allergic to dangerous nuts," said the Kid.

"I'm not sure about you, Kid." Ed laughed. "Half of what you say seems pretty switched on; the rest of it just sounds like gibberish."

"That's 'cause I'm a gibbernaut from the Planet Gibber."

"That's cool with me." Ed pointed out the kitchens and café where all the kids ate, the Waterloo Barracks, the Jewel House, which had once housed the Crown Jewels, although he explained that he had no idea if they were still in there, as it was impossible to get inside.

"So what do you reckon then, guys?" he said, sitting on a cannon outside the Jewel House. "You gonna like it here, d'you think?"

"It's great," said Sam. "I always dreamed of living somewhere like this, to be a knight and wear armor and carry a sword like you. Will I be allowed a sword?"

"If you want a sword we'll find you a sword."

"I love it here," said Sam. "It's all amazing. But I can't stay."

"What do you mean?"

"I told you I was looking for my sister."

"Yeah, but . . ."

"So I have to keep looking."

"But, Sam . . ."

"And I'm sticking with him," added the Kid. "Like chewing gum."

"As soon as we're ready, we're going to go to Buckingham Palace," said Sam.

"You can't." Ed looked appalled. "Don't be crazy. I mean, you can't just go wandering off out there."

"We did before."

"Yes, and with a mixture of stupidity and dumb luck and accidently finding your way here, you're still alive, but you can't risk it again."

"Come with us, then. You could look after us."

"What? No. I'm needed here."

"It wouldn't take long. You could bring some guards or something."

"I can't put other kids in danger, Sam. Not even for you. We need to plan and . . . Don't you get it, boys? To get to Buckingham Palace you'd have to go right through the no-go zone. . . . Unless . . ."

"Unless what?"

"Unless you went on the river, I suppose, took a boat."

"Hold your tongue," the Kid shouted, slightly too loudly, surprising Sam and Ed. "That just won't wash. Sorry to get on my high horse, Mister Ed, but Charlie don't surf. No boats for me. Not gonna play Pugwash. Water and me don't mix. In a nutshell—the Kid don't swim."

"Well, if you won't go on the river I don't see how you're gonna get through the zone."

"Did it once before, we can do it again," said the Kid.

"All right, listen," said Ed. "I'll make a deal with you. But you've got to stick to it."

"Depends."

"No, it doesn't. You have to agree now. Up front. I'll help you get to the palace, I promise."

"Sure, okay," said Sam. "So what's the deal?"

"Until we know what's out there, you're not leaving the castle."

"Well, how long's that going to be? That's not fair."

Ed looked at Sam. "Some guys set out from here the other day," he said.

"Yeah?"

"Yeah. It was a sort of exploration party. They were going west. Upriver. A friend of mine named DogNut and seven others. They took a boat. They've been gone a while now, so they should be back soon. The deal is, when they turn up and we know what's out there, and I think it'll be safe enough, I'll take you to Buckingham Palace. Myself. Okay?"

Sam thought about this for a while. Certainly the idea of setting off alone was something he didn't want to think about. A huge part of him wanted to forget all about Ella and stay here forever with Ed and the Kid. But just as Ed had made a promise to him, he'd made a promise to Ella. He was her big brother. He'd told her that he'd always look after her.

"Okay," he said at last. "It's a deal."

They shook on it and slapped palms.

Ed gave him a hard stare. "You're not to even think about it until DogNut comes back, okay? You can rest up, eat properly, learn how to use your weapons, do some basic training, and when he comes back . . ."

"What if he never comes back?"

"He'll come back. He knows what he's doing."

6

The Fear were on the move again.

That was the name that Shadowman had given to Saint George's army of strangers.

The Fear.

During the night they'd flushed out a small group of kids from a big house next to Hampstead Heath and sent them running. They'd caught and killed one on the spot; the others they'd tracked through the local streets and finally across the Heath. A few got clean away, but the Fear managed to catch several of the younger ones, the ones who were slower and weaker than the rest. The strangers had cornered them in a steep-sided hollow. The kids had been disoriented in the dark, exhausted and frightened, but the adults, using their sense of smell, had followed them easily. They'd fallen on them as a pack, killing them quickly. But what came next was not some mindless feeding frenzy. Having ripped the small bodies apart, the Fear had divided them up, Saint George taking the lion's share. There was a pecking order among the strangers, with Saint George and his gang at the top.

The oldest, feeblest, and most diseased of the strangers got nothing.

Shadowman wondered how long the weaklings could survive like this and how soon the stronger ones would turn on them and eat them.

The sun was coming up now and the Fear were moving off the Heath. If they followed their usual pattern, they would find a house and settle down to sleep until it got dark again.

From his hiding place, high up in a tree, Shadowman watched them closely. The way they congregated around Saint George. The way they seemed to move together, with a sense of purpose. How did they do that? How did they know what Saint George wanted them to do, beyond brute, slavish copying? They were organized the way an ant colony is organized, or the bees in a hive. There was a sense of purpose in everything that they did. Somehow they managed to arrange themselves into distinct groups, with set tasks. Nothing was said. Strangers' brains were so eaten away by disease they'd lost the power of speech.

Until now Shadowman had thought that all adults had lost the capability of rational thought. They hadn't. Their brains had *changed*, that was all. The higher level, the conscious reasoning level, might have been destroyed, but the animal part of their brains was still going strong. The brain stem, it was called. Shadowman had learned about it in science. It was the oldest, simplest part of the brain that humans shared with all other creatures.

And even the smallest creatures, worms, insects, microbes . . . even *they* had some kind of functioning brain.

Maybe flies didn't actually *think*. It didn't stop them from taking over the world, though.

Did the malaria parasite know what it was doing when it infected someone? Did it wonder what it was going to have for supper? What the other parasites were talking about? No. It just did what it did. *Plasmodium falciparum*, that's what it was called. He'd studied the parasite at school. A very successful creature. Spreading itself worldwide. It wasn't evil. It had no plan. It had no idea what it was doing. Like all animals, it simply had an inbuilt program that allowed it to survive. You couldn't blame the parasite for killing people, any more than you could blame a shark for having big teeth. Sharks were no more evil than hedgehogs or fluffy bunny rabbits.

So were these strangers evil? Or were they just doing what they needed to do to survive? And were they any more conscious of what they were doing than *Plasmodium falciparum*?

It made no difference. Scientists hadn't worried about morality when they'd set about trying to rid the world of malaria. Now the healthy, undiseased kids had to not question it when they killed strangers. And it was down to Shadowman to somehow try to stop the Fear from spreading.

The strangers had to be wiped out, because, like malaria, it was a case of *us* or *them*.

When Shadowman thought about the disease, he couldn't help but picture adults shuffling about like zombies. They had become the model of their own sickness. They acted like the disease itself. Spreading, destroying, growing, showing outward signs of purpose and intelligence, but with each individual member, each human cell, being essentially mindless.

They reminded him of something. A flock of birds. The way they seemed to anticipate each other, to move as a single unit, a single coordinated creature.

A flock of birds, a shoal of fish, a pack of hunting wolves . . .

A disease.

7

"There's something going down."

Ed looked up from his breakfast of lumpy porridge and blinked at Kyle. He'd been up late on guard duty and wasn't properly awake yet. As captain of the Tower Guard, he was meant to be ready for anything at all times, but the one thing he struggled with was early starts.

"How serious is it, Kyle?"

"Well, you know, like, *pretty* serious."

"What? A red alert? Orange? Purple?"

"Oh, come on, Ed. You know I can't get my head around those stupid colors."

"Okay, on a scale of one to ten, then. I've only just started breakfast and I don't want to come back to cold porridge. It was never very warm to begin with."

"I'd say a ten."

Ed swore and threw his spoon into his bowl. He slid the porridge across the table to one of his team, a quiet, curly-haired girl called Ali.

"Look after this for me, will you?" he said, standing up from the table. "Don't eat it."

Ali peered at the gray porridge and wrinkled her nose.

"It's safe."

Ed buckled on his sword and looked around the guard-room, which was situated at the bottom of the Bloody Tower. He picked out three girls and a boy who had finished eating and were playing cards at another table.

"You all, come with us."

They hustled out of the tower after Kyle, who explained what was going on as they went.

"The lookouts on Middle Tower heard shouting outside the castle about an hour ago. It was quite far away and they couldn't tell what was going on."

"Kids shouting?"

"You ever hear a zombie shout?"

"Guess not."

"It was definitely kids," Kyle went on. "I was on early watch, so they sent for me."

"They stayed put?"

"Yeah."

Nobody was allowed out of the castle unless authorized by Jordan or one of his captains.

"So have you seen anything?" Ed asked. They had come to Byward Tower. The gatekeeper hauled the gates open to let them through, and they ran across the causeway to Middle Tower. In the last few days the Sappers had made good progress in the moat; there were only a couple of inches of standing water left, and in some places patches of muddy ground showed through.

"We searched the whole area with our binoculars," said Kyle, struggling to keep up with Ed. "At first we couldn't see nothing, then Macca spotted someone."

"A kid?"

"Far as we could tell."

"Just one?"

"Just one *kid*. A whole mess of sickos, though. The kid was running from a gang of them."

They had arrived at Middle Tower, where they clattered up the spiral stairs to the roof. Four kids were waiting for them. Ed took a pair of binoculars off one of them.

"What direction?" he asked, putting the glasses to his face. "Where did they come from?"

"No-go zone," said the boy, Macca, who had given Ed the binoculars.

Ed swore.

"Since then they've moved northward, up by Trinity House." Macca had a screwed-up face and was always mucking about, but he had good eyes.

Ed switched direction, swinging the glasses around to the right, up past the ticket offices to the main street that ran along the north side of the Tower. They weren't in the best position to see what was going on up that way, and despite scouring the area for a couple of minutes, he could see nothing. He could *hear* something, though. A voice calling out, thin and high-pitched. A girl by the sound of it, or a very young boy.

"They shouting for help?" he asked. The lookouts stared blankly, except for a tall, athletic girl called Hayden.

"Could be," she said. "It's what I'd be shouting."

"Okay," said Ed. "We're going to have to find out."

There were groans from the others, all except for Kyle, who smiled and nodded his head, running his fingers along the blade of his new battle-ax. He was always up for a fight.

Ed ignored the complaints. "Macca, you come with us," he said. "And you, Hayden. Kate, you stay up here. Use these." He slapped the binoculars into her hands, then turned to the last of the lookouts. "Carly, you go around to Devereux Tower. There's a better view from there. Scare up some help on the way. Keep watch from there, okay?"

"Okay." Carly grinned as she hurried off, evidently relieved that she wasn't going to have to go out onto the streets. Ed leaned over the wall to shout down to her as she crossed the causeway. "And tell Jordan what's happening!"

Ed now surveyed his war party: Kyle, Macca, Hayden, plus the four cardplayers he'd dragged out of the Bloody Tower. He'd picked them just because they looked like they weren't doing anything, but he realized they'd make a good team.

Adele was a tough, chunky girl who could win a fight with almost any boy. It always amused Ed that Adele, as well as being one of his best fighters, was also one of the girliest girls in the Tower. Her hair was always full of sparkly hair clips and pins, and she didn't bother with armor or protective leather, preferring layers of bright colors and pretty patterns, beads and badges and bangles. To see her charging into a fight, all in pink and swinging her club like a baseball slugger, was really something. She was very popular with the little kids in the Tower, and you'd often see her walking around with several of them following after her, like a mother duck with her ducklings.

Partha and Kinsey were good, fast runners and often worked as a team with Hayden. Sometimes running was a more useful skill than fighting. Then there was Will. Will was smart and coolheaded, reliable, a good balance to Macca, who could be cheeky and undisciplined.

"Okay. There's eight of us," Ed said. "Should be enough. If it looks too dangerous we won't engage. Follow my lead and do exactly as I say. We haven't lost anyone in weeks, and I'm not losing anyone on my watch."

The kids nodded, their eyes shining and glassy. That familiar look of fear and excitement.

In less than a minute they were jogging north across the open space next to the ticket offices. It was a cold morning, the sky gray. Spots of rain were starting to fall. Ed realized he wasn't dressed for this. He should have put on a waterproof jacket of some sort, but hadn't been fully awake when Kyle had grabbed him.

Litter blew across the parking lot and pigeons wandered around, nosing through the piles of crap that had collected in every corner. When it rained heavily, the streets flooded. All the drains were blocked and there was no one to unblock them.

Ahead, the gleaming glass top of the Gherkin rose above the older buildings below it, including the ornate Trinity House, which looked like someone had looted a load of pillars, arches, and statues from ancient Rome and piled them up as high as they could, like a hyper kid with a Lego set. It was completely over-the-top and Ed's favorite building around here.

He didn't have time to admire it now, though. His mind

was on other things. Adrenaline was pumping through his system. He was preparing to fight or flee, depending on what they found. The others were jittery, red-faced, working themselves up, but Ed felt a familiar calm begin to settle over him, a weird detachment. A coldness. When it came time to fight—if it came time—he knew what would happen. He would explode into a ruthless killing frenzy. All the time, though, a part of him would be sitting back watching. Watching that other Ed. Ed the killer. It frightened his friends when they witnessed it. In battle he was the most ferocious of them all. It's what kept crazy Kyle loyal to him, always at his side.

The main difference between the two of them was that Kyle enjoyed all this running, fighting, hunting, killing.

Ed hated it.

Avoided it if he possibly could.

But a kid in peril, chased by sickos, that was something he couldn't avoid.

8

As they neared the main road, they could tell that there were sickos close. They were hit by the smell before they saw them. Sour, rotten, pungent; a mix of dog shit, bad drains, food left out of the fridge, gummi candy, toilet cleaner, and armpits.

Ed raised his hand and his team slowed down, moving more cautiously now, not wanting to run headlong into a swarm of grown-ups. You could always smell them, but you rarely heard them until you were on top of them, they made so little noise.

The kids turned the corner and there they were: sickos. About thirty of them, some wandering in the road, but most gathered on the porch of a Victorian office building next to a rib joint called Bodean's. The sickos were clamoring around the doors and windows, trying to get in.

There was a subway entrance on the other side of the arched doorway, and as Ed watched, three more sickos emerged from it. There must have been a nest of them down there. Jordan regularly organized sorties from the Tower to flush sickos out of the many tunnels in the area, and the kids were always trying to block them up. It would take them ages to make the area totally safe, though.

Ed quietly told his team to hold back. They hadn't been spotted yet. The sickos were too intent on trying to get into the building, and Ed wanted to keep it that way for as long as possible.

"I thought we'd cleaned out all the nests around here," he whispered to Kyle. They were squatting down, trying to keep a low profile.

"So did I," said Kyle. "But as soon as we get rid of them, they come back again."

"We'll bring a full unit later and properly clean that subway out. For now we've got to see what they're after, deal with them, and get back into the Tower quick."

"Why don't we just leave it?" said Kyle. "Go back now, round up an army, and come back and twat the lot of them?"

"Maybe we should."

It wasn't like Kyle to avoid a fight, which told Ed that he wasn't sure about this. And if Kyle wasn't sure of attacking, then it was bad. Maybe there were too many sickos to take on.

"This ain't our problem," Kyle added.

Just then a girl appeared at a first-floor window, opened it, and looked down at the sickos squabbling at the door below. She looked understandably frightened. She then looked over toward the Tower. She hadn't seen Ed's squad where they were hiding. She put her hand to her mouth and called out.

"Help me!"

Ed sighed. "It just became our problem."

"Why?" said Kyle. "We don't know her. She ain't one of us."

"You can be a real shit sometimes, Kyle."

"Yeah, I can, can't I?" Kyle snickered.

"I thought you were always up for a fight."

"I've got one rule, Ed. Never start a fight you can't win."

"That is a girl, Kyle. A kid. And any kid is one of us."

"All right," said Kyle. "Let's play Batman, then. Charge in to her rescue."

"We need more of a plan than that." Ed put his hand on Hayden's shoulder. "Hayden. You take Partha and Kinsey. You're the fastest runners. I want you to get the attention of the sickos over there. Look tasty, yeah? I want them drooling."

"Here he goes," said Kyle. "Ed with his plans."

Ed ignored Kyle and continued giving Hayden her instructions. "Get as many of them to go after you as you can. Lead them away eastward, along Tower Hill. You'll have to play it carefully. Keep close enough so that they don't get bored and come back here, but not so close that you risk getting caught."

"Don't worry," said Hayden. "We won't be getting too close to them. Trust me."

"Go on, then, and shout out to the girl. Let her know we're going to help her. Tell her to stay put until we get in there. We'll stay hidden here until the odds are a little better."

Hayden, Partha, and Kinsey moved out of hiding and gingerly crossed the road, creeping nearer to the siege. Ed watched as first one then another of the sickos stopped what they were doing and turned to stare at them.

The sickos were a mixed bunch of all ages, ranging from older teenagers to mothers and fathers in their sixties. You never saw them much older than that. Ed assumed that seniors had found it hardest to survive the illness and the madness that came on its heels.

As well as being mixed in age, this group was also in various different stages of decay. Some looked hardly touched, just pale-skinned and red around the nose and eyes, with dry lips and the occasional spot or rash. If he hadn't known better, Ed might have thought they were suffering from nothing worse than the flu.

Others looked like animated corpses, their flesh green and rotten, eaten away, with horrible growths and boils and blisters. Hair missing, ears and noses missing, lips gone.

He knew they weren't zombies. They weren't the living dead. But a lot of the kids called them that.

It suited them.

His head was aching. Was he doing the right thing? He had casually asked Hayden and the others to go and act as decoys. He knew how tense they'd be feeling as the sickos took the bait. Hayden was fast and not stupid. She'd know what to do and could easily outrun these diseased creeps.

It was still dangerous, though.

Hayden called out to the girl in the window, told her what was happening. She nodded frantically.

More and more sickos were becoming aware of the new arrivals. One by one they began to stop their assault on the office doors and focus their attention on the three girls.

And now they started to move, sniffing the air, salivating,

growing agitated by the scent of young flesh. Some shook violently; others hissed; one actually had a fit and lay in the road thrashing about like a landed fish.

"Go on," Ed murmured. "Fresh meat. Go get it. . . ."

Hayden's team had stopped, scared to go any closer; they waited nervously for the sickos to come to them.

"Hold on," said Ed, "just a bit longer. Let them all get a good sniff of you."

One sicko, bolder and fitter than the rest, moved ahead of the shuffling pack, striding on long legs, head held high. Finally he broke into a sort of half run, stiff-legged and awkward, like a drunk trying to look sober.

At last Hayden's nerve broke and she retreated, moving quickly backward. It seemed to trigger something in the bulk of the sickos; they came alive, keen to be first to the kill. They moved as a pack, keeping pace with the long-legged father. Hayden was forced to run now, she and her team looking back over their shoulders to make sure they were being followed.

Ed's group had ducked down completely out of sight. Kyle was still caressing his ax, a big heavy thing he'd recently discovered in a storeroom. It was designed for crushing and splitting armor in battle. Very different from the executioner's ax he'd been ready to use the other day.

Or had he? How much of that had been for show? He was a vicious hulk, with a cruel sense of humor. The best boy to have by your side in a fight, though.

Kyle leaned over and sneaked a look around the end of the wall.

"Well?" Ed asked.

"They ain't all left. Some have held back. Too interested in the girl."

"What d'you reckon? Can we take them?"

"Reckon so," said Kyle, and he turned to face the others. "You up for it?"

They all nodded, gripping their weapons tighter. Macca had a crossbow. He slotted a bolt into it, shuffled up the wall to see over the top, and leveled it at the sickos. "You want me to come with or hold back?" he asked. "Pick 'em off from here?"

"Hold back, Macca." Ed gave the order. "We need someone to stay outside and be our eyes and ears on the street. Will, you've got a crossbow too, you stay with him. We're gonna have to go inside and I don't think your bows'll be a lot of use in there."

"Sure, okay," said Will, and he took his place next to Macca, aiming over the wall. Ed, Kyle, and Adele joined them, quickly taking in the situation.

"Wait for it," Ed whispered. There were three stragglers limping after Hayden's group that looked like they might give up and turn back. Ed pointed to them, and Macca and Will got the message. They switched their aim and loosed a couple of shots. One bolt thudded into the back of a fat mother, who grunted and collided with a post. The second bolt took out a waddling father, and before the last sicko knew what was happening, Ed skittered over lightly, moving fast on the balls of his feet, and plunged his sword into his side, just below the ribs. As the father gasped and dropped to his knees, Ed stabbed him again in the neck.

Ed looked down the road, checking to make sure that the rest of the sickos were still following Hayden's group. They were. Like a pack of foxhounds, they were doggedly trudging along the north side of the Tower. Hayden should easily be able to outrun them and then double back to the Tower gates.

He left the three downed sickos to bleed to death and went back for Kyle and Adele. Adele was chewing something. She looked keyed up, her hands tight on her heavy iron club.

Ed waited for Will and Macca to reload and fire two more bolts into the mob at the doorway, and then he was off. He couldn't wait for them to reload again. Crossbows were powerful and accurate but had a low rate of fire. He wanted to move quickly and get it over with. It was always possible that there were more sickos down in the subway. The longer the kids stayed outside the castle walls, the more dangerous it became.

Kyle and Adele followed him over the road, hoping to move in before the rest of the sickos got a handle on what was happening. As they sprinted toward the buildings, Ed counted heads. There were seven of them still there that he could see. Could be more. It was cramped on the porch and the sickos were battering at the glass doors, crowding each other out. One had a crossbow bolt in his leg but was ignoring it.

Seven.

Not too hard to deal with.

The girl was still at the window. Watching but staying silent. Ed wondered why she hadn't simply found another way out. There must be more than one door to the place after all. He knew all too well, though, that when you're scared, you don't always think straight.

The sickos finally heard them coming. Or more likely smelled them. They turned. Started to come down the steps from the porch.

Ed felt a cold fist close around his heart.

"Do it quickly," he said.

Kyle raised his battle-ax and swung it, taking the lead sicko's head clean off his shoulders. At the same time Ed plunged his sword into the second sicko's guts. A third sicko went for Adele. One side of his face had been caved in, giving him a lopsided, cross-eyed look. Adele swung her club and caved the other side of his face in.

"Stay in the road," Ed commanded. "There's no room to fight in the doorway. Let them come to us."

And the stupid bastards did. As usual, their hunger and insane drive for food forced them to attack even when they were outgunned. None of them was armed, relying instead on strength in numbers, hands, teeth, and fingernails. They'd been whittled down enough for Ed to feel confident, though. Only four were left standing and one of them was already wounded. He had cut his wrist on something and his left hand was hanging half off, squirting blood down his pants.

Ed, Kyle, and Adele stood their ground, placing themselves far apart so that there was no risk of them striking each other with their weapons. Ed had found a Cromwellian military sword in the White Tower, nicknamed a mortuary sword. It was heavy and straight and brutal, not a fencing sword, not something to show off elegant swordplay with. It was designed to shatter and break bones.

And break bones he did, hacking at two more sickos as they came down the steps. Kyle and Adele easily dealt with the last couple, and in less than a minute all the sickos were dead or dying. Macca and Will trotted over to join them and retrieve their precious crossbow bolts.

"Keep watch out here," Ed told them. "And keep vocal. We don't want to get trapped in there like the girl. Any sign of danger, you let us know."

"Don't worry," said Macca. "We'll be here."

Ed called up to the girl, who was leaning out of the window.

"Stay there!" he shouted. "We're coming up."

9

Ed bounded up the steps and soon discovered how the father had cut his hand. The glass in the doors was broken in several places, and one jagged piece was painted with blood. Ed used his sword hilt to knock it out and then reached his hand in through the gap to open the door. Inside there was an entrance hall with a noticeboard on one side listing all the businesses that had once been based there. There was a small reception desk at the back with a blank TV above it, and behind it the elevators and a stairway.

So far there were no signs of life.

"Are you thinking what I'm thinking?" Kyle asked.

"Depends what you're thinking," Ed replied. "If you're thinking of tits, like you usually do, then no."

"I'm thinking there might be more of them in here. Otherwise why didn't the girl try to get out another way?"

"Nothing's ever simple, is it?"

"Nope."

Ed sighed. It had been easy outside. They'd been able to clearly see the threat and prepare for it. In here it would be a different matter. It was dark and cramped and unknown. He put his finger to his lips and they listened.

All quiet.

Ed went over to the stairs and looked up.

"Nothing. Stay close, yeah? We'll go slow and steady. Who's got a flashlight?"

Blank faces from the other two.

Ed grunted with dismay. "I should have brought one, I suppose," he said. "Left in too much of a hurry. Don't you have one, Kyle? I thought you were on early watch."

"Dead batteries, mate. We need to find some more of them windup beauties. You know Jordan don't like us to use up batteries."

"We'll bring it up in the next war council," said Ed. "Make it a priority to find batteries and more friction flashlights."

"It shouldn't be too dark," said Adele. "There's lots of windows."

"Yeah, but be careful."

"Will you stop telling us to be careful?" said Kyle. "It's not like we don't know."

"Are you ever careful, Kyle?"

Kyle grinned his big idiot's grin. "'Course not," he said. "Now let's go. Brain-biter is hungry."

"Brain-biter?" Ed tutted. "Don't tell me. You've given your ax a name, haven't you?"

"Yeah. I got it from a book. Ain't your sword got a name?"

"It's called Terry." Ed laughed and started up the stairs, he and Kyle side by side, Adele watching their backs. There was very little light in the stairwell, which wound up around the elevator shaft in the center of the building. They had to feel their way, creeping slowly from step to step.

"So did you give a name to that executioner's ax you were so keen to use the other day?" Ed asked Kyle quietly.

"Nah. It was just a replica. Don't even know if it would have worked."

"You were still going to use it, though."

"Dunno. Jordan told me what to do before the trial. I think he knew that killing Brendan was a no-no."

"So why go through with it?"

"Jordan wanted to look harder than hard. He was hoping all along that someone would come up with another plan. Talk him out of it. All he ever wanted was to kick Brendan out. Send him into exile."

"So why didn't he just say that in the first place and save us all that bloody drama?"

"I reckon 'cause he thought exile was pretty harsh, thought everyone might complain. This way it looks like he did Bren a favor, not crapping on him from too great a height. Makes Jordan look hard but fair."

"And what if I hadn't said anything?" Ed asked. "Would you have gone through with it and cut his head off?"

"Shhh . . ."

They had reached the second floor, where a corridor with offices off to either side ran from the front of the building to the back. It was full of dark moving shapes.

Hard to tell in the low light levels, but there were maybe as many as ten sickos there. Ed had a strong urge to turn tail. Was it worth risking any of their lives for this unknown girl?

They backed down the stairs and around a corner.

"Are you up for this?" he whispered.

"We've come this far," said Kyle.

"We could come back for her."

"Are you ducking out, Captain? Didn't you say she was one of us?"

"I don't want to force you two to do anything you don't want."

"We'd follow you into the mouth of hell, Skipper." Kyle put on a bad American accent.

"Shut up, Kyle. I'm serious."

"I told you, Brain-biter is hungry. Lead on."

"Let's do it," said Adele. "I can't go back to the Tower knowing I'd left that girl here. She must be terrified."

"All right. Let's do it, then." Ed led them back up to the top of the stairs and out into the corridor.

"Which door are you behind?" he shouted. There was no answer.

"She can't hear you," said Kyle. "How could she?"

"Must be one of the offices at the front," said Adele.

"But which side?" said Kyle. "Left or right?"

In reply the girl threw herself at the glass door to an office with the words MCKAY CONSULTANCY on it. She banged it with her fists, her mouth open in a silent scream.

"Go for it!" Ed shouted. The sickos were aware of their presence now. They advanced from both directions. "Barge through them!"

As Ed started to run, someone made a grab for his legs. Someone lying in the darkness of a doorway. Ed got a glimpse of long tangled hair. A hand took hold of the loose material of his pants, and he instinctively swiped down, cutting it off. Another slash and the body fell still.

Then a mother got hold of him from behind. He whirled around and stabbed her with the point of his sword. "Get off me!"

"Come on, Ed!" Kyle and Adele had gotten ahead of him and were by the office door already. Ed put his head down and powered through the corridor, knocking two more sickos aside. He jumped over a third who'd been killed by Kyle, and then he was at the door. The girl was still on the other side, pressed up against the glass. She looked about fourteen and was dressed all in green.

Kyle held off the sickos, using the shaft of his ax as a bludgeon in these cramped conditions.

"Open the door!" Ed yelled at the girl, and she did as she was told. The three of them piled in, almost falling over each other, and Ed pushed the door shut and bolted it at the top just as a knot of sickos caught up. Now it was their turn to squash against the glass. This group was mostly young, a couple of them not much older than Ed and Kyle.

"Ugly douche bags," said Kyle, and he spat at them, leaving a greasy gob to slide down the glass.

"That's disgusting," said Adele.

"Oh, right, and they aren't?"

"I didn't say that. It's bad enough having to put up with them slobbering all over everything without you adding to it."

"I'm so sorry, Mother." Laughing, Kyle wiped the gob off with his sleeve to a horrified "eurgh" from Adele. He then waved his damp sleeve in her face and she backed away, swearing at him.

In their relief at getting safely out of the corridor, they'd all but forgotten about the girl they'd come to rescue. Ed tore his eyes away from the angry sickos at the door and turned to her.

"Are you alone?" he asked. "Is it just you?"

The girl was frozen, her lips pressed tightly together, too scared to speak by the look of it. Ed knew she wasn't dumb—they'd all heard her shouting before.

"Are there any others?"

The girl burst into tears and Ed put an arm around her. She instantly stiffened, shrinking from his touch, and he let her go. She had short dark hair cut in an untidy bob. She was wearing jeans and a sweatshirt, both dark green, like she'd dyed them herself, and not too dirty, so she hadn't been sleeping outside. There was a wound on her forehead. It looked like it might be an old one, though. It was scabby and slightly infected.

Ed ignored the girl for a moment to take in their surroundings. They were in another reception area, filled with dusty office equipment.

"All right," he said. "Don't talk now; we're going to get you back to the Tower, okay? But you've got to do exactly as we tell you. Can you do that?"

The girl nodded. She had a round face and slightly too many teeth for her mouth. She picked something up.

"That all you got?"

Again she nodded.

"You're not going to do much damage with that. What is it? A walking stick?"

Another nod.

"All right. Listen. We stick close together till we're out

of the building, then we run. You can run, yeah? Good. We should be fine. Kyle, check outside."

Kyle went into the office that overlooked the street and leaned out of the open window. They could hear him calling down to Macca and Will outside. He waited a moment, listening, and then returned to the reception area.

"All quiet outside. It's just this group we have to worry about. Once we get past these goons, we should be fine. How many d'you reckon, Adele?"

Adele had been watching the door through all this. The sickos were still crowding around it, licking the glass, pressing their pimply, broken faces against it.

"I've counted nine," she said. "There could be more."

Ed took hold of the green girl's arms to get her attention. "Is there definitely no other way out of the office than through this door?"

This time the girl shook her head.

Ed swore under his breath. This girl was making a lot of trouble for them. He hoped she was worth it.

"We can't pull the decoy trick again," he said, letting her go. "Not in here. Won't work. Not enough of us. Too dangerous. Which means we've just got to fight our way out. I'll go first. . . ."

"Wait," said the girl, finally finding her voice. She put up her hand, then ran off.

"She's forgotten her handbag," said Kyle. "Typical girl."

Adele shoved him and Kyle laughed.

The girl returned with a backpack. She dropped it to the floor and opened the top. Started scrabbling around inside it for something.

"Can't find her purse," said Kyle, and Adele elbowed him in the ribs.

It wasn't a purse she pulled out, however; it was a pistol of some sort, with a wide, stubby barrel. Then she brought out a box. Ed read the label. They were flares. She cracked the gun and slotted a flare into it.

Ed smiled his approval. The girl put away the rest of the flares, stuffed her stick into the bag, then fastened it and straightened up, the gun heavy in her trembling hand.

"You ready, then?" Ed asked, helping the girl on with her pack. She spoke again, her voice hoarse from shouting.

"I'm ready."

10

'll pop the door, you let them have it. When I give the word, we break out of here."

Ed and Kyle went to the glass and jeered at the sickos, riling them, winding them up. They jittered and shook and clawed at the door in a frenzy. Once Ed was sure he had them all hooked, he took hold of the handle.

"Stand back. . . ."

He wrenched the door open, two sickos spilled in, and Kyle and Adele laid into them. Meanwhile, the green girl steadied her arm and fired the flare gun into the open doorway.

There was a bang and the next sicko in line fell back, a bright red ball of fire fizzing and hissing in the middle of his chest. His shirt caught fire, and in a moment the corridor was full of sparks and yellow smoke. The other sickos backed off in confusion, coughing and choking.

"Follow me," Ed yelled, and he was first out of the door, chopping to the left and right with his sword. It was hard to see anything and he tripped on a fallen body. Luckily he kept his balance and managed to cut through the sickos and get to the stairway. He was about to head down when Adele called out.

"Wait!"

Now what? Ed turned to look down the corridor. The green girl had stopped halfway and was squatting down by one of the doorways.

"Come on!"

Sickos were approaching the girl through the smoke. They were lit a demonic red by the still-blazing flare.

"Come on!"

He ran back to grab her, but she wouldn't move. Ed realized it was the doorway where he'd killed the thing that had grabbed his leg. He looked at the body on the floor. It wasn't a sicko. It was another girl. Also dressed in green.

He'd killed her.

Ed swore. She was missing a hand and her neck was slashed where he'd hacked at her. But then he saw that her stomach had been ripped open and her intestines had flopped onto the floor. The sickos had gotten her first—that's why she'd been on the floor.

"She's dead," he said. "Leave her."

The girl didn't move.

"Leave her!" Ed shouted, and pulled the girl up by her sweatshirt. A sicko came close and Ed angrily sliced his blade across his face, blinding him. Then he dragged the girl along the corridor to the stairs and almost threw her down. She found her feet and stumbled ahead of him, and he hustled after her, his heart pounding.

Mercifully they made it safely to the bottom and were

soon out in the fresh air, where Macca and Will were waiting for them.

"We need to leg it," said Macca, pointing westward to where another knot of sickos was approaching along Byward Street.

The kids didn't wait to be told twice; they raced across the road and down toward the castle gates.

Ed was grinding his teeth. He'd had a go at Kyle for almost killing another kid, and now he'd done it himself.

Brilliant.

He told himself that she would have died anyway—she was too badly wounded. Better a quick death than a long, slow one. He told himself that it had been an accident. That they wouldn't have been able to carry her out of there because of the sickos.

In the end, though, there was no getting around the fact that he'd killed a kid.

"Well done, boss," said Kyle as they helped the gate-keepers close the big black gates behind them in Middle Tower. They were both panting, their chests heaving.

"Another successful mission. No one hurt. One girl rescued." Kyle slapped him on the back. "Result."

It had all been worth it.

Hadn't it?

11

He supposed it was only a matter of time. The Fear had to eat. There were too many of them now to rely on the few children they caught. Shadowman had tried to count the strangers, but it was too hard. They only came out at night and he couldn't risk getting too close. It was difficult to get a fix on them through his binoculars. He'd pan over the horde and then lose track of those he'd counted and those he hadn't. There were definitely more than fifty, maybe even more than a hundred, and there were new arrivals every night, stragglers who seemed drawn to the bigger pack.

They'd been moving steadily across north London, from house to house, street to street, eating anything in their path, like a spreading stain. Shadowman followed along behind, trying not to think too closely about what they left behind: the bones, the scraps of skin, and clumps of bloody hair. But they also left in their wake food that they couldn't get at, unopened tin cans, dried food wrapped in tough plastic, unopened bottles and jars, and this Shadowman scavenged.

He was impressed at how thorough they were. What an incredibly destructive force.

Was it really only a few days ago he'd left the relative safety of central London where he'd been living and headed up this way with a group of friends looking for other children? It struck him just how useless they'd been, finding no one until it was too late. There *were* other children, though, and the Fear were finding them easily enough.

They marched slowly on, covering only a few streets a night. They could only move as fast as the slowest among them, and there were some very slow mothers and fathers in the pack: older ones, more diseased ones, those who'd been injured. They hobbled and crawled and staggered, twelve of them at his latest count. Easier to keep track of, as they were always at the back, closest to him. Shadowman almost felt like he was getting to know them. Had made up names for most of them.

Well, that had been a waste of time.

When it happened, it happened so quickly it had taken Shadowman completely by surprise.

The Fear had been sleeping through the day in an elementary school. Old redbrick buildings, long since abandoned. They'd found nothing to eat the night before, and as the sun had come up over the streets, they'd crawled inside to rest. Shadowman had found a good vantage point in an apartment building across the street and had himself settled down to sleep like the strangers. He was getting used to their rhythms and routines, tuning in to their behavior. He slept lightly, though, and could wake up and be on his feet in the time it took to flick a switch. When they stirred, he stirred.

He wondered sometimes if he was becoming infected by them somehow, turning into an insect, part of the swarm, the flock, the herd, the stain. Other times, when he was feeling less dramatic, he reckoned it was just their smell that woke him. They gave off a powerful stench, so powerful it masked his own smell and stopped them from finding him. He'd killed some of them the other day, a hunting party led by a mutilated stranger he'd dubbed the One-Armed Bandit. Afterward he'd drenched his cloak in their blood, just to be sure. He smelled like one of them now.

He'd woken at dusk as the first of the Fear emerged from the school buildings and spilled out into the playground. He'd gotten onto his knees and spied on them through a window. Watched as they congregated by a jungle gym. Just like the old days, when parents hung around, chatting to each other after dropping their kids off. They milled about, waiting for Saint George to come out with his little gang of officers, as Shadowman thought of them.

And then they'd come. Spike, who still had a crossbow bolt stuck in his ribs where Shadowman had shot him. Bluetooth, in the tattered remains of a business suit, with a Bluetooth earpiece embedded in his ear. Man U, in his red Manchester United shirt. And then there he was, Saint George himself, wearing baggy shorts, a pair of glasses that had long since lost their lenses, and the grubby vest with the cross of Saint George on it that had given him his name. He had a huge head, so grotesquely swollen by the disease that it was now almost too heavy for his neck to support. It lolled on his shoulders, and if his body hadn't been so stocky, his legs so sturdy, Shadowman might have wondered why he didn't just fall over, he was so top-heavy.

Saint George shuffled out into the middle of the playground, scratching his great bald head, looking around at his fellow strangers, staring them down, his officers flanking him.

Every day he appeared more human, less confused. Perhaps the disease was wearing off? Perhaps his body was fighting it, but if so, why did he continue with his murderous rampage? If anything, he was more savage each night.

Then he stopped. Stood there, the Fear in a big circle all around him, staring silently at him, as if listening. Was he communicating with them somehow? Were they tuned in to his thoughts? There could be no other explanation for what happened next. The Fear moved, as one, and grabbed the twelve weaklings. Tossed them to Saint George.

Shadowman had seen it all through his binoculars. Had watched as Saint George shuddered, turned his face, first to the darkening sky, then down to the pathetic pile of humanity crawling on the ground at his feet.

Then he'd smiled, and the Fear flowed inward and swarmed over the weak ones. Mercilessly and methodically they'd butchered their own kind and were now sharing the meat around. There were too many memories for Shadowman. Taking him back to a time before all this. He remembered summer fairs at elementary school, when all the parents had come to help out, cooking curries and kebobs, sausages and cakes and vegetarian fritters. A band in the corner made up of dads who still dreamed of being rock stars, playing old blues and rock-and-roll songs. Teachers in the stocks having wet sponges thrown at them. Goal-kicking contests. Tables where people sold old clothes and books and unwanted toys. Everyone talking away, eating and drinking and happy.

Well, this was like a horrible parody of those days. Now the parents were eating *each other*. Thank God there were no kids down there tonight. It didn't really upset Shadowman, watching adults being killed and eaten. And that bothered him a little. Bothered him that he wasn't bothered. How quickly he'd become hardened to it all. What did that say about him? Before things fell apart, this would have been the most horrific sight. He'd have needed to go into therapy to cope with it. Now he was mostly intrigued by the organization shown by the strangers, by the planning that had seemed to go into the attack.

Something did bother him, though.

The strangers would be stronger now, better fed, quicker. . . .

But still hungry. Always hungry.

Shadowman prayed that they didn't find any children tonight.

12

Her name was Tish. She was fourteen years old. She'd grown up north of here in Islington, with her mother, a brother named Neil, and a dog named Boris. This much Sam and the Kid had learned about the green girl. Once she'd stopped crying.

Ed had put her in with them, in their little house on Mint Street built into the outer wall of the castle. Mint Street was like a medieval street inside the Tower, with flowers growing in pots and clothes hanging out to dry on lines. The houses were self-contained, mostly single story, with two or three bedrooms each. They had little front doors and narrow arched windows that looked out onto the cobbled street, on the other side of which were the high battlements and old towers of the inner wall. There were some small windows at the back of the houses, little more than arrow slits for the most part, going back more than a foot through the stonework in a cross shape. You couldn't see much through them and Sam was okay with that. The less he saw of the world outside, the better. The Casemates were warm and dry and felt utterly safe. No sickos were ever going to force their way into the castle.

Sam and the Kid shared a room, with a bed each. A girl named Ali had another room, and Tish had been given the third bedroom.

Ed had told Sam and the Kid that they were to gently find out as much as they could about Tish. He felt he couldn't face her yet, felt awful about killing her friend, who he now knew had been Louise. He was keeping a distance and wanted all the other older kids to do the same. Tish needed to settle in and feel reassured.

"Anyone coming here from the outside world has valuable information," he'd told the boys. "When she's ready, Jordan can properly quiz her, but for now find out what you can."

He'd been right to keep away. Tish was really cut up about Louise, wouldn't stop talking about her, about what good friends they'd been. How she couldn't get the picture out of her mind, Louise lying there dead, her hand cut off, her throat slashed, her guts . . .

It had taken her a few days to bottom out, and now she was obviously still very sad, but she wasn't crying all the time. She would either have to bury her sadness or go crazy. Like most kids she had horrible memories shut away and had a sort of haunted look about her. She was calm, though, and quiet, and seemed to like being with Sam and the Kid.

It was nearly bedtime. They'd all four shared a communal meal in the café with the Tower kids—tonight it had been rice and beans—before returning to their house.

Ali had gone to bed to read a book. She read a lot. Had

been quite happy living there by herself, didn't seem to get lonely or need company; nothing seemed to freak her out. She seemed okay with the three newcomers. Hardly seemed to notice them really. Spent most of the time with her nose in a book. Books were valuable, the only real entertainment most kids had, apart from when they fired up the generator and showed DVDs in the pub. The kids who went out foraging always brought back any books they found, and there were a couple of libraries nearby that they visited regularly to pick up cartloads of new reading material.

Sam, the Kid, and Tish were in the living room of their house, their hobbit hole as the Kid called it, as if it had been burrowed out of the flinty stones of the castle.

Tish was sitting on the sofa with her legs curled up under her, drinking a cup of tea she'd brought back from the café, one hand absently picking at the dark scab on her forehead. She was wearing her green outfit: green sweatshirt, green pants. They'd been washed since she'd arrived, which had made the colors fade slightly, and they'd given her some other clothes from the store, but this was her favorite look. Tish liked green.

"What's with the green, sister?" the Kid had asked her the first night she was there, to try to distract her from talking about Louise.

"Living here in London, in all this gray, I need green. It reminds me of the countryside."

"I guess so."

"You should talk," said Tish. "You wear the weirdest clothes I've ever seen."

It was true. The Kid had a very individual dress sense.

His favorite item was a woman's battered old leather jacket that he'd cut the sleeves off of—"Too long. I ain't no gibbon." And since arriving here he'd taken to wearing a long dress over plaid pants that he'd picked up from the Armorers. He claimed the dress kept him warm. He'd also picked up a seventeenth-century helmet that he liked to wear when out and about, even though it was way too big for him. He and Sam were proud of their weapons and armor. Sam went for more of a medieval look. He'd found a leather jerkin that fitted him okay—Ed said it must have belonged to a very stunted soldier—and he had a short sword that he wore slung from a belt over his shoulder. He also had a dagger and a flintlock. The flintlock was unloaded and probably didn't work.

The room was lit by one small candle that gave off a gently flickering orange light. Everybody looked better in candlelight. It hid a lot. Sam and the Kid had been well scrubbed when they'd first gotten here, and Sam had been amazed at how the Kid's skin was now several shades lighter. His hair still stuck up in a wiry tangle, though.

Tish took a sip of her tea and smiled, enjoying the warmth. She stared into her mug, stuck on a memory. Sam hoped she wasn't thinking about Louise again.

"Mom used to make the best cups of tea," she said. "Neil was useless, though. Always made it too weak. Either that or he left the tea bag in so long it tasted rank."

"What happened to them?" Sam asked.

"Neil was older than me; he died of the disease early on. My dad had moved away before. He was in Leicester and we lost contact with him when everything went wrong. I assume he's dead along with most of the adults. I hope he is.

I wouldn't want to think of him as one of them, a Neph, you know, a sicko."

"You call them sickos too?" said Sam.

"Huh?"

"Just like the kids here. We just call them grown-ups, mothers and fathers."

"They're sickos," said Tish. "And when I think of Dad, I think of him like he was, not like them. To be honest, I didn't used to see that much of him. We spoke on the phone now and then, and a couple of times a year he'd come down to London and take me to the Rainforest Café, even when I was too old for it. Every time I saw him he looked at me like I was a stranger. Kept boring on about how tall I was, how I'd grown. And when I got boobs, he was well freaked out. Kept sneaking a look at them like he couldn't believe it. Said I was growing up too fast. Well, if he'd wanted he could've visited me more, couldn't he? He made his life. Made it in Leicester with another woman who wasn't my mom."

"Did your mom die?" asked Sam. "Or did she . . . you know?"

"She was killed, to be honest. It was really bad. Some looters broke into the house, right when things were at their worst. They were looking for food. Mom tried to fight them off, one of them hit her in the head, and that was that. She was killed. They didn't mean it, to kill her, and afterward they took me with them; they felt guilty, I guess, and wanted to look after me. One by one, though, they died of the sickness and I was glad. I hated them. The last one, the one who had done it, who had hit her, he was big and tough, lived longer than the others. I could see he wasn't going to keel over, was gonna become a sicko. I put him out of his misery, the bastard. Put him out of everyone's misery. Knocked him down with a hammer and cut his head off with a garden spade. Good riddance, I say."

Sam looked at Tish, sitting there with her legs tucked up, wrapped in a blanket, staring into her mug of tea. A fourteen-year-old girl. He tried to put this picture together with the other one—Tish cutting a man's head off with a spade. They'd talked about this kind of thing back in Holloway, around the fire in the evenings. Why they were the ones who had survived. Mostly it was luck, sure, but there was something else, something that had helped Sam get across London all by himself, had helped the Kid survive in the tube tunnels, had helped Tish make it here.

They all did what they needed to do to survive.

So many kids had cracked up, lost it big-time. Gone loony. Got so stressed they couldn't cope anymore. Curled up into balls like hedgehogs.

Died.

Tish hadn't curled up; she'd waited and waited, and when the time was right, she'd cut that man's head right off.

Just like that.

"I fell in with a gang of kids after that," Tish went on. "Tough nuts mostly. Knew how to fight but didn't have too much sense. Nobody really in charge. Arguing all the time. We moved around London trying to find a safe place. God, seems like a long time ago now, first with all the rioting and the looting and the murders, then the gangs fighting, then almost everyone dying, and after that the sickos everywhere. And there was fires to deal with and dogs and . . . Well, to be fair, you know how bad it got. I didn't think we were ever going to be safe, and then we arrived at the Temple."

"What temple?" Sam asked.

Tish laughed. "Oh, you know, that's just what we call our camp."

"What sort of temple is it?"

"It's not really a temple. It's just a name, to be honest."

"Does it look like a temple?"

"I don't know." Tish was starting to sound irritated. "One of the boys said it, like, you know, looked like a temple he'd seen in a PlayStation game or something, I think."

"Cool."

"It's not a temple, though, to be fair. It's just, like, a house, a building. Offices and things."

"Okay."

"So where do you hail from of late, wayfarer?" said the Kid. "Where's this temple of yours, and why on earth were you out there running around in Zombieland like a lost sheep?"

"We came from the center of town. You know? Our base is near Trafalgar Square."

"This temple of which you speak?"

"Yeah, this temple of which I speak." Tish giggled. "I'm sorry. You make me laugh."

"That's because I'm elemental, my dear Watson."

"So what were you doing all the way over here?" Sam asked.

"Yeah," said the Kid. "You were a long way from home without a paddle."

"There was ten of us came out," said Tish. "We were exploring. Seeing what other kids might be out there. We didn't mean to come this far. But then we bumped into some sickos, and they had other plans for us."

"You was ham-busted?" said the Kid. "Taken by surprise and blindsided, mashed up like pumpkins and done up like kippers?"

"We were attacked, yeah, if that's what you mean," said Tish. "They chased us all over. Half our group split off and went back; me and three others, we kept on running. Came farther and farther this way. Didn't really know where we were, to be honest. Then another group of sickos got us. And that's when Ed and his crew eventually found us, hiding in that building. Only he got to us too late. The others were all killed."

Tish stopped talking. There were tears in her eyes, and her voice was raspy and wobbly.

"That's bad," said Sam.

Tish nodded.

"We didn't know," she said quietly. "We were told we'd be protected, that no harm would come to us. We didn't have any idea how dangerous it was going to be on the other side of the Wall. How bad it is out this way."

"You came through the forbidden zone," said Sam.

"What's that?"

"The no-go zone. It's what the kids here call the whole area to the north and west."

"The badlands," said the Kid. "Full of outlaws and scum-crackers and professional no-goodniks. Sickos and ogres and blood-farmers, sniffing out the youngers. In the words of the prophet, 'Don't go there, man.'"

"Me and the Kid came all through the City of London,"

said Sam, trying not to sound too much like he was showing off. "You see where all the banks used to be? All the money-makers in their skyscrapers? We were like you: we didn't know where we were really or how bad it was. Maybe that's why we made it through. We were too stupid to be caught. The kids here couldn't believe we'd done it. They don't ever go there."

"Ancient evil," said the Kid. "Bad magic. The devil's playground."

"They only go out to the east and south over Tower Bridge," said Sam. "We're not allowed anywhere near the way you came."

"But if I'm going to get home, I have to go back that way," said Tish.

"You want to go back?"

Tish nodded. "Of course I do. It's my home. It's where all my friends are. They'll want to know what happened to us. I mean, don't get me wrong, in all fairness, what I've seen of it, it seems nice here; everyone's nice and friendly and it's safe and you have food and water, but it's not my home, is it?"

"It's not our food and water," said Sam.

"What do you mean?"

"This isn't our home. We're not staying, either."

"Really?" Tish sat up straight, listening more intently.

"Yeah," said Sam. "I have to find my sister, Ella. We got split up. She was heading for Buckingham Palace. I'd love to stay here, don't want ever to go back out there, but . . . I have to find her. I promised I'd look after her, you see."

"But to find her you'd have to go through the forbidden zone."

"Yeah. There's no way around it."

Tish thought about something for a bit, then smiled at Sam.

"We know the kids at Buckingham Palace," she said brightly.

"You do?"

"Yeah." Tish nodded. "We're really close to them in Trafalgar Square."

"Do you know if my sister made it there, then? She was traveling down from Holloway."

"Yeah." Tish's smile was so big it looked like it was going to split her head in half. "Did you say she was called Ella?"

"Yeah. Ella Brewer. Do you know her?"

"I do know that some kids arrived there recently from north London. It must be them. Ella must be there."

"I have to go and find her," said Sam, "but Ed won't let us."

"What's it got to do with him?"

Sam explained about the expedition that some kids had gone on and how Ed wasn't letting anyone else leave until they returned.

"What if they never return?" said Tish. "Then what?"

Sam shrugged.

"I'll tell you then what," said the Kid. "We're stuck here like bug-eyed flies on bug-eyed flypaper. In short, sweetheart, it's a bugger."

Tish stared into Sam's eyes.

"He'll never let you go," she said bluntly.

13

He'll keep you here. He doesn't want you to leave."

"Why do you say that?"

"The kids here are strong. They could put together an army and push their way through anything. But they sit behind their walls. They could get you to Buckingham Palace easy if they wanted. It wouldn't take them more than two or three hours at the most, to be honest."

"But it's through the badlands."

"I came through the badlands."

"And all your friends were killed."

"We weren't prepared. We weren't an army. Not soldiers like the kids here. We thought it would be easy. We were dumb. I'm not dumb anymore. If we were prepared, if we did it right, we could get through."

"What do you mean 'we'?"

"Us three. We could do it. In the daytime when the sickos are asleep. Go quickly. Properly armed."

"But—"

"Ed won't ever take you. Believe me. And he won't let

you go with me neither. I know it. They don't want any kids to know what's really out there. If you stay here you'll never see your sister again."

"Why would Ed want to keep me here?"

"You've heard the rumors?" said Tish.

"What rumors?"

"You know the ones. I've heard them too. People have talked to me; they know I'm living here with you two."

"What rumors?"

"They all talk about you. How you're special."

"I'm not special," said Sam.

"Special needs maybe," said the Kid.

"It doesn't matter whether you believe it," said Tish. "*They* believe it. They believe that if they keep you here they'll be safe. Ed will never let you go. You're too important to him. But us three . . ."

"That way madness lies," said the Kid. "Us three traipsing off like dilly-dallies, bog-eyed silly billies. You were big kids and you got sliced and diced, they murdered your faces. What chance would us three musketeers have?"

"You lived on the streets by yourself," said Tish, "and Sam made it all the way here from Holloway, didn't you?"

"Yeah, but—"

"Two squirts like you. You're lucky. Maybe you *are* special."

"You're wearing green and you ain't so lucky," said the Kid.

Tish smiled at him, then smiled at Sam. "You two will bring me luck. You feel lucky. I just know it."

"It doesn't make any sense what you're saying," said Sam.

"First you tell us how bad it is out there, and then you say us three could make it back to your place, to the palace."

"An army is right," said the Kid. "An army is what we need."

"It's only the first bit that's dangerous, to be honest," said Tish. "The no-go zone."

"They call it that for a reason."

"Yeah," said the Kid. "So we no go there."

"We'll think of a way," said Tish. "We'll work something out."

"I'm going to talk to Ed again," said Sam. "Try to persuade him. This isn't right."

Tish looked anxious. "You won't tell him what we've talked about, will you?" she said. "About our plan?"

"Not that bit, no. If he thought we were even *thinking* about going by ourselves, he'd probably lock us up."

Tish got up and hugged him. "We can do it. We'll be all right."

She sat back down. Sam's cheek was wet where she had pushed her own tear-streaked cheek against him.

"Hey, hold on, babe," said the Kid. "Don't the Kid get a hug?"

Tish looked at the Kid, and for a moment she seemed fearful. Then she smiled and gave him a quick stiff hug.

"Boobalicious!" said the Kid.

Tish looked awkward and Sam understood. The Kid was weird. He freaked some people out. Sam knew he had a good heart, though. He was loyal and brave and tough as anything.

He was the best kid in the world.

Sam would make Tish understand that.

14

Ed scratched his head and yawned. It was another early start for him. The sun was barely up, and the war room in the White Tower was freezing cold. Even though he was wrapped in his winter coat, knit hat, and gloves, the cold had gotten into him. His breath hung in the air in a frosty cloud. Once a week General Jordan Hordern pulled all his captains together for a meeting, and he insisted on doing it at dawn. Jordan never seemed to need any sleep. You could see candles burning in the Queen's House long into the night, and he was always the first up.

Ed sometimes found it funny. You'd have thought that a bunch of kids, young teenagers mostly, left to themselves with no adults to tell them what to do, would have slept all day and partied all night. But it wasn't like that. They usually went to bed at sundown and woke at sunrise. Ed really could have done with a sleep-in this morning. But as captain of the Tower Guard, he had to be there.

He'd hardly slept. There'd been trouble with one of the girls, Zosia. She'd gotten hold of some vodka from somewhere and made herself horribly drunk. She'd smashed a window in the Queen's House, screamed abuse at Jordan, and then started throwing up everywhere before she passed out. Ed had had to sit with her and make sure she didn't choke on her own vomit in her sleep.

Ed's lieutenant, Kyle, was explaining what had happened to Jordan.

"She was Brendan's girlfriend."

Jordan nodded, his eyes unreadable behind his thick lenses. They were sitting directly above the room in which they'd held the trial, where Jordan had ordered Brendan's execution.

"I thought that girl, what's she called? The one that went off with DogNut? I thought she was Brendan's girlfriend."

"Jessica?" said Ed.

"That's her."

"She used to be his girlfriend," said Kyle. "Only they split up. That's why she went with DogNut. To get away. Then Brendan took up with Zosia."

"What are people saying about it?" asked Jordan.

"That Bren was cut up about Jessica. Went a bit crazy. Tried to impress Zosia by jacking that stuff. He was showing off to his new wifey. Showing her he could look after her with all that loot."

"Do they think I was too harsh?" said Jordan.

"It's mixed," said Ed. "Some think Bren had to be punished for stealing; others—his friends, Zosia obviously—reckon the punishment was too cold. It frightens them, thinking about what's out there, wondering how they'd cope if it was them."

"That was kind of the idea."

"We don't want everyone to be scared," said Tomoki. Because Tomoki had been in charge at the Tower before Jordan arrived, the kids who'd been there before looked up to him, although none of them would ever dare challenge Jordan as leader. Brendan had been one of Tomoki's kids, and it was among them that the bad feeling about how he'd been treated was strongest.

"Fear doesn't do anyone any good," Tomoki went on. "Some of the kids here, if they're not part of one of the more active regiments, haven't left these walls in months. That makes them bored and scared; actually, not so much scared, more anxious, nervous, worried. . . . What's the word I'm looking for?"

"Neurotic?" Ed suggested.

"Yeah. That's it. And those two little boys arriving . . ."

"Baaaa," said Kyle, and a couple of the other kids laughed.

"It's kinda freaked everyone out," said Tomoki. "Some people are talking about them bringing bad luck."

"Oh, for Christ's sake," Ed spluttered. "Grow up, Tomoki."

Tomoki blushed. "It's not me," he said. "It's not my group. It's your group, Jordan, the ones who were at the war museum. They think those boys are special in some way."

"They *are* special." Ed was trying not to shout. "They're special because they're brave. They're bloody heroes. They're special because they made it here all by themselves. But they are *not* some kind of spooky magic figures out of World of Warcraft or something. Just because of a stupid coincidence that they happen to look vaguely like the kids Mad Matt painted on his poxy banner. So I don't want to hear any more rubbish about people being freaked out by them."

"It's not just that," said Tomoki.

"What is it, then?"

"It's everything. It's being bottled up here. Kids are starting to think that this is it." He indicated the four walls with his hands. "They're starting to think they'll just hang on here until they get old and die. We need to think about doing something more. Giving them something to look forward to."

"Like what?" Jordan asked.

"I don't know. Breaking out of here. Taking the City back. Maybe going on the attack instead of always being on the defense."

"You saying we need to get into the forbidden zone?"

"Sooner or later we're going to have to," said Keren, who was captain of the Pathfinders until DogNut got back.

"Keren's right," said Tomoki. "The zone sits there on two sides of the Tower, like a constant reminder, and it makes the kids nervous."

"Neurotic," said Jordan.

"Yeah. Neurotic. Why can't I remember that word? I mean, the thing is, Jordan, you've got troops. Why not use them? Let's take war parties in there and kick some heads in."

"There's still loads of sickos out there," Ed interrupted. "Why risk kids' lives?"

"I think it might help—what's the word . . . making everyone feel good?" said Tomoki.

"Morale."

"Yeah."

"How good would it be for morale if kids got hurt, Tomoki? Got killed?"

"We just have to make sure we get more of them than they get of us," said Kyle, and he chuckled.

Kyle never seemed to get bothered by anything. He was probably a psychopath. But in these changed times psychopaths were useful. At least he was Ed's psychopath. He'd hate to be on the opposite side of Kyle in a fight.

Ed's scar was itching, like it always did when he was stressed. He couldn't forget seeing that girl in the corridor, Louise, the one he'd killed. Couldn't forget the effect it had had on Tish. There was no way they could go out there into the streets and not be in danger. And risk more moments like that. More kids dead, more kids wiped out by the loss of a friend.

Ed sighed and pushed his hair back off his face. "I just don't think we should do anything until DogNut gets back," he said. "He can give us a much better idea of what's out there."

"Sounds to me like you're just scared," said Keren. "Us Pathfinders go out into the streets every day."

"Not into the zone you don't," Ed snapped. "Like I did to rescue Tish."

"Scared you, did it?" said Keren with a smirk.

Kyle gave Keren a dirty look, full of murder. "Ed ain't scared," he said bluntly.

"If you say so," Keren muttered.

Ed hung his head in his hands. Kyle knew the truth. Ed *was* scared, but not of sickos. He was scared of himself. Kyle might have been a psycho, but deep down Ed knew that he himself was worse. When Ed got into a fight, he became a different person, capable of terrible violence. That was why he didn't want to lead any war parties into the no-go zone looking for sickos to slaughter. He didn't want to be plunged back into a killing frenzy.

"I'll think about it," said Jordan. "But I ain't making any decisions until DogNut's back. I'm not moving without intelligence."

"He ain't coming back," said Kyle.

"We'll talk about it at the next council," said Jordan. "I want to hear some real ideas."

He stood up. The meeting was over. He walked across the wooden floor to the stairs. The others began filtering out after him, chatting excitedly about the meeting. Ed had to admit that Tomoki was probably right. The kids needed some focus. Something to do. A feeling of power, of taking control.

He didn't want to talk about it anymore now, though. He waited for the others to leave, then made his way down the stairs and out into the sunlight. It was a cool, crisp morning. The Tower ravens were hopping about in the big vegetable planters, rooting for grubs. The day was warming up. Ed was thinking about breakfast. He stretched, loosening his stiff muscles, and heard someone call his name.

He looked around to see Small Sam and the Kid hurrying toward him across the cobblestones. They were clumsy in their armor and with their swords hanging at their sides. He smiled. They looked so eager and happy.

"We want to talk to you," said Sam.

"I gathered that. What's up?"

"When are we going to be able to go and look for my sister?"

"Whoa, hang on. Who said you were?"

"You promised."

"Yeah, but Sam, I told you we need to wait for DogNut."

"If you won't help us, we'll go by ourselves."

Ed couldn't bear to imagine these two young boys going back out into the streets.

"No, you won't," he said angrily, sounding like a bossy parent. He tried to calm down. "Not yet," he said. "You need to wait and be patient. Things are happening. We just had a meeting."

"What about?"

"Well, one of the things we talked about was you. . . ."

"What about us?"

"It doesn't matter. We talked about you and the forbidden zone. We're making plans."

"Will they affect us?"

"They'll affect everyone. But you know what? You two, you're *special*, okay? And whatever happens, I'm going to keep you near me. So don't worry about anything."

Ed could see he hadn't convinced Sam. He'd been trying to reassure him and he'd failed. Sam looked utterly gutted. Like a kid who'd been told he couldn't go on a longed-for outing. He was too young to hide his feelings.

The Kid just scowled.

Ed squatted down so that he was on their level and put his hands on Sam's shoulders.

"Please be patient, Sam," he said. "I'm not bullshitting

you. I *will* help you find your sister. Just not yet, okay? In a week's time we'll talk about it again. Do you trust me?"

Sam bit his lip and nodded once, staring at the ground.

"Come on, maggot," said the Kid. "There's nothing for us here."

He dragged his friend away.

Ed swore. It was clear Sam hadn't believed a word he'd said, but he'd just have to wait. Ed would show him. In fact, he'd start making plans that night. Present them to Jordan at the next war council. Yeah. He'd surprise Sam and the Kid. Go and visit them in their little house in the Casemates and sort it all out. And he'd talk to Tish. It would be an opportunity to break the ice with her. He was being oversensitive about killing her friend. The sickos had ripped Louise's guts out, for God's sake. It wasn't his fault. He had to stop feeling guilty.

Life had to go on.

15

The Thames was low, exposing a stretch of muddy beach on which a cargo ship was stranded, jammed halfway under the Tower Pier. The pier was a relatively new construction that had been built for river cruisers and passenger ferries to dock. The Tower kids now used it themselves. They were starting to explore the river in rowboats, learning to read its tides and navigate its strong currents. The wrecked boat, which must have slipped its moorings some way upriver, would damage the pier if left where it was. Plus, it was valuable salvage.

It was pretty big and its ancient oak timbers were splintered down one side. A work party of older kids was busy on the beach dismantling it with axes, saws, and crowbars. As they freed a section of planking, other kids hauled it across the beach to the foot of the embankment, where pieces were tied with rope and hauled up.

Tomoki was standing behind some railings watching the activity below. He turned to see three kids at his side. Tish and the two little boys. He had to admit the boys looked pretty normal to him—except that they were both laden with armor and weapons, and the dark-haired one appeared to be wearing a dress, like they were on their way to a fancy-dress party.

"You won't need all that stuff today," said Tomoki, trying not to laugh.

The Kid patted his sword. "We never go anywhere without our hardware, squire," he said. "Forearmed is forewarned."

"I tried sleeping with my sword one night," said Sam, adjusting his scabbard. "Kept waking me up, though. Sticking into me. I leave it by the bed now."

"Fair enough," said Tomoki. "But you might find it's going to slow you down a bit."

"We'll be all right," said Sam. "So what do you want us to do?"

"It'll be your job to help load the salvaged wood onto those dollies over there and wheel them to the sorting area by the ticket offices."

A shout went up from the beach, and they craned over the railings in time to see two big boys carry a steel barrel out of the wreckage.

There was evidently more plunder on the boat than just the wood.

It was mostly wood that the three kids were going to be shifting, though. They got to work, grabbing the salvage as it was hauled up and piling it onto their dolly. Once they had a full load, Sam and the Kid took hold of the bar at the back and Tish gripped the arm at the front, and they began to wheel it up to the sorting area.

"I'm really not sure about this," said Sam.

"We might never get another opportunity this good," said Tish, straining to keep the heavy dolly moving.

"It all feels kind of sudden," said Sam.

"We've got to grab the chance while we can."

"Yeah, but I'm still not sure."

They had sat up half the night planning how to escape from the Tower when they were ready. And this morning, when they'd been told that they'd be working outside the walls, Tish had gotten very excited. Had tried to convince them that it was the perfect opportunity to get away unnoticed. At first Sam had been caught up in her enthusiasm, but now he was having second thoughts.

"What exactly did Ed say to you again?" Tish asked as the dolly bumped over the uneven, cobbled ground.

"That we're special," said Sam, "the Kid and me, and that he wanted to keep us near him."

"You see. It's what I said."

"But I don't really know what he meant," said Sam. "I'm muddled. It doesn't feel right, us three running off into the forbidden zone. It's too dangerous. It's crazy."

"What's crazy is staying here, to be fair," said Tish. "You never meant to come here. You've got to get to Buckingham Palace. Your sister needs you."

"Yeah. I'm still scared, though."

"It's the middle of the day. The sickos will all be asleep. Us three can travel fast and light. It's only about three miles. If we're quick we can do it in an hour. The hardest part will be getting clear of the Tower guards. If we try to just walk away, they'll stop us. We need a diversion."

"Hold your horses, Captain," said the Kid. "All of it,

every word you say, all the spouting of it, you make it sound too easy. I don't like it. It's too quiet. There's Indians out there."

"We've got to go for it," said Tish.

"Well . . ." The Kid turned to Sam. "I'm with you, little boots. What you say goes."

"I don't want to be stuck here forever."

"We'll be fine," said Tish.

"So what do we do?"

"The guards are looking for sickos coming in, not kids going out. I'll think of some way to distract them."

Tish had a map book, and last night they'd discussed routes. In the end Tish had said that they should head for Great Tower Street, then along Eastcheap, Cannon Street, past St. Paul's Cathedral, into Ludgate Hill, Fleet Street, the Aldwych, and on to the Strand, which would take them all the way to Trafalgar Square. Almost a straight line all the way. She'd shown them where her hideout was, the place she called "the Temple"; it was a large building behind the London Coliseum, although you couldn't tell much about it from the simplified black-and-white maps in the book.

This morning, when she'd heard about the salvage operation, Tish had packed some emergency rations into her backpack, as well as a flashlight, some matches, a knife, and a few other useful bits and pieces.

"We'll get to the Temple, pick up some support, and go straight on to the palace," she'd explained. "You'll be with your sister by this evening, instead of being stuck here polishing armor for the rest of your life."

They crossed the wide-open area by the ticket offices and

unloaded the dolly. A group of older kids was breaking up the wooden sections further, separating the planks and stacking them in neat piles ready to be carted into the castle to be reused.

Tish took the opportunity to look around. She timed some boys guarding the perimeter. In the past, crowds waiting to go into the Tower had gathered here, joined by sightseers who just wanted to take pictures or gawk at the old castle. There had been food stalls, entertainers, and sometimes marching bands and displays. Now the kids used it as a sorting area before stuff was taken into the Tower. They didn't want to fill their living space with too much junk, so there were a couple of Dumpsters here as well. Once they'd built up a big pile, it was tossed in the Thames to be washed out to sea.

That morning a unit of Pathfinders had found three cars in a private garage with gas in their tanks and their keys hanging on a Peg-Board. Two matching silver Mercedes C-Classes and a red Porsche 911 Carrera. They'd driven them to the sorting area and parked them with the vehicles they'd collected over the months. Some small boys were standing around admiring them.

"Let's get another load," said Tish, and they wheeled their dolly back down to the river.

"The longer we wait, the less I want to do this," said Sam.

"Don't worry," said Tish. "I've got an idea."

"What?" Sam's heart was pounding. He was filled with a mixture of fear and excitement. Everything was happening too fast for him to know if he was doing the right thing.

"I'll start a fire," said Tish. "When we get back up there, you talk to the boy racers with their shiny cars, keep them busy. When you see smoke, head for the shop. We'll go together from there."

"Okay."

Back at the river's edge, there was a stack of wood ready for them to load onto their dolly. They plunked it on in silence. Sam's throat was too dry to talk. He couldn't figure out if he was most worried about getting away from the Tower kids or of what they might have to face if they were successful. He looked at the Kid. Couldn't read him at all. If the Kid was okay with the way things were heading, then Sam was okay. He'd survived alone out there. He knew all about danger.

But what was he thinking?

Sam caught his eye and the Kid winked at him.

What did that mean?

"Come on." Tish was ready to be off and Sam took hold of the bar. The dolly rattled and squeaked as it got under way.

Was he right to trust Tish? Shouldn't he trust Ed instead? Ed had promised to take him to find Ella. Was he just lying, though? There was all that creepy stuff about the lamb and the goat. Sam was too confused to straighten it all out. Best just to keep moving.

Into the no-go zone . . .

He'd spent time in there before. It was where he'd been held prisoner by two grown-ups, Nick and Rachel, in their subway car down in the tunnels beneath Bank Station. They hadn't seemed to be affected by the disease. They'd said they wanted to help Sam, told him they were keeping him safe.

Just like Ed.

And just like Ed they hadn't wanted him to go. . . .

Of course the grown-ups weren't normal. They had the disease in them. Deep down and hidden. And they'd been fattening Sam up so they could eat him. It was the Kid who'd rescued him. Sam had escaped the forbidden zone one time. And now here he was getting ready to run back into danger, like an idiot.

Was he really planning to leave the safety of the castle? Somewhere he'd always dreamed of living? He looked across at the high yellow-gray walls.

Tish was right.

This place might be a castle, but for hundreds of years it had also been a prison. If he stayed here too long, he'd never get away. He'd forget about Ella; she'd fade from his memory like his parents had. It was less than three weeks since he'd last seen her, but so much had happened in that time. He'd moved from one world to another. He tried to picture her now, but all he could remember clearly was a photograph that had been on the mantelpiece at home. Him and Ella with Father Christmas. Ella looking like she was about to cry, Sam looking embarrassed.

She was two years younger than him. Preferred to wear boys' clothing to girls' and had short dark hair.

That was about it.

It wasn't enough.

He had to find her. She was all he had left of the past.

They unloaded their delivery and he strolled over to the cars with the Kid while Tish slipped away.

He stood watching the older boys, who were taking turns sitting in the driver's seat of the Porsche. Out of the corner of his eye he saw Tish going over to the end of the row of older cars. He was supposed to be distracting these boys, wasn't he?

"How fast does it go?" he asked one of them.

"About a hundred and eighty."

Sam nodded. "Cool." In truth he didn't really know very much about cars, but 180 miles an hour did sound pretty fast.

"Has it got a full tank?"

"Half full. It drinks a ton of fuel as well."

"Yeah." Sam nodded again. He was running out of things to talk about. "I like the color."

"You want to sit in it?"

"No. I'm all right." What was taking Tish so long? He nudged the Kid in the ribs. "Help me out here," he hissed.

"It's got four wheels," said the Kid, who evidently knew less about cars than Sam. The older boy laughed.

"You're weird," he said.

"I'm no weirder than a dog with the head of a cat and the heart of a humming bee."

"I guess not."

Mercifully Sam saw a puff of black smoke waft above the row of cars.

There was a shout.

"Hey!"

The smoke thickened, turned into a column. Kids were shouting and running toward the cars. There was a hubbub of voices.

"It's on fire."

"Fetch some water."

"Don't get too close, it might explode."

"What happened?"

Sam and the Kid edged away from the commotion, moving backward through the crowd of kids who were congregating around the fire. They reached the ticket offices and found Tish waiting for them.

"I thought it would never catch fire," she said. "But look at it go now!"

The guards were wandering over from the perimeter, drawn by the fire, forgetting what they were supposed to be doing. In the end they were all just children and couldn't be expected to have the discipline of trained soldiers.

"What did you do?" Sam asked, staring at the flames that were leaping above the cars.

"Set fire to some crap on the backseat of an old Ford Focus."

"Will it be all right?"

"Of course it won't be all right!" Tish gave a short, slightly crazy-sounding squeal of laughter.

"Now let's go."

16

They ducked behind the ticket offices and made their way quickly around the big modern building in back. In fact it was two buildings, joined by a huge glass wall and roof. A pedestrian walkway led between it and an old church. They pounded along it, fully expecting to hear someone screaming at them to stop.

It didn't happen.

Sam realized he was crying. This wasn't right. To be running away from other kids. He was letting them down. He felt really bad for Ed. Ed had been the kindest. He'd only wanted to help Sam, keep him alive. Ed was sensible. Tish seemed reckless and a bit strange.

Sam knew he'd be getting Ed in a lot of trouble—all of them. They'd wonder what had happened, probably put together a search party. Ed would worry about him. And he was clever. He'd work it out. He'd know that Sam had gone off to look for Ella. Sam hoped he wouldn't try to follow. He didn't want to put any of the castle kids in danger. He remembered what Ed had said, about how he couldn't risk other kids getting hurt for Sam's sake.

And now look what he'd done.

It was Tish's fault. She'd rushed him into it. Dragged him into the forbidden zone. Even the bravest fighters from the Tower didn't come here. Not Ed. Not Kyle. Not anyone. And there was only this green-shirted girl to show them the way.

Already his legs were aching, his chest burning. He knew he wouldn't be able to keep this up for long. His sword slapped painfully against his side, and twice now he'd almost tripped over it. His helmet was heavy on his head; the breast-plate he was wearing, part of a child's suit of armor, cut into him. He wished now that he'd left the armor behind.

"Can we slow down?" he gasped, trying to catch up with Tish and the Kid.

"Whassup, shortstuff? Ain't got the legs for it?" said the Kid.

"I'm getting a stitch."

"We need to make sure we're well out of sight of the Tower," said Tish.

Sam stopped and looked back. The road had curved to the left and he couldn't see anything of the castle past the tall buildings. And if he couldn't see the Tower, then surely nobody in the Tower could see him.

"They can't see us here," he said. "We're miles away." He bent over and rested his hands on his knees.

"We should keep going," said Tish.

"Should we?" Sam said angrily.

"Of course."

"We're running from the wrong people," Sam muttered, and stretched his aching side.

"Chin up. We made it," said the Kid. "Out of the frying pan."

"You know the rest of that saying, don't you?" said Sam.

"What saying?"

"Out of the frying pan."

"I just made it up."

"No, you didn't."

"Yes, I did. I'm a wordsmith."

"Oh, never mind." Sam straightened up and looked around. They were on a boring street of offices and banks. Ed had told him that this part of town was where people had come to work during the day. No one had really lived here. There were no normal shops, just a few sandwich bars and coffee places.

He hoped it would stay boring. The last thing he wanted now was excitement. Maybe he'd worried too much. It was still and quiet. There was nobody else around. No signs of life at all apart from a few pigeons flapping about.

So far so good.

He knew that it could be a trick, though. Tish and her friends had been attacked by grown-ups close by here, hadn't they? He just hoped that all the grown-ups were asleep now, down in their cellars.

"We have to hurry," said Tish. "The quicker we get through the zone, the better."

"How long did it take you before?"

"About an hour."

"That quick?"

"Maybe two. It's hard to say, because when we got chased, we lost our way. Get moving, though, Sam, yeah? We can talk as we run."

"Fast walk," said Sam. "I can't run for two hours. I'm not Superman."

"We won't have to; it's only till we're out of danger."

"And how far is that?"

"To be honest, I don't know. It's the kids at the Tower that made up the idea of the zone. We don't call it that. We don't measure it or anything."

"But you don't usually go this way?"

"No. Everyone knows it's dangerous. So let's hurry, yeah?"

"Okay."

Sam jogged off after Tish and the Kid. He had drawn his dagger and was gripping it tightly in his hand. It gave him some degree of comfort, though he knew that if he saw any grown-ups he would simply run as fast as he could in the opposite direction rather than stop and fight.

A couple of minutes later they came to some burned-out buildings. There was rubble strewn in the road that they had to pick their way through, and Sam spotted a couple of dirty skeletons in the ruins, their bones jumbled up with steel girders, broken masonry, cables, and charred furniture.

It was as they were clambering over the last stretch of rubble that they heard a rhythmic tapping noise. It seemed to be coming from a side street. Like metal hammering stone.

The sort of sound you used to hear coming from construction sites. As the children stopped to listen, the sound stopped. They waited. Nothing.

They moved on, and as they did so, the sound started up again, this time appearing to come from a different direction.

"Can you hear that?" Sam stood frozen in the road.

"It's nothing," said Tish. "A bird or something."

"Why? How do you know? Have you heard it before?"

"No, but what else could it be? Let's keep going."

"What bird makes a noise like that?"

"To be fair, it could be anything."

"I think we should go back. I don't like this."

"We can't go back now. We've come this far."

"But there's still a long way to go. I shouldn't never have listened to you. This is a dumb idea. We should go back and talk to Ed. Persuade him."

Tish suddenly grew angry and yelled at Sam. "We are NOT going back! Don't be such a wimp. We're okay." Then she grabbed him and pulled him along the road.

Her shout had sounded horribly loud, reminding Sam of how quiet it had been before.

Except for the clicking, that is.

For a moment after her rant there was a deep, empty silence, then the clicking, tapping, knocking sound started up all around them, seeming to come from every direction.

"Tap, tap, tapping on my cough-cough-coffin," said the Kid.

"Great," said Sam. "That's made me feel a lot better."

"I don't like it, Captain."

"It's just something banging in the wind," said Tish. "It doesn't mean anything."

"What wind?" said Sam, and he jerked his arm free of her grip, stuffed his dagger in his belt, and drew his sword. The Kid did the same.

"Ready for anything," said the Kid. "Come at me, varlet, and I will spike thy gizzards."

They moved on down the street at a fast walk, the noises keeping pace with them. Up ahead they could see the white stonework of St. Paul's rising up into the sky. Sam's head was throbbing, filled with a dull ache. His muscles were sore with tension.

He spotted a sign for Mansion House tube station and the throbbing in his head got suddenly worse. He associated the London underground sign with dark tunnels and hungry grown-ups.

And then his heart sank into his boots.

The road was completely blocked. There was a sort of barricade made from a burned-out bus and a pile of cars all tangled together with junkyard bits and pieces. The kids would have to climb over it or go around it via one of the side streets.

The street from where the noises were still coming.

Tap-clink-tap-clink-tap-tap-tap . . .

"What do we do?" Sam asked Tish. "Did you come this way before?"

"It was all a bit of a panic, to be honest with you."

"Oh God," said Sam. "Please, let's just go back."

"We're nearly there."

"No, we're not. Don't be stupid. Trafalgar Square's ages away still."

"I meant we're nearly out of the zone."

"I'm going back."

"I never had you down for a chicken," said Tish.

"He ain't no chicken, matron," said the Kid. "He's just got a sensible head under his hat today. We didn't think this through. We got a choice. This is fifty-fifty. Danger one way—home the other."

"This way." Tish turned her back on the two of them and started to climb over the barricade. Sam and the Kid had no choice but to follow her, clambering over the pile of junk.

When they got to the top, they heard Tish swear and found her standing there trembling.

There were five grown-ups waiting in the road on the other side. Crouched low, curious and wary.

17

"That's just great," said Sam. "That's really great. What do we do now?"

"You want to phone a friend?" asked the Kid.

"No. I want to go back to the Tower."

"Is that your final answer?"

"Yes." Sam turned and started to scramble back down the barricade. Just before he got to the bottom his scabbard caught on something and he tripped and fell, bashing his arm on a car door as he went. He landed in a heap, swearing and trying not to burst into tears again. The Kid and Tish came down and helped him up.

"You okay?" Tish asked.

"No, I'm not. I feel like an idiot. What are we doing here?"

"You want to phone a friend?" asked the Kid again.

"Shut up," Sam snapped, not amused by the Kid's jokes anymore. "Just shut up, can't you?"

But as he picked up his sword, he saw that they were trapped. A larger group of grown-ups was shuffling along the road toward them. And more of them were coming from the south.

They were wary like the first group. Like wild dogs he'd seen on nature programs, staying in a pack, holding back as they studied their prey, getting ready to move in for the kill. They were a mixed bunch, all ages and states of decay, their clothes and skin so black and greasy they looked like they were wearing wet suits.

Sam swore, felt his whole body shaking with a toxic cocktail of fear and fury and self-pity.

"This way," said Tish, and she headed down a narrow alleyway that cut off the main road to the north. Sam and the Kid stayed hard on her heels. No time to think. No time to plan. Just run and keep running as the blood hammered in your ears.

If it had been an organized ambush, then it hadn't been very *well* organized. The grown-ups had left the alleyway clear.

Unless, of course, that was the plan, to funnel them down here . . .

Ambush? Don't be stupid. Grown-ups don't make plans.

Except this was the forbidden zone, wasn't it? Where the normal rules didn't apply. Where the grown-ups behaved differently. That's what Ed had said. They were unpredictable. Strange things happened. That's why it was so dangerous.

That was why it was no-go.

Why-why-why had he listened to Tish? Why? This was horrible. He'd been so safe in the Tower he'd forgotten just how scary it was out on the streets. He'd blanked it out of his mind. Those awful days getting from Holloway to the Tower. Wetting his pants, blubbering with fear, frozen into a terrified little ball of nerves. Part of him wanted to do that now. Lie down, curl up, and wait for it all to be over.

But a bigger part of him made Sam run.

It was dark in the alley, the high walls seeming to lean inward. There were old tailor's shops and black-and-gold-painted pubs on either side, so different from the modern buildings on the main road. This was a part of historical London, like something out of a Dickens film on TV.

Except Dickens films didn't have cannibal grown-ups chasing kids.

As he ran, Sam could hear the tapping sound echoing all around him. It seemed much closer, coming from right next to him . . . up above . . . inside his head. . . .

He could see nothing, though. Nothing.

Just run.

They came to a junction, but the road to the left was blocked with another barricade.

"Keep going!" Tish shouted.

Keep going where? Sam thought. They should be heading back to the Tower. Not trying to press on deeper into the zone. Well, it was up to the grown-ups now, wasn't it? It all depended on which way they chased the three kids.

There was a large redbrick church ahead of them, with another passageway running off to the left.

Sam called out to Tish.

"Do you know where we are?"

"Go left."

They ran down behind the church and came out into a small square. There was a single twisted tree and the statue of a man who looked a little like a pirate.

The clicking was even louder than ever here, and Sam gradually became aware that the dark places, the doorways, the corners and steps, even a couple of parked cars, were filled with grown-ups. They were sitting squashed together in groups, and they all had something in their hands—bottles, cobblestones, bricks, bones, bits of metal—and were banging them together, like ghostly street performers.

For the moment, though, they weren't attacking.

"What do we do?" Sam asked.

Behind them their pursuers were coming up the passageway.

"We're so close," said Tish.

"Close to what?" said Sam. "Don't be stupid, we're not close to anywhere."

"I'm not stupid," Tish hissed. "Don't call me stupid."

"You brought us here, didn't you?" said Sam, careful not to raise his voice. "Right into the middle of . . . grown-ups."

"This is Nibelheim," said the Kid.

"Maybe if we just keep going they won't chase us," said Tish, ignoring the Kid.

"What are they doing?" Sam asked.

"How am I supposed to know?" said Tish. "Stop asking me questions."

"Them's dwarves, hammering out their gold," said the Kid, and again the others ignored him.

They started walking slowly, slowly, not wanting to disturb the grown-ups, heading for the north side of the square, where it was open onto the main road. Expecting every step of the way one of the grown-ups to jump up and come after them.

For a few seconds it looked like they were going to make it. The grown-ups just stared at them with dull, lifeless eyes, tapping out their rhythm. There was a powerful, evil stench hanging in the air, trapped by the buildings. Sam tried not to look too closely at the mothers and fathers, at their pock-marked skin, their boils and swellings, the rotting patches in their flesh. The green flowerings of mold.

While the sound of their tapping drilled into his skull.

"Different drummers," whispered the Kid.

Sam shushed him.

"We need to go into Alberich's cave."

"*Shut up. . . .*"

And then there was a movement. A bloated mother squirmed out of a car and started to limp toward them. It acted like a signal. Everywhere now grown-ups were stopping their tapping and standing up, advancing toward the three children.

18

S am spun around and quickly saw that the exit from the little square was blocked. And the grown-ups were closing in.

"I'm telling you, Siegfried," said the Kid, no longer bothering to whisper, his voice harsh and urgent. "We need to go into Alberich's cave."

Sam swore at him. "We don't have time for this!" he snapped.

"Listen to me, bonehead. I know this place," the Kid kept on. "I been here before. That statue there, that's old Alberich. And that tree is the white ash, the great white hope. And down under its roots is Alberich's cave."

"What are you talking about?" Sam's voice was jittery and hoarse with panic. He glanced at the statue. "That's not Alberich. It's someone called John Smith."

"Trust me," said the Kid. "I'm the tunnel king, remember? Monsewer Rat. There's a way out of this mess."

"Are you saying there's a tunnel entrance near here?"

"Yes, dumbbell, what did you think?"

The Kid darted off and the other two kept close behind. More and more grown-ups were coming alive, pressing in from all sides.

"We're gonna have to cut the cake!" the Kid yelled, and he raised his sword above his head, charging at a knot of grown-ups, his dress flapping. He slashed the sword wildly in the air and the grown-ups fell away. Sam was right behind him, swinging his own sword and screeching a wordless war cry.

They battered a path to the side of the square, and there, close to the wall of the church, was a large iron manhole cover. The Kid slid his sword into its scabbard and dropped to his knees. Humming maniacally to himself, he slipped a metal tool out of his jacket pocket, stuck it into one of the handles on the cover, and began hauling it up. Tish squatted down to help him shift it sideways while Sam kept the grown-ups back, thrashing his sword in the air and screaming.

Once the cover was off, the Kid wriggled down into the dark hole beneath. Tish came next and finally Sam. He turned his back on the grown-ups, made his sword secure, and hurled himself into the opening in such a mad rush that he bruised himself all down one side and took the skin off his shins.

There was a ladder fixed to the wall below. Sam just managed to get ahold of it and he descended into the darkness. There was no time to replace the manhole cover. Above him three grown-ups peered through the opening, dribbling saliva that fell past him and spattered on the floor a couple of feet below.

One of the grown-ups started to crawl headfirst through the square hole, blocking out the light.

"Look out!" Sam yelled as suddenly a heavy shape fell past him. He heard a wet slap as it landed.

"Stupid bastard," he said with some relish. "Stupid grown-up bastard."

A flashlight beam came on and played up the wall, guiding Sam down the last few steps. Tish and the Kid both had flashlights out. The Kid shone his on the grown-up that had done the nosedive. It was a young father, still alive, but with a broken back. It flopped about, hissing. Tish kicked it in the head and it stopped moving.

"Follow me," said the Kid, trotting off along a low tunnel, his head bowed. There were damp brick walls with ancient cabling running along them. Dirty warning signs. Puddles on the ground.

"Where are we?" said Sam. "Where does this tunnel go?"

"They all link up," said the Kid. "The tubes, the dirt-pipe sewers, the gas and 'lectrics and waterworks and wormholes. Don't ask the Kid what's what, is all just tunnels to him. Tunnels and caves. I gave them all a name so's I could member 'em. This place is Alberich's cave, the place of dwarves. Thought I recognized that tap-tapping. Heard it before when I was sploring once."

"Who's Alberich?"

"That statue up there, I know it ain't really Alberich. Alberich's a dwarf. My dear departed grandpa, God rest his battered soul, was an opera-loving geezer. Piles of old black records filling his little flat with warbles. Some of it rubbed off on me. One piece I used to listen to all the time, fierce and loud it was, all clanking and banging. The Ring Cycle,

Das Rheingold, going down into Alberich's cave in Nibelheim and all the anvils hammering out a sound to wake up the slumbering hills. The Kid loved that sound, so he did."

"So where will this take us?" asked Tish, shining her flashlight ahead down the twisting tunnel. "Is there another way out?"

"There's a million. Depends where you want to go."

"Okay. Wait."

Tish stopped walking and the three of them stood there, crouching down so as not to bump their heads on the tunnel roof.

"Does it link up with the tube system, did you say?" Tish asked the Kid.

"The train tunnels? Yeah."

"Not the tube," said Sam, and Tish shushed him before asking the Kid if he could get them to St. Paul's station. The Kid scratched his head.

"Which one's that?" he said. "The Kid don't read—he's not much cop with the old hieroglyphics."

"The Central Line—the red line. We must be very near it. St. Paul's is on the other side of the Wall. If we go west."

"East, west, north, south, each, peach, pear, plum. Don't mean anything to the Kid."

"Yeah," said Sam. "And I really don't want to go into the tube tunnels. They're always full of grown-ups. Anywhere but there."

"What choice do we have?" said Tish. "The Kid knows what he's doing. He's used these tunnels."

"Don't like them, though," said the Kid. "Specially not

'round here. In Nibelheim. This place used to freak me out of the house. With Alberich's dwarves up there. Didn't want nothing to do with the old Clickee Cult. No, sir."

"We'll go carefully," said Tish. "But whatever happens, we've got to get back up to street level."

"I suppose so," said Sam.

"Quickest way, I s'pose," said the Kid. "Easiest for me to remember is along the tracks and up through a station." He squeezed Sam's hand. "You with me, or are you with the Woolwich?"

"I'm with you," said Sam, and the Kid winked at him and continued down the tunnel, humming again and muttering to himself about dwarves. Sam fell in beside him.

"I'm sorry about that," he said.

"'Bout what?"

"Back there, in the square, having a go at you. I was just scared."

"Forget it, Samphire," said the Kid. "If I could speak more clearer I would, but the words get all jumbled and twisted and convulsive and they don't come out like I want them to. We did okay, though, didn't we? Showed them Clickees who's the boss. Showed them the old snickersnee."

"Yeah." Sam laughed, feeling slightly hysterical. He knew they weren't out of danger by a long shot. Tried not to think about going into the tube system.

There was another ladder at the end of the tunnel. It only led down, deeper underground, rather than up toward the daylight. The Kid put his flashlight between his teeth, hopped lightly onto the ladder like a monkey, and dropped into darkness. Tish was less sure of herself, and Sam went slowly and carefully, worried that he might get tangled in his scabbard again.

At the bottom they found a cramped room filled with electrical equipment. There were two doors.

"That way leads to more of the same," said the Kid, pointing to one door, and then he pointed to the second door. "That way leads to the train tracks."

"Which way would be quicker?" said Sam. "To get back up there?" He looked at the ceiling.

The Kid nodded toward the second door.

"Okay," said Tish. "We check it out and if it's all clear we go. And go fast. I don't want to stay down here any longer than anyone else."

The Kid opened the door and took the others along a short passageway, at the end of which was an oval-shaped opening. He went into a crawl as he neared the end, then lay on his belly and stuck his head out through the hole, shining his flashlight around.

"All clear," he said, and climbed down a third ladder. Soon all three of them were standing on the tracks by the glinting steel underground rails. There was no sign of any life.

Didn't make Sam feel any better. His chest was heaving. This was bringing back too many memories for him. He felt a rising wave of panic. He'd never been claustrophobic before, but now he was feeling both trapped and exposed. His legs were shaking and they threatened to buckle at any moment.

"Can we get out of here as quick as we can?" he said, trying to stop his voice from breaking. Tish took her pack from her back and fished out the map book. On the back was a tube map. She studied it by the light of her flashlight.

"Look," she said. "It makes sense that this is the Central Line. We would have been almost directly above it up in the square. We have to hope it is. And if we go west we get to St. Paul's."

"There's a tube station at the Tower," said Sam. "We could try to get there."

He grabbed the map off Tish and tried to make sense of it. And then he felt a cold flush pass through him.

He passed the book back to Tish. "We go to St. Paul's," he said, his voice shaking.

"What's the matter?"

"If we go the other way we get to Bank Station."

"What's wrong with that?"

"Oh, it comes back to me now," said the Kid. "That's the boneyard; that's where Sam was held by the blood-farmers. That old witch, she might still be there. We don't want to go back that way."

"So which way is St. Paul's, then?" said Tish.

"I'm trying to remember."

"I've lost all sense of direction, to be honest," said Tish. "You must have some idea."

"That way," said the Kid, turning to face one way down the tunnel, and then, as the others joined him, he abruptly turned in the other direction. "No, that way."

"Which way, Kid?" Tish was growing angry.

The Kid peered along the tunnel through narrowed eyes. "I got a sense that that way is hope and freedom and the buzzing of the bees in the lemonade trees." He jerked his thumb back over his shoulder. "And that way madness lies."

"We've got no choice anyway," said Sam miserably, and he had to steady himself against the Kid as his knees gave way.

"Whassup, doc?"

"Shine your flashlight down the tracks."

The Kid did as he was told and the beam lit up three grown-ups, pale-skinned and bald, like cave lizards, with wide dark eyes and long fingernails. They looked tough and wiry and were moving quickly.

"Leg it," said the Kid, and the next moment the three children were stumbling along over the tracks, flashlight beams madly scribbling a route in front of them.

Sam could hear the grown-ups hissing and panting behind him. The ones who lived underground tended to be faster and healthier than the ones up top.

He could only see about thirty feet ahead as the tunnel went into a curve. He prayed that there would be a platform on the other side, or at least a way out. And he prayed that they wouldn't be back at Bank Station. The horror of the tube train where he'd been held prisoner, with its butcher's carriage full of body parts, had almost been too much for him.

The curve was agonizingly long, so it was a while before they could see any distance ahead.

"Yes!" Sam blurted as they emerged into a straight section. Tish's flashlight beam had caught the edge of a station platform. What if it was the wrong stop, though?

"Can you see?" he gasped. "Can you read the name on the signs?"

"Not yet," said Tish.

They ran on a little while in silence, and then Tish cried out. "St. Paul's! Yes! It's St. Paul's! It's the right one. Well done, kiddo."

Soon the tunnel opened out and they were in the larger space of the platform area. It stank there, a sharp reek of human waste that caught in Sam's throat, and there were piles of bones and other garbage strewn along the platform.

Except for the three grown-ups who were chasing them, though, there didn't appear to be any others around so far. The children clambered up onto the platform and looked for an exit sign among the jumble that hung from the roof. Sam was staring up when suddenly a body came hurtling out of the darkness and bowled him over. He went down hard, all the air forced from his lungs, a spray of bright lights in front of his eyes.

Someone had barged into him, but luckily their momentum had kept them going, and they had tumbled over the platform edge onto the tracks. Sam was too jolted to move for a moment. He lay there, aware of movement all around him. The breastplate had protected him a bit, but it had also dug into him painfully.

He knew he couldn't stay like this. He sucked in a lungful of air and struggled to sit up and clear his head. Tish had been knocked aside in the attack and had dropped her flashlight; it was rolling along the ground, lighting the legs of several grown-ups on the platform. The Kid had found the exit and was yelling at the other two to follow him.

Tish pulled Sam to his feet just as the three original grown-ups emerged from the tunnel. They were obviously part of a different group, because a fight immediately broke out between them and the father who had fallen onto the tracks. A couple of mothers joined him, sliding over the platform edge.

All this confusion gave the children the start they so desperately needed. They were off and running again, through the exit and onto a long frozen escalator. They scrambled up, taking two steps at a time, coughing as they kicked up clouds of dust. Sam found it hard going, tried to ignore the pain in his legs. His pants were wet with blood. He hobbled and limped up the steps, trying to keep up with the other two. His whole body felt like it had been hammered with a baseball bat. He was covered in cuts and bruises, and there was a stabbing pain in his chest. He wondered if he was having a heart attack.

Is this what it felt like?

Tish took his hand.

"Come on, Sam," she said. "We're not leaving you behind."

Sam realized he'd lost his helmet in the fall. Tears came into his eyes. Behind him he could hear the grown-ups. Following. Low moans echoing off the walls, the scrape and thud of their feet.

"Keep going up," Tish shouted. "I can see daylight. . . ."

Sam was sweating and exhausted when they reached the ticket booth at the top. The other two leaped over the turnstiles, but he clumsily flopped and crawled. Light was streaming down through the exits to the street, blinding them. Sam shielded his eyes and ran. Wanting nothing more than to be out in the sun.

They went to the left, up a short flight of steps.

And then they stopped.

The folding metal gates had been pulled across the exit and chained together. The chain was fastened with a padlock.

19

Sam put his hands to the closed gates and shook them, swearing. He could see through the dark crisscross pattern made by the bars. On the other side was sunshine, an empty street.

On this side . . .

There came a whine from the station depths, coughing noises, a deep rattling groan. The grown-ups had reached the ticket booth.

"Bloody hell!" said Sam, and he kicked the gates. There was no way they could force them.

"I should have thought," said Tish. "I forgot."

"Now what?" said Sam, knocking his forehead over and over against the metal gate.

"There was another exit," said Tish.

"We'd have to go back down there," Sam said angrily, pointing down the stairs to the ticket booth. "And what makes you think the other exit won't be locked as well?"

"Well, what's your idea, then?" Tish shouted back at him. "What's your bloody plan?"

"You brought us here," said Sam.

"No, I didn't," Tish replied. "The Kid did. So, Kid, come on, how are we going to get out?"

"Search me," said the Kid.

Now Tish grabbed hold of the bars and she screamed at the top of her voice. "Help! Help us!"

"That's no good," said Sam. "The only people who'll be able to hear you are grown-ups. You'll just attract more of them."

Tish ignored him and continued yelling for help.

Sam turned to the Kid. "Maybe we *could* try the other exit," he said, his mouth so dry he could hardly get the words out. "We've got to try something."

They left Tish shouting for help and crept down the stairs. The first of the grown-ups had reached the top of the escalator. These were the fitter, healthier ones, five of them, three fathers and two mothers. Luckily they were having even more of a problem with the sudden bright light than the children had. They cowered back, cringing and hissing. Close enough for Sam to get a good look at them, though.

He could see their red eyes, their rotten teeth, the scabs and boils on their skin.

He knew it was only a matter of time before they got bolder. Once a grown-up had your scent, nothing would stop it.

He drew his sword from its scabbard.

"We can't fight them all," said the Kid. "They're just gonna keep coming."

"We can fight some of them," said Sam, holding his sword tightly. It was heavy in his hand, though, and he felt weak and useless. Who was he kidding with his bright shiny blade? He wasn't a knight. He was a nine-year-old boy. He might cut a few of the grown-ups, but what chance did he have of killing any? He'd joined in a couple of the training sessions back at the Tower. He'd enjoyed it. This was different.

This was real.

One of the grown-ups grew brave enough to advance, squinting through tightly pressed eyelids. He hobbled over to the turnstiles and tried to squeeze through. Finding that impossible, he flopped onto the solid turnstile housing and started to crawl across it. Just like Sam had done.

"No, you don't!" The Kid darted forward and smashed his sword down on the father's head. The blade glanced off, struck the metal housing, and snapped in half. The blow had at least taken a chunk out of his skull, though. Thin, watery blood spilled out and some grayish jelly, exposing a patch of bright white bone. The father writhed in agony. The Kid hit him again, with the broken stub of blade, hacking off his ear.

Sam had been concentrating so hard on what the Kid was up to he hadn't noticed that the other grown-ups had come forward as well and were all now trying to get across the barriers. He ran over to them and jabbed a bald mother in the shoulder with the point of his sword, not wanting to risk breaking it like the Kid had done to his. The point barely pierced the mother's skin. She looked at him with dull eyes and her tongue flopped out of her mouth. He stabbed her again, aiming at the same spot, and only succeeded in making the mother angry. She tried to grab hold of the blade, and when her fingers closed around it, Sam yanked it free.

It came away bloody, and Sam saw that it had cut into the tendons of the mother's fingers.

It wasn't enough to stop her, though.

Normal humans might have held back, scared of the weapons, not wanting to get injured. Grown-ups didn't think clearly enough for that. They had no sense of danger.

And that made them dangerous.

Above them Tish was still calling for help and battering her fists against the locked gates.

The first grown-up finally made it over the barrier. The Kid had taken chunks out of him and was still chopping at him with his broken sword. Each time he cut another bit off him, and each time it wasn't enough to stop the father from advancing.

Sam broke away from the wounded mother and went over to help the Kid, stabbing the father in the back. He felt his blade scrape against the man's ribs, cutting him. He knew he would have to try harder if he was going to hit anything major inside him.

He tried aiming lower and dug into the soft fleshy area below the rib cage, and this time the point penetrated deeper. Before he could try again, however, two more grown-ups got over the barriers. Sam turned and swung his blade wildly, slashing one in the upper arm.

Again, not good enough. Not a killing blow.

Sam and the Kid were forced to retreat now as the rest of the grown-ups swarmed over, all five of them advancing as fast as they could. And more were coming up the escalator.

The three at the front were bleeding, but there was just

one thought in their heads. To take the children down, kill them, and eat them.

The only thing that gave Sam any advantage was that the grown-ups still seemed to be disturbed by the bright light. They turned their heads to the side and rubbed at their skin as if the sun's rays were burning them.

Sam swung again, aiming low. He was more successful this time. The end of his blade cut through the belly of the mother whose fingers he'd sliced. She belched and gurgled and vomited up a stream of dark blood, which spilled down her front and joined the spreading stain on her dress.

With more confidence he swung again.

And missed.

With the Kid at his side, he backed steadily toward the stairs, guided by Tish's shouts.

What was the use of calling for help?

Sam swore. They were beyond help. Soon it was going to be hand-to-hand combat. And what chance did they have then? One of the fathers was twice his height, with wiry muscles showing on his scabby, spotty, naked arms.

Sam wasn't strong enough to do anything. He was just a boy. Not strong enough to make the sword any use. His arm ached as he pathetically swung it back and forth, back and forth like a pendulum.

His eyesight was blurry with tears.

He stumbled up the stairs. It was only a matter of time before he'd be backed up against the gates at the top. The grown-ups were hungry; they were beating their fear of the sunlight, dribbling as they advanced.

Sam should have stayed at the Tower. Should have listened to Ed.

And then he heard voices—boys' voices—and he turned around.

There were three boys outside, on the other side of the gates. They were wearing soldiers' camouflage jackets, green and black. Two were carrying short spears.

One had a gun.

"Stay back!" he said, and the three trapped children cleared the opening. The boy fired his gun through the gates. There was a loud bang, and a gout of stinking smoke puffed into the stairwell. If the bullet hit anything, it didn't show. For a moment, though, the grown-ups stopped in their tracks.

One of the other boys was fiddling with the padlock. He had a bunch of keys hanging from a chain on his belt.

"I can't remember which one it is," he said.

"Hurry up!" said Tish.

The grown-ups were still holding back, trying to make sense of this new development.

"Fear of the cutter!" the Kid shouted, and he darted back at them, hoping to finish off the father whose head he had shredded. He raised his broken blade, then chopped once, twice down the man's face, splitting his nose in two.

"Got it!" said the boy with the keys.

"Come on!"

There was a rattling noise as the chain was pulled free of the gate.

The Kid hacked again and at last the father went over. He tripped and fell backward down the stairs, trying to stop the rest of his face from falling off with his hands. Encouraged by the Kid's success, Sam stabbed the tall father in the throat. It was enough to stop him, and then Sam felt himself being yanked out through the open gate.

He was dumped in the street. The two boys with spears poked them through the opening to keep the grown-ups back while the one with the keys fought to slide the gates shut, before refastening them with the chain and making the padlock secure.

Sam noticed that there were four more boys out here, all dressed in variations of army combat clothing. For a moment he allowed himself to feel safe. He couldn't stop his body from shaking, though, and his stomach was burning with acid. He leaned forward and threw up on the pavement.

The soldier boys formed a protective group around Sam, Tish, and the Kid.

"Can you walk?" said the one with the keys and the gun. He was tall, looked like an athlete.

Sam nodded and the boy helped him to his feet. "It's not far."

Sam was too numb to say anything. Tish took his hand and he walked in dazed silence down a paved area between some modern buildings. Ahead of them was the side of St. Paul's Cathedral. A mass of white pillars, arches, statues, windows, and carved stonework rising high above the streets to the great black dome at the top.

"They got past the barricades again, Nathan," Tish said to the tall boy.

"We'll sort it."

Sam wasn't really paying attention. He felt sick and numb, the blood pounding in his ears. He looked at the imposing bulk of St. Paul's. It must have seen a lot in the hundreds of years it had stood here—riots, fires, the Blitz—but surely nothing as strange as what had happened in the last few months.

Sam found it quite reassuring. That it was still here. Whatever happened, whoever lived and died, the cathedral would still be here. The world carried on.

They turned as they reached the cathedral grounds and walked around the edge. Where exactly were these boys taking him? Sam looked at them properly for the first time. They'd been at the dress-up box. It was funny what the different groups around London wore. They'd had no uniform in Holloway where Sam had been living. Not like the kids at the Tower with their armor and their swords and their medieval outfits. This bunch, whoever they were, obviously preferred the modern army look. Tish fitted in very well with them in her green shirt and pants.

She fitted in too well.

One of them had an identical wound to hers on his forehead.

Sam almost stopped—it suddenly struck him: she knew them. How else had she known they'd hear her shouts? And she'd used the boy's name—Nathan—just now, hadn't she? But this wasn't Trafalgar Square.

Sam looked more closely at the boys. What he had thought were army clothes weren't necessarily that. Some of them were wearing green-dyed pants and hoodies.

They came around to the front of St. Paul's, and Sam was amazed to see a load more kids there, standing quietly, as if waiting for them. There was something odd, and yet familiar, about them, and it was a moment before it hit Sam.

They were all wearing green.

Like the soldiers.

Like Tish.

He looked up at her and she smiled at him. "You'll be all right now," she said.

Why didn't he believe her?

The world spun around him.

If he hadn't already emptied his guts, he'd have done it now.

Why didn't he believe *anything* she had told him?

20

Sam and the Kid were hustled up the steps at the front of St. Paul's and in through the great central doors that were standing wide open.

Sam wasn't sure if he'd ever been inside the cathedral before. If he had, he must have been so little he couldn't remember anything about it. It was vast in here, like something out of a fantasy computer game; the ceiling looked impossibly high, held up by pillars and arches. Marble statues stood everywhere. Painted scenes, gold and red and blue, covered every surface. You couldn't take it all in at once. Sam noticed, though, that there were plants in there. The kids had brought in branches and fixed them around the walls, and there were more things growing in pots—jungly plants with big leaves, climbers, great sprouting things.

He heard a squawk, and something scurried across the aisle in front of him. It was a chicken. He saw now that there were loads of them, wandering around all over the place. Crapping on the tiled floor. Running in between the legs of the children who were sitting on a field of chairs, dressed in green. As Sam went past, they dropped to their knees and stared at the floor. It was freaking him out. This huge open space, large enough to fit twenty houses inside it. The plants. The chickens. The quiet kids falling to the floor . . .

All his senses were being bombarded at once. There were fires smoldering in garbage cans, and incense burners hanging everywhere he looked. They filled the cathedral with smoke. It hung up by the ceiling like a cloud, and the light streaming in through the high windows caught in the blue haze, so that Sam felt like he was entering heaven.

The smoke stung his eyes, though, and they were already watering so badly that he had to wipe away tears. His dry throat was further irritated. He was soon coughing and spluttering. The sickly scent of the incense mixed with a woody smell from the fires and the occasional waft of something harsh and bitter.

Then there was the noise. A group of kids was playing musical instruments, and their din filled the cathedral like the smoke, adding to Sam's confusion. Some of the musicians were banging percussion instruments—bongos, cymbals, drums, cowbells, tambourines—hammering out a rhythm in exactly the same way as the grown-ups outside.

What had the Kid called them? The Clickee Cult.

Others were playing violins and guitars, saxophones, flutes, and trumpets, anything they could get their hands on. Those who didn't have an instrument were singing, or rather chanting, wordless ums and ahs. They were like some deranged school band. There didn't seem to be a tune or even any kind of set pattern. They were all just blowing and scraping and banging, setting up a hypnotic drone. Most of the time it made a horrible discord, but every now and then the different sounds came together, and a melody of sorts would rise up and open out and fly, only to collapse and return to the chaotic musical stew.

Sam's whole body was throbbing and tingling. Waves of pain pulsed through him. There was a growing ache behind his eyes. He was suddenly hungry and thirsty and tired. . . .

A few minutes ago he'd been in a blind panic, trapped in the dark tunnels, the worst place on earth, and now he was here. It was a weird dream whose parts didn't fit together. Just as the music kept drifting between beautiful and ugly, between order and chaos, his own mood kept swinging— between relief that he had gotten away, and fear of what was going on now, between happiness and confusion. . . .

"Between the devil and the deep blue sea," said the Kid, almost as if he had been reading Sam's thoughts.

"What's going on?" said Sam.

"Beats me with a stick," said the Kid.

Sam asked the same question, louder, to one of the boys who were escorting them. The boy said nothing. Made a point of ignoring Sam. Wouldn't look at him. Kept marching forward.

They came to two rows of carved wooden seats facing each other across the narrower end of the cathedral. In the past, when there had been services, the choir would have sat here. Now it was where most of the musicians were sitting. They didn't stop playing as Sam passed, but lowered their eyes so that they weren't looking directly at him. Some muttered a word, the same word as far as he could tell—Sam couldn't make it out over the din of their music.

The musicians looked glassy-eyed, drunk, dazed, almost like diseased adults themselves. They had played themselves into a trance.

The smoke haze was thickest around the altar, at the very end of the cathedral, an elaborate construction of twisting pillars, shiny marble, and gold leaf. Sam could just make out a group of six boys standing there, waiting for him to arrive. As Sam got closer, he saw that they were wearing some kind of religious robes, and they too had been dyed green.

There was a boy at the center of the six, watching Sam as he was led down the aisle. He was the only kid in the whole cathedral who looked at Sam.

Slowly he swam into focus out of the smoke haze, a sharp, hard object, as if carved from stone like one of the white marble statues.

He was smiling.

He looked to be about sixteen. Quite short, though there was something about him—a stillness, a confidence that made him seem taller than he was. He was skinny, almost like a skeleton, with a narrow, bony face. His head was shaved and his skin was so pale it was almost transparent. Sam could see blue veins beneath it. His eyes were sunk deep in purple sockets above his long straight nose and looked dreamy, shining.

He had a black scab on his forehead, crusty and oozing pus from one infected spot.

"Welcome," he said, dropping to his knees but keeping his eyes fixed on Sam the whole time. He then raised his hands up toward Sam, as if begging.

"Welcome," he said again. "We've been waiting for you. My name is Matt and it is my honor to welcome the Lamb to his Temple."

21

Shadowman couldn't sleep. He'd been trying to match his own rhythms exactly to the Fear, but he still found it hard when he was exposed and couldn't do anything to block out the sun. He was in the cab of a truck that was sitting opposite a small tire center on the edge of an industrial park in Kilburn. The tire center sat behind a large courtyard. It had an open-fronted area where cars would have been fitted with new tires, and behind that was a warehouse piled high with tires and car parts. That was where the Fear were sleeping. Shadowman could picture them, all crowded in there, pressed up against each other.

He'd nearly been caught out in the open by a small raiding party yesterday and had just managed to duck into the truck before he was seen. He'd waited ages for them to go away and in the end had decided he might as well stay in here. With the doors locked he was safe from the strangers, and he was high enough to get a good view of the tire center.

Beyond the warehouse were railroad tracks running up from West Hampstead Station. A wall and a high barbed-wire fence blocked access to the tracks, so there was no danger of the horde going out that way and giving him the slip when it got dark. Saint George had been leading his army through the local housing developments, working his way from street to street. They hadn't found any kids since they'd left the school the other night. And Shadowman was happy for it to stay that way. However, while the lack of fresh food was making the horde sluggish, it also made them angry and unpredictable. There were a lot of them to feed. They occasionally found scraps in the houses they raided, but it was clear that what they really craved was children.

Shadowman tried to straighten out and groaned, rubbing a stiff muscle in his neck. He'd been trying to sleep across the front seats. Unfortunately the truck wasn't big enough to have its own bed in the cab. It was squashed and uncomfortable in there, and the low afternoon sun was now shining directly in through the windshield.

He sat up and looked out. All quiet. A flat, dead, dull street. He picked up his binoculars from the dashboard and trained them on the tire warehouse. Nothing moved. It would be at least another hour before it was dark and they would stir.

He thought he might risk getting out and stretching his legs. He didn't want to get a cramp. He took the plastic bottle out of his pack and drank a little water. Broke his rules and ate a hard, dry cookie he'd found in a sealed tin in someone's kitchen the day before. He was trying to save the cookies and only eat them at mealtimes, but he was feeling at a low ebb. The sugar hit him and he felt a fizz of dizzy light-headedness. He mashed the cookie against the roof of his mouth with his tongue, turning it into a paste so that it would last longer.

He took a last look around, then popped the lock on the passenger door and swung it open. He climbed down the steps and carefully closed the door, trying not to make any sound.

He sniffed the air. If any strangers were close, he'd detect them. He was becoming more like them every day, relying on his animal senses. He thought he could vaguely sense the bulk of them, over the road in the warehouse, detect a warm, rotten smell wafting in the afternoon air. He was probably imagining it. They were all inside. It was unlikely their stink would reach him here.

He pulled his homemade camouflage cloak around his body and set off to explore. The Fear had stopped abruptly last night before he'd had a chance to scope the area out properly.

He moved quickly and silently around the nearby streets, getting his bearings, learning the lay of the land. It was important to know your territory. Plus, it was possible the Fear might use the tire warehouse as a base for a while, so he needed to find a better place to sleep. Just in case.

Be prepared.

He selected a three-story apartment building not far from the truck. It was easy enough to break in with the tools he always carried with him, and he made his way to the top front corner apartment. The windows here would offer the best view of the tire center.

There was a musty, moldy smell in the airless apartment. It had been left too long with the doors and windows sealed.

He waited a good minute before going in, letting out any noxious fumes and allowing the fresh air in.

Then he took a deep breath and stepped in through the door, his knife held tight in his hand.

You never knew what you'd find when you entered an apartment like this.

The first thing he saw were two corpses sitting side by side on the sofa. They were holding hands. Rats and maggots and bacteria had long since eaten their flesh away, leaving only the bones, leathery patches of skin, and the ragged hair on the top of their skulls.

There were the remains of a meal laid out on the low table in front of them. Plates with dark smears of something, inedible bits and pieces.

Once Shadowman might have been panicked by something like this—panicked, revolted, and scared—but he'd gotten used to all sorts of sights in the last year.

You didn't need to be scared of dead things.

He nodded to the corpses and said, "Afternoon."

What really would have panicked him was if one of the corpses had replied.

Well, thankfully a lot of weird stuff had gone down in the last year, but, as far as he knew, people didn't come back from the dead. Some people called the strangers zombies, but they weren't the walking dead, and if you killed one it didn't get up again.

He wondered how long it would be before the scales tipped and all the strangers were wiped out, from their disease, from hunger, or from being killed by children. At the moment they might just have the upper hand; kids lived in constant fear. It couldn't last forever, though, could it?

Unless . . . Unless . . . Unless . . .

Saint George's mob were showing worrying signs of . . .

What was it?

Organization?

Intelligence?

Motivation?

The scariest thing was that they were changing. Was the disease entering a new phase? That's why Shadowman had to keep on their tail. Learn as much about them as he could. Start planning how to stop them.

He went over to the window and checked the view.

There was the warehouse. Good. He had clear sight of the courtyard and into the workshop area. This was perfect. A shame he hadn't had time to come here the night before. He had an uninterrupted view both ways along the street. He could see the top of the truck, the railroad tracks, what looked like a shopping center some distance off to the right. And there . . .

Something moving.

He checked the sky. Still too light for the strangers to be up and about. He lifted his binoculars to his eyes and scanned the streets.

Where was it? Had he imagined it?

He was pretty sure he had spotted a movement, and he was pretty sure it had been a person.

Now there was nothing.

He moved the glasses slowly, methodically. . . .

Yes. There. He could see a human shape. Someone was squatting down. Hiding behind a garden wall in the shadow of a big tree.

Strangers didn't hide. Not like that.

A kid, then?

If it *was* kids he'd have to warn them not to go blundering about and wake the adults. He couldn't shout out a warning for the same reason. Saint George's troops could be up and on the move surprisingly quickly if they scented prey.

Shadowman stared at the spot where he'd seen the person, but whoever it was had shrunk back farther behind the wall, and now he could see nothing.

He swore. He would have to go down and find them, although that held dangers of its own. If it was a hunting party of kids, patrolling their streets, they would be ready for the attack. They might go for him before they knew who he was. It was safer to strike first than risk being attacked by a stranger.

A stranger. That's what he was to them.

He unslung his crossbow from his back and headed over to the door, saying good-bye to the two lovebirds on the sofa on his way out. He moved fast down the stairs, then went more cautiously out into the street. Keeping close to the buildings, using any cover he could find, his crossbow up and ready. He was soon at the garden he'd been watching from above. A narrow, overgrown strip between a low front wall and a house.

There was nobody there. Except for a kid's bike with one wheel missing, the garden was an empty tangle of long grass and weeds.

Had he imagined it, then? Humans were very good at seeing patterns in random shapes. Faces in clouds, monsters in a pile of rumpled sheets, the image of Jesus Christ on a piece of toast. Had he created a living person out of some shadows and weeds?

He had to admit that he'd been lonely lately, with only the shambling Fear for company. Saint George and his lieutenants, Bluetooth, Man U, and Spike. He really didn't need any imaginary friends right now.

He hopped over the wall into the garden, looking for some clues, anything that told him a person had been there. There was nothing obvious. He looked closer. *Yes.* He wasn't losing it. A flattened patch where the grass and weeds had been crushed.

Someone *had* been here.

Unless it was a dog or a cat.

He suddenly flinched as a shape moved fast past him and then another. He froze.

It was only two squirrels chasing each other. He smiled and let his breath out in a rush. Watched as the squirrels scampered up the tree, darted about up there, chattering. Then one jumped down into the street and dashed across to the other side.

And that was when Shadowman saw the three kids.

22

Instinct kicked in. The habit of survival. Without it he would have been dead long ago. He'd ducked down behind the wall before he'd even thought of doing it. He waited, and when nothing happened, he risked peeping over the bricks.

The three kids weren't looking his way. They were camped behind a car and all their attention was focused on the tire center. Shadowman had a quick look around, in case there were more of them.

Couldn't see anyone else.

Now he studied the kids more closely. They were two boys and a girl, about his age. One boy carried a crossbow similar to his own, the other had a homemade spear, and the girl carried an iron bar.

They looked pretty streetwise. They'd have to be to have survived this long. They all had long hair, tied back behind their heads, and were wearing protective bike leather pumped up with skateboard elbow and knee pads. The boy with the spear also had on what looked like a police stab-proof vest over his jacket. Shadowman would have loved one of those.

Another movement caught his eye. It was a father. Old and skinny, nearly naked. He wandered out of the tire center and began to cross the courtyard.

That was bad. They were waking up.

There was a whizzing noise and the father fell over, a crossbow bolt sticking out of his ribs.

What were these kids doing? Attacking his strangers? What had been the point of that? The father had been old and weak. . . .

Shadowman stopped himself. Was he really feeling sorry for a stranger?

It was the kids he had to worry about.

They were still crouching behind the car. The boy had reloaded his bow. Now the girl said something and they moved forward. Started to creep toward the gate into the tire center courtyard.

No, you idiots. Not in there.

He had to warn them. This wasn't a small nest of dozy adults. This was the Fear. There were nearly a hundred strangers in there. Tough and organized. The kids wouldn't last two seconds. To take on an army, you needed an army of your own.

He was shafted either way. If he did nothing the kids would stumble in there and be overwhelmed. If he shouted out then the strangers would surely hear him, and that would bring them out like a swarm of disturbed bees.

He hissed through his teeth. . . . "*Sssss* . . ."

Nothing. They hadn't heard him.

He raised himself up a little higher. Tried a hoarse whisper. "Hey . . ."

Still nothing.

He picked up a small stone. Threw it at the girl. It hit her in the back, made a little *pock* sound.

The boy with the crossbow spun around, bringing the bow up as he turned, and he fired the bolt straight at Shadowman all in one swift, clean movement.

Damn, he was fast.

But Shadowman was faster. He dropped to the ground and the bolt whizzed harmlessly over the top of the wall and embedded itself in the side of the house.

Shadowman stayed down, hugging the wall, pulling out his knife just in case. He heard the three of them coming back across the street.

Well, he wasn't going to let himself be killed like this.

"I'm one of you," he said, just loud enough for them to hear. "I'm a kid."

"Show yourself." The girl's voice. Making no attempt to keep quiet.

Bloody idiot.

"Keep your voice down," he said. "There are strangers nearby."

"What are you talking about?"

"Please. . . . Be quiet. Whatever you call them. Grownups, zombies. There's a hundred of them across the street. If you disturb them we'll all be up shit creek."

"Why should we believe you?"

"Why shouldn't you?"

"Show yourself."

"As long as you promise not to fire another bloody bolt at me."

"Okay . . ."

Shadowman was furious. All the time he'd put into studying the Fear—tracking them, learning about them—could all be wasted by these bloody kids. They were going to ruin everything. If the strangers woke now it was the end for all of them. He had to try to convince the others of the danger they were in.

He got into a crouch, then gently eased his head up over the top of the wall. The three kids were spread out, weapons ready, the lethal crossbow trained at his chest.

"Put that crossbow down," he whispered as loudly as he dared.

"Who are you?" asked the girl. "Are you alone?"

"Yes. But please believe me. We have to get away from here now, and we have to do it fast."

"I'm sorry, mate." The girl was doing all the talking, seemed to be in charge. "We don't trust no one."

"You have to listen to me. You have to trust me. There are adults in there and they're not nice ones. If you disturb them . . ."

"We know there's something in there," said the boy with the spear. "And how do we know you ain't lying to us? Might be food or something. Something you want."

"There's no food in there, only grown-ups."

"We ain't scared of no zombies," said the second boy. "This is our turf and you shouldn't be here. Where you come from?"

"Buckingham Palace."

"Yeah, right. Where you from?"

"The center of town," said Shadowman wearily. "I've been following these grown-ups for days."

"What for?"

"Jesus Christ! That'd take too long to explain. And you all are making too much noise. Now I'm going to come out from behind this wall and I'm going to start walking slowly away from here. I want you to follow me."

"You might just lead us into a trap."

"Why the hell would I want to do that? I'm one of you. I'm a kid. We have to get away from here now. And when we're at a safe distance, I'll explain everything."

"We don't trust you," said the girl.

"Well, then, just let me go. I'm no threat to you. The mothers and fathers inside that building are the enemy."

"We'll merk them," said the boy with the spear. "They don't scare us. We cleaned out every zombie around here. We own Kilburn."

Shadowman wasn't listening. His sharp ears had picked up a noise coming from inside the tire center. He was sniffing the air. The three kids didn't move.

"Listen," he said. "Please get away from here. I'm going to start running any second now. You don't know how dangerous these grown-ups are."

"'Course we do," said the boy with the spear, almost shouting. "How d'you think we're still alive? We know everything there is to know about zombies, and we kill any we find, that's why we're here. We saw some last night and we've been hunting them. And now we've found them. So now we're going to kill them."

Shadowman saw movement in the tire yard. Dark shapes emerging from the buildings. He vaulted over the wall, yelling at the kids to run.

But he saw that it was already too late.

Somehow two groups of strangers had gotten out another way and were advancing down the street from both directions.

23

I don't get it, Ed. Yesterday you were telling everyone we shouldn't mess with the zone. Now you tell me you want to get in there."

"Things have changed, Jordan. It's like this game. . . ."

Ed pointed to the two armies set out on the tabletop. He and Jordan were in Jordan's rooms in the Queen's House, reenacting the Battle of Austerlitz, where Napoleon had crushed the combined armies of Russia and Austria. Jordan was obsessed with war games. He'd brought a load of tiny painted soldiers with him in his backpack of essentials and had found loads more in a collection at the Tower. He liked to re-create famous battles and see if there could have been a different outcome. He studied the rule books for hours and ate up history books, learning all he could about the different troops and their abilities.

The soldiers on the table were an odd mix: about half were authentic Napoleonic figures, the others were mostly made up from later wars—the Crimean War, the Boer Wars, the First and Second World Wars—but there was also a regiment of

Greek hoplites standing in for French grenadiers. Truth be told, Ed found these games a bit boring—they could go on for hours—but he knew that if he wanted to talk to Jordan for any length of time, the best thing to do was suggest a war game.

As usual, Ed was losing, even though he was commanding Napoleon's superior army, the army that won the original battle.

"What d'you mean?" Jordan narrowed his eyes, magnified behind his thick glasses, and studied the troop layout, leaning in very close to check he hadn't missed anything. "What's like this game?"

"Well." Ed leaned back in his chair, relieved not to have to think about the game for a minute. "You know what it's like. You decide on your tactics, but you have to change them as the battle goes on. What's that quote you're always throwing at me? About tactics?"

"No battle plan ever survives contact with the enemy?" said Jordan.

"That's it." Ed nodded. "That's exactly what I mean. We both started this game with a plan. We both thought we were going to win, but you didn't do what I wanted you to do. Your moves didn't fit my plans. So I changed my plans and you changed yours, and, the way it goes—things change."

"Yeah," said Jordan. "Things change. You're right. You got to keep an open mind."

Ed nodded. "And you need to change it now and then," he said. "Like I've changed mine. Because things have happened that I need to react to. Yesterday I wasn't sure about charging into the no-go zone and getting people hurt. And for what? To stop people from getting bored? To expand our territory?"

"Yeah, all of that."

"But, as far as I can remember, I sort of agreed to it in the end. When we were ready for it. But now—things change. Sam's gone. And it's my fault. He kept on asking me to go with him, and I kept telling him to wait. He didn't wait."

"What were you waiting for, Ed? For DogNut to get back?"

"Mainly."

"He ain't coming back, Ed," said Jordan. "I think we've got to accept that."

"Yeah, maybe you're right."

"Which means one of two things."

"What?" Ed sneaked a look across the table at Jordan. He knew Jordan didn't like people to look at him, but sometimes, when you were having a conversation, it helped to look at the person you were talking to. He wanted to know what Jordan felt about DogNut. He never discussed his emotions, so Ed had to try to read them in his face.

It was hard, though. Jordan's face rarely gave anything away, and his glasses changed his eyes. Right now the general had his eyes fixed on the game, bent over, his nose almost touching the little soldiers, so he wasn't aware that Ed was studying him.

"It means that either he's dead," said Jordan, "or he's found a sweeter deal than what he can get here. Found someplace he'd rather be. That boy always was ambitious. Never liked being the underdog. Top dog was the only position he wanted. The soldier knew he could never be better than number two as long as I was here. So maybe, just maybe, he found somewhere he could be number one."

"Maybe." Ed looked away as Jordan raised his face. "But DogNut was loyal. He had respect. You know that. He wouldn't do something like that without reporting back."

"Wouldn't he?"

"I don't know." Ed shrugged. "As I was saying, things change."

"They surely do. Your move," said Jordan, nodding at the two armies.

Ed sighed and set about laboriously moving blocks of troops, checking everything with the rulers and charts and the various compasses and protractors that were strewn all over the table.

"My heavy cavalry division is charging your Jaeger Regiment."

"You sure?" Jordan frowned. "They'll come within range of my grenadiers."

"Yeah. I just want some action, Jordan. All this creeping about is getting frustrating."

"It ain't creeping about, Ed, it's maneuvering."

"It's dull is what it is, Jordan. I want to see some blood on the table."

"Go ahead, man, but you'll be wasting a lot of troops."

"Unleash hell!"

In this case unleashing hell wasn't quite as dramatic as it sounded; it meant rolling several dice and making complex calculations on a piece of paper, and the end result was exactly as Jordan had predicted. Ed took out a few skirmishers but came too close to the grenadiers, who shot his cavalry to pieces.

At least it had livened the game up a bit. Ed didn't have the patience to be a great tactical player. He would have made a terrible general. It had always been the same with him. He was happier playing sports like soccer or cricket, where all you had to do was go out there and do your best. Games like chess did his brain in. He'd always start well, bold and decisive, and then he'd get bogged down. Couldn't cope with the strain of trying to think ten moves ahead, checking all the possible outcomes of moving one small piece on the board. He'd do something reckless, take down a bishop, say, even though he knew it was risky and would leave one of his own more valuable pieces exposed. And if he was playing someone like Jordan, who was patient and calculating, never flustered, able to look twenty or thirty moves ahead, he would lose.

Every time.

Just as he knew he was going to lose this battle.

Jordan now set about marshaling his own forces.

"So how many people you want to take with you?" he asked as he slid some hussars a few inches across the table.

Ed ran his fingers through his hair. It had come to the crunch. "Twenty," he said. "To be on the safe side."

"Can't spare twenty," said Jordan bluntly. "We need all our troops to guard the forage parties or we won't be able to bring enough food back."

"I'll only be gone a day."

"That's what DogNut said."

"Yeah. Well, I thought you might say that." Ed smiled

and shook his head. "So over to you. How many can you offer?"

"I don't want you to go at all, Ed. You know that. You're important to me here. The kids like you. If anything goes belly-up you're a good man to have around. Specially now that everyone seems spooked by what I done to Brendan and them two little boys tipping up. Baa baa black sheep and all that. I mean, what if you do a DogNut on me?"

"I won't. You know me, Jordan. You can trust me."

"Yeah. You could get taken down, though."

"Not if you give me enough fighters I won't."

"What's your plan?"

"Sam wanted to go to Buckingham Palace. That's miles away through the most dangerous part of town. He got a head start this afternoon. We only just realized he's gone, unfortunately."

"And the other two? The weird kid and the girl?"

"Yeah. She must have gone with them. I can't try to follow them now. It's too late. It's getting dark, dark and dangerous. I'll leave tomorrow when it's light."

"You'll move faster with a small squad."

"Maybe."

"Pick from your own unit. You and five others. I can't spare no more than that."

It wasn't enough, but Ed knew that it was all he was going to get. Jordan liked to play it safe, keep troops in reserve. It was one of the reasons he always won these war games. "All right," he said. "Thanks. I just need to know Sam's all right. You understand?"

Jordan looked at Ed for the first time. His eyes seemed to

bulge behind the lenses. "Ed, dude," he said. "If something was going to happen to the youngers, it would have happened today. It would have happened in the first hour they was gone. That out there is the badlands."

"I know. And it's my fault he went there. I promised to look after him and I didn't, and now he's gone." Ed was on the verge of tears. He had made himself responsible for Sam and he'd let him down. He knew it was just his own guilt that was making him mount an expedition. The chances of finding Sam if he was in trouble were pretty small. But he had to do *something*.

"I've lost friends before," he said. "People I should have looked after. I don't want it to happen again. I don't care how dangerous it is. I'll risk that."

"It's happened, though, Ed. It's done."

"No. I'm not going to believe that Sam's dead. He might be holed up somewhere. Under attack. Praying that someone will come and get him, Jordan. And I can't just leave him. I can't."

24

Sam was sitting wide-eyed at a table that had been set up in the center of the main aisle in the cathedral. A feast was laid out on the table. There was chicken and rice, canned vegetables, dried fruit, cookies, cans of Coke, even chocolate. Sam couldn't remember the last time he'd had a meal like this. He was drunk on the luxury of it all. Shaking. He still couldn't quite believe what was going on. He'd stumbled into a strange dream, and he had to admit that at this moment it was a very nice one.

Just as long as he didn't think any further than his stomach. And he was having to go carefully there. Unused to such rich food, and so much of it, his stomach was gurgling and clenching, and he was worried that he might be sick again. That wouldn't be good, not after everyone here had been so kind to him.

He was the guest of honor at the feast.

He'd never been a guest of honor before.

And guests of honor didn't throw up all over the table, did they?

He hoped the Kid didn't mind being left out. Not being special like Sam. He was sitting on Sam's right, staring at his empty plate and fidgeting in his seat. Sam could tell he wasn't comfortable here at all. The other people around the table were making him nervous. Tish was on Sam's left and opposite them was the boy in charge, Matt, as well as a chubby kid named Archie Bishop and the four other boys who'd been with Matt when Sam arrived. They were younger and didn't say much, just stared at Matt in awe and nodded furiously at everything he said.

Sam was worried that their heads might fall off with all that nodding, because Matt hadn't shut up since Sam had met him. He just went on, talking, talking, talking.

Sam had stopped listening a long time ago. His voice was just a drone, something you had to get used to, like the music and the smoke. It was just *there*. So that you either learned to ignore it or you went mad.

It was hard, though. Sam's eyes were still watering from the smoke, and the racket from the kids in the choir stalls hadn't stopped since they'd arrived. Whenever one musician got tired, another took his place. Everybody in the cathedral seemed to be expected to join in. He hoped he wouldn't have to. He'd be terrible. His mom, who'd sang in a choir and loved music, was always trying to get him to learn an instrument. He'd started piano lessons, then guitar, trumpet, even drums. But he didn't take to any of them and hated practicing. The thought of having to join the band made him nervous.

Surely the guest of honor wasn't expected to play at his own feast.

No. Sam tried to think about only two things: the food and his stomach. He didn't want to think about anything else. He didn't want to think about *why* he was the guest of honor. What these kids wanted from him.

He knew it was something to do with religion, because that was all Matt talked about. It wasn't any kind of religion Sam recognized, though. His family had never been very religious, but a year before the disaster his parents had announced that they wanted to send Sam to a different school. A church school.

"It's got a very good reputation," his dad had explained. "They get far better results than any of the ordinary elementary schools around here. Their test scores are very high."

"And the discipline's very good," his mother had added. "You won't get bullied there."

Sam had wanted to explain that he didn't get bullied at school, but he knew his mom was convinced that there were too many rough kids there.

"But what about my friends?" he'd asked.

"You'll make new friends."

Sam hadn't wanted to make new friends. He liked the ones he had.

He hadn't been able to argue his parents out of it, though. And there was a catch. They would have to start going to church to convince the priest they were religious and make sure they could get a place. So Sam had been dragged over to the church near the school every Sunday. The stories the priest told about things happening a long time ago were sometimes quite good. Sam liked the ones about armies and fighting and swords and spears. Usually, though, he didn't understand the stories and couldn't really see what they had to do with him. He'd enjoyed some of the hymns, except when his mom sang the ones she knew too loudly.

Mainly it had been boring, and he would much rather have been back at home playing on his PlayStation.

He'd often wondered since then what good any of it had done. His parents were both dead, and Sam wasn't at any kind of school at all. Maybe Mom and Dad had gone to heaven. He hoped so. He preferred to think that they'd gone to a lovely tropical island and were having a really long vacation. Maybe that was what heaven was like.

Wherever they were, it was probably better than being here. In the hell that the world had become.

So Sam wasn't that experienced with church stuff and religion, but the things that Matt was coming out with were weird. Sam had tried to concentrate at first, because he was guest of honor, and because of the other thing. . . .

The thing he was *really* trying not to think about.

The *Lamb* thing.

He wished he'd paid more attention when Ed had told him about Matt, but the thing was, Sam had never expected to actually *meet* him.

Mad Matt, Ed had called him. And there was something about a banner, with two boys painted on it. The Lamb and the Goat. Ed had said that he and the Kid looked a bit like those two boys, and that was why some kids at the Tower had looked at them funny.

And why Kyle had made a sheep noise.

Well, *all* the kids here looked at him and the Kid funny.

If they looked at all. They were still doing that spooky thing where they stared at the floor. *So what* if they thought he looked like the Lamb, if that meant he got feasts like this. The Kid was a bit left out, though. It obviously wasn't as good being the Goat.

Sam giggled. It was all quite stupid, and it was clear that the Kid hadn't listened to *anything* Ed had said. He was acting as if none of this had anything to do with him. He'd quickly stuffed his face and now kept muttering to himself and humming little bits of tunes, as if he was trying to sing along with the crazy music. He refused to join in any conversations and had turned inward. Sam was feeling a little alone and was really trying to be polite to Mad Matt.

He realized that Matt had asked him something. He was staring at Sam with his dark-rimmed eyes.

"Say that again," said Sam, and Matt smiled.

"Don't you see?" he said. "Everything that's happened—the disease, the death, the rise of the Nephilim, it's all our fault."

"I don't know what you mean," said Sam. "Whose fault?"

"All of us."

"You're saying the disease is your fault? How can it be your fault?"

Matt smiled even harder at him, like someone talking to an idiot. "Isn't it obvious?"

"Not really, no. Nothing's obvious. I don't get it."

"Why else would all this be happening?" Matt went on. "Some people blame scientists, or the army, or aliens from outer space, but it's all God's punishment for how we were behaving. We weren't worshipping Him properly, not following the true path as shown to us in the teachings. It's just like the great flood and all the plagues before. This is the last plague. Once we have been punished we will be allowed to enter God's kingdom here on earth."

Sam couldn't follow this. "Why would we need to be punished?" he asked.

"For our sins. This is the great cleansing."

Sam tried to keep himself from laughing. Nobody said "cleansing," not even in ads. He turned the strangled laugh into a cough, a machine-gun burst of harsh barks that hurt his throat. Again Matt smiled at him. Sam was beginning to be really irritated by his habit of doing this.

"The revelations were first shown to me in smoke," said Matt. "So now we live in the smoke so that we'll keep seeing new visions."

"But won't it give you, like, cancer or something?"

"No. How could it? We are the chosen ones. God won't let any harm come to us."

"So none of you ever get hurt?"

"Not unless we do something wrong. Obviously, wrong-doers are punished."

"Okay. Right." Sam remembered learning about witch-craft in history. How in the past if they thought a woman was a witch, they'd throw her in a pond. If she floated she was a witch and would be burned at the stake. If she sank she wasn't a witch . . . and would drown. Either way the poor woman wound up dead. Even though there never really were any witches in the first place. Matt's religion seemed to work the same way. The proof that you weren't religious enough was if you were killed. And the proof that you *were* religious enough was if you stayed alive. Matt couldn't lose.

"That's why we keep the song going," said Matt.

"What song?"

"The music you hear is the Great Song; we started it last summer and we haven't stopped singing it since. It will go on until God's kingdom is established on earth. It's our way of praising Him, of letting Him know our devotion to Him. He can hear us."

"But you stop to go to sleep, yeah?"

Again that smile. The shake of the head. "No. The song will only end when God is triumphant. *I heard the voice of harpers harping with their harps, and they sang as it were a new song before the throne, and before the four beasts, and the elders, and no man could learn that song but the hundred and forty and four thousand, which were redeemed from the earth.'"*

"Right," said Sam. "Yeah. Um. Can I ask you something, Matt?"

"Of course."

Sam wiped his mouth on his sleeve and pushed his plate away. If he ate any more he would surely explode. "How come you all sort of seemed to be expecting me?" he said. "As if you knew I was coming here."

"It was foretold."

"How could it have been?"

"It's God's way."

"But *I* didn't even know I was coming."

"Tish knew."

Sam turned to look at Tish. She was beaming, her face seeming to glow in the candlelight.

"How did you know?" he asked.

"It was told to us."

"There never was a place near Trafalgar Square, was there?" said Sam. "You tricked me. This is the temple you told us about, isn't it? You planned all along to bring me here."

"She was sent to fetch you from the Tower," said Archie Bishop.

"The whole thing was a lie, then," said Sam.

"Not a lie, no," said Matt.

"Just by saying things you can't make them real," Sam snapped. "You can't just sit there and say 'It's not a lie' and that makes it not a lie."

"She had to lie to others at the Tower," said Matt, "because they were Babylon's instruments, keeping you imprisoned there. They were the ones who were *lying* to you. Tish had to fight their lies with her own ones."

"I don't understand any of this. How did Tish even know I was there?" Sam turned to Tish again. "Did you have a vision or something?"

"We were shown the truth," said Tish. "I came to save you, and then this morning I signaled the Temple to let them know I was coming back."

"*Hallelujah!*" said Matt. "*The smoke from her goes up forever and ever.*"

"The burning car?" said Sam.

"It's how it was all meant to be," said Matt.

Sam didn't say anything. He was too angry and frustrated and confused. Tish had lied to him, and he'd let Ed down, and he had no idea what these weirdos wanted. He stared at his empty glass wishing they would all just go away and leave him alone.

But that wasn't going to happen. Matt was still going on.

"A year ago we came here to the Temple to wait for you," he said. "We've been waiting all this time and finally you have come."

"I just don't get it!" Sam shouted, trying to get through to them and make them talk some kind of sense. "How were you shown? What were you shown? Who showed you?"

"It was all done through His messenger," said Archie Bishop.

"What, like an angel or something?" Sam scoffed. He was light-headed from the food and the smoke and music. He was still in the dream where nothing fitted together or made sense. If he stayed too long holed up here in this cathedral, he'd go as mental as the cathedral kids.

Matt didn't reply to Sam; instead he signaled to one of the three younger boys at the table, who jumped up and hurried off into the dark depths of the cathedral.

The Kid leaned over and whispered in Sam's ear, "Listen, shortstuff, I don't always get things. I take the wrong end of the stick sometimes. Other times I don't manage to get hold of either end of the stick. People say I'm a weirdo from space, but these loons are doing my nut in. I never did like church monkeys, and these guys are church chimps through and through. They give me the creeps and shivers. First thing in the morning, when we have stuffed our bellies, we are gone from here. Bottom line, sunshine. I don't want to live with monkeys. See you later, crocodile."

Sam watched as the Kid got up from the table and wandered over to the choir stalls. How he wished he could go with him, get away from these "church monkeys," as the Kid had called them, but that would be rude.

In a little while the boy Matt had sent away came back. He had someone with him. Tall and fair-haired. His face was bruised. Sam thought he recognized him but wasn't sure where from, and then it hit him.

It was Brendan, the boy who'd been exiled from the Tower by Jordan Hordern.

"Hah!" Sam exclaimed. "So Brendan is God's messenger?"

"Yes," said Matt. "God arranged for Brendan to be sent here to show us the truth. He told us all about the Tower, and your arrival, so we sent Tish and the others to fetch you."

"And the others got killed. Thanks, God."

"The others must have done something wrong," said Matt. "We can't be sad for them, we can't mourn them. They were sinners and they've been punished. It seems that only Tish was pure."

Sam bit his tongue. Tish obviously hadn't read the part about not being sad. For the entire first day at the Tower she'd hardly stopped crying, wailing about her dead friends. Particularly Louise, the girl Ed had accidentally killed. Now here she was, smiling away like she was glad about it, going along with Matt's craziness.

Well, whatever Matt said, Tish had lied to him. And now she was lying to Matt. Pretending she was a true believer, a pure nun, pretending she hadn't been sad, pretending that God had planned it all.

As far as Sam was concerned, if this was all God's plan, then God had made a right mess of things. He rested his elbows on the table and planted his chin in his hands.

Let them talk. He wanted to hear the full explanation.

25

The Kid was wandering along one of the choir stalls, studying the musicians. They kept their eyes fixed on their instruments. Wouldn't look at him. One boy was banging an old metal garbage can with a wooden spoon. Another was honking on a saxophone. There was a girl with a cello. Not bad, not brilliant. Then there was a boy playing a bent and battered cymbal that made a sort of dull, clanking noise. He was hammering it rhythmically with a stick, beating it further out of shape.

"That don't sound so well, Lionel," said the Kid, sticking his fingers in his ears.

The boy turned his head and stared off into space, dull-eyed, in a trance.

"Let me put it to you, sir," said the Kid, "that a cymbal should go *tingaling*. It should clash. It should shimmer. In a nutshell it should shimmy, Jimmy. That cymbal is a dead cymbal. It goes *whap. Whap-whap-whap-whap whap* . . ."

Getting no response, the Kid moved along to the next musician. A girl with long fair hair who was playing the violin. She had her eyes tightly closed, and the Kid could tell that she knew something about her instrument. There was a sweet tone coming out of it.

"That's cool," said the Kid, nodding. "You got the music in you. The Kid loves music. You've played before, I'll bet."

"Shhh," said the girl, her voice a whisper. "I'm not supposed to talk to you."

"No? You church monkeys are a weird bunch, Yo-Yo."

"Yo-Yo Ma played the cello," said the girl. "I play the violin."

"Who was that other one, then? The Chinese fiddler? Vanessa Doodah?"

"Vanessa-Mae?"

"That's her. My granddad said she could play the angels from out of the sky. But I think he just had the hots for her."

"Shush. Go away. I'm not allowed to talk."

"What's your name, Yo-Yo?"

"Charlotte."

"Hi there, Charlotte. I'm the Kid."

"I know who you are, and I'm not allowed to talk to you. If Matt sees me he'll punish me."

"That's worse than school days," said the Kid, and he whistled. "Oh my word, he is *strict*."

"He's the only one that fully understands the word of God," said Charlotte, sounding like she was quoting a book. "He gets visions and revelations and he explains them to us. Without him we'd be godless and lost."

"Yeah? Seems like there's plenty of other youngers in London who get on just fine and dandy wine without him."

"That's what they think."

"No point in arguing with a church monkey," said the Kid. "But why the zipper lips?"

"Please. Don't talk to me."

The Kid watched Charlotte's fingers dancing on the strings of her violin. "What grade you at, Yo-Yo?"

"Sixth."

"That's good, I think. You're good. Not like these other monkeys. I reckon their organ grinder wants his money back. I guess Matt, he's the organ grinder here."

"I don't know what you're talking about."

"You're not the first, Yo-Yo. Sounds like me and Matt got a lot in common. *You* don't know what *I'm* talking about, and *I* don't know what *he's* talking about, but apparently *he* knows what *God* is talking about. Everybody's saying something and I can't hear a word they're saying."

The Kid watched the other musicians for a while, working away at their instruments. None of them was in the same league as Charlotte. A trumpeter fell asleep and nodded forward, banging his trumpet on the bench in front of him and waking himself up with a sore lip. He rubbed his eyes and stood up. Walked over to where a girl was sitting with a bunch of kids who had no instruments. He gave her the trumpet and disappeared into the darkness near the great altar. The Kid spotted a group of boys gathering there, Nathan, the tall one who'd saved them from the tube station, among them. Giving orders by the look of it. He pointed at the Kid. The Kid waved to him and turned back to Charlotte.

"I like your style, Yo-Yo," he said. "Reminds me of home, my old granddad. The sounds that came out of his old record spinner. Whoo. The Kid liked them sounds. I'd like to hear you play a solo sometime, Yo-Yo."

"This is all we're allowed to play, the Great Song; all other music is evil. We have to open our minds and just play what God tells us."

The Kid leaned over and whispered in Charlotte's ear. "You don't fool me, Yo-Yo. I can tell what you're playing there. That's Beethoven. That's the old *Kreutzer* Sonata."

Charlotte blushed and scraped her bow over the strings, making a discordant racket.

"It's okay. Your secret's safe with me," said the Kid. "I like you, Charlotte. When you stop that sawing, you come and find me; we'll be friends. Any girl can play like that I'd like to get to know. If you want, you can even be my girlfriend."

Charlotte suddenly opened her eyes and glared at the Kid. "Go away!"

The Kid winked at her and strolled off.

"I am *in* there," he said to himself, snapping his fingers.

He didn't notice Nathan give a signal to his group of boys, who nodded and set off after him.

26

still don't get it," said Sam. "Why would you even want to send Tish to get me? Why's it so important to you? Why am I guest of honor here?"

"Because you are special, Sam," said Matt. "I told you, we are only here because of you. You are the Lamb."

"No, I'm not," said Sam stubbornly.

"The truth is inside you," said Matt with one of his horrible smiles. "We need to free the truth. At the moment you are being held back by your shadow. Your dark half is hiding the truth from you. Only when we free you from your shadow, from this human realm, will you fully understand who you are, and then you can show us the way to salvation, and we will bring God's kingdom to the earth."

Sam wasn't listening. He had spotted the Kid going over to look at a big statue of a soldier. There was a large square structure next to it, covered with a green cloth. Sam vaguely wondered what it might be. Something stupid, probably, like everything else here. A group of boys seemed to be following the Kid. He looked very small and alone. Sam wanted to go to him, to be with his friend. He'd had enough of Matt and his nonsense. He felt hemmed in, suffocated, wanted to run around screaming and yelling and telling them all to shut up and leave him alone.

"I'm tired," he said, standing up. "I want to go to bed. Where do you sleep? If you ever go to sleep."

"It's important that you understand about—"

"No, it's not!" Sam shouted. "None of it's important! You're making it all up. I don't want to hear any more about it, okay? You think I'm something that I'm not."

He took a few steps into the darkness that surrounded the table, feeling sick and dizzy. Matt's voice stopped him.

"You have one dark shadow. The Goat, the demon, the dark one. It must be cut from you. You will never be free until we make a sacrifice."

Sam forced a laugh. "You're mental," he snorted. "I don't want you to kill some poor animal for me."

Matt came over and put his bony hand on Sam's shoulder. "You are the Lamb," he said, "and when we sacrifice the Goat, you will know the truth and we will all rejoice."

"Please, I'm tired," said Sam, Matt's words washing over him. Just so much noise. "I want to go to bed." He glanced over at the Kid. Nathan's boys were all around him now, and Nathan was saying something to him.

"We will sacrifice the Goat to the great demon, Wormwood," said Matt. "Wormwood will eat the Goat and will be destroyed by it, and we will be free of him, and the light will enter you, and you will understand the truth, and you will show us that truth."

"What are you talking about?" said Sam, struggling to

pull free from Matt's grip. He couldn't see the Kid at all anymore, and his mind was racing, trying to make sense of what Matt was saying.

Scared of making sense of it. Didn't want it to mean what he feared.

Another group of kids was moving the cloth-covered structure into the middle of the cathedral. It must be on wheels.

Matt was talking again. Sam had missed some of it.

". . . he goes by many names," he was saying. "The Goatlord, Abaddon, the First Beast, the Whore of Babylon, but you know him as the son of the Goat—the Kid."

"Not the Kid, no," said Sam. And at that moment his friend broke free from the ring of boys and made a mad dash down the aisle toward the cathedral doors.

"Run!" Sam cried. He leaped to his feet to go after him, but Matt reached out and held him fast.

"He's a trickster," he said, leaning close to Sam's ear. "A master of illusion. He's a demon with a thousand faces. He speaks in tongues and carries a broken sword. He has tricked you and fooled you into thinking he is your friend."

"He *is* my friend!" Sam shouted. He struggled against Matt as he watched Nathan catch up with the Kid and bring him down. Hot tears stung his eyes.

"He is the Goat," said Matt, signaling to the kids by the square structure. They pulled the cloth away and Sam saw that underneath it there was a big cage.

"And only when he is killed will the final revelation be shown to us."

27

Shadowman struggled back into consciousness. He was covered with blood. Lying in a pool of it. He realized he was facedown, his head twisted to the side so that his cheek was on the ground. The bottom half of his body was raised. He could feel something soft beneath his legs and hips.

It was dark, but a shaft of moonlight picked out the blood and a scattering of broken glass. That was all he could see. He felt light-headed, starved of oxygen. Tried to take in a deep breath and winced in pain. There was a terrible pressure on his chest.

He couldn't move. Had no idea where he was, how he had gotten here. His head was filled with a cold ache, making it hard to think. He closed his eyes and instantly found himself falling asleep. He couldn't think straight, but he knew enough to know that if he fell asleep now he might never wake again.

He forced his eyes open. Saw the jagged lumps of glass. The blood.

He struggled to move again. Felt something sharp

digging into his ribs. Something else pressing down on the back of his neck.

He stopped moving. It was hopeless. He was stuck here. Thirsty. Breathless. Hurting all over. Lost. Slowly, memories began to form. Dull flashes that slipped and slithered and flipped about inside his head as if he was dreaming.

Come on, focus. . . .

A squirrel . . .

He laughed, despite himself, and felt a stab of pain.

A squirrel . . .

But there *had* been one, hadn't there? Hopping across the road. It had led him to the three kids. The girl and the two boys.

Yes. He felt a bitter taste in his mouth, and his memory came roaring back, full of blood and noise and pain. He almost wished it hadn't returned. Wished he'd stayed in ignorant bliss.

The last few hours had been a nightmare. It had started badly and got worse. If only those kids hadn't shown up. So cocky. Knew it all, didn't they? Weren't scared of strangers.

Not them.

He coughed, releasing a gush of blood from his nose.

He saw the grown-ups again.

It was vivid. That first moment, when they'd appeared from either end of the street and time had stopped for a beat. Shadowman and the other children had frozen where they stood, and the reality of their situation had utterly changed.

Shadowman was back there now, hiding behind the wall in the overgrown courtyard, opposite the tire center, his brain turning. Trying to add up this new set of facts. Trying to work out how he'd gotten suckered. Trapped here.

How had the strangers gotten out of the tire center without any of them noticing?

Another entrance obviously, another way in and out.

How many of them were there?

Maybe ten in each group? So there was a chance. If he and the other three kids could stick together, work together, fight side by side, they might be okay. They had to be quick, though. If the Fear were on to them, then they'd soon be streaming out of the tire center.

Another eighty of them.

Shadowman vaulted over the wall.

"We have to get out of here," he shouted, and the girl threw him a pitying look.

"We've dealt with worse than this, you noob."

"No, you haven't."

"We don't run. We lock them down. End of story."

"We've been following these creeps all day," said the crossbow kid. "Ever since we first eyeballed them up in Willesden, near the Jewish cemetery."

Shadowman tried to make sense of this. How could these kids have seen the Fear near Willesden earlier? The grown-ups had been asleep in the tire center all day. And in all the time he'd been following them they'd never gone anywhere near Willesden. He could picture the route they'd taken since he'd joined them by Arsenal Stadium. He'd followed it carefully across the pages of his map book. Unless some of the strangers had sneaked out while he was dozing in the truck, he couldn't see how they could have been spotted in Willesden.

No. Not possible. He was too sensitive to their movements to have missed something like that.

There must be another explanation.

He studied the nearest group of strangers, who were shuffling closer along the road to his left. He tried looking for a familiar face or item of clothing. It was difficult. Their skin was darkened, lumpy and rotten, making them all look similar. A lot of them were bald, and what clothes they wore were identically black and greasy. They came closer. Something was definitely different about them. Was it their smell? Or was it that they seemed less organized? Not in sync.

That was it. They weren't working as a group. Shadowman knew the habits of the Fear well enough by now. If they ever split into smaller groups, then one of Saint George's lieutenants would nearly always take charge. Man U or Bluetooth or Spike. Nobody seemed to be in charge of this group.

No point trying to explain that to the three kids. They'd laugh at the idea of strangers being organized.

These must be a completely new group of strangers. And if these *were* newcomers, it was worse than he'd imagined. There were still at least a hundred of the Fear waiting inside the tire center.

"We have to get away," he shouted, his voice hoarse with panic. That and the fact that he hadn't spoken to anyone since his friends had abandoned him at King's Cross station.

How long ago was that? Two weeks? Three weeks? He'd lost all track of time.

"We told you, noob," said the girl. "We don't run, we fight."

"Well, *I'm* running," said Shadowman. "Or I'm gonna try. The only thing is, four of us could easily punch our way through. By myself it's gonna be hard."

"Then stay and fight. We'll show you how we deal with zombies."

"But we're trapped here," Shadowman pleaded. "There's 'zombies' coming at us from both sides. At least break through one group so that you don't have the others biting your asses."

"He's got a point," said the boy with the spear, turning around to watch the slower group coming up from the right. The girl thought about this for a few seconds, chewing something.

"Yeah, all right," she said, and raised her iron bar in readiness. The boy with the crossbow slung it over his shoulder. He evidently didn't want to waste bolts if he didn't have to. He drew a machete from where it was hanging at his belt. It was straighter than Shadowman's machete. Chipped. Looked like it had seen a lot of action.

The three of them stood shoulder to shoulder, ready to charge the nearest group of strangers. They didn't ask Shadowman to join them. Obviously thought he was a waste of space. Expected him to stand back and marvel at their technique.

"We'll smash through, then turn and take them from behind while they're still confused," said the girl to her friends. "You ready?"

"Let's do it. . . ."

Shadowman had to admit to being impressed by their combat skills; they moved fast and efficiently, slicing, clubbing, spiking, and the strangers fell back from them, two of them badly wounded, bleeding from deep cuts, a third reeling from a blow to his head.

Shadowman tucked in behind the three of them, his own machete at the ready. He lashed out a couple of times as strangers got too close, but it looked like they were going to make it through without too much trouble.

Now if only he could convince the others to keep moving, they'd be safely away and he could get back on plan.

As soon as they were clear, however, the other three stopped and started laying into the strangers from behind.

"Leave them!" Shadowman yelled. "Leave them and get away. What difference will it make killing a few more?"

"It's what we do," said the boy with the spear. "You run if that's what *you* do."

If I have to, thought Shadowman. Yes, I will. But what I really do is stay alive. I survive.

This was just stupid. They were taking a pointless risk. The kids were good, well trained and not afraid to kill. If those ten strangers were all they had to worry about, it would have been a breeze.

The Fear were waiting inside, though.

The kids continued hacking and chopping, and pretty soon half the pack of strangers was injured in some way. Two lay dead in the road. Others were down and writhing on the ground. Shadowman didn't join in. He was looking past the fight to where the second group of newcomers was getting closer.

And then, behind them, he saw what he had most feared. A great dark mass of grown-ups emerging through the gates of the tire center. Moving fast. Saint George's army had woken and were coming out to hunt.

28

"Run!" Shadowman screamed. "They're coming."

"See ya," said the girl. "Don't forget to write."

"Can't you see? There's too many!"

If he ran now he'd make it. He could get his act together and return to spy on the Fear when everything had calmed down. It would be easy. The Fear would be too slow to catch up. They probably wouldn't even bother chasing him. They'd stay to eat the three kids. . . .

Shadowman swore and then yelled at the kids again. "You stupid bastards. You can't win this fight!"

He had to get away now. Before it was too late. He turned and ran. Three yards, four, five . . .

He stopped.

Swore again.

Turned around.

The Fear had spread across the road and were coming fast—much faster than the kids were used to—and only now, too late, they realized the danger they were in. They were badly outnumbered and would very quickly be swamped.

Strangers had no fear; when they wanted something, they wouldn't stop until they'd got it. They would climb over dead bodies to get at you.

Shadowman knew what would happen next. He'd seen it too often in the last few days. The strangers would surround the kids, move in as a solid mass of flesh, and smother them, making it difficult for them to use their weapons, not caring if the front ranks were cut down, chopped up, and killed. There would always be more behind to take their place.

The girl was shouting at her two friends to break off the fight and get clear, but as they backed away from the thickening mass of strangers, the boy with the spear tripped over a dead body and stumbled. A father lying bleeding on the ground got ahold of his leg and sank his rotten teeth into the boy's calf. He shrieked and went down. His friends instinctively grabbed him to try to pull him free, but it was their second big mistake. Maybe they weren't such skilled fighters after all, because now they couldn't use their weapons properly. It was weapons that gave kids their big advantage over strangers; without them they were horribly vulnerable to attack. As they slowly dragged the boy along the pavement, the two of them barged with their elbows, kicked out, the iron bar and machete flailing limply in their free hands.

Shadowman knew he couldn't leave them to it. Not this time. He'd seen too many kids get killed lately. It didn't mean he had to be happy about it, though. He swore once more, using the worst words he knew, and ran back to help, barreling into the mob of strangers, knocking three of them over and nearly falling over himself. He swung his machete in a wild circle but was scared of hitting the kids, so he quickly sheathed his blade and snatched up the spear where the boy had dropped it. He could stay clear of the strangers this way. He jabbed it at them, twisting it so that it wouldn't get stuck, concentrating on the ones that were trying to surround the other kids.

It was hopeless, though; he didn't stand a chance of holding back this huge press of bodies—the strangers filled the street from side to side, a stinking, rotten press of diseased humanity. The boy and the girl were too slow, desperately pulling their friend along, as hands reached for them and mouths dribbled in anticipation. The injured boy was screaming and sobbing as more strangers clawed at his legs, attacked him with teeth and lips and tongues.

There was too much going on to be able to keep up; grown-ups came at them from all sides now. The boy with the machete wasn't even looking at his blade as it flapped uselessly in the air.

And then a big father ripped the weapon from his hand.

"Hey!" the boy snapped, surprised and indignant. Zombies, as he called them, weren't supposed to do that. They didn't use weapons.

Well, he was learning fast; *these ones* did.

He'd learned his lesson too late, though. The father who had gotten ahold of the machete was one of the Fear. Cleverer, more organized, more lethal. He brought the machete down in a huge clumsy arc and it severed the boy's arm at the elbow. The boy cried out, let go of his friend, and as the strangers smelled blood, they fell on him in a frenzy. He went down with a hideous screech. The girl tried to pull him along as well.

It was no use.

"Leave him," said Shadowman. "You can't do anything for him."

"I'm not leaving him."

Already, though, the boy had disappeared beneath the press of strangers as more and more of them collapsed on top of him. Shadowman saw his chance. The pack was distracted, intent on getting to the fresh meat. He ducked down and got the other boy around the waist, hauled him to his feet with one mighty heave. His legs were covered in blood, but he could walk.

Just.

"We can't fight this bunch!" said Shadowman, staggering down the road with one arm around the boy. "We'll all be killed."

The girl had no choice but to follow them. She ran to catch up and then supported her friend on the other side. The three of them lurched along as best they could. The injured boy was limping and moaning with each step he took. Shadowman glanced down. Blood was pouring from the wound, soaking the bottom of the boy's jeans, which were ripped and tattered, his skin underneath shredded, covered in bite marks. There were a couple of deep gouges with ragged edges. The cuts would be difficult to heal without stitches, and then there was the risk of infection.

It was unlikely he'd survive.

It had all been so unnecessary.

"I tried to warn you," said Shadowman.

"Shut up," said the girl bitterly. She was right. It was pathetic to be scoring points now. They had to concentrate on getting away. "We should never have left Ricky behind."

"You had no choice," said Shadowman. "His arm was gone. No way he could recover from that."

"You don't know that."

"Whatever," said Shadowman. "It makes no difference now. How far away is your base?"

"About two miles."

"Two miles? You're joking. What are you doing so far from home?"

"We told you. We were tracking zombies. We cover a lot of ground."

"I'm not sure your friend's going to make it two miles."

"No worries. We got wheels."

"A car?"

"Yeah."

Shadowman looked back. Most of the strangers appeared to have stopped to eat the fallen boy. But some were advancing along the road. The closest were only about ten yards away.

"Okay," said Shadowman. "I hope it's nearby."

"Not far."

"I don't think I can make it," the boy gasped. "My leg hurts too much."

"Keep going," said Shadowman.

"There," said the girl, nodding up a side street where a big black Lexus RX was parked in the middle of the road.

"Just don't tell me your friend back there has the key," said Shadowman.

The girl swore. Stopped dead in her tracks. Swore again.

Brilliant . . .

29

"Oh Jesus," said the wounded boy. "I can't walk, Jaz. I'm gonna be sick."

"Is it locked?" Shadowman asked.

"'Course not. Why would we lock it? Zombies don't drive."

"Let's get him in there, and we'll figure out what to do. If we keep on slowing down like this, they're gonna catch up with us."

"We'll be trapped in there."

"We'll work something out." Shadowman twisted around; the lead strangers were nearer and closing every second.

"Come on." He put on a burst of speed, dragging the other two along with him.

When they got to the car, the girl, Jaz, wrenched open the back door and bundled the boy onto the seat before climbing in after him. Shadowman got into the front. He slammed the door and hit the central locking button. The locks snapped shut with a satisfying clunk.

He took a quick look around the car. It had once been

a luxury four-wheel drive, but the kids had given it quite a battering. The seats were dirty and ripped in a couple of places. There was trash piled up all over the floor. He noticed the passenger window was open a crack. He tried to close it with the window button, but it was dead.

"Won't work without the ignition on," said Jaz.

"Yeah, well, I don't think even the skinniest zombie could crawl through that," said Shadowman, and he checked the rearview mirror to see where the strangers were.

Nearly at the car. Six of them, more strung out in the road behind them.

He scrunched himself back in the seat and sighed. "Well, this is cozy," he said as the first of the strangers arrived and started pawing at the windshield, leaving greasy smears across it. Soon all six of the first bunch were crowding around the car. There was a whimper from the backseat. The boy was crying and Jaz had her arm around him. It looked like she might be crying as well, but her face was so crusted with blood it was hard to tell. The two of them were a mess, and Shadowman supposed he didn't look much better. The blood that had soaked through his clothing felt sticky.

"We're never going to get out of here," said Jaz. "We're going to be stuck in this car until they either smash their way in or we starve to death."

"This was your idea," said Shadowman. "Maybe if you'd remembered you didn't have the keys—"

"My leg really hurts," the boy interrupted. "It's not good, Jaz. It really, really hurts."

All the boy's swagger was gone. He was like a five-year-old with a cut knee being comforted by his mom. A big part of Shadowman wanted to join him. To break down and weep and have someone look after him.

There was no one, though, was there?

He took off his cloak and removed his backpack. Fished out a roll of bandage and some antiseptic.

"Here," he said, passing them to Jaz. She sniffed, wiped her nose, and smiled at him for the first time.

"Thanks."

"Yeah, thanks. I'm Johnny, by the way," said the boy.

"I'm Carl." Shadowman lied automatically, his habit of secrecy kicking in. He didn't know these kids well enough to tell them his real name.

Whatever that was.

He'd been christened Dylan, but nobody used that name anymore; most called him Shadowman, but others knew him by different names. Carl was the name of one of the kids at the squatter camp he'd been living in before he'd set off on his doomed trip to north London looking for other groups of surviving kids.

Jaz set about patching up her friend, all three of them trying to ignore the strangers who were all around the car now, pressing their faces to the windows, scratching at the glass with grubby, broken nails. One mother had found the open window and was wiggling her fingers through it. Shadowman could hear her panting.

"Bug off." He slashed at her fingers with his knife and she quickly withdrew them. Moments later she was back, dripping blood down the inside of the window. This time he ignored her.

What was the point?

He took his map book from his bag, tried to figure out where they were. Better to be doing something than to just sit here.

"What's this street?" he said.

"I'm not exactly sure where we are," said Jaz. "We were following the zombies for ages. They kept leaving the road, wandering in the developments, cutting through yards, getting in the houses. We couldn't always keep up with them in the Lexus. Had to keep getting out and going on foot. One point we lost them for, like, two hours. We think they were down on the train tracks. It was like they were looking for something."

Shadowman folded up his cloak and put it in the top of his backpack. He didn't want it to slow him down if they had to run again.

"Where you from, Carl?" asked Johnny.

"West, originally. Notting Hill way. This last year I've mostly been living in the center of town."

"Were you really at Buckingham Palace?"

"Some of the time, yeah."

"Cool."

"Why don't you two get a room?" said Jaz, and Johnny told her to shut up.

"So you got a plan yet, then, Carl?" Jaz asked with an edge of sarcasm. "You gonna magic us out of here?"

"Listen to me, Jaz," said Shadowman. "You chose to ignore me when I warned you about these creeps. You treated me like an idiot. Wouldn't listen, would you? Thought you knew better. But if you'd listened to me, we wouldn't be stuck here like this right now. You'd have the car keys and you'd have your friend, what's-his-name—"

"Ricky."

"Yeah, Ricky. So don't put the blame on me. I could've run. I could've left you there. You don't mean anything to me. But we're all in this now. So let's try and work together."

"Yeah, okay," said Jaz, though she didn't sound entirely convinced.

"Listen to him, Jaz," said Johnny. "He knows what he's talking about, I think."

"Maybe."

"We've got a choice," said Shadowman. "We can leg it. All three of us get out of this car before the rest of the pack arrives, and we try to find a safer place to hole up until Johnny feels strong enough to walk again."

"No way," said Johnny. "I ain't leaving this car. We wouldn't get two feet."

"Yeah," said Shadowman. "You're probably right. So there's another choice. You and me, Jaz, we get out of the car and leave Johnny here. We go back to your camp and get help."

"You are *not* leaving me," Johnny wailed. "Not in this car by myself. That is *not* happening."

"Then just one of us goes," said Shadowman.

"That's too long," said Jaz, "even if we could get past that bunch." She waved a hand at the dark ugly faces that were squashed against every window, licking the glass and blocking out the light. "It's a good half-hour walk to our camp, maybe more, then we got to get back here. In the meantime this car's going to be crawling with zombies. They'd get to whoever was left here with Johnny before we made it back."

"Probably right," said Shadowman.

"Good plan," said Jaz. "Really good plan."

"There's a last option," said Shadowman.

"Which is?"

"One of us goes out there now, before the rest of the horde gets here."

"And does what?"

"Tries to lead most of them away, then doubles back and gets the car key."

"Would that work?"

"If we were fast enough. Most of the grown-ups will be strung out between here and where we left Ricky. If we ran, got back here before they arrived . . . These are the fastest ones, the strongest. The others are slower. I know them."

"That sounds very risky," said Jaz.

"It's a good plan," said Johnny. "If we got the key, we could drive away from here."

"It's all right for you to say that," Jaz sneered. "You're obviously not the one who's going back out there." She leaned forward, closer to Shadowman. "What if there's still loads of them back there with Ricky? And what if there's loads here when you get back?"

"What d'you mean when *I* get back?" said Shadowman. "Who said I was going? He's your friend."

"Well, I just thought . . ."

"If I leave this car I could just leg it," said Shadowman. "You weren't exactly nice to me when we met. I don't owe you anything. All you've done is screw things up for me."

"You've got to do it," said Jaz.

"Why?"

"Because I'm scared, that's why. All right? I couldn't do it. Not go out there alone. No way."

"Jaz," said Johnny, his voice breaking. "Jaz . . ."

Shadowman stared at two fathers who were thumping on the windshield. One had a missing nose, and the other had a mouth full of growths that bulged out as if he was trying to see how many golf balls he could cram into his mouth for a bet. Shadowman couldn't believe it had come to this. Trying to save these bloody kids. He'd had it all sewn up. He was on top of things. Studying the Fear. Following them at a safe distance. And these stupid kids had thrown it all away.

Was he really prepared to die for them?

That's what it came down to. Getting out of this car was almost certain suicide. He knew what the Fear were capable of.

He closed his eyes. Tried to clear his mind. Counted slowly from one to ten. Felt his heart pounding in his chest.

Then jabbed his finger at the door-lock button.

30

Shadowman kicked open the car door, spilling two strangers onto the ground. He came out fast and brought the spear up while he was on the move, using the shaft to bat away more strangers. A bigger pack was advancing, and more were coming around the corner at the end of the street.

Don't think about it.

Just run.

He smashed his way out of the knot of strangers around the car and sprinted away in the direction opposite from the one they'd come.

Once he was at a safe distance he started jumping up and down and shouting at the strangers. "Come and get it, you bastards! Come on. Dinner! Over here."

He was getting their attention. A few broke away and ambled toward him. Trying to get in the car was like trying to open a can without a can opener. Shadowman was all unpacked and ready to be served. He smiled as the new arrivals coming down the road switched direction and headed for him instead of the Lexus.

"That's right. Over here. Come and get it. Fresh meat. Still on the bone. Come on. . . ."

The father with the mouth full of growths was the keenest and the fastest. He loped along, eyes fixed on Shadowman. Shadowman waited until he was nearly upon him, then hurled the spear at him. It took him cleanly in the center of the chest and flung him backward. More and more of them were coming now, and Shadowman started to retreat, drawing them away from the car. Once he was sure enough of them would follow, he looked at his map book and set off at a slow jog, plotting a route as he went. He stopped every few yards to check that he still had company and to study the map. He had to judge it right: get too far ahead of them and they'd give up and go back to the car; let them get too close and he risked being caught. He knew that at some point, though, he would have to speed up and get well away from them or he wouldn't have enough time to look for the car key.

He was the Pied Piper today and wished he could lead the pack over a cliff or something.

He figured out a route that would take him in a wide circle, ending at the apartment he'd checked out earlier. He'd be able to hide there and get a good view of where Ricky had been attacked.

Why the bloody hell was he helping these dorks? Why should he risk sacrificing himself for them? Why not just turn his back on them? Run away and keep on running. Leave Jaz and Johnny to look after themselves. He had no doubt that's what they'd have done in his situation.

He remembered how his best friend, Jester, had abandoned him by the railroad tracks at King's Cross after they'd been attacked and Shadowman had been concussed, unable to walk. Jester had simply left him there to die. It was the sensible thing to do. It was the way to stay alive.

Hadn't Shadowman done exactly the same thing? Persuaded Jaz to abandon Ricky?

He knew now how Jester had felt. Why he'd done it.

But he also remembered how he himself had felt.

It was the worst feeling ever.

Was it really the same? He and Jester had been best friends. He didn't know Ricky. Ricky had been too badly wounded to live. . . .

The worst feeling ever. No getting around it.

That's why he was out here, leading a pack of strangers away from the car. He was showing he wasn't like Jester. Making it up to all the kids he'd watched being hunted and killed by the Fear. Proving he was one of the good guys.

After about five minutes he put on a burst of speed and dashed off, leaving his pursuers for dust. He raced around the streets, his feet pounding a steady rhythm on the asphalt, and was soon near the tire center, approaching the apartments from the other end of the street. He ran up to the doors, barged them open, and bounded up the stairs to the top floor.

Once inside the apartment, he secured the door, put his back to it, and slid down to the floor. He was exhausted, his throat raw, his legs burning. His stomach suddenly lurched and he bent forward and puked on the carpet between his boots. He knew it was a basic defense mechanism. The stomach needs a lot of energy for digestion, ties up a lot of your blood flow. When the body urgently needs more blood to work the leg muscles, or extra energy to help you run or fight, it automatically empties your guts. Even if you haven't eaten anything you'll be hit by the heaves.

He took a glug of water from his canteen. He only now allowed himself to acknowledge that he had been terrified. From the moment he'd first seen the new grown-ups up until now, he'd been in the grip of raw fear, but he'd used some survival instinct to block it out.

Jaz had admitted she was scared. Which must have taken something. He wondered if she'd seen that he was just as scared.

Probably not. He was good at hiding things.

He spat and got up. This was his last chance to run and leave Jaz and Johnny to look after themselves. After all, they'd ruined everything for him.

He laughed. Remembering how he'd felt protective about "his" strangers when Jaz and the others had attacked them.

What had it all been about really? Following the Fear?

He walked into the living room, nodded to the bodies on the sofa, and went over to the windows. The tire center appeared empty. The grown-ups must all have emerged. He opened the window and leaned out. Could just see where they'd had the fight in the street. There was an oily, dark, wet patch, bits of body and clothing strewn about, several dead strangers, some already half eaten. Nine living strangers were fighting over the remaining scraps of good meat. These were the weakest and feeblest of the Fear. Always the last to eat. Hanging on for a few more days before they too were killed. Really they were doing little more than fattening themselves up for when Saint George decided it was their turn to be dinner. He was clever, Saint George, Shadowman had to admit. He had a sort of admiration for him. Saint George was toughening up his army, gradually culling the weakest and slowest, and using them to feed the rest. And now it looked like others were searching for him, joining up. That's why the Willesden pack had been coming here.

Somehow word had gotten out. Saint George's army was on the march.

Shadowman took out his binoculars and focused on the group of feeding strangers. He was tempted to try to shoot them from there, but figured it would be a waste of bolts. He could see Ricky's bow lying on the pavement. Too complicated even for these clever strangers to use.

And then he spotted something weird. There was a lone father standing about ten yards from the group. Still as a statue, his arms out in front of him as if he was holding an invisible box. He had his eyes open, unblinking, staring into the distance. Waiting for something.

Shadowman hadn't seen this behavior before.

He swiveled around and checked the other direction. No sign yet of the strangers who'd been following him from the Lexus.

Only a matter of time.

He slipped his bow off his shoulder, checked it, said goodbye to the dead couple, and went down the stairs.

Once he was back on the street he moved cautiously toward the feeding strangers. As soon as he was close enough, he aimed at the back of an aging mother and pulled the trigger. The bolt thumped into her and she fell forward. He put the end of the bow to the ground, slipped his foot into the stirrup, and hauled up the string, snapped it in place, fitted in another bolt. The whole action took him less than thirty seconds. He'd had plenty of time to practice. The other strangers didn't seem to have noticed that one of their gang had been shot, and two minutes later four more of them had been hit. Two lay still, killed outright, but the rest were crawling around with the bolts embedded in their diseased bodies right up to the feathers. One was flipping about on the ground, arms and legs twitching.

Shadowman reckoned he'd done enough. It was safe to advance. He was fast with the bow, but time was running out. He had to get back to the car before the main mass of the Fear reached it. He slung his bow over his shoulder, drew his machete from its sheath, and walked quickly up to the surviving strangers.

A mother had Ricky's head and was smashing it on the ground trying to break the skull open so that she could get at the brain. It looked like an old rubber Halloween mask found in the bottom of the dress-up box, floppy and out of shape.

Shadowman fought back a wave of nausea as he lifted the machete and swung. The mother had wanted brains, well, here they were. The top of her head came off like the top of a boiled egg.

"That's how you get to the brains," he said, but he had to turn away so as not to look at the shiny pinkish-gray gloop that spilled out.

He shivered as he laid into the other strangers, and soon they all lay dead.

Except for the one who was standing still as a rock up the

road. As Shadowman checked him out, he noticed that there were two more, spaced the same distance apart, about ten yards or so, waiting, with their arms held out.

A word came into Shadowman's mind. Sentinels.

No time now to figure out what they were doing. The main thing was that they were ignoring him.

So he would ignore them.

He had to find that key.

31

Shadowman tried not to think too hard about the mess that was strewn everywhere. He remembered going on family trips to the countryside when he'd been small. Remembered the first time he'd seen roadkill. He'd been struck by how hard it was to tell what the animal had once been. So many cars had gone over it, smearing it into the road surface, and so many birds had pecked away at it that it was an unidentifiable smudge of fur and blood.

Ricky looked the same. The horde had made quick work of him. A hundred hungry mouths had torn into him. There wasn't a lot left. Bones, shiny bits of gristle, a length of intestine, shredded clothing. He could see a hand lying under a parked car; one of the strangers had been trying to get to it when Shadowman had shot him.

He saw the stab-proof vest, which was still in one piece. He removed his backpack and bow and put the vest on. It hadn't done much to protect Ricky, but it was better than nothing. Nearby was his leather jacket, also still in one piece, but covered in blood and feces. Shadowman picked it up and hurriedly went through the pockets. There were a few pathetic reminders of Ricky's life. A crumpled photo of his mom and dad, a Valentine's Day card, the membership card for a sports center, a ticket to a soccer match, a lucky rabbit's foot (ho, bloody ho), and a penknife that Shadowman pocketed.

But no keys.

"Damn." He tossed the jacket away and wiped his hands. *Keep moving.*

There was a pile of stuff in the gutter by the side of the road, a disgusting mangle of skin and hair, inedible body parts, and torn clothing. He poked through it with the toe of his boot, turning it over, trying to find something he recognized. This was taking too long. He sucked in a deep breath, got down on one knee, and went to work with his machete, lifting the layers to see what was underneath. At the bottom he found what he was after—a pair of jeans. They were filthy, covered in what looked like the entire contents of Ricky's stomach. Some vile scraps of flesh clung to the inside. He felt the pockets and his fingers closed on something hard.

The key to the Lexus.

He fished it out, wiped it clean on his own jeans, and zipped it into a jacket pocket.

He checked—the sentinels hadn't moved—then looked the other way. Just in time. His pursuers had finally arrived, hobbling along the street, bunched together. He grabbed Ricky's crossbow and slung it over his shoulder next to his own and set off back to the car, sticking to the route they'd originally taken when they were running from the Fear. The only problem was that he would have to go past the sentinels.

Oh well. They were spaced out, unmoving and unarmed,

and he had his machete. He nevertheless gave the first one a wide berth, expecting him at any moment to come awake and run at him. He didn't even blink. If it wasn't for the fact that his eyes were open, he might have been dead or asleep. It was the same with the second sentinel, and the third, and as Shadowman turned the corner, he saw more of them strung out along the length of the road at regular intervals. He counted them as he ran past. Three, four, five, six, seven . . .

And then he spotted the rear of the main pack, a seething dark mass, shambling slowly in the direction of the car. It hadn't taken them long to eat Ricky, but it had delayed them long enough. With luck, there wouldn't be too many around the Lexus yet, and Shadowman would be able to get back in.

He couldn't run through this mob, however, so he bypassed them by ducking into the next street, which was mercifully free of grown-ups. He ran as fast as he could. It was vital that he overtook the strangers. His legs ached, felt as if they'd been filled with concrete, and his body was flooded with lactic acid. He pushed on, ignoring the pain. How long had he been gone? Five minutes? Six? Probably more like ten. He hoped Jaz and Johnny would still be there after all this.

When he came to the next junction, he cut through and caught sight of the car. There were a lot more strangers crowding around it than he had hoped. The main body of the Fear had yet to arrive—there was no sign of Saint George—but there were still maybe thirty of them there, three deep around the car, with more arriving every second.

Once again he had a powerful urge to turn tail and get as far away from there as he could. He'd watched plenty of kids die in the days he'd been following the Fear. He clearly remembered that first one at Waitrose, his head coming out on a stick. He could watch these die as well if he had to. There was no point in risking his life if there was really nothing he could do.

Seriously, could he fight his way past thirty strangers to get to the car?

He stopped running. Started to back away.

And then the car horn sounded. A long unbroken blast that caused the startled strangers to cower away for a moment, clearing a space. Shadowman got a brief glimpse of Jaz sitting in the driver's seat, her face white with fear, mouth and eyes stretched wide.

She'd seen him somehow and was signaling to him.

Damn her. Now he'd have to help.

And he had to move fast while there was an opening.

He unslung Ricky's crossbow and started to run, faster and faster, with no real plan except to somehow get into that car. The strangers hadn't seen him; they were too interested in the Lexus.

Closer. Closer. Closer still. He sped up.

At the last moment he let out a roar and fired the bow directly into the wall of bodies. A father went down. A fresh gap opened up. Shadowman raised the bow and used it like a club, battering his way through. Diseased faces turned toward him. Faces deformed by growths, by blisters and festering wounds, missing eyes and ears, noses, teeth.

In a movie this might all have happened in slow motion, clear and beautiful like a rehearsed dance. But this was real life and it all happened too fast. It was choppy and messy and confusing. Shadowman was in among the strangers. They swarmed around him in a blur, arms and hands with clawed fingers reached for him. He was in a hot, stinking world of open mouths, bulging eyes, yellow flesh. And then he recognized a dark blue business suit, a familiar face. It was Bluetooth, still with his earpiece in. He'd gotten ahold of the spear and was pushing through the crowd.

So he was in charge here, was he?

Shadowman dodged him, hooked an elbow around his neck, and hauled him backward, throwing him into the scrum of bodies and bowling several over. Shadowman hurled Ricky's bow after him. It wasn't any use to him in these cramped conditions.

He powered into the strangers nearest the car, shoving them out of the way. Now was his chance. The door was clear. There was Jaz peering out at him.

"Open it!" he yelled, but Jaz shook her head.

"I can't risk it. They'll get in."

Shadowman heard the clunk as she engaged the central locking.

"Open the bloody door, you idiot."

"Pass me the keys through the window."

Jaz waggled her fingers through the open crack at the top of the door.

"Let me in!"

Jaz shook her head again.

Idiot.

Shadowman pressed the unlock symbol on the car key and before Jaz knew what was happening he tugged the door open. Unfortunately Jaz was holding tight to the handle on the other side and, as the door swung wide, it tugged her out of the car, spilling her on to the ground. There was a surge of strangers rushing to get at her.

She screamed.

Bluetooth was at their head. He lunged with the spear and the point went into Jaz's shoulder, cutting off her scream with a gasp of agony. Shadowman tore his machete from its sheath and took a swing at Bluetooth, but a mother got in the way and the blade crashed into the front of her skull, spraying the car with blood and pus. Shadowman pushed her into Bluetooth, whose spear became entangled in the crush of bodies. Taking advantage of the clear space, Shadowman managed to scoop up Jaz. But he had to let go of his machete to do so. It clattered to the ground.

He threw Jaz into the car, a small diseased teenager going with her. Shadowman hauled the teenager out and then, elbowing, head-butting, and kicking all the way, he squeezed in after Jaz, half lying on top of her. He rolled onto his back and, using both feet at once, he repeatedly booted the faces of the strangers who were massing at the open door. And then he was aware of a movement from the backseat. Johnny wasn't completely out of action; he was using the end of Jaz's iron bar to jab at the grown-ups.

It was all Shadowman needed. He sat up, took hold of the door handle, and pulled it. A mother had her hand in the way, however, and the door bounced off it. It took him two more slams before she removed her mangled fingers and he was able to close it properly. Then he squeezed the lock button on the key.

Thunk.

He was still on top of Jaz, who was whimpering and panting and bleeding into the seats. Shadowman slid off her onto the passenger seat, pushing her legs out of the way. He was covered in blood from head to foot, but he couldn't tell yet if any of it was his.

"Well done, mate," said Johnny. "That was awesome."

"Yeah, thanks." Shadowman was trembling and felt like he might throw up again at any minute. The strangers had gone into a frenzy, hammering on the car with a noise like thunder. Shadowman tried to ignore them. They weren't in the clear yet.

"I assume Ricky was the driver?" he said.

"Yeah," said Johnny.

"Can either of you two drive?"

"I've done a bit. But the way my leg is, I don't think I could use the pedals."

"What about Jaz?"

"She's had a bit of practice. Can she do it, though, like that?"

"She's gonna have to."

32

Shadowman helped Jaz sit upright. She leaned forward against the steering wheel for support. Her shoulder was soaked with blood. Shadowman pressed a hand to her wound, trying to stem the flow.

"Can you drive?" he asked.

"I don't know." Jaz was even paler than before. "It hurts like hell. I'm gonna die, aren't I?"

"We just need to get away from here."

"That spear was dirty, had zombie blood on it. That was like an injection of shit."

"Don't think about that now," said Shadowman. "The main thing is to get moving."

"I don't know if I can. I'm gonna pass out."

"No, you're not."

Jaz jumped as a grown-up whacked the windshield with something hard and heavy. Cracks appeared.

Shadowman rammed the key into the ignition and turned it. The engine rumbled into life. Outside, Bluetooth was using the spear to try to smash a side window; another father was chopping into the hood with Shadowman's machete.

"Just drive!" Shadowman shouted. "Go, go, go. . . ."

Jaz winced as she tried to put the car into gear. She couldn't move her left arm, though. Shadowman checked the gears. It looked like an automatic. He pulled the gearshift to the drive position with his free hand. Jaz stamped on the accelerator and the Lexus lurched forward, bumping and jolting as it plowed through the strangers. Johnny gave a cheer from the back.

"So long, you mugs!"

The car sped down the road, swerving slightly from side to side as Jaz tried to steer with one hand. It banged and the bottom scraped horribly as they went too fast over a speed bump. The windshield was so cracked and streaked with filth it was hard to see ahead.

"Slow down," Shadowman croaked. Jaz said nothing. There were tears streaming down her face.

What a mess.

Jaz didn't slow down; if anything, she sped up. Johnny was giving directions from the back, but he wasn't confident of the route, which was making Jaz more and more tense. Shadowman couldn't risk getting his backpack off to reach for his map book. He didn't want to take his hand away from Jaz's puncture wound. The point of the spear looked like it had gone all the way through her shoulder. He was already slick with her blood. She was losing a lot of it. Only fear and adrenaline and a deep-rooted sense of survival were keeping her going.

Was it enough, though, to get them back to her camp?

They bounced and rattled around corners, Jaz only just managing to keep control of the big heavy car. It was clear that she was desperate to get home. They might have made it if they hadn't spotted another group of strangers. About twelve of them, wandering down the road in three strung-out groups.

"Jesus. Where are they all coming from?" said Johnny.

"Who cares?" said Jaz. "But I know where they're going."

"Leave it," said Shadowman. "All that matters now is getting back safely."

"They killed me," said Jaz. "The filthy bastards killed me."

She stomped on the accelerator and the Lexus roared straight into the first knot of strangers. Shadowman realized he didn't have his seat belt on. None of them did. There hadn't been time. He braced himself with his free arm and there was a grating thump as they hit the first stranger, then another and another; bodies flew past the car and then the Lexus was out of control, veering wildly across the road toward a lamppost.

Jaz cried out and wrenched the wheel around so that they swung back the other way, plowing through the rest of the strangers. Now they were in danger of hitting a parked car on the other side of the road. Again Jaz hauled on the wheel, oversteering and causing the car to swerve back too sharply the other way. It was completely unstable now, driving on two wheels, and as Jaz tried to right it, it twisted around completely sideways, slamming into the last few strangers before at last tipping over. Shadowman's head banged into the roof as they went into a roll.

He could still hear the noise, the thudding and crunching, the rattle of breaking glass, screams. He remembered the weird, unreal sensation of being upside down in a car, the world outside spinning around, as they went over and over and . . .

Now here he was.

How long had he been unconscious?

Long enough for it to get dark.

He must still be in the wrecked car. Lying in a cocoon of twisted metal. He was on top of a body. Was it Johnny? Jaz? One of the strangers?

At least he hadn't been eaten. Had the Lexus miraculously wiped them all out? Or had they pulled the other kids free and were eating them before they moved on to him? Had they tried to pull him out and failed? After all, he was well and truly stuck here.

"Hello? Johnny? Jaz? Hello . . . Is there anyone here with me? Anyone? Anyone . . ."

He had to get out.

Christ. What if they'd already started to eat him? He couldn't feel his legs. Could they have chewed away at them?

He growled in fear and fury and frustration.

Too many questions.

Too many unknowns.

One thing was clear, though. And it was a big positive. Whatever had happened, he was still alive. And he was going to get out of this somehow.

He heard the scuff of footsteps.

Froze.

Someone was moving around out there.

More than one person by the sound of it.

They'd come for him.

He closed his eyes and opened his mouth and howled. . . .

33

We found seven more Nephilim this morning. God knows how they're getting through. We've repaired any damage to the Wall we could find, but there were no obvious weak points. Without knowing exactly where they got over, we don't have a clue where to start fixing things up. It's too big a job to reinforce the whole Wall. It took us nearly a year to build it. We need more soldiers out on the streets, regular patrols."

"The Lamb will look after us, Nathan."

Archie noticed Nathan give a little look that Matt missed. Nathan sighed. "But he'll take any help he can get from us, yeah? You should see it out there, Matt; it's like Glastonbury for the diseased. There's more Nephilim rocking up every day, and they're massing on the other side of the Wall like flies around poop. I never seen anything like it, man. It's getting really crowded. Is like they're after something."

Nathan was Matt's main man at the cathedral when it came to security. In charge of all their soldiers. He was tall and well built, had been a keen soccer player before the collapse, had dreamed of getting a tryout for one of the London teams. Archie liked him. He didn't take any crap from anyone and he didn't dish any out.

Nathan, Archie, and Matt were plodding up the endless spiral staircase inside the south wall of St. Paul's. Their feet clattered on the wooden steps that were fixed on top of the stone ones underneath.

"How many Nephilim did you say you found on this side of the Wall this morning?" Matt asked, slightly out of breath.

"Seven." Nathan was glugging from a can of Coke and wasn't finding the climb difficult. Archie was too knackered to even speak. Sports had never been his thing, and since arriving at the cathedral, he hardly exercised anymore. He stayed indoors, eating unhealthy food.

"Were they all together?" Matt asked.

"Nah, one group of two, one group of five."

"Were they any trouble to get rid of?"

"Not really. There were enough of us to sort them out. We wasted them and dumped their bodies off the Wobbly Bridge. Big splash. Bye-bye, Neph."

Matt stopped and turned to Nathan as they reached one of the small landings.

"Then what's the problem?" he asked. "You can deal with the few that get through, can't you?"

"Yeah, but there's more and more of them out there, man. You need to look for yourself."

"Well, that's what I'm doing, aren't I? I'm not hacking all the way up here for my health, Nathan."

"Won't do you no harm," Nathan joked.

Matt tutted and continued up the stairs. Archie filled his aching lungs and followed.

Eventually they came to the Whispering Gallery. Archie had never liked it up here. From the gallery you could look right down inside the dome to the floor, miles below. You felt like you were hanging in this vast, open, empty space. Archie was scared of heights and had a crazy urge to throw himself off.

When they'd first arrived, the kids had all come up here. You could whisper into the wall and someone on the other side of the dome could hear you perfectly clearly. The kids had spent ages whispering rude words and giggling. Now they hardly came up anymore.

Archie tried not to think about that sickening view down to the black-and-white-tiled floor and was relieved that they weren't stopping there this time. They were heading up to the Golden Gallery, at the top of the dome, with its 360-degree views of the outside world.

It meant more stairs, however, and Archie was already out of breath, his heart hammering at his ribs, and his legs burning. Nathan and Matt had gone on ahead. He could hear their voices echoing down the stairs. He struggled on behind, swearing quietly to himself. There were benches for resting every twenty steps or so, and Archie had to use every one. The smoke wafting up from below didn't help. It got everywhere, and as he passed through the thick haze trapped in the stairwell, he started to cough and choke. It was a relief to get out into the fresh air when he reached the Stone Gallery that ran around the bottom of the dome. Archie preferred it out here to the Whispering Gallery. The cathedral felt more solid and secure. Somehow, looking straight down inside the building was worse than looking out at the view across London.

He had a faint hope that they might stop here, but the high stone balustrade made it hard to see clearly, and the extra height from the Golden Gallery gave a better view.

Besides, Matt would want to go right to the top. It was easier to play God from up there. Lord Matt Almighty looking out across his kingdom.

Archie sighed as he saw Matt and Nathan slip inside the small doorway that led to the next group of stairs.

This was the worst part.

The dome had an outer shell and an inner shell, and between them was a narrow space. Cast-iron spiral stairs had been built inside this space, and Archie would have to climb them to get to the top.

He hated those iron stairs. Not only were there hundreds, but you could also see down through the holes in them.

He was nauseated and sweating and shaking by the time he got to the Golden Gallery, and as he ducked his head to get through the doorway to the outside world, he gulped in lungfuls of cold air.

He concentrated on the spectacular view until he had calmed down, then edged his way around the narrow gallery until he was next to Matt and Nathan, who were leaning on the rusted iron railing, pointing downward.

In the early morning light Archie could clearly see the Wall, the series of barricades that they'd laboriously built over the last year, blocking off every street around the cathedral and creating a safe area on the inside.

He could also clearly see a great crowd of grown-ups—Nephilim as Matt had named them, after some giants in the

Bible. It looked like every sicko in London was heading this way. They were pressed up against the barricades.

And he could hear them, tap-tap-tapping.

Dumb clucks.

Matt had started the Great Song soon after they'd arrived, trying to keep it going all day and night. In those days the grown-ups could come right up to the cathedral walls at night. And they clustered there, copying the kids inside. It had spread like a craze among them. As if music still lived on in some deep animal part of their brains.

Archie was amazed that all these new arrivals had joined in so quickly. They were making quite a racket down there. You couldn't hear them from inside the cathedral, but when the wind was in the right direction, the sound rose up here loud and clear.

"What do they want?" Archie asked, not really expecting an answer.

"It's the Lamb," said Matt.

"What?"

"The Lamb. They know he's here. They've come for him. They want to destroy him."

"So you'll admit it's a full-on army, then?" said Nathan.

"They are the Emim, the Awwim," said Matt. "The Terrors, the Rephaim or Dead Ones, the Gibborim, the Devastators."

"They're a bunch of sick bunnies is what they are," said Nathan.

"They are the Nephilim," Matt went on. "The fallen ones, the cursed ones. And this is their city, Kiriath-arba."

Nathan sighed. Archie could tell he was trying to stay

patient. Nathan was more interested in practical things, didn't have much to do with the religious side of life in the cathedral.

"They're something we need to maybe worry about, though, yeah?" he said.

"No," said Matt. "I don't worry about anything. We have the Lamb. Our faith is strong. We will win this."

"How, exactly?" said Nathan, almost losing it. "I mean, seriously, Matt, what are we going to literally *do*? How does it work? Is he going to lead us, the Lamb? Are we going to go out there and fight them Nephs? Is he going to shoot laser beams from his fingers, or will the clouds open up in the sky and a big, like, ray of light come down and turn them into dust? I mean, *literally*, Matt, are they all supposed to just drop down dead or something? Tell me how it works."

"It will be shown to us."

Archie bit his lip and turned away so that there was no danger of Matt seeing his expression. Sometimes he wanted to hit Matt. He could be *really* annoying. He'd known him since he was eight. They'd been together seven years, first at Rowhurst elementary school and then at middle school. To say that Matt had changed would be something of an understatement.

Archie's father had been a priest, but Matt had never been religious, until he'd seen the light in a big way a year ago. Archie remembered sheltering from the sickos in the school chapel. They'd been burning wood and Bibles and anything they could get their hands on to keep warm, and the fumes had built up until they'd all nearly died from carbon-monoxide poisoning. When Matt came around, he'd changed. A strange religious mania had come over him, and he was now absolutely sure that he was right and everyone else was wrong. He knew some hidden truth.

Archie often wondered how much of it all he *really* believed. If he confronted Matt he knew what the answer would be. . . .

All of it. Every single word.

But he changed those words, didn't he? Nearly every day. To suit himself. To fit the situation. The truth was slippery.

Matt was completely crazy. Archie was a hundred percent sure of that. But maybe in a crazy world you needed a crazy person to lead you.

And so far they'd done pretty well, hadn't they? Whenever Matt had said that the Lamb would look after them, it had come true. Like a series of miracles. Unbelievable really, if you thought about it.

They'd survived the boat wreck in the Thames. They'd found their way here. They'd beaten off the Nephilim. Built the Wall. They'd found the food supply that kept them all alive. They'd found Wormwood. They'd even found the Lamb and the Goat.

Just like Matt had said they would.

Maybe, when it came down to it, Matt was the sane one and the rest of them were crazy.

A hundred percent crazy.

"When we sacrifice the Goat, all will be clear," Matt said. "We'll know what we have to do. Today we'll take him to Wormwood. And we'll see what's what. So let's get on with it."

34

Sam felt like he was going mad. The chickens running around everywhere, the smoke, the noise, the messed-up kids. He'd hardly slept at all, and whenever he had managed to doze off, his dreams had been filled with horrors. He'd lost count of the times he'd woken up in the night, anxious and shaking, drenched in sweat. It didn't help that he was under guard. There were always two older kids watching over him, working in shifts, sitting there silently, forcing themselves not to look directly at him.

His bed was a camping mattress rolled out on the hard floor. All the other kids appeared to sleep in the main body of the cathedral, except for Matt and his closest circle, who had some rooms in another part of the building somewhere.

Sam sat up and looked around, making doubly sure that this wasn't just another nightmare. His head throbbed; the cuts and bruises he'd gotten yesterday were very painful, particularly his shins where he'd bashed them climbing into the tunnel. The smoke that filled the cathedral had made his throat raw, and he still felt jittery from all the rich food he'd eaten last night and all the Coke he'd drunk.

A few kids were still churning out a drone from the choir stalls. They'd kept it up all night, just as Matt had warned. It was the thing Sam found hardest to deal with. He'd gone on a trip with his family to Spain once. They'd stayed in a nice hotel, with a pool and waterslides, but their rooms had been directly over the hotel disco, and all night the *thump, thump, thump* had come up through the floor, mixed in with people laughing and cheering and shouting. Sam had found it impossible to sleep, and his dad had been driven nuts. Sam had never seen him like that before, stamping about in his room in the middle of the night, screaming at them all to shut up.

Sam yawned and rubbed his face. His eyes felt all itchy and gritty; they hurt if he moved them too much. Above him the early morning light made a milky-white glow in the smoke-filled dome. Two pigeons flapped around up there. He coughed. Spat on the floor. Then a big fat tear ran down his nose and splatted next to the pathetic little blob of phlegm. This was all so unfair. He wasn't supposed to be here. The grown-ups were the ones you had to worry about, not other children. How could the kids here pretend they were good, claim they were helping him, claim they worshipped him even, when they treated him and the Kid like this?

They'd put the Kid in a cage last night. That wasn't right. They shouldn't do that to someone. After they'd caught him they'd dragged him down the aisle to where the cage stood waiting. He'd gone quietly, realistic about his chances of being able to fight so many people. Sam had gone berserk, though, spitting, cursing, yelling, screaming, and kicking the bigger kids who held him back. In the end he'd exhausted himself and they'd let him go. He'd sat in a side chapel and cried and cried until they put him to bed.

The cage sat in the middle of the cathedral, under the dome, where they'd dragged it last night. It was metal, looked a bit fake, like it had been made for a film or a play, or the old London Dungeon. Maybe that's where they'd gotten it from—they certainly hadn't made it themselves. But the lock on its door worked all right; that wasn't just for show.

Sam looked over to his friend. The Kid was sitting up straight with his legs crossed, unmoving, his dark eyes glinting in the milky light.

Sam started to get up. One of the boys who was guarding him spoke.

"Stay there, please."

"Can't I at least go and talk to my friend?"

"Matt said you weren't to go anywhere."

"I'm not going anywhere. I'll only be over there."

"I don't know. I was told to keep you here."

Sam swore at the boy, who kept his head bowed and his eyes on the floor.

"What's going on?" Tish came over with another girl. They looked bleary-eyed. Sam wondered if anyone ever got any sleep around here with that racket going on all night. Maybe Matt wanted it that way, wanted to keep everyone half crazed, unable to think straight, like zombies. Sam had seen a program about brainwashing once, how the American army tortured people by not letting them get any sleep—and playing loud heavy-metal music at them. It broke their minds eventually.

"Are you all right?" Tish asked with a sappy smile, as if she was talking to a baby. At least she looked at him, though.

"What do you think?" said Sam. "Of course I'm not all right. Please, can't I just go and talk to the Kid? I feel sorry for him, all by himself over there."

Tish bit her lip as she thought this over. The scab on her forehead looked black. At least half the other children here had similar wounds.

They freaked Sam out.

"If you want me to go along with things," he said, "then you'll have to let me do what I want."

Tish looked around the cathedral. There was no sign of Matt or Archie Bishop or any of the acolytes.

"Okay," she said. "If it'll cheer you up. But just for a minute, and then will you behave, yeah? Cooperate?"

"I suppose so."

"Come on, then." Tish smiled again. "To be fair, I can't see what harm it can do."

She took Sam over to the cage. The other girl and the two guards came with them. Sam felt a bit self-conscious, but when he got there, all he could think about was how miserable the Kid must be. He laced his fingers through the bars of the cage and tried not to start crying again. That wouldn't help his friend any.

"I'm sorry about this," he said. "I didn't know. It's not my fault. I'm not what they think I am. I'm sorry we ended up here."

The Kid said nothing. Didn't move or speak, just stared

into infinity. Sam felt awful. The Kid must be blaming him for everything. Sam would've done the same in his position. He turned angrily on Tish.

"How can you say he's bad?" he said, trying not to shout. "How can you say he's this goat you all keep talking about? Some evil thing? He's not evil. He's a boy like me. He's my friend."

"He's deceived you."

"I don't even know what that means."

"He's pretending to be your friend when really he's the Goat."

"That's mental. He's not a goat. How could he be a goat?"

"It's not literal," said Tish, looking slightly confused herself. "To be fair, I don't think he's, like, I mean, he's not *literally* a goat. I don't really understand it. It's all symbols, hidden meanings, words inside words. You'd need to be in the inner circle to understand it. I don't understand half the stuff. Matt and Archie and the acolytes, they have meetings and study groups, and Matt tells them the words and they write them down. The religious books get longer every day, and sometimes they change, like when Matt tells us he's heard the words wrong or misunderstood something, then he changes things. Writes new rules. That's what the smoke's for, to give us all fresh visions."

"Since when did smoke ever make anything clearer?" said Sam. "That's just stupid. Like everything here."

"Matt can explain it better."

"But I mean, wouldn't I know about it?" said Sam. "Just a little bit? If I really was the lamb, wouldn't I have some idea? It doesn't make any sense."

"You *are* the Lamb."

"No, I'm not!"

"It was prophesied."

"Don't keep using long words to try and confuse me."

"Matt was told you'd come here."

"How could he have been? I'm *not* the lamb."

Suddenly the Kid spoke. "He's not the Messiah," he said. "He's just a very naughty boy."

Sam laughed. He'd seen that film, *Monty Python's Life of Brian*. It was one of Dad's favorites. The Kid laughed too. Maybe he didn't blame Sam after all.

Sharing a joke like this broke the spell, made everything more normal. Sam noticed that even one of the guards was trying not to laugh. They couldn't actually believe all this garbage, could they? Had Matt really brainwashed them so completely?

It felt very different in the cathedral when Matt wasn't around. There was a much more relaxed and normal atmosphere. And now, right on cue, all ready to spoil the party, he came in. Swishing in through the side door that led to the stairs, followed by Archie and Nathan.

Sam felt the place go cold. The smile died on the guard's lips.

Matt had his own smile, big enough for all of them. He approached Sam and did a little bow with his head.

"How are you today, my Lord?"

"Terrible," said Sam. "I hardly slept at all."

"Your mind is troubled," said Matt. "You are waking up. The light of truth is entering and pushing out the darkness. Maybe it's too bright for you to sleep."

"No, it's too bloody loud. That so-called music is doing my head in."

"The truth is waking inside you."

"You twist everything," Sam snapped. "That's not what's happening. Why don't you just let me and the Kid go? We don't want to join in your stupid games."

"He casts a strong spell over you, the Goat."

"He's not a goat, he's a kid. He's *the* Kid and I don't mean like a young goat, I mean that's his name."

"His name is the Kid?"

"Yes, that's what we call him."

"And what's his real name?"

"I don't know. He's never told me. He's just the Kid. That's it. Full names don't really much matter anymore, do they?"

"You see how he's deceived you?" said Matt. "How he's hiding who he really is from you?"

"No, I don't see that at all. He just uses a nickname."

"But most people with a nickname, they'd tell you their real name, wouldn't they?"

"He's not like most people."

"Ah . . ."

"I don't mean anything like that, stop twisting things. He's just different."

"He is truly different." Matt now turned to the cage. "Tell us your real name," he said.

"Rumpelstiltskin," said the Kid.

Sam saw the mask slip. A flicker passed across Matt's face and he looked annoyed for a moment. He was used to everyone there listening carefully to everything he said, looking up to him, worshipping him even. The Kid knew how to get to him.

Matt moved closer to the cage, leaned toward the Kid. When he spoke, it was quiet and intense.

"What should we call you?" he said. "What is your true name? Are you the First Beast? The Second Beast? The Whore of Babylon? The dragon? Beelzebub, Satan, Lucifer, Leviathan—"

"Dave Dee, Dozy, Beaky, Mick, and Titch," the Kid interrupted.

Again there was a flicker of irritation from Matt before he pressed on. "Baphomet, Iblis, Shayatan, Belial, Azazel . . .

"Pugh, Pugh, Barney McGrew, Cuthbert, Dibble, Grub . . ."

"You see." Matt turned to Sam, holding his arms wide. "He's trying to confuse us with his magic."

"No, he's not," said Sam. "He's having a joke with you. This is all wack."

Again Matt spoke to the Kid. "Just tell us your real name," he said. "It'll save us all a lot of time."

"I'm the Kid is all you need to know."

"What kid?"

"The Milky Bar Kid, the Silky Bra Kid, Billy the Kid, Billy the Fish, Super Meat Boy, Kid Jenson, kid leather, I kid you not."

"Tell us your name!" Matt screeched at him.

"What difference does it make what his name is?" said Sam. "Leave him alone."

"The first step to taming the beast is to find out its name."

"He's not a beast, though, is he?"

"And you shall know him by what he brings. He shall carry a sword, but that sword shall be broken. By his dress also shall ye know him. . . ."

"What are you talking about?"

"It was all in the prophecy. It was all written down. *'By his dress also shall ye know him. . . .'* And see, he's wearing a dress."

Sam gave a snort of laughter. "Don't be crazy," he said. "That just means dress, like in what he's wearing, not dress as in a *dress.*"

"It's all written down," said Matt, ignoring Sam. "And it's also written down that we have to find out his real name."

"Where's it written?"

"It is written. That's all you need to know."

"I bet it's not. I bet you're making it up."

"We have to know his name."

"Well, he's not going to tell you, is he?"

"We'll get him to talk."

"Good luck," said Sam. "If he doesn't want to do something he won't."

"The truth is stronger than lies," said Matt. "It will always win and it will always show itself in the end. Unlock the cage."

Sam felt his heart lift. They were going to let the Kid out. Maybe Matt was starting to see sense. One of Sam's guards unlocked the door and swung it open. Matt's acolytes had come over to watch. Matt spoke softly to them and they nodded.

After a while the Kid got up and climbed out; he looked stiff and awkward and took a few moments to straighten up and stamp some life back into his feet. Sam gave him a hug.

"Kiss me, Hardy," said the Kid.

"Kiss yourself," said Sam.

"I'll fettle thee!"

Matt watched them for a few seconds, then made a sign, and what happened next shocked Sam. One of the acolytes grabbed hold of the Kid and pulled his sleeveless leather jacket off, then two more of them pulled down the top of his flowery dress. This time the Kid struggled, but it was no use, he was overpowered. The acolytes took him over to stand facing the cage. Matt then tied his skinny wrists to the bars with two thick leather boot laces. They cut into the Kid's skin, and his hands started to go red.

"What are you doing, you perverts!" the Kid yelled. "Take your stinking paws off me, you damned dirty apes!"

Sam turned to Tish for support, for some sort of explanation; he was too upset to speak. Tish looked embarrassed and slightly ashamed. She shrugged and turned away.

An acolyte passed Matt a horsewhip. Sam couldn't believe he was going to use it on the Kid. But then Matt stepped forward and touched the tip of it to the Kid's back.

"Tell us your name."

"No," said the Kid quietly.

"You will tell us or I will beat it out of you."

"It's none of your bloody business."

"You can't hide behind your lies any longer. We *will* discover the truth."

"You can shove the truth up your hairy ass, you church monkey."

One of the acolytes had gone up into the pulpit and now started to ring a handbell, *clang-clang-clang*. One by one the children in the cathedral, all except the ones playing the music, drifted over and formed a semicircle around the cage. A sea of green.

"Only in pain will the truth be revealed," said Matt. "We must force the demon from the flesh."

"If you hurt him I swear I will kill you," Sam sobbed.

"Whoever spares the rod hates his son," said Matt. "But he who loves him is diligent to discipline him."

"I swear I will!"

"Tell us your name!" Matt cried out, his voice echoing in the vast emptiness of the cathedral.

"No!"

"You'll tell us eventually. Tell us now and spare yourself the pain."

"O bondage, up yours."

"Your name!" Matt brought the whip down and it cracked into the Kid's back, a deeper thud sounding under the harsh slap. The Kid leaped and writhed, straining at the cords that only cut deeper into his wrists. An ugly red stripe appeared diagonally across his skin.

"Tell us your name."

"No."

The Kid yelped as Matt brought the whip swishing down again. He sagged against the bars, sweat pouring down his back. He was muttering and mumbling. The second lash made a squashed *X* on his skin, and welts were beginning to rise up. Sam couldn't move; one of the boys was holding him still. He looked around at the green-clothed congregation. Some looked upset, hands clamped over their mouths, staring wide-eyed; others looked at the floor; a few of them were snickering and pointing.

Matt had a wild look. He was enjoying this. Sam thought this was about nothing more than showing off his power. That and getting his kicks. This was the worst bullying Sam had ever seen. And it was so unfair. The Kid hadn't done anything. He was a nice guy. To see him beaten like this was more than Sam could bear. He tried to pull away from his guard, to kick his shins. But it was useless. The boy was strong and knew what he was doing. Sam obviously wasn't the first person he'd held like this.

Thwack. The whip lashed down for a third time, and the Kid jumped like a kicked cat.

"Tell us your name. I won't stop until you tell us your real name!"

Tell him your name, Sam pleaded silently, *please.*

"It's Angus," the Kid wailed as if he could hear Sam's thoughts. "My name's Angus Day. Now just leave me alone, will you?"

Matt suddenly stopped. His arm went limp. All the kids stood shocked and silent. Sam didn't know what had happened, why the Kid's real name was so important.

"You're lying," said Matt.

"I'm not," said the Kid. "Why would I lie? What difference does it make if that's my name? Angus Day? It's what you wanted to know, isn't it?"

Sam heard a girl standing nearby whisper to her friend, "We've made a mistake."

Matt scratched his bald shaven head quickly, like a monkey.

A church monkey, thought Sam.

Matt nodded to Archie and the two of them moved away to talk quietly and excitedly with each other. Tish went forward and asked the Kid something. He shook his head. She gently stroked his back, trying to comfort him.

The boy finally let go of Sam, who called him a bastard and a few other things. The boy looked away, not wanting to catch Sam's eye.

Presently Matt returned with Archie, both looking worried.

"Untie him," Matt said. "It's possible we've been deceived. Things might not be as straightforward as they appeared. The Goat is a trickster. He can't be trusted."

Sam grinned. They'd bought some time. The Kid's real name obviously meant something to these children, but he had no idea what.

Matt approached him, stared into Sam's face, searching for something.

"Okay," he said. "We need to put them both into the cage."

35

This is your last chance to back out. I don't want to force any of you to do anything you don't want to, and nobody's gonna say anything or think badly of you." Ed looked along the row of familiar faces: impossible to read. They all looked pretty grim, but that could mean anything.

None of them said anything.

"Okay, this is my idea," Ed went on. "To be honest with you, Jordan Hordern didn't want me to do this at all. He'd rather I stay here and not risk losing anyone else. And it *is* a risk. I can't lie about that. We don't know what to expect when we get into the no-go zone. It's going to be bad, though. We know that much. You all came with me the other day to rescue Tish, which is why I asked you. You know what to expect."

"Yeah," said Kyle. "Sickos."

"Exactly," Ed went on. "We took down a few of them, but there's gonna be more. So, as I say, anyone have any doubts, you can step down now and that'll be the end of it."

Still nobody said anything. Nobody moved.

Ed smiled, his scar pulling his face out of shape.

They were standing by the big black gates of Middle Tower. Beyond those gates was the outside world.

There were five of them in all. They were the first people he'd asked, and none of them had refused. They respected him and wanted to help. As well as crazy Kyle, who rarely left Ed's side, Ed had chosen Hayden, as she was the fastest runner in the Tower and had a cool head. Then Macca and Will. The two of them had fought well the other morning and hadn't panicked. Will was smart; he'd help Ed make any tough decisions. Macca enjoyed a fight, had very good eyesight, and was pretty handy with a crossbow. And lastly there was Adele, dressed from head to toe in pink and silver, a ladybird pin in her hair, but you still wouldn't want to mess with her.

"Okay." Ed checked his mortuary sword, hanging from a scabbard at his belt, and tightened the straps. He was wearing his lightest armor, and, as well as his sword, he carried a mace in his backpack, the heavy iron head sticking out of the top.

"All we know is that Sam was heading for Buckingham Palace," he said. "About three or four miles west. The most direct, and the safest, route would be to stay close to the Thames and follow it along. That way we have the river at our shoulder the whole time. No risk of getting lost and no risk of attack from that side. If I was Sam that's the route I'd have gone."

"Why don't we do what DogNut did and take a boat?" Macca asked. "We could skip the whole zone, then."

"No." Ed shook his head and took a map out of his pack.

"We need to be on Sam's trail. He might still be in the zone somewhere. We have to follow the way we think he went. Look for signs, anything."

He unfolded the map on top of a collection box that had once taken visitor donations for the upkeep of the castle and pointed out the route to his gang, following it with his finger.

"We cut along Lower Thames Street onto Upper Thames Street, then we go along Victoria Embankment until we reach Charing Cross Station. That's where we'll move away from the river. Up through Trafalgar Square and along the Mall to the palace. It's almost a straight line. If we keep our speed up, it should take us an hour and a half, two hours max. It all depends on what we find along the way. Streets could be blocked, there could be too many sickos, God knows what, so we have to be prepared to change our route if we have to, and just hope that if we come up against anything bad we can ram our way through. From what we know, this first part's gonna be the most dangerous. Hopefully once we've cleared the zone the streets will be safer."

"Why do we assume that?" asked Will. "We don't know anything about what's out there."

"Tish came from some camp near Trafalgar Square," Ed explained. "And from what Sam told me, some kid turned up where his people were hiding out. He was from the palace and he persuaded all Sam's friends to go into the center of town because he said it was safer there. The part between here and Charing Cross is the part we don't know about. The sickos in there don't follow the rules. They don't always sleep in the daytime. They're smarter and pretty unpredictable. So we go fast, but not so fast that we might miss any signs of Sam and the others."

"What sort of signs?" asked Hayden, who was doing some warm-up stretches as if she were about to run a race.

"I don't know, Hayden." Ed shrugged, trying not to sound too clueless. "Signs of a fight, blood, dead sickos. I can't say right now. We just have to get a feel for the streets as we go."

"So we head for the palace?" said Hayden. "And what do we do if he's not there when we turn up?"

"We work our way back, I guess," Ed replied. "At least we'll have a better idea of what's in the zone."

"So why don't we just search the zone properly first?" asked Will.

"It's too big, too dangerous, and, if Sam *did* make it through, we'd be wasting our time, putting ourselves in danger for no reason. We can't try and guess what might have happened to him along the way; all we can do is try and guess the route he took."

"Why don't we just—" Macca started to say, but Kyle interrupted.

"Why don't we just get going?" he said. "We're wasting time here. Let's get out there and crack some sicko skulls."

He swung his heavy battle-ax and leered at the others with a wicked grin. They backed away from him, some complaining, some laughing, some swearing at him.

A bunch of kids—that's all they were—getting ready for a school trip.

Ed watched them, hoping that he wasn't leading them into disaster. They were good kids. Tough. Fit. All fighters.

They had a pretty good chance. If only Jordan had let him take more, though. They were hardly an army, barely even a raiding party, but Ed had promised to stick by Jordan's rules.

He thought about Small Sam, setting off out there with just the Kid and Tish for protection. He was struck again by how brave the two boys were, how lucky to have survived on the streets by themselves. He just hoped their luck was holding out. Hoped they'd be found safe and unharmed at the palace, reunited with Sam's sister. Feet up, roasting their toes at the queen's fireplace.

Ed had to accept, though, that this was a fool's errand, crazy, doomed. The chances of finding Sam if he *was* stuck somewhere were tiny, and the chances of him making it through alive were even tinier.

Ed had to try, though.

Because he'd also made a promise to Sam, hadn't he?

His scar was throbbing, burning with a cold fire, like it always did when he was tense. Best not to think anymore. Best to just get out there and take it moment by moment. He remembered what he'd said to Jordan last night, that the first thing to go out the window in a battle was your plan.

He stuffed the map into the back pocket of his jeans. "Open up," he called to the gatekeeper, who unlocked the gates and wished them luck as they trooped out of the castle.

It was a dull, overcast day, looked like it might rain later. Ed rubbed his scar as they regrouped on the wide terrace. "Thanks, guys," he said. "I appreciate this."

"Will you stop yapping and get a move on?" said Kyle. "Brain-biter grows hungry." A couple of the other kids laughed a touch nervously as Kyle kissed the blade of his ax.

"Any sicko wants to mess with us will end up a dead sicko—the best kind." He rested his ax on his shoulder. He wasn't bluffing. He was enjoying this.

"Let's go, then." Ed walked off, and after a moment's hesitation the others gave a cheer and followed.

They went down to Lower Thames Street, the road that ran closest to the water. Like so much of London, it was a jumbled mix of old and new. It didn't run directly along the embankment; large buildings lay between it and the riverside, mostly converted warehouses, factories, and offices that had once served the busy river trade, with narrow alleys running between them. It would only be when they reached Victoria Embankment that the road would actually pass directly along the river's edge.

They moved at a fast jog, sticking close together, with Ed and Kyle slightly out in front. Now that they were on the go Ed felt the familiar cold calm settling over him. There was nothing more to think about. He had made his move. What would be would be.

He could sense Kyle's mood. Very different from his. Kyle was hyped up, jittery, looking for a fight. He was the most likely to disobey Ed's commands, and Ed needed to keep him under control.

"Our first rule is to run," Ed said. "If we can avoid a fight we will. We're not doing this to kill sickos, okay?"

"You might not be, boss, but I am."

"Don't you dare put any of the others in danger."

"Wouldn't dream of it."

Ed sometimes wondered why Kyle was so loyal to him. They had nothing in common, came from very different worlds, and had very different views of the world. If everything hadn't turned upside down, they'd never have been friends, but they'd fought side by side at the battle of Lambeth Bridge, and Kyle had seen something in Ed. Had latched on to him and now treated him as a brother. Maybe he'd seen that deep down they weren't really so very different. Ed had to admit he liked having Kyle around. Most of the time he made Ed laugh; the rest of the time he appalled him. In a fight, though, they acted as one and were a pretty unbeatable force.

In these changed times it was good to have a wingman like Kyle.

They ran past the old Billingsgate fish market, a Victorian building with arches along its front and a statue of Britannia on the roof. The next building was a modern construction of blue glass and steel. Any of these places could house a hundred sickos, more, but so far all was quiet. In Ed's experience sickos didn't gather together in big numbers anymore. There wasn't enough food around to feed large groups. They mostly hunted in packs of between ten and twenty.

This was the no-go zone, however, and as he'd tried to get across to the others before they'd set off—the normal rules didn't apply here.

The sickos had to eat, though, didn't they? They were still human. That couldn't change. A person was still a person, even if they might be so badly diseased they acted like some lower species. And as there were no children around here, no plants, no animals, why would a sicko stay?

Ed was just starting to relax and feel a little more confident about the day when Kyle shouted out, "Hold up!" and stopped running. The rest of them fell in beside him.

They'd spotted their first sicko.

It was a father, standing on a walkway that crossed over the road. He was very still, his arms held out stiffly in front of him, his head tilted up to the sky, eyes wide open and unblinking. The kids stared at him and nudged each other.

"Is he dead, do you think?" asked Hayden.

"Dunno." Ed shrugged. "He's not moving, that's for sure."

"We could get up there," said Kyle. "Take him down."

"For God's sake, Kyle. Leave him." Ed shook his head. "He doesn't look dangerous. Let's keep going, yeah, but we need to be extra careful now."

They hurried under the walkway and continued on. There was a church to their left. Ed remembered it from his map—the Church of St. Magnus the Martyr; that meant that the structure spanning the road on the other side of it was the end of London Bridge. Lower Thames Street dipped slightly as it went under it.

As they got closer, they spotted another sicko, a mother this time. Standing by the side of the road in exactly the same position as the father they'd left behind, still as a statue, with her arms held out in front of her, as if waiting to embrace someone.

"This is freaky," said Macca.

"Freaky, my ass," said Kyle. "They're just dumb sickos. And—Merry Christmas—there's another one."

He pointed with his ax to where a third sicko stood frozen a few paces up the side street to their right.

"I'm gonna whack that mother for sure," said Kyle. "That

is easy meat. Too good to leave." He took a few paces, but Ed went after him and held him back.

"Listen," he said.

Kyle stopped and they all listened. They could hear a distant, rhythmical tapping noise.

"What is that?"

"Sounds like builders," said Macca. "Or a mad percussionist." He mimed a drummer going around his kit with a pair of drumsticks.

"What would make a noise like that?" Ed asked.

"A builder in a rock group," said Kyle, and Macca laughed; the two of them shared the same sense of humor.

"Seriously."

"Seriously I don't know," said Kyle. "And I don't really want to know, neither."

"Can you tell where it's coming from?" said Will, squinting as he concentrated.

"Sounds like it's coming from all around," said Hayden, an edge of nervousness creeping into her voice. "I reckon we need to keep moving."

"Aw, let me fix the sicko," Kyle pleaded.

"No." Ed turned and strode on toward London Bridge. As he went, the weird clicking sound seemed to swell and grow louder, closer. . . .

Tap-tap-tap-tap-tap-tap-tap . . .

He shivered.

Like someone tapping on your coffin lid . . .

That was a phrase his granny used to say. He'd never really understood it until today.

Tap-tap-tap . . .

"Slow as ever," said Kyle as he pushed past him. Then came Hayden, trying to outrun them all. Soon all six of them were speeding up, sprinting into the underpass. Like a herd of deer spooked by a hunter.

And then Hayden yelped, staggered to a halt. Deep in the shadows beneath the bridge, standing close to the wall at the side, was another sicko.

"Jesus," Hayden said accusingly, as if she was blaming the others. "I nearly ran into him."

It was a father. He could have been a wax statue, he was so still. Kyle crept closer and waved his hand in front of his eyes. No response. Not even a flicker.

"He's an ugly bastard," said Kyle, and nobody argued. The father's skin was a deep, ripe purple and was split all over, bright pink flesh poking out of the slits. A run of livid yellow boils studded his forehead, and his eyes and tongue were bulging out of his head. Both his ears were missing, rotted away, leaving a pulped, scabby, pus-oozing mess on either side of his skull.

"You are one krutters piece of roadkill," said Kyle, and he gagged on the stench of the man. An unholy perfume of feces, urine, sweat, and decay with a sickly smear of sweetness over the top.

"I am definitely taking this one down," said Kyle, spinning his ax in his hands. Macca giggled.

"Leave him," said Will, sensible as ever.

"I'll leave him," said Kyle. "I'll leave him for dead."

"What's the point?"

"It's fun, Will, and Brain-biter is thirsty for blood."

"It's not a game, Kyle."

"Will's right," said Ed. "We're wasting time."

As Ed spoke, the father moved, or at least his eyes did; they seemed to pulse as if something was pushing them from the back. They bulged out farther from his head for a moment, then sank back.

"Holy crap," said Kyle. "Did you see that? He's got rats in his brain."

The eyes pulsed again, followed by a thin dribble of brown liquid that trickled from his tear ducts.

"Gross," said Kyle.

Adele came and joined him, peering at the father and turning her head to the side. "You hear that?" she said.

"No? What? You mean the clicking?" Kyle frowned at her.

"No, listen."

Ed strained to hear, but aside from the distant *tap–tap–tap* he had no idea what Adele might be talking about.

"What are we listening for?"

"Like a sort of whining sound."

"No."

"Yeah, I can hear something," said Hayden, and she came over to stand next to Adele and Kyle.

"There's a really high-pitched sound," she said. "Like a radio signal or something."

"I can't hear nothing," said Macca. He looked to Ed, who shook his head.

Then Kyle and the two girls jumped back as the father's whole body pulsed. A ripple passed through it, starting in his stomach and rising to his head, as his eyes almost popped completely out of his skull. The aftereffect was pretty revolting as the father belched then puked up a sticky wash of yellow bile that forced its way past his swollen tongue and spattered on to the road, causing the kids to jump back.

Through all of this the father had remained standing upright, his arms stiffly extended.

"I am going to finish this rude boy before he bursts on us," said Kyle. "Stand back!"

"I'm not staying for this, you dickhead," said Will, and he marched out into the sunlight on the other side of the underpass.

"Wimp," said Kyle, and he swung his ax in a clean, powerful sweep. From hours of practice at the Tower, his aim was good. The blade sliced cleanly through the father's neck and his head flew off, bounced against the wall, and hit the asphalt with a crunch.

Macca cheered as the body crumpled and fell. Kyle gave a whoop of delight and kicked the head to the other side of the road. The girls swore at him.

"You'd better come and look at this. . . ." Will's voice echoed under the bridge. He had retreated back into the shadows and was looking up at something.

"What is it?" Ed and the others hurried over; as they got closer, Will indicated that they should go carefully, then pointed upward.

Ed sneaked out so that he could see what was happening up on the bridge.

Sickos. A whole mob of them, slowly shuffling along from the south, moving silently and purposefully. Ed hadn't been worried about sickos coming from that direction. The far side of the Thames was filled with blackened ruins from when a huge fire had nearly destroyed London a year ago.

What were they doing? What had brought them here and where had they come from?

Ed withdrew under the bridge. Shushed the others as they all fired questions at him in urgent whispers.

"There's an army of sickos up there," he explained quietly. "But they can't get down here. We're okay for now." He quickly scanned Lower Thames Street in both directions. Except from the sicko Kyle had killed, he could see no more on their level.

"We go fast," he said, "and hope they don't spot us. God knows what they're up to, but I don't reckon they're after us. Not yet at least."

Macca tried to say something, but Ed stared him down and he fell silent.

"On my count," Ed said. "One, two, three, go, go, go!"

As they ran, none of them saw what was happening to the severed head in the underpass. Even though it had been separated from the father's body, the eyes were still pulsing, the tongue still moving, as if the dead man was trying to speak. Then slowly, slowly, slowly, the eyes bulged, forcing their way out between the tight, boil-encrusted eyelids. Farther and farther they came, smeared with pus from the bursting boils, until, with a soft, breathy hiss, they plopped free and rolled out of the skull, followed by a writhing mass of something gray and jellylike.

36

"Mate, I didn't know. They're nutjobs. I didn't know. Sorry."

Brendan was standing by the cage talking to Sam and the Kid. Talking quietly so as not to attract any attention. He had no idea what all the rules were yet here at the cathedral, couldn't keep up with them, but he was pretty sure he wasn't supposed to be talking to the prisoners.

"It's not your fault," said Sam.

"They didn't say," Brendan went on, desperate to explain to the two little boys. "If I'd known what they were planning to do . . . Ah, Sam, I'm so sorry, mate. This is so wrong."

Sam was too miserable to say anything much, just let Brendan talk.

Brendan leaned closer, resting his forehead on the bars and looking at the floor. "Thing is," he said, "I was really vexed when I got here. My head was all over the shop. Being kicked out of the Tower like that. Jordan threatening to execute me. Losing all my friends. I was mucked up. And it was crazy out there, man. You saw what it's like, with them sickos on the streets everywhere. I was chased all the way here—thought I was gonna be massacred. Some of their guys found me trying to climb over this big wall they've built. Whoa, that felt good, I'm telling you, being rescued like that. I was on a high when they brought me in.

"So there's all these things going nuts in my head—I was mad and I was mad, you know, like angry and crazy and relieved to be alive all at the same time. Matt was good to me. Said I was safe here, gave me anything I wanted. You see, like, they've got all this food? And bottles of water. I thought, Okay, Bren, things ain't gonna be so bad as I thought. And Matt wanted to talk to me. Said nobody'd ever come here from the east. He knew Jordan from, like, back in the day, and he wanted to know all about what he was up to now. I was happy to tell him what a bastard he is and everything that had happened there. Told him about you two as well. Big mistake. You should've seen him. Like he was on fire. Mad eyes he has. I didn't know what it meant, about all that Lamb and Goat crap. Didn't know what it was all about. If I had . . ."

"It's all right, Brendan," said Sam. "It's not your fault."

"If there was anything I could do. Any way I could help you. But they're freaky here, they give me the creeps, never take their eyes off of you. I don't know what they'd do to me if I helped you escape. Matt's as bad as Jordan; the two of them, they're the same, crazy and cold. I want to get away from here. But they watch you all the time . . . and out there." Brendan swallowed, remembering his journey here. "I'm not sure I could do that again. That was the scariest half hour of my life. I was a wreck, man, run out, rinsed."

He stopped talking and looked up at the boys; they were huddled together; the Kid had his arm around Sam. He couldn't bear to see them like this.

"I don't know," he said. "Maybe it's not so bad, maybe it's all a big bluff, yeah? You see, like Jordan? I mean, they can't seriously be thinking of killing you. I mean, human sacrifice? Come on, it's nuts."

"It's the blimp, Frank, it's the blimp," said the Kid in a spooky, high-pitched voice.

"You what?"

"Ignore him," said Sam. "He's in one of his weird moods. He hasn't said anything that makes sense since they shut me in here with him."

"Harry, Harry, I'm back, I'm back. Tell Frank."

"Who's Harry?" said Brendan.

"I don't know," said Sam. "Harry Hill? Harry Potter?"

"Harry Houdini," said the Kid. "Escape artist. Now there was one clever piece of work. Harry will look after us. He'll find a way to spring us. God bless Harry and God bless me. Thank you and good night."

"You've thought of a way to escape?" asked Sam, his face lighting up.

"Not yet," said the Kid. "Give me time."

"Mate, you haven't got any time," said Brendan. "I heard them saying they're going to come and take care of you in a few minutes. That's why I came over. I had to explain. It's not my fault."

"No," said Sam feebly.

"You're out of time, guys. I'm sorry."

37

Don't slow down!" Ed yelled.

They were running through another underpass. This one went beneath Cannon Street Station. The last few minutes had not been fun. There were sickos coming out of the woodwork on all sides now. Waking up from their hidey-holes. Crawling into the light. There was no telling what had triggered it, but a big pack of them were on their tail, lumbering along the road behind them, and Ed could see more of them silhouetted against the light at the far end of the underpass.

"Up ahead!" Hayden yelled. She was out in front, her long legs pounding the asphalt. Running came easily to her.

"Yeah, I've seen them," Ed shouted back, drawing his heavy sword from its scabbard. "We have to keep moving."

"How long do we run for?" Macca asked, short of breath.

"As long as we need."

"We should turn back."

Ed glanced over his shoulder; the road was thick with sickos. "No chance," he said. "There's a lot more behind us than there is in front. We push on. Cut through them if they try and stop us."

"Don't worry," said Kyle, overtaking Ed. "They're gonna try!" And he let out a war cry as he burst into the sunlight and slammed into the waiting sickos.

The kids hacked and slashed their way through the first line of sickos before they knew what had hit them. They left five of them lying dead and five more reeling from their wounds.

The kids ran on, whooping and cheering, but their joy was short-lived.

The whole road in front of them was filled with a great crowd of sickos. They were streaming across Southwark Bridge and spilling out as they hit the junction with the road the kids were on. They were way too many for them to be able to batter their way through. Ed had to make a quick decision. They could go back, they could turn northward and head away from the river, deeper into the tangle of streets that made up the no-go zone, deeper into the part of town that the sickos themselves seemed to be heading for, or they could go the other way, down toward the river. Take their chances there. It was low tide, so there might be enough beach to walk on. It was possible they could use it to get past this milling horde.

"This way!" he shouted, and turned to his left into a narrow alleyway called Cousin Lane that ran along the side of the station.

"Are you insane?" Macca screamed. "We'll be trapped down there."

"It's our best bet," Ed replied. "Believe me. You can take

your chances with that bunch if you want, but I'm getting out of here."

"Stick with him," said Kyle. "He knows what he's doing."

"It's crazy."

"Yeah," said Kyle. "Innit?"

Cousin Lane sloped gently downhill, with the great brick arches that supported Cannon Street Station running down one side, each with some kind of workshop built into it. At the far end was a pub, the Banker, also built in one of the arches. It reminded Ed that before everything had fallen apart this area of London had been the financial center. Past the pub was the wide expanse of the Thames with the Cannon Street railroad bridge jutting out across it.

Just before the pub there was a dark opening to their left with a sign saying STEELYARD PASSAGE. One of the arches was open there, and as the kids drew level with it, a group of sickos lunged out at them, and they found themselves in a desperate, sweaty, close-up fight. Ed laid into the sickos with a cold, brutal fury. The first few went down quickly, and the others shrank back into the passageway underneath the station.

The killing frenzy had come over Ed. He wanted to follow the sickos and kill every one. Chop them into small pieces. He had retreated into himself, withdrawn all the nice civilized parts of his personality and hidden them safely in a hard shell, leaving only the harsh, emotionless, animal part of him. The part that hacked and cut and killed and delighted in the bright sprays of red blood.

"Ed, come on, they've gone!" Will shouted, and Ed stopped, taking a big shuddering breath. He stared at Will and Will backed away from him.

"Christ, Ed," he said. "You look like you want to kill me."

Ed sighed and wiped his face. "Sorry, Will."

There were some steps next to the pub that led down to the water. Ed led his group over to them.

"Yes!" He punched the air triumphantly, flicking drops of blood into the air from his sword. "What did I tell you, Macca? Stick with me and you'll be all right."

There was a narrow strip of muddy beach, about two yards wide. They leaped down the steps and were soon squelching their way west again, their feet sinking into the thick London clay.

No sickos, thought Ed, and no Sam either. As he'd feared, his plan to get a feel for the streets, to look for any clues as to what might have happened to him, had gone out of the window as soon as they'd come across their first sicko. If the poor kid *had* come this way yesterday he wouldn't have lasted five minutes.

They clambered over two beached trash barges laden with rusting containers that were blocking their way. Will stopped on top of one of them.

"Would you look at that?" he said. He was gazing ahead at Southwark Bridge, its jolly green-and-yellow ironwork looking out of place on this gray day filled with violence. There was a steady flow of sickos crossing over it from the south.

He started to recite some lines.

"Under the brown fog of a winter dawn, /A crowd flowed over London Bridge, so many, /I had not thought death had undone so many."

"What's that?" Ed asked.

"Just some poem I had to study at school. It's near here."

"What is?"

"My old school. City. It's on the river near St. Paul's. We'll be able to see it from the other side of the bridge. We'll go right past it. I haven't thought about it in all this time. That poem just came to me."

"That's typical of you, Will. You see a bridge full of sickos and you think of a poem."

"What do you think of?"

"More killing, more blood. No end to it. That's why we need people like you, Will. To stop us all turning into, I don't know, turning into Kyle."

Will hesitated before going on. "You really looked like a monster back there, you know, Ed? You really looked like you were going to kill me."

"It's this scar. Makes me look creepy."

"No, it's not. It's *you*, Ed."

Ed shrugged, went to move on. Will put a hand on his shoulder. "Are we going to live?" he asked.

Ed kept on moving. "Yeah."

They slogged their way under the bridge, the mud coating their lower legs and making their sneakers thick and heavy. There was a strong smell from the river. But it wasn't a bad smell. Not compared to the sickos. It was the smell of life.

Ed looked at the flow. The tide was rising. The beach wouldn't be there much longer. He sped up, urging the others on.

They came to a big building that looked like a classical Greek temple. Will explained that it was Vintners' Hall. Something to do with the wine trade in the City. Its fancy architecture would only be visible from the far side of the Thames or on the river itself. There was a raised terrace with steps leading down to the beach. Ed wondered whether maybe barges had once put in there to unload wine barrels, but then he noticed that the building was actually quite modern, faked up to look old.

They climbed the steps and leaned on the balustrade, exhausted, staring out at the great gray-green muddy Thames.

"Anybody hurt?" Ed asked.

"No," said Hayden. "Don't think so."

"I grazed my finger," said Macca, wincing.

"You grazed your finger?" said Kyle, wide-eyed, and left his mouth hanging open.

There was a moment's silence and then they all started laughing, relief flooding out of them. They'd done it, they'd gotten this far in one piece, and Macca's complaint about his grazed finger seemed to them to be the funniest thing they'd ever heard. They held on to each other and heaved and groaned until the tears were rolling down their faces.

"He grazed his *finger*!" Kyle gasped.

"You idiot, Macca," said Adele.

At last they stopped, settled down into silence, each of them alone with his or her thoughts.

To their left was Southwark Bridge, to their right the Wobbly Bridge, as everyone called the Millennium Footbridge, and opposite, the burned-out ruins of the old power station that had been converted into the Tate Modern art gallery.

All that art, thought Ed, up in smoke. All those paintings, sculptures, gone forever.

All those people.

The end of the world.

I had not thought death had undone so many.

"So what now, boss?" Kyle asked, propping his elbows on the low wall next to Ed.

"We can keep going along here," Ed replied, putting his arm across Kyle's shoulders. The laughter had cleared his head and cleaned out the blood fever. The overfriendly hug was half for show and half for real. "When it looks safe, we'll go back up onto the road."

"Or if the tide gets too high," said Kyle.

"Yeah."

"We ain't gonna find the boys down here, though, are we?"

"Nope."

"Let's face it, Ed, we ain't gonna find those boys nowhere."

"I'm not giving up on them, Kyle." Ed straightened up, feeling bone-tired. "And we've done okay so far. If the worst we've got to worry about is a grazed finger, then . . ."

"*If* that's the worst," said Kyle.

"Yeah. Thanks for that. Always look on the bright side of life, eh? Let's go."

38

Shadowman realized he'd been awake for a while, staring at a ceiling light without really understanding what it was. He hadn't expected to be looking at a light fixture, so his brain hadn't accepted it. He blinked, trying to get his eyes to focus. He wasn't supposed to be here—wherever *here* was. It didn't fit. The last thing he remembered, he was in the Lexus and they were dragging him out. . . .

Must have blacked out again. A toxic mix of pain, fear, and shock had switched his brain off.

One thing was clear: he wasn't in the car anymore. He was indoors. He forced himself to sit up and look around. His felt a single massive throb in his head, as if someone had attached a bass drum pedal to his skull. It was followed by a queasy lurch from his stomach. He fought against throwing up and closed his eyes for a moment until the pain and the nausea went away.

He opened his eyes.

He was in bed. In a neat, orderly room. Almost too clean and perfect. The world wasn't like this anymore. Fresh, crisp sheets. Matching pillows. Walls covered with subtly patterned wallpaper. Some wooden blinds. Closed, so that he had no idea what time it might be, whether it was even day or night. All the furniture looked brand-new. A chair, a dresser, and a wardrobe. A rug on the floor. A bedside table with a lamp on it. None of the lights were working, of course. No electricity. The room was lit instead by a tea light in a glass holder.

The door was closed.

He rested back against the pillows.

This was weird.

He rubbed his head. It was pulsing like it was about to hatch. Was it possible, he wondered, for a head to just spontaneously split open? Certainly it happened to strangers occasionally. They burst in the sun like overripe fruit.

There was a glass of water on the bedside table. He sniffed it, then took a sip. It tasted clean. He noticed his clothes, neatly folded on a low table, his backpack and weapons leaning up against it.

He was wearing his T-shirt and underwear. He felt dirty in this clean, orderly room. He was aware of how much he smelled. Couldn't remember the last time he'd had a bath or a shower. He tried to fumigate his clothes in smoke whenever he could and used the smell of it to mask his own pungent scent. Out on the streets, surrounded by evil-smelling strangers, he was positively fragrant. In this sterile room, though, he was a stinking, grubby monster.

And he hurt all over.

He ran his fingertips over his scalp. There were some fresh lumps to go with the one he'd gotten when his friend Jester had accidently whacked him with a baseball bat. If he kept on getting knocked about like this, he was going to become punch-drunk. It couldn't be doing him any good. He pictured himself as a shambling, dribbling head case, fitting right in with Saint George's army.

He coughed and felt a sharp pain in his chest. He lifted his grimy T-shirt. There were some nasty bruises across his ribs.

Oh well, could be worse. At least he was still alive.

But where the hell was he, and how had he gotten here?

He struggled out of bed, groaning as his muscles cramped and twitched with pain.

He hobbled over to the blinds and tugged on the cord. They rose up to reveal . . .

Nothing. No window, just more blank wall behind.

Weirder and weirder.

He'd thought there was something too neat about this room, too perfect, and as he looked at it again, he realized the whole thing was fake, like a stage set. It wasn't a real bedroom at all. He went over to the door. Knew what he was going to find—it would be locked. He was a prisoner here.

His fingers closed on the handle, turned, and . . .

The door popped open.

It wasn't locked.

He raised his eyebrows. Let go of the handle.

Stupid.

If he was a prisoner here, why would they have left his weapons? His clothes? He wasn't thinking straight. He'd always lived by his wits, had been a quick thinker. One step ahead of everyone else. He hoped the blows to his head hadn't permanently affected his brain.

He got dressed. Picked up a bow. Better to be safe than sorry. He slung his backpack over his shoulder and went over to the door again. Swung it slowly open and peered out. There was an almost identical room opposite, except it had one wall missing. He saw other rooms, odd bits of furniture standing around. Prices on them. Funny Swedish names.

He laughed. He was in a furniture showroom. And not just any showroom.

He was in IKEA.

He'd been here before, a couple of times with his parents.

They'd bought tea lights, hundreds of them, in big plastic bags.

He spotted a couple of kids sitting reading books by candlelight, another boy writing on a pad. The boy looked up at Shadowman. Smiled. Came over.

"You're awake."

"I guess so—unless this is a dream."

"It isn't—least as far as I know. Sometimes wish it was. I'm Dan."

"Carl," Shadowman lied, and they slapped hands.

"Yeah, Johnny said."

"Johnny? He's alive?"

"Yup. And so are you, thanks to him. Come on. He's been waiting for you to wake up."

Shadowman followed Dan through the maze of the showroom. It had been designed to make shoppers pass as many items as possible, to encourage them to buy things they hadn't intended to. Like tea lights.

Shadowman could see where the kids who lived there

had made living spaces for themselves in the dummy rooms. It all seemed very peaceful and quiet. Shadowman felt the pain and tension slipping away.

Dan led him to the front of the building, where there were windows and natural light. They went down a stairway to ground level and out into the huge parking garage. Johnny was waiting there by himself, sitting in a wheelchair, his leg propped up and heavily bandaged. He was surrounded by patio furniture, umbrellas, and tables, a carpet of fake grass, walls made out of trellises, and plants in pots. Shadowman smiled. The local kids had made a sort of backyard for themselves.

It was a gray day but not too cold, and it felt good to be out in the fresh air.

Johnny grinned at Shadowman when he saw him, but made no effort to move. He looked tired, his face pinched and drained. One of his eyes was twitching. Shadowman went over to him and they gripped each other's wrists for a moment.

"I thought you were toast for sure," said Shadowman.

"Me too."

"What about Jaz?"

Johnny shook his head.

"I'm sorry," said Shadowman.

"Yeah," said Johnny. "Still can't believe it. It's unfair. It's too bloody unfair." Tears came into his eyes and he wiped them away, sniffing.

"There was a body underneath me when I came around," said Shadowman. "I thought it was you."

Johnny shook his head again.

"She was wounded by the spear, battered in the crash," he said. "But then she had the bad luck to lie there with her foot sticking out of the car. Stinking zombies chewed it off. She died from loss of blood."

"So what happened then?" Shadowman asked, sitting down in a bright blue plastic garden chair. "I still don't get how we're both here."

"Crazy bastard crawled all the way here," came a voice from behind him.

Shadowman turned as a group of kids arrived carrying weapons. The boy who had spoken was tall and fit-looking with glossy black hair twisted and tangled into something like dreadlocks. There were various bits and pieces knotted into his hair: lucky charms, ribbons, tiny bones, and plastic figures. He reminded Shadowman of a character from *Pirates of the Caribbean*. He was good-looking and he knew it. His shirt was unbuttoned to his belly, and he was wearing the tightest pair of black jeans Shadowman had ever seen on anyone.

"It's thanks to Johnny that you're still alive, dude," said the boy. Shadowman didn't need to be told that this guy was in charge here at IKEA. He carried himself with a certain swagger. Shadowman had been expecting a cool, understated, blond Scandinavian type. This guy was very much not that.

"I'm Saif," he said. "Welcome to my yard."

Shadowman nodded. "You got a good thing going here."

"I know it, brother."

I bet you do, Shadowman thought. You really like yourself, don't you?

"This is my kingdom," Saif went on. "We got plenty of space. Dirty big fence all the way around. Good lines of sight. Plus—it gets better, dude—I got rides. Yeah? Ain't no one else in London got what I got." He shook his hand, snapping his fingers together. "They was even food when we first come. The joint was well stocked. Had all we needed, furniture, food, water. Now of course we got to go out scrounging for stuff. But there's lots of houses 'round here, the pickings is good." Saif stopped and gave Shadowman a cold look. Poked him in the chest with a long, thin finger.

"Yeah, my friend," he said. "All was going well until you showed up."

39

"Wasn't me killed your people," said Shadowman. "It was *zombies*. Ricky didn't stand a chance. He was swamped. Didn't expect them to use weapons. One of them cut his arm off with a machete, and then Bluetooth got Jaz with a spear."

"Say what?"

"A zombie stabbed her." Shadowman felt foolish for letting that slip. Pushed on, running out of steam. "And then she crashed the car."

Saif wasn't going to let it go. "No, before that, man," he sneered. "What'd you say?"

"A zombie got her with a spear."

"That's not what you said, though." Saif turned to his friends. "That's not what he said, is it? Noob said something about a man."

"He said 'Bluetooth,' I think," said a short boy with a flat head.

"It's nothing," said Shadowman. "Just a name."

"A name for what?"

"One of the zombies I was following. He has a Bluetooth phone thing stuck in his ear."

"You give them *names*?" Saif had an exaggerated look of amazement on his face. "Whaffor? They your friends or something? You know them personally? You want to be in their gang? Have tea with them?"

"It's not like that."

"Listen, noob." Saif flicked his fingers dismissively at Shadowman. "Zombies don't bother us, man. They're no sweat. Jaz could have coped with them fine. The only thing different yesterday was you."

"I told you, Saif," said Johnny. "This guy tried to help us."

"Lot of good that did." Saif slumped into a deck chair, tried to stare Shadowman down. Shadowman held his gaze until Saif looked away.

Shadowman turned his attention back to Johnny. "You really crawl all the way here?"

"Nearly all the way. I was picked up by a patrol who were out on the streets looking for us."

"But you could hardly move."

"I guess when you want to keep on living you can do things you couldn't do normally. Luckily I wasn't hurt in the crash and could get out of the car, but the front was all, like, squashed in and I couldn't do nothing for you and Jaz." He paused as fresh tears welled in his eyes. "I tried. I really tried. Jaz was still alive then. By some weird luck we'd taken out all the nearby zombies in the wreck. But I could see there was more coming for a look. That's when I started crawling."

"Thanks, man," said Shadowman. "How you doing now?"

"Not good. My leg's all chewed up. Don't think I'm

gonna feel up to walking for a good while."

"Gotta watch out for infection as well," said Saif. "A zombie bite's got more germs in it than a fresh dump."

"Nice," said one of Saif's friends, and giggled.

"You got medicine here?" Shadowman asked. "Antiseptic? Otherwise I got some."

Saif gave Shadowman a withering look. "'Course we got medicine, dude. What do you think we are? Savages? I told you, I fixed this yard up the finest in London. Everything was cool here until you showed up."

"And I told you it's not my fault," said Shadowman. "I've been tracking that bunch of zombies for days."

"What for?"

"What do you mean what for?"

"I mean what I mean," said Saif. "Why was you tracking zombies?"

"You know . . . to find out about them. They're different, this bunch. They're organized."

"Hah!"

"Listen to him, Saif," said Johnny. "He ain't bullshitting. I saw them, they're weird, not like other zombies."

"Zombies is zombies," said Saif. "We've had a year to get to know what they're like. They don't change, man. They do their thing and we do our thing, by which I mean we splatter them."

Shadowman sighed. "That's what Jaz said," he pointed out. "And that's what got her killed."

"No, sir," said Saif, hauling himself up out of the chair. "Like I say—the only thing different yesterday was you. You are what got her killed. You pulled her out of the car and your pal, Bluetooth, speared her. You gonna deny it? No. Soon as you are ready, I want you gone from my yard. Seen?"

Saif made a sign to his friends and they all trooped off across the parking garage toward the main road, checking their weapons as they went.

"He's proud," said Johnny, watching them walk away. "But he knows his business. He's a good leader."

"Good leaders listen to intelligence," said Shadowman. "Good leaders show some *signs* of intelligence."

"He ain't stupid."

"Come on," said Shadowman, rubbing his face. "I'm not making this up. I'm not imagining it. You were *there*; you saw what they were like. They're different. And they get cleverer every day. I mean, like, did you see any of the sentinels?"

"Sentinels?"

Shadowman stood up and adopted the pose—arms stretched out, staring up at the sky.

"Yeah," said Johnny. "I did see a couple when I was getting away. First one I saw I thought she was gonna come after me, but she just stood there."

"You ever seen anything like that before?" Shadowman asked.

"Don't think so."

"So what's it all about?"

"Reminds me of this wildlife program I saw once," said Johnny. "One of those, like, David Attenborough things, you know? Was about jungles or insects or something."

"Reminded you how?"

"There was all these, like, ants, yeah?" Johnny fiddled with the piece of knotted cloth that held his long hair in a loose ponytail. "Soldier ants or some shit. In the Amazon, I think. And there was millions of them, but they all had their own things to do, as if they'd had a big meeting and agreed on it. 'Okay, you, like, you're going looking for food, you guys is gonna guard the queen, you're gonna protect the workers, and you big guys, you're gonna just stand on the edges like signposts, making sure the other ants don't get lost.' Reminded me of them."

"Yeah," said Shadowman. "I know what you mean. They're, like, showing the other zombies the way."

"One of the lookouts spotted another one this morning," said Johnny, pointing in the direction that Saif and the others had gone. "She's still there, over the other side of the North Circular. Been standing there all day. Saif's gone to take her down. Said he was gonna use her for target practice."

Shadowman saw that Saif's group had climbed up onto a footbridge that crossed over the main road and were waiting there.

"I gotta talk to him." Shadowman went over and squeezed Johnny's shoulder. "Thanks again, Johnny," he said. "What you did was really brave."

"Carl?" Johnny had something on his mind. Shadowman waited.

"What I did back there? It wasn't because I was brave. It was because I was scared. More terrified than I've been before. I never want to feel that way again. Alone. Do you ever have those dreams where you're in a house somewhere with a bunch of friends and something's trying to get at you, only you can't wake anyone up?"

"Used to," said Shadowman. "When I was little."

"It was like that. A nightmare. You and Jaz were out. I was alone and the zombies was coming closer. It was fear made me crawl away. Desperate bloody fear."

"Doesn't matter why you did it," said Shadowman. "The thing is you saved my skin. I'll always owe you one." He smiled at Johnny and set off across the garage.

He saw that the IKEA kids had fenced off the bottom of the footbridge with barbed wire and concrete blocks so that no grown-ups could climb it. They'd made a way to get to it from the garage, however, by building a protected ramp.

Shadowman clambered up the ramp and onto the footbridge. Climbed the steps to the top. Saif and his gang were laughing as one of the boys fired a crossbow.

"Nah, missed," the others jeered.

"Jaz got *herself* killed, Saif," said Shadowman.

"You still here?"

"She panicked," Shadowman went on. "She took on more than she could handle and panicked."

"Jaz was a good soldier. She never panicked."

"She did, Saif. I was there."

Saif turned angrily on Shadowman, grabbing his jacket and shoving him up against the railing of the footbridge. Shadowman looked down at the wide four-lane road several yards below.

"She was my best soldier," said Saif, "and she was my girl, seen? She never panicked."

Saif let him go and returned to his friends. A tall, skinny guy was lining up a shot at something on the far pavement. Shadowman went to look. It was a mother, standing in the familiar sentinel pose, oblivious to the boys up on the bridge. She was middle-aged, bald, half naked, and covered in growths.

The crossbow clicked and the bolt flew silently off, narrowly missing the mother's head.

"Whoa! Yeah! Nearly."

"Why won't you listen to me?" Shadowman asked quietly, standing at Saif's shoulder.

"Don't know you, man. Don't trust you. You seem to like them zombies. *Oh, they're so clever, oh, they're so organized, they're better than you.* You still ain't explained what you was doing tracking them. Maybe you wanna be one. Is that you? A zombie wannabe? Maybe you *are* one already. One of the clever ones. Don't know nothing about you, man. Where you from? Where's your yard?"

"In the center of town," said Shadowman. "There's a few settlements there. I came up this way looking for other kids. I got split up from my friends, and instead of kids I found this bunch of zombies who behaved differently."

"And you thought you'd follow them? That don't make no sense."

Shadowman couldn't really explain it. He wasn't sure himself. It had felt like the right thing to do.

That was all.

It was now Saif's turn to shoot at the mother. He leaned forward and rested his crossbow on the railing, took very careful aim.

"Die, you sick bag of pus."

He grunted as he pulled the trigger, then shouted in triumph as the bolt hit the mother at the base of her throat, just above the sternum. As she toppled over, the other boys cheered. They cheered even more as the mother's body writhed and jerked on the ground before erupting in a bubbling mess of boils and her insides came gurgling out of her mouth. A minute later there was nothing recognizably human left of her, just a putrefying pile of flesh and blood.

The boys slapped Saif on the back, congratulating him.

"Nobody craps on my party," Saif said to Shadowman. "That's what I'm gonna do to the zombies that killed my girl. It's payback time."

"What are you planning to do?" Shadowman asked.

"We gonna wipe them diseased freaks off of the streets, dude."

"You reckon?"

"I reckon."

"How many soldiers you got in all?"

"Enough. By the end of today there ain't gonna be a living zombie within five miles of here."

"Are you sure you've got enough soldiers?"

"Won't take more than twenty of us, twenty-five tops. We got weapons, we got rides, we got God on our side, so it's bye-bye, zombie, bye-bye."

"You'll need more bodies than that. . . ."

"Don't you tell me what to do, boy," said Saif, pushing past Shadowman. "You're just some sad straggler with no home to go to. I don't need no advice from a loser like you. Now, we gonna go collect our arrows. When I come back, I expect to see you gone."

40

A procession of children was advancing out of the doors at the front of St. Paul's and moving slowly down the steps. They were all dressed in green and several of them were carrying branches. At their head was Matt, wearing a full set of bishop's robes, originally embroidered in red and gold but now dyed green. Behind him came Archie Bishop, in similar gear. Then came the four acolytes, one carrying the banner that showed the Lamb and the Goat, a crudely painted image of two children, one shining and bright, the other dark and shadowy. Another acolyte was carrying the book of Matt's revelations and was reading lifelessly from it as they went.

". . . How long, Sovereign Lord, holy and true, until you judge the inhabitants of the earth and avenge our blood . . . ?"

Next came a group of the best musicians, including Charlotte, the little girl who the Kid had latched on to the night before, playing sweetly on her violin. Others were hammering away on drums or blowing trumpets, and one had a saxophone.

Behind the musicians walked Brendan and Tish, both looking thoughtful and none too happy. Then came Sam and the Kid, with dog collars around their necks. Not the sort of dog collars priests wore, rather the type that dogs wore, with chains attached. Nathan and one of the oldest and biggest guards were holding the chains.

Bringing up the rear were the rest of the cathedral kids. The only ones who had not joined in the procession were a skeleton crew of guards and a second group of musicians.

Sam could just hear the acolyte's voice over the music.

"The fifth angel sounded his trumpet, and I saw a star that had fallen from the sky to the earth. The star was given the key to the shaft of the Abyss. When he entered the Abyss, smoke rose from it like the smoke from a gigantic furnace. The sun and sky were darkened by the smoke from the Abyss. And out of the smoke came an army of the fallen, and they ate all in their path like locusts. They were told not to harm the grass of the earth or any plant or tree, but only those people who did not have the seal of God on their foreheads."

The procession turned south and began a circuit of the cathedral. Sam saw the long walkway that sloped down to the Wobbly Bridge and, in the distance, the bridge itself, cutting a straight line across the Thames. If only he and the Kid could break free and run and run, across the river, away from these crazies. He wondered if he was ever going to see Ella again. He had to cling to the hope that he would. It was the only thing that kept him going.

They came to the back of St. Paul's and turned to their left. This had been the most ancient part of the City, but aside from the cathedral, there wasn't a lot left of old London. Sam had learned at school how the whole area had been bombed in the Blitz, how all the buildings had burned down, except for St. Paul's, the dome of which had risen triumphantly above the flames. The new buildings were ugly and looked even worse now that they'd been abandoned for a year.

When they got around to the other side of the cathedral, Matt led the procession over to an arch and through into a modern square where a pedestrian walkway curved away to the north.

"When they have finished their testimony," the acolyte droned on, "the beast that comes up from the Abyss will attack them, and overpower and kill them. Their bodies will lie in the streets of the great city."

Sam felt miserable and stupid and self-conscious. He'd never liked being the center of attention, and being paraded like this, chained up, was embarrassing. He'd had a good look at the banner when they were getting ready to leave the cathedral. You'd need a good imagination to think that the childishly painted boys on it looked like him and the Kid in any way. This whole thing was a joke. Except for that one thing. The name on the banner in big letters—Angus Day.

The Kid's name.

"I'd never have guessed you were called Angus," he said quietly, not sure if he was allowed to speak or not. Matt had so many rules, and they kept on changing.

"What did you think my name was?" the Kid asked.

"I don't know, could be anything, could be Frankenstein or Dracula or Brian. I can't think of you with a real name. Your nickname suits you fine. Though I guess Angus does sort of fit."

"You think, yeah?"

"Yeah."

"Think on, midget brain. The Kid don't give out his moniker freely."

"What d'you mean?" said Sam. "That you're really called Monica?"

"No way, Horace."

"So is Angus your real name or isn't it?"

"'Course it isn't."

"Well, how come . . . ?"

"I ain't no dumb-ass," said the Kid. "I keep my earlugs flapping and my peepers peeping. I sponged up all the info I could back at the Tower. When I hear something, it goes in my brain and sticks. It's all in there, but it's a bit of a jumble. Well, I talked to the Tower kids, didn't I?"

"What d'you mean? What about?"

"I got interested in those fairy tales of the lamb and the goat. The Kid loves a good fairy tale, doesn't he? So I boned up on it, found out all I could. There was quite a few of the population knew Matt from way back when. They knew him when he was daubing up his banner all fancy like. Big joke it was. They all loved that story. Ho, ho, yes, indeed, ladies and gentlemen."

"What happened?" Sam asked. "I don't get it. What was the joke?"

"Well, one of Matt's microlights . . ."

"You mean acolytes."

"Is what I said. Boy called Harry was given the job of writing up some old Latin words on their big flag. *Agnus Dei*, if I'm not mistaken. Which I'm not. Only he got his ass and his tits mixed up, and made a right pig's elbow out of it. Harry doesn't spell so well—my sympathies go out to him. Me and writing don't always get on."

"You might get your words muddled," said Sam, "but you make more sense than some people I've met. So are you saying that's why it says Angus Day on the banner? Harry got it wrong?"

"As I say. Big joke. The Kid likes jokes, appreciated it, stored it away in the hamster cheeks of his noggin to chew on at a later date, savvy?"

"So why did you tell Matt that was your name, then?"

"Well, first of all to stop him whacking me like a bad dog. But mainly 'cause I thought it might buy us some ticker-ticker-timex, throw the cat-o'-nine-tails among the pigeon fanciers. Bamboozle them right and proper. Only thing is, it seems to have landed you in the Shinola with me. Apologies, my learned but stunted friend."

"I'm no shorter than you," Sam protested.

"Inside I'm ten miles high," said the Kid.

"Yeah, well, inside I'm twenty miles high and have laser beams that can shoot out of my eyes."

"That's nothing," said the Kid. "I can make cheese out of wine."

"Numbskull."

"Deviant."

"Twassock."

"Whippersnapper."

"Fish lips."

"Slimy sculpin."

"Gibberfish."

"Gurnard, grunt, flabby whalefish, banjo catfish . . ."

"Seriously, though, Kid," said Sam. "What's going to happen to us, d'you think?"

"Bad things," said the Kid. "Mad things."

"I still don't seriously believe they'll do anything."

"Are you nuts?" said the Kid. "They've been playing too much Twister. They are *around* the twist and we are without a paddle. You were there, Spam, you saw him take his whip to me."

"How's your back? Does it hurt?"

"What d'you think?" said the Kid. "Red raw and sore as brambles it is. I tell you, I hope they *do* sacrifice me and put me out of my misery and torment."

"Don't say that." Sam was on the verge of crying. This was all too much for him. Playing his silly games with the Kid was the only thing that took his mind off what was happening.

"Don't despair, little guppy," said the Kid. "We'll find a way. We always do. We're the dynamic duo."

"I don't feel very dynamic right now."

"You don't look it. You look like an upright poodle with a bad case of the singing squitters."

"Yeah? Well, you look like a shaved baboon who's been got at by a blind face painter."

"That's what I am, Sam, green eggs and ham."

They had come to a section of the Wall strung out across the road between two low modern buildings. The Wall was piled high with junk and salvaged building materials. Through the gaps in it Sam could just make out a horde of grown-ups on the other side.

Matt held up a hand and the procession halted; another wave of his hand and the musicians stopped playing. A ghostly echo of the music seemed to continue on all around them, however, and Sam realized it was the grown-ups outside the wall—the Clickee Cult, as the Kid had named them—tapping on anything they could find. It was as if the City had been turned into a giant ticking-clicking-clanking machine.

Matt waited while Archie Bishop selected a key from the collection that hung from his waist. He went over to a door that was chained and padlocked shut, fiddled with the lock until it snapped open, and then unthreaded the chain. Meanwhile, many of the kids in the procession were busy lighting candles.

Once the doors were open, Matt led them all inside. There were more candles in here, fixed to the walls. Kids lit them as they went past. They went through two more locked doors, and each time Archie had to unlock them with a different key. The noise of the chains as they rattled loose was very loud in the enclosed space. They seemed to be in some kind of industrial building. The walls were rough and undecorated, and the doors they passed through were made of metal.

Finally they came to a stairwell and Matt took them down, their feet scuffing on the concrete steps. At the bottom they passed through a final door into a vast underground room. Their candles now seemed feeble, unable to penetrate the dark depths. But Sam could see enough. His mouth dropped open.

He hadn't been expecting anything like this.

41

They were in a massive warehouse, filled with tall shelving units piled high with cardboard boxes. And it was clear what was in the boxes.

Food.

Sam read the labels on the nearest stack—rice, pasta, canned vegetables, soup, cereal, baked beans, fruit juice. The next shelving unit was filled with an endless supply of drinking water in plastic bottles. Then there were oils and sauces, spices, salt and sugar and jam and peanut butter, chocolate bars and candy, cookies, canned fish, canned fruit, dried fruit, currants, raisins . . . Sam's head was spinning.

He'd wondered about the kids at the cathedral, why they put up with Matt's madness and his rules, his cruelty, his smoke, and his music. Well, this answered all his questions. You'd put up with anything, you'd believe anything, you'd go along with any garbage for a taste of this.

There was enough here to last them for years.

Sam remembered when he'd first gone to live in the Waitrose supermarket back in Holloway. A lot of kids had broken in there looking for food. There had been hardly anything left, just a few boxes of stuff hidden in a storeroom upstairs. They'd stayed, though. Lived there for a year. Their leader, Arran, had looked after them all. It had been good. Until that day when the grown-ups had gotten into the parking lot and captured him.

He hadn't seen any of his friends since.

He missed them. Not just his sister, but Monkey Boy, Maxie, Josh, Freak and Deke, Maeve, Achilleus . . . Arran would be looking after them, though, wherever they were.

If only they'd found somewhere like this a year ago, their lives would have been so different. So much better.

Maybe, though, it was like this in Buckingham Palace. Sam pictured them all sitting around a big table having a feast with silver goblets and waving big turkey legs. He smiled. The picture gave him some comfort. Took him away to a good place.

Matt waited in the center of the warehouse for the kids to form a wide circle around him. Nathan and the guard unfastened the dog leashes and released Sam and the Kid. They couldn't run anywhere—they were surrounded by the ring of children.

"We have reached the holy place," said Matt. "This is the Tree of Life. Which was shown to us by the Lord, just as was prophesied. . . ."

He closed his eyes and turned his face up to the ceiling, began to shout out some lines from his book.

"The angel showed me the river of the water of life, as clear as crystal, flowing from the throne of the Lamb down the middle of the great street of the city. On each side of the river stood the Tree of Life, bearing twelve crops of fruit, yielding its fruit every month. And the leaves of the Tree are for the healing of the nations. No longer will there be any curse. The throne of the Lamb will be in the city, and his servants will serve him. They will see his face, and his name will be on their foreheads. There will be no more night."

He paused, looking around at the faces of his followers. "Everything that was told to me, everything that I tell to you, is the truth. And our Lord watches over those who are true. So, to give thanks to Him, we come here to make our offerings. Today we offer up our greatest gift. Today we destroy the evil one forever. Today we sacrifice the Goat. And his blood will water the roots of the Tree."

A murmur passed through the waiting kids and Matt silenced them by raising his voice. "I promised to provide you with everything you needed. And here it is. I promised to deliver the Lamb and the Goat. And here they are. But which is which?"

Sam felt suddenly cold, even though it was no cooler down here than it had been outside. Matt walked over and stared at him and the Kid.

"Beneath us lies the Abyss," he said. "One of you must go down to meet your fate. Wormwood is there and he will devour you, and we will all be cleansed. The Lamb will see the light and he will follow it and take us to victory against the Nephilim. But the Goat is a trickster. He is playing his games with us, trying to fool us. He is good at hiding. He has had thousands of years' practice. So we must decide. . . . Has he disguised himself as the Lamb and made the Lamb look like the Goat, or is that only what he wants us to believe? He has cast doubt among us. That is his way. So which one of you is pure and which of you is evil?"

"Neither of us!" Sam shouted. "Why won't any of you listen to me?"

Matt ignored him, strode off, and started to walk around and around the circle of kids, shouting into their faces. "Which of them must go down into the Abyss to be devoured by Wormwood, and which of them will remain in light and live in the clouds of eternal bliss?"

"By jingo," the Kid whispered. "This boy spouts more gibberish than me. I ain't never heard such a crock of witless drivel."

"Two boys!" Matt shouted, staring once again at Sam and the Kid. "One called Samuel, one called Angus Day. One dark and one fair. One good and one evil. But which is which? We must not be deceived. There is only one way to find out the truth. We must ask each in turn who should be sacrificed today."

"Hey," said Sam. "That's not right. You can't make us."

Matt hurried back to Sam with long strides and put his hand on his forehead, spreading the fingers wide. "Just answer my question," he said, lowering his voice.

Sam couldn't help but stare at the scabby mess in the center of Matt's own forehead. Matt realized what he was looking at. "It is the mark of the Lamb," he said. "A holy blessing, a stigmata that proves I am a true believer, a righteous follower."

"A dickhead," said the Kid, but Matt ignored him.

"So, Sam?" he said. "Which of you should we sacrifice today?"

"Me," said Sam quietly and full of misery. "Sacrifice me. I can't let you hurt the Kid any more."

Matt released Sam and strode over to the Kid, but when he put his hand on his forehead, the little boy suddenly started to shake and shudder. Tears rolled down his cheeks, he sniffed, threw his arms around Matt.

"Please," he said. "Not me. Don't do it to me. Do it to Sam. Please. Please not me."

Sam swallowed hard. Tried to be brave. His own face was wet with tears now.

"It is decided, then," said Matt. "The Lamb has shown us the truth, and the Goat has tried to hide behind a lie. We know for certain which one is which." He paused, like a judge on a TV talent show, looking from one boy to the other, building up the tension, making them wait and enjoying the power he held right then.

All his kids were standing silently, watching him. Gripped. Trying to guess what he was going to say. Finally Matt fixed his eyes on the sniveling Kid.

"You," he said, drawing out the pause. "Angus Day, you . . . are the Goat! And you must die today."

"What? No!" Sam threw himself at Matt, beating him with his fists.

Matt held him still. "You are the Lamb," he said. "Only one as brave and pure and true as the Lamb would sacrifice himself for a friend. Now!" He turned to the musicians. "Drive the darkness out with your music!"

Clutching Sam to his chest and muffling his protests, Matt bowed his head. All the kids in the circle copied him, except for the musicians, who started playing again. Sam wrenched his head around and looked at the Kid, who winked at him and mouthed one word.

"*Morons.*"

Matt let go of Sam, who ran over to the Kid before anyone could stop him. Gave him a hug. "I tried. I did try."

"Not hard enough, buster," said the Kid. "I outfoxed you with my acting skills."

"How did you know what Matt was going to do?"

"Their twisted logic is wastepaper thin," said the Kid. "I've seen enough daft films to know how this was going to play out. Lemons all around. Farewell, brave companion."

Matt pulled Sam away, and Nathan and the guard took hold of the Kid. He didn't struggle, just raised his head and smiled at the circle of children. "Remember this day," he said. "Remember what you did to me. Now, so long, suckers!"

Sam watched as his best friend ever in the world was taken away, looking tiny between the two big boys. He couldn't believe that he would never see him again. Couldn't let himself believe it.

"We'll find a way, small fry!" the Kid shouted, his croaky voice getting lost in the vastness of the warehouse.

"Talk all you want, demon!" Matt shouted back. "There's nobody can save you now."

42

Ed grunted as he swung his sword, bringing it down hard at the place where the father's neck joined his shoulder. Blood exploded from the severed artery, and the father seemed to split open, as if he were an overstuffed suitcase being unzipped. His skin separated and a foul mess bubbled out from inside. A mixture of pink flesh, bright red blood, and a shiny gray jellylike substance that Ed had never seen before today. The father fell to his knees, his head flopping to one side, his bones coming apart. He had become a shapeless sack that was slowly melting into the road. Guts and hideously swollen internal organs spilled out of him until he was just a stinking heap of offal.

It wasn't over yet, though; there was another father behind him, and another. They'd come from nowhere, and Ed's group was surrounded.

It had all been going so well. They'd made good progress along the beach at the side of the Thames, but the rising tide had forced them back up onto the road at Victoria Embankment. It had been quieter now that they'd gotten clear of the zone. They'd ignored the few lone sickos who were wandering around, and the three frozen ones, standing stiff and vacant, like shop window dummies with nothing to sell. They'd hurried past them, anxious to press on, knowing that the frozen ones weren't a threat. Even Kyle seemed to have had his fill of killing. Their last brutal fight back at Steelyard Passage had been enough for him.

They'd felt relatively safe walking along the Victoria Embankment. It was a wide, tree-lined road with the river on the left and a string of public gardens and big, old office buildings set back behind spiked iron railings on the right. Ed felt like they'd definitely left the zone behind and were in the more secure area they'd been hoping to find on the other side.

But then, as they'd headed up toward Trafalgar Square, they'd run straight into a gang of sickos. After a moment's panic Ed had switched direction, with similar results. Whatever route he picked seemed to be blocked by sickos plodding doggedly along.

This behavior was totally unexpected. Ed had never seen anything like it before. The whole day had gone wrong. He'd watched sickos pouring over the bridges all morning. And now there were more of them, wandering the streets of London in greater numbers than he'd seen since the first days of the disaster.

Where were they all coming from?

There had been no time to fuss over these questions. Ed had to get his group away from danger. In the end he'd taken them back to the Embankment, where he'd hoped to outflank the sickos, but then, not far from the Houses of Parliament, they'd been ambushed.

Thirty, maybe forty sickos had come streaming out of a side street, fast and determined. Now Ed's group were once more fighting for their lives. As fast as they cut one sicko down, another took its place. Ed would have ordered the kids to run if there had been anywhere to run to, but they'd used up all their options. Their only hope was to kill every one of the sickos in this attack party.

And that was just what Ed was trying to do. He'd gone beyond all rational thought and was like some unstoppable killer robot, cutting, hacking, slashing, stabbing, moving on. Some of those he whacked just fell dead; others, though, split open and erupted from their skins. The bursters made the surface of the road dangerously slippery. Ed was literally up to his ankles in human remains.

He was dimly aware that he was tired. His arm ached. His shoulder was crying out in pain. This was just information, though. It didn't affect him. It was happening to someone else.

More information ticked in a corner of his brain. Kyle was at his side, as always, working away mercilessly with his ax. Of the others he had no information at this moment. The conscious, rational part of his brain, shut away behind a closed door in a dark corner, hoped that they were holding up. Hoped he hadn't lost anyone.

The killing part of him didn't care.

"There's more of them, boss," Kyle shouted.

Ed flicked his eyes to the side—saw another gang of

grown-ups approaching. This was rapidly becoming a big hungry mob. He summoned up a fresh burst of energy, went into overdrive, sped up the rate of his sword strikes, washing himself in the blood of the sickos he cut down. There were too many, though, even for Ed and Kyle to deal with. Slowly they were being forced back. Ed couldn't keep it up: his arm was growing numb; his body was covered in scratches, cuts, and bruises. As he turned to swipe at a father who was trying to get past him, he saw the rest of his group had formed into a tight huddle. They looked terrified.

"We're totally outnumbered," Macca screamed. "What are we going to do?"

Ed wanted to snarl at him, *We're going to die*, but he couldn't speak. Nothing would come out. Instead he turned back to the advancing sickos and waded into them. It was all he knew right now. The blood was singing in his head.

And then Ed became aware of a new sound. A crazy roaring, yelping din. A ripple passed through the attacking sickos. They too were aware that something had changed. Their attack seemed to lose energy. Ed hissed between his clenched teeth and laid into them with a final, desperate fury, Kyle matching him stroke for stroke.

And then the sickos' attack completely fell apart. The mob broke up, started trying to get away, and Ed saw a gang of kids with big fighting dogs attacking them from their rear, driving a wedge through their ranks toward Ed and Kyle.

"The helicopters have arrived!" Kyle yelled. "Come on, let's show them what we can do!" With a high, ululating war cry, he swung his ax around his head and plunged into the nearest knot of confused sickos. Ed was with him, hardly aware of what he was doing, lost in a red mist, animated only by his killing frenzy.

The newcomers fought well and hard, as merciless as Kyle and as cold-blooded as Ed. Very soon there were only wounded or dead sickos left. The others had moved on, heading eastward, drawn by something the kids could only guess at, some silent call on the wind.

"Let them go," said the leader of the newcomers, a wild-looking boy wearing a leather mask.

Ed's group stood there, panting, exhausted, drenched in sweat, their clothing stained dark red, their weapons hanging limply by their sides. Ed wearily checked the numbers, a bored shelf-stacker counting cans of soup.

They were all still standing. A thought came into his mind—it was good that they were still standing, but there was no emotion to go with the thought.

Just that.

It was good.

"Who's in charge here?" asked the boy in the leather mask, his voice muffled.

Ed was still too wired to speak. Kyle nodded toward him, and the newcomers came cautiously closer. Ed just stared blankly back at them.

"Where you from?" the boy asked. Ed shrugged. For the moment he couldn't remember. He'd wanted to say, *Kent—Rowhurst School.* For years it had been his automatic response to that question. A deeper, wired-in memory than the memory of his time at the Tower.

But that was a long time ago. Another life. With Jack and Bam and all the others he had lost.

"Tower of London," Kyle replied for him. "Out east along the river."

The boy in the mask sniffed and took a long look in the direction that Kyle was pointing.

"That's the badlands," he said. "We don't go nowhere near there. The dogs don't like it. They can hear something we can't, start whining and pulling on they leashes."

"We don't usually go through there, either," said Kyle, still speaking for Ed. "I mean, like, we don't *never* go through there."

"These is twisted times," said the masked boy.

"True that."

"You guys look like you can take care of yourselves, though."

"We were just a bit outnumbered," said Kyle.

The masked boy chuckled. "About a hundred to one."

"We're looking for someone." Ed finally spoke. He was slowly returning to life, like a dead leg coming awake. It was painful. If it was possible to get pins and needles in the brain, that's what it felt like to Ed.

"Looking for someone?" the masked boy asked.

"Yeah. That's why we came through the badlands from the Tower. We were looking for someone. Didn't know how bad it was going to be."

"Ain't usually like this."

"No?"

"No. Strange days . . . I'm Ryan Aherne, by the way."

Ryan offered his hand for a high five and Kyle slapped it.

"Ain't nothing goes down on these streets I don't know about it." Ryan pushed the mask from his face. He was an ugly bugger, covered in acne.

"We're hunters," he said, as if he expected Ed's group to understand what that meant. His whole gang, maybe twenty-five of them in all, were dressed in leather and furs, and Ed noticed that Ryan had a string of dried human ears hanging from his belt.

Noticed—but didn't feel any reaction.

The kids all introduced themselves and started chatting. There was a lot of news to share. Ed watched Adele and Hayden and Will and Macca. He was glad that none of them had been killed. That was due to Ryan and his hunters. Ed at last felt human enough to thank him, and they locked grips.

"I saw you making hamburgers of them bastards," said Ryan. "I don't know your story, man, but if you ever want to join my pack, there's a space for you."

"Thanks." Ed forced a smile. "I'll bear that in mind."

He felt a growing sense of relief that he was alive, but it was soured by a heavy weariness and a headache. Behind it all lay a gloomy depression. The fight had taken a lot out of him.

"We been chasing down bastards since we woke up," said Ryan, scratching his dog's head. It was a big Rottweiler, with a thick studded collar. "Streets 'round here are usually safe in the day."

"We thought we'd be okay once we were through the badlands," said Ed. "Never expected this." He indicated the vile mess in the road. A truckload of blood and guts, already covered in flies.

Ryan went over to one of the bodies and poked about with his boot.

"They've started arriving a couple of days ago," he said, and spat into the road. "First just a few, ones and twos, you know, heading east mostly, into the badlands. Then they started coming over the bridges. At first they only came at night, then they started coming at all hours." He kicked a head and sent it skittering across the road. "It's messed up," he said, and then spotted something, knelt down next to a heap of dead flesh.

"Would you look at that," he said. Ed joined him. There was a pile of gray jelly, slick and slimy. It looked a bit like frog spawn, and there were what looked like translucent eggs in it.

And something else.

Something moving.

Like tiny gray maggots.

"You ever seen anything like that before?" Ryan asked.

"No."

Ed straightened up. He didn't want to think about any of this right now. "You said it, Ryan. These are twisted times."

"Too right. We need to get you somewhere safe. Let's roll!" He called this last command out to the waiting kids, and they set off down the road in the direction of the Houses of Parliament. Ed could see the familiar tall tower that housed Big Ben, like something out of a dream. Something from the past that was lost a long time ago.

"So who you looking for, then, soldier?" Ryan asked Ed as they trudged along.

"A boy, two boys, traveling with a girl."

"Through the badlands?"

"Yep."

Ryan sucked his teeth and then whistled. "Don't fancy they chances much, to tell you the truth."

"Me neither."

"I ain't seen no one about," said Ryan. "Anyone with any sense is staying off the streets till these bastards pass through."

"But not you?" Ed smiled.

"Told you, soldier." Ryan grinned back at him. "Is our job to keep the streets safe. We're like the Old Bill, I guess. Your friendly neighborhood police force. Where was your friends trying to get to anyways?"

"Buckingham Palace," Ed replied.

"Wouldn't advise rocking up that way right now, to be honest. There's a lot of sick bastards coming through. Besides, we don't have a lot of truck with them palace dudes. You guys need to rest up for a bit, get yourselves clean before you go dancing in that party. Safest bet is I take you to Nicola. She'll look after you."

"Nicola?"

"Yeah." Ryan laughed. "She's the prime minister, man. Didn't you know?"

Now it was Ed's turn to laugh. "You're not serious."

"Well, in her own mind she's the prime minister. She's holed up in the Houses of Parliament. Bunch of real serious kids she got with her. They have votes and everything in there. Makes no difference to anyone else, but if it keeps them happy, you know? She's good news, though, Nicola. She does all right by us. Not like some. You'll like her."

The air was suddenly filled with screams. Shadows swarmed across the road. Ed flinched and then looked up.

Seagulls.

Hundreds of them, wheeling and swooping, come to clean up the mess. Like vultures.

There were rich pickings for them back there.

43

It was dark as midnight down in the hole, and there was a right stinko in the air. The Kid knew that stink.

Old man's stink.

Sick and rotting. Plus the other thing.

Everybody poops.

The Kid stood very still, feeling the vibrations in the room. He was bat and moth and radar, all in one.

The bad boys upstairs had stripped him of his precious jacket, frisked him, and whisked him away. Four of them, the two with the dog chains and two others, bristling with spears and slick with fear. They had the shakes on them bad. They'd tied his wrists with leather twine and taken him to a hole that they'd knocked through a wall in the warehouse. Big black hole it was, and they'd slipped him through it, stepping from the new world into the old. From concrete and cinder blocks, ducts and cables and metal shelves, into a musty, dusty, fusty, dry old world of stone and brick and wood that had stood there so long it had turned as gray as a senior citizen in a Werther's candy ad.

There were Roman buildings down here. His granddad had told him that. It was the Romans who had first built London, long time no see. Like in the olden days. Dates had never been his thing. And underneath all the new stuff was the old stuff. Buried deep. Whenever they wanted to put up a new building these days, they had first to excavate. Send in the Time Team. See what the Romans had left behind.

The Kid wondered if this old place they'd walked through had been built by some long-gone Julius or Claudius or Caligula, back in the days of Latin and sandals.

There were stone steps down, all worn and broken up, taking them deeper between narrow walls, pressing in from the sides. Then the corridor had opened out into a vault with brick arches holding up the roof. Wine barrels hiding in niches, forlorn and forgotten.

The Kid had smiled, felt a familiar, friendly warmth in his belly. This was *his* world. The underground. Alberich's realm. He was the tunnel king. He'd been in cellars like this before, exploring beneath the city.

That was the olden days too. Many moons ago. There had been a heap of them back then, girlies and boyos, all mucking in together where they'd lived in Spitalfields Market. They'd done all right for several good months. And then they'd gotten sick. Not the old man sickness of the grown-ups, some other disease, the flu or the pox or the flux. It had come to walk among them, and one by one by one they'd passed away.

The Kid knew then he'd have to skedaddle. Being another victim wasn't for him. He'd taken his chances on his own.

And then he'd met Sam I Am, his right-hand man.

Never had a friend like Sam before. He hoped he'd be all right up there without him.

These thoughts had clattered about in the haywire tangles of the Kid's mind as down they'd gone, the candlelight slipping and crawling over the old gray-and-yellow-stone walls.

And then at last they'd come to a door.

Big door. Black door. Iron studs and a key as big as your head. Nathan had unlocked it. *Rattle-click-clunk-clank.* The Kid had thought of the Clickee Cult, up there, banging away until kingdom come. And he'd thought of sweet Yo-Yo, his violinist. He had to get back to her somehow. Make her see sense. He liked Yo-Yo. He liked anyone who could play music like that. His granddad had made him hear music. All music. What there was inside it. Where it took you. How the best music didn't shout at you and tell you what to do. How you could find your own way through it.

Then the big boys had made ready, spears held out, the fear dripping off them so you could almost see it. They didn't like what was on the other side of that door.

Nathan had turned on a powerful bright flashlight. Dazzling it was. And they'd counted . . .

One . . . two . . . three . . .

Then it was door open, spears jabbing into emptiness, the flashlight shining bright, all shouting and yelling fit to frighten the devil away. And they'd shoved the Kid through the door.

There were more steps on the other side and he'd almost fallen, but somehow he'd danced down them, and by the time he'd reached the bottom, the door had banged shut behind him, and—*BANG*—the lights went out.

He'd had half a moment to get a picture of the place they'd flung him into like a dirty rag. It was another ancient wine cellar, most of the barrels gone, arches and dust, lots of dust. Tracks in the dust where something had walked. . . .

Then darkness.

The smell of death.

It was the darkness he stood in now, trying to herd his thoughts somewhere useful.

He wasn't alone down there. The vibrations told him that. And the smell. Poo. Wee. Worse.

The smell of a hungry fellow.

He'd smelled that smell many times before, in the tunnels, knew if he got a whiff of it he had to turn back and go another way. There wasn't no other way to go down here, though, was there? This was the end of the line. This was a dungeon. And there was a dragon in it.

He kept very still, keeping his breathing quiet, trying to sense where the monster might be. Trying to build up a picture.

Not much luck.

Give it time.

He waited, still as a frightened mouse, and at last he heard it. Sniffing. Sniveling. The monster was sussing him out.

And then he heard something else.

A voice.

"Hello."

A man's voice. Soft and low and gentle. A kind voice.

Don't be fooled, kiddo. It was the monster, all right. The blimp, Frank, it was the blimp.

The Kid held his counsel. Didn't deign to reply.

"Don't be frightened," came the kindly voice, floating over the darkness. Like honey it was. "I only want to talk to you. It's lonely down here. What's your name, child?"

Everybody wanted to know his moniker of late. Well, that was between him and the gatepost. He had to keep some things to himself. A person needed secrets, private things, needed to keep a part of himself hidden away in a money box for a rainy day. You never knew when you might need it. His name was his to have, his to hold, his and his alone.

If you shared too much of yourself you eventually found there was nothing left.

Hold your counsel. Still your tongue. Let the cat have it.

"Why don't you come over here and sit with me? You must be scared in the dark there. I'll look after you. There are rats down here, you know."

Yeah. One big fat talking rat who smelled of rotten sneakers and toilet gifts.

"We'll have a party. I don't often get visitors. But when I do, I always make them feel at home."

A party? Right. Yeah. The Kid had heard enough. It was time to put his four-step plan into action. He raised his hands to his hair, his joyous, thick tangle of locks. Like an explosion, sprouting from the top of his head. Stiff as wire wool it was. Matted solid.

His granddad used to read him stories. The Kid loved stories more than anything. One of his favorites was about the Twits. Old man Twit had a beard to write home about. Yes, indeed.

He'd kept things in his beard.

And the Kid kept things in his hair. Oh, the big boys had frisked him, all right, but they really weren't up to the job. They weren't professionals. He had all sorts stashed away in his hair. He felt carefully for one of his razor blades. A good trick that, to keep razor blades hidden in your locks. If any grown-ups tried to grab your hair and pull you into their dens they got a nasty shock, and sometimes lost their fingers.

The twits.

In a matter of moments he'd cut through the leather twine and freed his hands.

Step two. His cigarette lighter. That was there to be winkled out, nestling in a pocket of hair like a bird's egg in a nest.

Step three. He used his blade to cut a strip of material from the bottom of his dress.

Step four. He started to move slowly to his left. He'd seen just enough when the boys had shone their flashlight in to know that there was a wine barrel over there and some rickety old wooden props and supports.

"There's no point in moving about in the dark," said the voice. "It's not safe. You must be scared and lonely. Come here. We'll be great friends, you and me."

The Kid ignored him and kept shuffling along, hands stretched out in front of him. Had a good sense of space, learned from many months exploring in the dark. Went like a blind boy until he felt the hardness of a wooden post. His fingers ran over it, reading it, looking for a crack. The wood was ancient and dry and half rotten. He found a loose strip, dug it out a little with his blade, then prized the strip away.

It was about a foot long and slightly thicker than a pencil. It would do.

"I've got things you'd like—candy and chocolate and, I don't know, sometimes I forget. Do you like chocolate? What's your favorite color?"

The Kid put his blade back for safekeeping and then wound the length of cloth around the end of the wood and secured it in place with the leather twine, binding it tightly into a wad, but leaving a strand flapping loose.

All the while the monster had been talking, talking, wheedling, syrupy, trying to hypnotize him, like Kaa the snake in *The Jungle Book*.

"Come to me, child, sit with me a while. They always do. In the end."

The Kid was finally ready. The big boys had shown him the best weapon to use to slay the dragon. Light. They'd shone that big brightness of theirs right in here, trying to scare the monster away from the door.

He walked quickly toward the sound of the voice, and when he was close, he rolled the flint at the top of his lighter, and as it sparked into life, he put it to the scrap of loose cloth. It flared and lit. Burned bright for a few seconds.

Long enough for him to eyeball the monster.

He was a father. Maybe forty years old, bald, with long skinny arms and legs and a round potbelly. Just sitting there on a stone bench, his arms by his sides, his hands resting on the bench, with long fingernails, horny and twisted. He appeared to be naked, but it was hard to tell; his skin was marked by the disease, distorted by lumps and growths and swellings, and covered all over with a soft fur of green mold. His skin was pulled tight on his face, making his pale eyes bulge and exposing his gums. The sort of face the Kid used to make in the mirror to amuse himself, pulling the loose skin back with his hands.

As the Kid shoved the flames toward him, the man raised one hand to his face, shielding it, fingernails rattling.

He swore at the Kid. "How'd you get that? Why'd they let you down here with fire?"

"Because they're stupid," said the Kid. "Because they believe too strong in one sole thing. Their brainboxes is all facing one way. They don't think that there might be other things in the world. I'm not like them. My mind don't go in a straight line. The steering wheel is loose."

"Who are you?"

"I'm the Kid. Who are you?"

"Who do you think?" The monster's voice turned cold and hard. "I'm Wormwood, the Green Man."

44

Shadowman was making his way back to the Fear. He had a strange, sick, out-of-joint feeling that he was more at home with his strangers than he was with other children. He hadn't bothered to argue anymore with Saif. What was the point? The guy was an arrogant prick. Arrogant like Jaz and Ricky had been, and if Saif wasn't careful he was going to wind up as dead as them.

True, he had a lot to be arrogant about. He had organized the camp at IKEA well. The big garage was secured all around and they were growing a lot of food there. He had a collection of cars with gas in them, so his scavenging parties were fast and efficient and relatively safe. The kids were well armed and the distinctive blue box of the main building was warm and dry.

Something happened to people when you gave them too much power, though. They started to believe they were special, that they were always right, all-powerful, invincible.

Saif almighty.

Shadowman had seen it happen to other kids around

London. A girl called Anita had been in charge of the first safe house he'd camped out in after the illness hit. It had been out west in Notting Hill. Had been her family home. They'd done well there to begin with, survived the early days of chaos and rampage. They'd lived through the first weeks when the streets had been thick with strangers, and Anita had begun to think that it was because of her, that *she* was the one making a difference. She couldn't see that it was mostly luck.

She got cocky, started taking risks, making rules, ordering her kids to do stupid things.

It had gotten her killed. Her and most of the kids in the house.

Shadowman had had to move on. Tried various groups of other kids, but always found he preferred being alone. The last place he'd been living had been a wild camp of hooligans run by a head case called John. He was violent, stupid, unfair, but his people did what he told them, looked up to him even.

Then there was David, lording it up at Buckingham Palace, thinking he was king of the shit heap. That guy was *definitely* nuts, like every dictator that had gone before him. Nero, Caligula, Henry VIII, Napoleon, Stalin, Hitler, Mussolini, Margaret Thatcher, Colonel Gaddafi, that crazy North Korean bastard who was in *Team America*, Kim Jong whatever.

The dear leader.

They all thought they were God. Nothing could knock them down. But they all got knocked down. They all lost it in the end. They were no more God than he was.

Overconfidence could kill you, believing you were invincible. Shadowman was all too aware of that. You had to speak softly and carry a big stick.

Who had said that? It was a quote from somewhere. Just another power-crazed tyrant probably.

All that power, that long run of good luck, had made Saif overconfident. Stuck there behind his high fence in his cozy blue box. He couldn't get it into his head that things might change, might not always stay the way he wanted them to be. Which was pretty dim when you considered what had happened a year ago.

The whole bloody world had changed, hadn't it? So why couldn't Saif see that it could change again?

Saif was a moron and Shadowman was going to have to live with that. He was not going to keep on hitting his head against the wall.

Leave them to it.

In the end he hadn't wanted to stay at IKEA anyway. It had weirded him out, waking up in that fake room. He didn't feel comfortable in a real bed, with clean sheets, anymore. And he hadn't been made welcome. The kids had their castle and they didn't want any outsiders coming in and taking what was theirs. Only Johnny and his friend Dan had wanted to listen to what he had to say. They'd shown him some kindness and tried to make him feel welcome. They'd said they could make Saif change his mind about kicking Shadowman out, but he'd told them not to bother. He didn't belong there.

At least he'd gotten something out of it, though. He'd refilled his water bottle and picked up some fresh supplies, including a new machete. Johnny and Dan had seen to that, apologizing all the while. He'd tried to assure them that it didn't matter, and the last thing he did was try to warn Johnny one final time.

"Don't let Saif attack the horde unprepared," he'd said as he was leaving. "At least get him to check them out for himself before he goes blundering in there without enough muscle. Even with cars and weapons, twenty-five kids is not enough to take on . . . you know . . ." He had been going to say "Saint George," but worried about how that might make him look. Giving names to zombies again.

So he'd left it hanging. Johnny knew what he meant.

"I'll do what I can," he said. "But once Saif has an idea in his head, you can't change it."

"You don't say."

It felt good to be back on the streets, alone. It felt right, though walking was painful at first. He'd downed some painkillers. They weren't enough, only knocked the edges off his pain. Both his legs were cut and bruised, and his chest was extremely sore. He thought he'd maybe cracked a rib or two. Gradually his muscles loosened, the pain dimmed, and walking became easier. It was late afternoon and the sky was darkening, not just with the sun going down; the clouds were thickening, massing for a storm by the look of it. That was something else he'd learned in the last year, how to read the weather. Hadn't ever really given it a thought before. Hardly ever even looked up at the sky.

He'd only been going a few minutes when he spotted his first sentinel. A father with a collapsed belly hanging over the filthy, tattered remains of his jeans. He had adopted the standard pose—arms out, head slightly tilted back, eyes staring—though with one difference. He was missing a hand. A cloud of flies buzzed around the rotten stump. Crawled up his arm.

He ignored them.

"All right, Stumpy," Shadowman said as he walked past, and laughed at his little joke.

He spotted three more sentinels along the way, despite switching routes and trying different roads. They seemed to be everywhere. He got the impression that they were fanning out from a central point. Presumably that would be where the bulk of the Fear were. If they'd moved from the tire center he should be able to find them by following the sentinels.

He remembered what Johnny had said about ants, and wondered if the sentinels really were part of some kind of primitive communication network, reaching out to other strangers and drawing them in to join Saint George's army. He'd certainly seen a few lone wanderers heading in the same direction he was, plodding along in broad daylight. One of them was even carrying the body of a small child. Like a cat bringing an offering of a dead mouse.

He had to find out what was going on. He couldn't live in ignorance like Saif. The sentinels were the most obvious indication that the strangers were changing, getting better organized. If the Fear were somehow using the sentinels to attract other strangers, their army could grow very quickly. How many would they be now? Shadowman and Jaz's crew had taken down a few yesterday. Twenty maybe? But would that make much difference?

There was only one way to find out, which was why he was heading back to the tire center. Of course the horde might have moved on, but all the signs told him otherwise.

It took him a long while to get to his lookout apartment, and as he got closer there were more strangers around. He had to be very careful he didn't blunder into a big group of them. He went slowly and didn't take any chances. So it was nearly two hours after leaving IKEA before he was safely up in the apartment. Nothing had changed; his puke was still there, drying on the carpet. The dead couple were still on the sofa, holding hands and staring sightlessly at a dead television.

He went to the window, put his binoculars to his eyes, and looked out.

The Fear were still there. The sentinels were out in the road, and there was a steady trickle of new strangers shuffling up and going into the building.

Shadowman wondered what would happen next. If the Fear stuck to their normal routine, they'd come out as darkness fell and start to hunt. Which way would they go tonight? If there were sentinels as far north as IKEA, then Saint George might know about the kids there.

Was that how it worked? Had they really become that organized? A swarm of ants ready to clear the whole area. That was scary.

It would be impossible to attack Saif's kids if they stayed put behind their defenses. Would Saint George know that? How clever had he become? What might he be planning to do?

It wasn't long before Shadowman got his answer. He was watching the front of the tire center, only about twenty minutes later, when he saw dark shapes emerging. At first a slow trickle, then a great mass of them. Too many to count. Shadowman couldn't be sure, but it looked like they'd at least doubled in number.

Saint George was at the front, with two of his lieutenants, Man U and Spike. As usual, no words were spoken, no commands given, but the strangers knew exactly what to do, even though a lot of them must have been new arrivals. They spilled into the street, and for a moment it looked like they might go either way, left toward IKEA or right toward . . .

Toward where? The road ran roughly north to south, which meant that if they went right and kept on going, they'd eventually reach the center of town.

Now he was being ridiculous. Putting his own thoughts and fears into Saint George's head. They could go anywhere.

He waited, scanning the faces of the horde with his binoculars. The weak sunlight was burning their skin, ripening the spots, painting red-raw streaks across their cheeks. They didn't seem to care anymore, though. Something was more important to them than the pain; something was driving them on.

They had a purpose.

At last Saint George started walking. Right. South. Directly past the block of apartments where Shadowman was hiding. He felt like one of those dictators, surveying his troops. They didn't exactly march—they were too far gone for that—but there was a definite sense of order about them.

It took a long while for all of them to pass. At the back were the stragglers, the weaker ones, the older ones, the most diseased. Bluetooth was with them, in his dirty blue suit. He had a small group of fitter strangers with him, almost as if he was herding the weaklings along.

Just like a medieval army on the march, with oxen ready to be slaughtered when they were needed to feed the troops.

At last all that was left were the sentinels in the road, still standing there. Waiting. Shadowman packed up his gear and went down the stairs. Moved cautiously out into the road.

Froze.

There was a stranger coming from the north, limping along all by himself.

Shadowman ducked down out of sight. Realized he recognized the lone walker; it was Stumpy, towing a cloud of flies in his wake. He walked right past Shadowman, who let him go.

Once he was sure it was okay to move, he came out from behind the wall and crossed over the road to the tire center, curious to see how the Fear had left it. The stink as he got close was appalling; a huge number of diseased adults had been in there for two days. He covered his mouth and nose with his cloak and crept in.

He wished he had squashed his curiosity. There were bones everywhere—animal bones, children's bones, adult bones—all mixed in with human waste, clothing, hair, vile bits and pieces.

A movement.

They hadn't all left.

A twisted little stranger with bent arms and legs, his shirt front coated in drool, was crawling about, picking over the remains for something to eat. He had big watery eyes and a few strands of long lank hair stuck to his face.

He smiled at Shadowman. A warm, welcoming smile.

All the frustration, pain, rage, and fear of the last twenty-four hours welled up inside Shadowman. He walked over to the father and smashed his skull in with his machete.

"I'm not one of you," he said.

And then he heard the rumble of engines.

45

So you're the bogeyman, are you? The Green Man. Green bogeyman. Mr. Wormwood. The toad in the hole. I can hear you moving there in the dark. I've sharp ears and a sharper blade. I seen you, before my flames died down, licking your lips. You want your dinner, don't you? But you try and come for me and I'll cut you and burn you and make you cry. Is that understood?"

"I wasn't doing anything. I was just—"

"I know what you were doing. Don't play me for a fool. Sit back down and listen, 'cause you and me, Mr. Green, we've got some talking to do. A lot to catch up on. I've got some questions to ask you, Old Wormwood."

"I've got questions too, little hairy kid. I've been down here too long. Don't know what's going on in the world. I hear them sometimes up there, chattering. Louder and louder lately. I try to say hello, but they're too stupid. It's like talking to the bugs back in the big green."

"Well, that's why you don't want to eat me just yet, do you? I ain't stupid. I ain't a bug. I can answer your questions.

Let's talk first, yeah? Before dinner. You and me?"

"Mm. I *do* have some questions. I surely *do*."

"Fair's fair and all that, bogeyman. Here's how it works. You ask one question, I ask one question. Play it straight and I'll play straight by you. Way I see it, Mad Matt and his microlights, they ain't been playing straight with you. They keep you locked up here."

"It's not fair. You're right. It's really not fair. I'm an important person, a VIP. I was king of the jungle. Something like that."

"You think you're king of the Kop, Wormhole, so how come you're buried underground like the worm you took your moniker from? You're the underground man. You're dead and buried, sunshine. Except there ain't no sunshine anymore. Just dust and darkness. And the Kid can't believe that's what you want, Colonel Bogey. He thinks you want to walk in the sunshine."

"Not the sunshine. No, not that. The sunshine hurts. Brings on the itch."

"And when you itch, you got to scratch. Scratchy and itchy, that's you. The big itch. The Jolly Green Giant."

"You're confusing me."

"I'm confusing myself."

"I hate them. They say they worship me, but they keep me down here like, like a, like a . . ."

"Like a bad smell. A toe rag. A dirty secret. Mrs. Rochester. The mad one in the family."

"It's not right, Kid, I should be shown some respect."

"You should, Wormy, you really should."

"It's like this, though. I've sort of forgotten who I am."

"You're flotsam and jetsam, squire. You're on the seabed, sleeping with the fishes. Blind to everything."

"I don't understand a word you're saying."

"The feeling, as my granddad used to say, is mutual. We're both experts at spouting gibberish, which means we spikka da same lingo, you and me, and neither of us can follow the threads. Ain't that a laugh? We've got to iron some things out."

"I'm so, so hungry, Kid. I've got to eat. You smell so good. I want to hear the news, but—"

"Sit still."

"Sorry."

"When you're sitting down again, you can ask away, Wormy."

"I'm sitting now."

"Good. So what do you want to know?"

"What's going on? Tell me what's going on. It's been so long since I've seen a newspaper."

"Same as it ever was. Dog eat dog. The cycle of boom and bust."

"I could eat a dog, but I'd rather eat you. They bring me dogs sometimes. Tough they are. Perhaps you could sit here? With me. You sound so crunchable."

"We've got to get to the bottom of this, Wormy. You want to eat me? Well, I'm just a scrap, a gristly morsel, one bite and I'm gone. Poof. Gone with the wind. You will fart me out and sneeze, and you will be emptier than you were before."

"I need to eat. I need to eat you."

"I'm a scrap. All they feed you is scraps. You don't want scraps, you're the king underground. The fishing king, fishing for herring and trout, but only catching boots and old bicycles. And shrimps. Which is all I am. Just a shrimp. My very good friend, Sam I Am, he reckons I'm the smallest of the small. I reckon he's the smallest. Who knows the answer? Thing is, though, we're the bottom of the heap, the tiniest, we are plankton."

"Plankton? That makes me the whale."

"And I am Jonah. Soon to be inside you. Or are we Pinocchio and Gepetto, the two of us, in our boat in the belly of the whale? This cellar with its ribs and arches. Could be a whale, d'you think?"

"You're confusing me again. I can't keep up."

"Just go with it, Wormy."

"Tell me what's going on. You said we would take turns. Asking questions."

"I did, I did. But it's my turn now. I ask one, you ask one. You've had yours."

"Have I? What was my question?"

"That's cheating, Wormy, that's another question."

"Sorry. What's your question, then, Kid?"

"I've a riddle for you. What sleeps in a hole and wakes up in hole and spends its day in a hole?"

"I don't know. A worm?"

"Prezackly. A worm. Mister worm king himself, emperor worm. Wormwood. That's you. You are naught but a worm in a hole."

"You're bamboozling me."

"We're just a couple of old bamboozlers, bamboozling each other in the dark. Now it's your turn. Next question, worm."

"All right. I've a riddle for you as well. And if you don't answer it, I get to eat you."

"That doesn't seem exactly fair."

"The world isn't fair. Have you not noticed? This is my house. My house, my rules. I'm holding all the cards. I could crush you like one of the bugs that used to be my friends."

"All right, baldy, keep your hair on. Riddle-me-ree."

"Hee-hee-hee . . . Who am I?"

"Easy, you are the Green Man, the bogeyman, Wormwood, old Wormy, old snotter, crusty snot rag, the Jolly Green Giant, Colonel Bogey, the goblin king in his mountain hall, the Cyclops in his cave, the underground man, emperor worm, Alberich the dwarf, watching over his hoard of gold."

"No, who am I really?"

"The troll under the bridge."

"What?"

"Three billy goats came over your bridge, remember? And you were skulking down under there, up to your ass cheeks in cold water. Warty old troll. And the first billy goat gruff, he was the littlest, he comes trip-trap-trotting over. And what does he say to you?"

"I know this story."

"Ah, now we're getting somewhere."

"I used to tell it to my boys at night."

"You had kids, Wormy? Pray tell. I am all ears, like an elephant. I never forget. Tell me once, tell me twice, tell me three times. Then take it to the bridge."

"Stop. Stop your babble for a minute. I want to remember . . . my three boys."

"Tell me about it, wormhole, tell me about your three billy goats gruff, the big one, the middle one, and the little one. Your three sweet boys."

"At night, yes, it's clear to me now, I remember, I would go to my boys' bedrooms. Three boys. You're right. There were three boys. I won't tell you about the other one. That one came out all wrong. But the boys . . . I read them stories, and each one grew up and I lost them. I lost them way back there."

"Keep going."

"Except the youngest. He was still my boy when . . . when . . ."

"Don't think about the bad parts, when the sickness came, remember back when they were all three boys."

"Yes. Yes, I will. It's a good memory. You see, at night, I'd read them stories. The oldest first. I'd read him stories at night until he got too old for it . . . *Each Peach Pear Plum*, *Peepo!*, Paddington Bear . . . and then he grew up, didn't want me to read to him anymore, so there was the next one, and the same thing happened. He grew up too. Not the youngest, though. He was always young. Always will be, because I got sick and the world turned upside down, and—"

"Don't go there, Dad. Remember the story you were telling. The three billy goats gruff."

"Yes. They went trip-trap-trip-trap over the bridge."

"Tell it to me now, Wormy. I'm still a younger. I could be your boy. I still want to hear the stories."

"There was a troll," said Wormwood, his voice sounding like it was coming from far away and long ago. "There was a troll who lived under a bridge, and there were three goats. They lived on a hillside and they'd eaten all their grass. On the other side of the river was another hill, full of rich, sweet grass. . . ." Wormwood sobbed.

"Don't stop, Dad. I like to hear the old stories."

"Are you really my boy?"

"Yes. Right now. Here in the dark. I'm your boy. Go back there, Wormy, back to when all was quiet and still. The world was fine. You told stories to your boys at night. And it was good night, boys, good night, John-Boy, good night, moon."

"Okay. Yes . . . Yes. Well, the smallest of the goats, he couldn't stand it any longer. He went trip-trap-trotting across the bridge to get to the fresh green grass on the other side, and the troll came out, the ugly old troll, and he said, 'Who dares cross my bridge?' And the little goat, he said, 'Don't eat me, my brother's bigger than me, there's more meat on him. You eat him and let me go. . . .' I can't go on."

"My granddad used to tell me that story. He loved the old stories. 'Cinderella,' 'Rumpelstiltskin,' 'Rapunzel,' 'Hansel and Gretel,' 'Jack and the Beanstalk,' 'The Twelve Dancing Princesses.' Do you remember them, old troll?"

"I remember them all, son. I remember there used to be a time before, when it wasn't all darkness and disease. When I could sit like this with my boys by their beds at night and tell them stories. How did I end up here?"

"Beats me with a stick, Wormy. But here you are. And here I am. Now you've got a choice, Green Man: you can tell me some bedtime stories or you can eat me. You can be a dad or you can be a troll. The choice is yours."

"I don't know what I am. I thought I knew. I can't think straight because of them up there; they're all shouting at me, trying to get my attention. There's another memory, you see? Of the big green."

"Tell me about the big green."

"I remember a forest, a jungle with trees as tall as skyscrapers. And I was very small, just a germ really. I lived there for a million years, I think. Until I escaped, jumping like a flea from bug to beast. Except I don't think that was me. How could it be? How could I be two people? One inside the other like those dolls. How could I have lived in the jungle with the bees and the fleas and the bats, and also have been that man who read stories to his boys at night? That's why I asked you the riddle, son. Who am I? I need to know."

"You're the man who read those stories."

"What is my name?"

"You're wasting questions, Wormy. You only have so many; why are you asking me when you already know the answer?"

"Do I?"

"Yes. Now it's my turn."

"No, wait. . . ."

"My question is this. How long you been down here, troll?"

"Long enough to count my days with coffee spoons."

"Oh, Spoony, you are breaking my feeble heart. Tell me this: do you have a heart?"

"I'm a man, that much I know."

"Prezackly. Pre-flaming-zackly. You are a man with a beating heart and bellowing lungs and a long, giggling stomach."

"Giggling?"

"Giggling, gurgling. Same difference."

"What are you talking about?"

"You keep wasting your questions, Daddy-o."

"No, that wasn't—"

"Yes, it was. Now here comes my next poser—wouldn't you like to get out of here? What can you do down here under your bridge? Shut away forever, waiting for them to toss you some salad?"

"I don't want to be here."

"Okay, troll. We're getting somewhere. Now you get another question."

"Can you help me?"

"Let me tell you how the story goes, Dad. The troll comes up from under his bridge, and the little billy goat turns around and says to him, 'Mister Troll, what kind of a life is it living under a bridge? Waiting for your lunch to come trip-trip-trapping along? Just as I've seen fresh green grass on the other hill, why don't you come up here and see that the world is bigger than what's under your cold stone bridge?'"

"Can you really set me free?"

"That's why I'm here, greenback. This was always meant to be. You and me. I've come to save you, Mr. Green. To take you back into the world."

"Will I see my boys again?"

"I can't promise you the moon on a stick. Can't even

promise you a stick. You can fly away home, but your house is on fire and your children are gone. There's been a lot of water flowing under your troll's bridge. Time is a river, flowing on, and you can't stop it. Granddad told me that. When he got so old his poor dry bones gave up the ghost. Buried him in a box we did. Never cried so much."

"I'm scared, though, son. I fear the daylight."

"Not you, Wormy, the thing inside you, the sickness, the doll living in the doll. The thing that came from the big green and got inside you is driving you, Wormy. It ain't you, babe. It's the sickness fears the daylight, fears the sun and the air and all the good things. You're not your sickness. You said it yourself. You're the other one, not Wormwood, not the Green Man; you're the father of those boys."

"I'm Mark Wormold."

"Yes. You are. And I have answered your riddle. You don't get to eat me now."

"How can you get me out of here, though? You're just a kid."

"I am *the* Kid. I'm King Rat, the burrower. Listen, good father, we are underground and underground is my domain, my stomping ground. I'll find a way. I know these old places, these tunnels and dungeons full of wine and dust and spiders. I can get us out of here. But you've got to make some stone-hard promises."

"What?"

"First, I am *not* your lunch."

"You do smell good, though. You smell like life, and that's what I need."

"Not you, Mark Wormold, that's the sickness talking.

You are one and it's another. You are a father; *it* is Wormwood, the fallen star, growing back there in the big green. Wormwood wants me. You got to fight him, tell him who's the daddy. Don't let your sickness be the boss of you."

"No."

"You don't want to eat me. There's bigger billy goats than me. Let them be your lunch. It's them who've kept you down here under the bridge. Not me. I wouldn't even make a meal. I'm less than a bite, so put your teeth away. Is that a deal, old troll?"

"If you can get me out of here, then we are friends for life, little billy goat gruff."

"I'll take you home, troll. Trust me."

46

Sam had never known a feeling like this before. He was all churned up inside. Oh, he'd been angry before, and sad and confused and frightened and bored, all those things, of course he had, and often, as now, he'd felt them all at the same time. The difference now was that even though he felt all that, even though he was deep in the blackest of moods, he was being treated like a king.

A bloody god!

And for the first time in his life he realized that maybe it wasn't such a great life being a king. He hated being a celebrity. It would be much better to be just ordinary.

Basically, being God sucked.

Matt had forced him to wear some ridiculous home-made green robes, he'd put a garland of dead leaves on his head and had plunked him on a throne under the dome at St. Paul's, where he'd been made to sit for God knows how long.

Ha! God didn't know, did He? God was bored out of His mind. Sitting there with an aching butt, listening to the horrible racket of the musicians, breathing in the smelly smoke, while Matt read endless passages from his book of truth . . .

". . . These are they who have come out of the great tribulation. They have washed their robes and made them green in the blood of the Lamb. They are before the throne of God and serve Him day and night in His Temple; and He who sits on the throne will spread His tent over them. Never again will they hunger. Never again will they thirst. The sun will not beat upon them, nor any scorching heat. For the Lamb at the center of the throne will be their shepherd. He will lead them to springs of living water. And He will wipe away every tear from their eyes. . . ."

Oh yeah? Sam thought miserably. And just how am I supposed to do all that?

Matt had promised that once the Goat was sacrificed, the Lamb would see the light and understand who He really was.

That wasn't happening yet, was it?

Which meant one of two things.

It either meant that the Kid was somehow still alive—which gave Sam a tiny warm glow of hope in his guts—or it meant that he wasn't the Lamb. That this was all bullshit.

He knew one thing for sure, though. Whatever happened, Matt would have some handy excuse. He'd make up some story or change an old one, find some dumb quote to explain it all. So long as he had all that food in the warehouse, his "Tree of Life" as he called it, he would literally have these kids eating out of his hand. Look at them all, sitting there, heads bowed, soaking up all this drivel. . . .

". . . Each one had a harp and they were holding golden bowls full of incense, which are the prayers of the saints. And they sang a new song: 'Salvation belongs to our God, who sits on the throne, and to the Lamb. . . .'"

Sam had picked up the Kid's leather jacket from the floor of the warehouse and slipped it on over his hoodie. The Kid would need it. Sam was holding on hard to the belief that he was still alive. The Kid was a clever little sod. Because of the way he spoke and the odd way his brain worked, people made the mistake of thinking he was a fool. He wasn't. Oh, Sam thought there was probably something wrong with his friend, but he was tough and clever, and he had the skills he needed to survive in this twisted new world. If anyone could work out a way to survive in the Abyss, it was the Kid.

But just what was down there? Who or what was Wormwood? How did the sacrifice thing actually work? That's what Sam had to find out, because when he did find it out, he was going to start plotting. He was going to rescue the Kid, and he was going to kill Matt, and he was going to make everything all right.

Yeah. Somehow he was going to fix everything.

He smiled despite himself.

Finally he was thinking like a god. . . .

47

"oes it hurt?" The red-haired girl touched her fingers gently to Ed's scar.

"No. Not really. Sometimes, I guess. If it's really hot or really cold or I'm tired. You know. It sort of aches. Hurt like hell at the time. A grown-up on the turn got me with a blade."

"I hope you killed him."

Ed hesitated, remembering that awful day a year ago when he'd lost his two best friends.

"I didn't," he said flatly, then shrugged, trying to make light of something that still lay heavy on him. An incident he still had nightmares about. Always would. "He's probably dead now, though, like most of them."

Greg, the butcher. He'd promised them all he was immune to the disease. He wasn't. It had just taken him a little longer to get it. And when he did . . .

"I bet you had all the girls chasing after you before."

Ed blushed. The girl, Nicola, was sitting just a little too

close to him. She had a mane of thick red hair and green eyes, and smelled of perfume and soap.

The prime minister.

"I don't know," he said lamely. "They don't chase after me now. Mostly run screaming."

"I like it."

"Yeah, right."

"It gives you character. I never was one for pretty boys. I don't like things to be too perfect."

"Well, you got that right. My face certainly isn't too perfect."

Nicola laughed. They were sitting alone on an uncomfortable narrow sofa in a small private office in the Houses of Parliament. Ed had been amazed to see the inside of the place. The view of the outside was so famous you didn't really notice it anymore, and he'd seen the inside of the House of Commons on the news often enough. He'd never really given much thought to how the rest of the place might look, though.

Well, it was like a palace. In fact, as Nicola had pointed out proudly as she'd led him through the buildings to this room, it *was* a palace. The Palace of Westminster was its proper name. The kids who lived here, and there seemed to be a lot of them, only used a tiny part of it. Ed might live in a castle, but it was pretty basic at the Tower. This place was full of grand chambers and Hollywood staircases, corridors lined with paintings, statues, gold everywhere you looked, tapestries, wood paneling, stained glass in all the windows.

He had to admit it was pretty impressive.

Nicola and the other kids here had been wary of Ed's crew when Ryan the hunter brought them in. Like all kids these days they were suspicious of outsiders, but Ed had explained what they wanted, and Nicola relaxed. She'd told them to hand all their weapons in and had then taken Ed to her office for a private chat.

Her office? What kids had offices?

Well, this one did. Nicola was about Ed's age, but she seemed much older, more mature. She was very pretty and reminded Ed of girls he'd known when he was at school. Rowhurst had been single sex, strictly boys only, but he'd mixed with girls from other private schools, like Walthamstow Hall in Sevenoaks. They were mostly strong and confident and seemed to know who they were and what they wanted from life.

Just like he had been back then. Not anymore. He'd lost all his certainty. Saw the world in murky shades of gray now, not the clear black and white he'd grown up with. Nicola hadn't had the confidence kicked out of her yet. He could still picture her starring in the school play or leading their hockey team out onto the field.

It was strange being alone with her, here in this tidy office. It was like he'd been taken out of the dirty, chaotic world he'd gotten used to and had somehow been transported back to simpler times.

"I'm sorry this is all a bit stiff and fussy," Nicola was saying. "But you know what it's like, we can't trust anyone, and . . . well, to tell you the truth, you're not the first kids to tip up here from the Tower of London."

Ed leaned forward. "D'you mean DogNut and his crew?"

"Yep. They came through here about, I don't know, three, four weeks ago. It's so easy to lose track of time. We were scared they might be spies or something, checking us out, with an idea to take over our patch, take what we've got here."

Ed laughed. "DogNut wasn't interested in any of that," he said. "He was happy at the Tower. Jordan Hordern, the guy in charge, doesn't even know this place exists. We've got a bloody great castle, the safest place in London, why would we want to move in here? No, DogNut was just looking for some friends."

"I know, I know." Nicola ran her fingers through her hair, untangling a knot. "But still people are suspicious. You can't blame them."

"No."

"And you turning up like this, it just adds to the rumors, the paranoia. Coming here with the same story—looking for someone."

"Well, we *are* looking for someone. Don't you believe me, then?"

Nicola touched his scar again. "I believe you, scary face."

Ed tried to ignore her. "So what happened to DogNut?"

"He tracked his friends down to the Natural History Museum. Definitely went over there; don't know what happened to him after that, though. We don't have much to do with those kids."

"So he found Brooke?"

"Is that the girl he was looking for?"

"Yes."

"Then, yes, he would have found her. As far as I know, she's still there."

"I can't believe it. After a year." Ed was curious to see what he felt about this. Brooke was a little like Nicola. A strong girl, not afraid to say what she thought. She'd come on to him and then backed off when his face was mutilated. He had a brief flare-up of emotion, remembering all this. And then nothing. He packed it all away. Too complicated to think about any of this now.

"She's one of the lucky ones, I guess," said Nicola. "A survivor."

"Yeah. And DogNut too!" Ed slapped his leg, happy for his friend. "I thought he'd given himself a crazy mission. Thought Brooke would be miles away or dead or, I don't know. Jesus, they must have made him so welcome he never wanted to come back to the Tower. The sly hound."

Nicola put a hand on his knee.

"So you're looking for two small boys and a girl who were trying to get to Buckingham Palace?"

"That's where we reckon they were headed."

"Funny thing is, Ed." Nicola gave him a knowing smile. "I think you know the guy in charge there as well."

"Do I?"

"Boy called David."

"David?"

"DogNut certainly seemed to know him. From back in the day."

Nicola occasionally tried to use slang, and it didn't sit

right, like she was trying too hard. It was wasted on Ed. He'd never been exactly street.

"It was a long time ago," he said. "I don't remember any David."

"Serious boy," said Nicola. "Acts a lot older than he is."

"Wait a minute." Ed was amazed. "Did he have a lot of kids with him who used to wear red blazers?"

"Still do."

"*That* David. Jesus. He's in charge at Buckingham Palace?"

"I'm afraid so."

"Do you have any dealings with him?" Ed asked.

"We have a sort of alliance with the palace."

"You guys are really organized." Ed laughed.

"We have to be," said Nicola. "Or we'd all be dead."

"So if you have dealings with David at the palace, then maybe you know whether Sam's friends ever made it there?"

"Sam?"

"Small Sam, the boy we're looking for."

Nicola looked thoughtful. "I do know that a group turned up from Holloway not long back. One of David's guys had found them, persuaded them to come to the palace. David made a big deal of them. How they were the 'greatest fighters in London.'"

"Yeah, that fits."

"It was a bit embarrassing for David, though, because he wound them up the wrong way and I don't think they stayed long."

"Why's that?"

"David's weird," said Nicola. "Not everyone takes to him. He lays it on a bit heavy and a lot of kids don't like it there, but he's trying to build up an army, so he's desperate to get more fighters. *Too* desperate. Like a sweaty boy at a party coming on too strong. He puts people off."

"What's he want an army for?" Ed asked.

"Wants to rid London of every oppo and unite all the kids."

"Oppo?"

"Is what we call grown-ups."

Ed put his head in his hands and sighed. "This is too much to take in right now."

They'd been very isolated at the Tower. Secure in their own little world. He'd had no idea that there was this whole other life going on out here, so close, if only they'd ever braved the no-go zone. It had become like the Middle Ages, when someone could spend their whole life in one village and never even visit the next one up the valley. Well, he'd crossed the mountains now and discovered not another village on the other side, but whole towns full of busy people.

Nicola stood up, tugged her sweater down automatically. "I think I can trust you," she said. "So let's go and talk to the Cabinet. I told them to get ready in the House of Lords."

"The Cabinet? Right."

Ed hauled himself up off the sofa. It wasn't the most comfortable piece of furniture he'd ever sat on, but he was tired and sitting down for a while had been bliss.

He walked alongside Nicola as they made their way back downstairs. She kept close to him, and he made no attempt to move away. In a different life he might have flirted with her. It was clear she liked him. But these days he didn't think about stuff like that. Boy-girl stuff. He kept himself to himself. Concentrated on what needed to be done. Girlfriends were a distraction. He didn't need anyone else to worry about. Couldn't fight with a girl hanging on his sword arm.

Besides, since he'd gotten his scar he'd lost all confidence in that department.

And yet . . .

No, Ed, put it out of your mind. Like Brooke.

Ryan was still there, sitting sprawled on the plush red benches of the House of Lords with his hunters. A sea of black leather. Thankfully they'd chained their noisy dogs up outside when they'd come in.

The rest of Ed's crew were there as well, comparing their wounds and reliving the day's events. There were also about ten of Nicola's kids. All three groups were sitting apart and chatting among themselves.

Nicola gave a quick roundup of what she knew and what Ed wanted.

"It was definitely them," said Ryan when she'd finished.

"Who?" Nicola asked, sitting down with her kids.

"The ones who rocked up at the palace. They was definitely from Holloway. That raggedy-assed kid in the disco coat, Jester, found them and brought them in like you said. About two weeks ago they all left in the night. David don't want no one to know about it. He's got a red face over that one. Everybody knows he's trying to fit up an army, and they was really good fighters is what I hear."

"Where did they go?" Ed asked.

"Natural History Museum is what I been told—same as

your man DogNut. Ain't heard nothing about them since. Is been well quiet over that way. With all that's going down these last days, we ain't been near the place."

Kyle settled back in his seat and leaned over toward Ed. "Seems you've got to take us on an outing to the museum, boss."

"Seems so."

A boy with a buzz cut and no front teeth stood up and called across the floor to Ed.

"Can I ask a question?"

"Fire away."

"Did you really come through the City of London?"

"Yeah. I wouldn't advise it, though."

"Did you know there were all these oppoes about?"

"No. Yes. Well, no, we knew there'd be more of them in there, knew it wasn't exactly going to be fun, but we had no idea just how bad it was going to be. No way did we expect all these new arrivals to be out on the streets in the daytime."

"I told you, soldier," said Ryan. "We don't even go in there."

"We weren't overjoyed about it," said Kyle.

"It'd be interesting to know what goes on there," said Buzz Cut. "Specially now with all these oppoes heading that way."

"So nobody round here goes into that part of London, neither?" said Kyle.

"No," said Buzz Cut. "The Aldwych, Holborn, that's about our limit. I mean, we sometimes get one of the Greens to come out, but you can never trust what they say."

"What do you mean?" Ed sat up straighter, something

tugging at his thoughts. "Who are the Greens?"

"This bunch of kids that live in St. Paul's Cathedral," said Buzz Cut. "They got some screwy religion, cult type thing going on. They used to send out what they called missionaries, holy rollers trying to convert other kids and take them back to join in their prayer meetings. Ain't seen one of them for a long while. Probably 'cause a couple of them faked it, came out as missionaries, and—what's the word? Deserted?"

"Defected," said Nicola.

"That's it," Buzz Cut went on. "We got an ex-Green here. Come out of St. Paul's singing hymns, done a bunk, moved in with David for a bit, and when he's found that's worse than St. Paul's, he's come here."

"Why do you call them the Greens?" Ed asked.

"They all dress in green," said Nicola. "It's part of their cult."

This wasn't good. Ed's brain was grinding, trying to make sense of this information. The facts were rearranging themselves into a new pattern.

"Who's in charge there?" he said. "Who runs the show?"

"Guy called Matt," said Buzz Cut.

Mad Matt. All this time he'd been there, at St. Paul's, just a mile away from the Tower. Ed felt sick. He'd gotten it all wrong. An image came into his mind of Sam and the Kid sitting in the pub at the Tower while he told them about the Lamb and the Goat. Memories came barging in. Matt coming out of the smoke with his visions and crazy ideas. Matt causing the boat on the Thames to sink. Floating off on a piece of wreckage. The kids at the Tower whispering about Sam and the Kid. Matt's wacky banner. Tish's friend Louise, slumped in the doorway, her hand cut off, her throat slashed. Blood on her green clothes.

Green like Tish, who he'd put in with Sam and the Kid in the Casemates.

Green.

They all dressed in green.

Shit. Shit. Shit. He was in the wrong place. Sam hadn't been heading for the palace at all. Tish must have been taking him to St. Paul's, whether he knew it or not.

Ed stood up. "I've got to go there," he said.

"Go where?" Nicola looked surprised.

"St. Paul's. I've made a mistake. The boy you were talking about—the Green, the missionary, the defector, whatever—I need to see him."

"Here we go again." Kyle clapped his hands. "The game is on."

48

The Kid was worried that Wormwood was going to get stuck. It was okay for him, scurrying around down here in the tunnels; he was skinny as a pin. The Green Man was a bigger deal, though, and had that round tummy on him. He had to slither along on his front. Now and then the Kid turned around to check on him. Shining the flame on him and making him squirm. He'd ferreted a slim candle out of his hairstack—not much bigger than the ones people used to put on birthday cakes. It was already burned down to a stub. But there was still just enough flame left in it to show him the fuzzy green naked skin of the man, his bulk filling the tunnel from side to side and top to bottom, his arms reaching out, long fingernails waving, stretched face leering at him, gums bright and shiny, little silvery-gray teeth.

The way his skin was pulled tight made him look like he was smiling the whole time as he shifted slowly along, inch by squeezed inch. The Kid was scared to stop and wait for him to catch up, though, because the damned bogeyman wasn't smiling. He was hungry. If the Kid let his guard down, he was going to feel those nasty sharp little teeth in his backside.

He just hoped they'd reach the end of this tunnel soon.

It had taken him ages to find a way out of the cellar, but he'd done it in the end, like he knew he would. These places usually had drains of some sort, and there had been one there, hidden under years of dust and rubble and God knows what bits and bobbins. He'd searched the floor, over and again on his knees, feeling with his hands, sniffing for fresh air currents, the reek of sewers, anything that would give him a clue to another way to escape this dungeon than by the big black iron-hard door.

He only had the one candle and he'd been saving that. So he worked in the dark, talking, talking all the long while, making sure the Green Goblin kept his mind off his supper and his eyes on the target. He wanted the troll to forget about ribs and loin and thighs and breast, and think instead about freedom and fresh air and a change of scenery.

Twice as he'd searched, the Kid had flicked on his Bic and, in the bright sudden flare of light, he'd seen that Wormwood had gotten up and was creeping across the floor toward him. Then the Kid would kick up a storm and roar and yell and threaten the bogeyman with bright fire and remind him that he was getting them both OUT OF THERE.

Then, grumbling and moaning and rubbing his swollen, aching belly, Colonel Bogey would shuffle off back to his bench and sit down again, arms at his sides, teeth bared, waiting.

The Kid liked to talk; he had a lot of words stored up in his head, every one he'd ever heard, it sometimes seemed, but he was running out of chat by the time he found the drain hole. Sensed it was there in the dark. He scrabbled and cleared the debris away. And then, just as his fingers found the metal bars, he felt hot breath on his neck, rolled quickly aside, and screamed blue nuns at Wormwood. Spun the flint on his lighter and there he was, crouching over him, dribbling.

"Can't you get it into your fat head?" he'd shouted, dancing with that hot lighter in his hand. "That if you eat me you will never be gone from this place?"

"I'm sorry," whined Wormwood. "It's not my fault. It's not me. It's the other. The falling star, a million years old, that's not me, how could it be? That's what you said. I'm Mark Wormold. I work for Promithios."

"We been over this a million times," the Kid protested. "I don't want no more excuses. I want you to fix on this: I am your Salvation Army. Now put those gnarly claws of yours to good use and dig this drain hole clear."

Wormwood had been obedient. He'd gotten to his naked knees and groveled and scratched away at the garbage until he'd cleared the grille that covered the hole. Just big enough to fit through. Only just.

The Kid had had a lot of experience of grilles like this. It was an old friend. Old and rusted. It was easy enough to smash it to smithereens with a wooden shelf he ripped from the wall. Then he slipped down to investigate. There was a short drop into a long brick-lined tunnel with cables running along the side of it.

The Kid had lit his candle then. Taken a good look-see, crawling on hands and knees like a newborn. Maybe once upon a time this had been a sewer, and then, as they made new sewers, these old tunnels found new uses. The Kid knew from experience that the ground under London was riddled with such tunnels, all now carrying cables and wires. He went far enough to check it wasn't blocked anytime soon, then scurried back for Wormwood.

Found him dangling down through the drain hole, upside down, arms out, fingernails combing the air. A dangling bogey.

"Hey, Struwwelpeter!" the Kid had snapped at him. "You wait for me and do as you're told."

"I'm stuck."

"No, you ain't. Go back up and then come down feet-first."

It was easier said than done, but done it was, eventually, and Wormwood had joined him in the tunnel.

Which is where they still were. Making slow progress. They struggled and sweated and scraped along, and the stink of the Green Man made the Kid want to throw up his guts.

His candle was about to burn out, and they had to find a way up soon or Wormwood would give in and just eat him and then die down here wedged in the tunnel like a toad in a drainpipe.

"Is this the way to work?" Wormwood asked.

"Come off it." The Kid started giggling. It was either that or start crying. "It's a wormhole for a worm."

"I was working somewhere," Wormwood went on. "Near here. Promithios. I had a white coat then. Not green. It was washed white. And at night I'd go home and tell stories to my boys and kiss my wife and watch the television. Is there still television?"

"No, sir. That's all gone," said the Kid. "The juice has run dry, old bean. Maybe one day it'll come back. Never used to like the old goggle-box myself, to tell you the God's own truth. There was too much in there. It used to set my poor head spinning, fill it up with words and pictures and the old sound and fury. I hear something, it goes right into my brain and sticks there, you see? Yeah? Sure you do. Once the words go in I can't rattle them loose. Granddad and Grandma, they said it wasn't good for me. TV. Said it overstimulated me. That was a fine big word, 'overstimulated.' That one stuck. There's a lot of useless words stuck in my head: 'testosterone,' 'Toblerone,' 'mallard,' 'affidavit.'. . . And sometimes the words get broken and mixed up with each other if I get overstimulated. Back then, with Granddad and Grandma, it was the worst thing to be, *overstimulated*. Did you used to watch the box with your childers, Mr. Worms?"

"Yes. Yes, we did. Me and my wife and the three boys. Those were happy times. All of us together."

"It's a long way from there to here," said the Kid. "And you can't get back there. No, sir. It's a long way from watching TV with the family to eating small fry like me. You need to join the dots. How did you end up down here playing the Minotaur?"

"They came to my workplace," said Wormwood. "I do remember that. All very hush-hush. That was the word they used, 'hush-hush.'"

"Hush-hush?"

"Yes. They came from the jungle, you see? Little brown men. It was my job to make sure they were healthy, to check them over."

"Who are you going on about now?" asked the Kid. "Am I supposed to know?"

"It hurts my head to answer your questions," said Wormwood. "These memories hurt. The past is a heaviness. Because, you see, something got inside me. Something spoiled everything I had. My home, my wife, my children, all gone. Something got inside me and made me do things. There are two of me. Like you said. There's Wormold and there's Wormwood. We're not the same."

"Change the record, Mr. DJ, that one's stuck."

"It was all my fault," said Wormwood.

"You got sick," said the Kid. "Wasn't only you."

"Oh, but I was one of the first."

"Tell me more about you and the boys and the lovely wife and Christmas 'round the Christmas tree, Wormy. Those are the bits I like."

"Yeah, that was nice, that's a happy memory. You see? We were working for the company. And it was all hush-hush. And the sickness got in us. The sickness made us do things. Hide things. We had another child. A girl. I've tried to forget her. She was twisted, you see? Didn't come out right."

"Now here's a new story," said the Kid. "Tell me about the poor twisted girl."

"She came out all wrong," said Wormwood sadly. "She wasn't alone. There were others. We were all working there. Hush-hush."

"Working where, old Wormster?"

"Promithios. I am Mark Wormold. I work for Promithios. I study tropical diseases. Parasites. How do you do? 'No, don't shake my hand, ha, ha.' That was my joke. 'You don't know what you might catch. Have you met the wife?' I'm Mark Wormold and I have a wife and three boys. We have a fourth on the way, a lovely girl. My wife always wanted a girl." Wormwood fell silent. All the Kid could hear was him snuffling and panting and wriggling along on his potbelly, fingernails scritch-scraping on the bricks. And then, after a long pause, he went on, sounding very sad and lost.

"But she came out wrong," he said. "We were all there, we all had children, and they all came out wrong. She'd be about fourteen now. It was hushed up, hush-hush. All hushed up. You know the only way to make it right?"

"Lay it on me, Daddy-o."

"To eat the world. To taste the flesh of the ones who aren't sick. The ones like you. That's what I hear them shouting at me. All of them up there. That we must eat the world and I must show them how. I try to tell them to keep it buttoned, but they won't shut up. Their chittering is in my head. They're louder now. Up there. The bugs. I tell them there's another way. But will they listen? No, because like me, they're two in one. I tell them there is a way. I tell them that good blood will force out bad, but they won't listen. All they want to do is eat the children."

"Not me," said the Kid. "We got a deal, remember? A cast-iron, copper-bottomed, blue-chipped mug of a deal. You can't eat me, buster balloon."

"No. No, I don't want to. You're right. I'm sorry. I want to talk to you about the old days, the good old days, the TV and the bedtime stories and the Christmas tree, my three boys, stars in the sky and the big green all around, back there with the bugs and the bats, thinking that was the whole world. Oh, yes. Things happened, but we got together and promised not to tell, and we raised the twisted children in secret. And . . . and everything went wrong. The sickness got in me from the start, I think, and it got in the bugs, and then it got in the men, and they came blinking out of the jungle, and the sickness came over the sea and it got in me, and I became the Green Man."

"You're losing me, Dr. Green. And I was already lost."

"It's important I remember. Good blood will force out bad."

"You know, Wormy," said the Kid, "you're really telling all this to the wrong person. I won't remember but one word of it and that'll be the wrong word. 'Toblerone.' I like the stuff about you and the boys and the stories. The other stuff . . . Save it for the judge. You and me, right now, we need to concentrate on getting the hell out of here."

49

W ell, I guess I'm just stupid," said the boy in the policeman's helmet. "I should have stayed at St. Paul's with Matt. All that food he's got there. It's a survivalist's dream come true."

"Where'd it all come from?" Ed asked.

"Maybe it was something to do with the government hoarding stuff when the disease started? Making sure they kept the City of London going, like in a war or something, you know?"

The boy, Bozo, had been telling Ed all about Matt's secret store of supplies, his "Tree of Life." Bozo was a couple of years younger than Ed, and the helmet he was wearing was several sizes too big for him so that it fell over his ears.

"Or maybe Matt was right," he went on. "Maybe it was a gift from the gods. But it's definitely what's keeping him going. I couldn't stick it any longer, though. 'Blah, blah, blah, the Lamb did this, blah, blah, blah, the Lamb did that, there will be endless weeping and sorrow, blah-di-blah-di-blah.'"

"But how do they protect it from grown-ups?" Ed asked.

"They built a wall, blocked up all the roads, so no oppoes can get close."

Bozo drew a circle on Ed's map with his finger, ringing the cathedral. The two of them were sitting on a great Gothic porch at the front of the Houses of Parliament. The rest of Ed's group were waiting nearby, all except for Adele, who was playing a game with some of the younger kids. Small children seemed to be drawn to her, and their game involved a lot of running up and down a long corridor and screaming. Seeing Adele like this, a blur of happy pink, it was hard to imagine that less than two hours ago she'd been smashing in the skulls of deranged sickos with her club.

The others were sitting eating the rations they'd brought with them. Nicola hadn't offered them any food and Ed hadn't asked for any. It wasn't up to her to feed every open mouth that tipped up on her doorstep. Food was precious. People fought over food. That's why Matt was on to such a good thing with his Tree of Life.

"Yeah," said Bozo. "Matt may be mad, but he in't stupid. Not like me. I could still be there, growing nice and fat on all that food or, even better, at Buckingham Palace. Yeah. Used to live there too. David's like Matt, got it all figured out—food, water, security. But like the moron I am, I came here. Now I get to vote on everything and listen to speeches and, you know what? It's nearly as boring as Matt's sermons. I'm just too stupid to look for something better."

"Yeah, okay." Ed tried to stop him from going on. "Can we stick to the cathedral? I need to get there, but there's grown-ups out on all the streets, and now you reckon there's a wall as well. Could we get over it?"

"If you knew the right spot, but you'd have to fight through oppoes all the way to get there. Matt's kids know the ways in and out, the barriers you can climb over, the buildings you can go through. You'd be chancing it going in blind, probably wind up as an oppo's breakfast. No. If you were cleverer than you looked, you'd go along the South Bank."

Bozo indicated the route on the map, running his fingers along the opposite side of the Thames.

Ed slowly shook his head. "It's a mess over there," he said. "Not somewhere we ever go. The fire turned it all upside down."

"It's not so bad. . . ."

A loud bark followed by an outbreak of snarling and yelping distracted the two of them. Ryan's hunting dogs were chained up nearby, one of his boys guarding them. Bozo was on gate duty this afternoon, which is why Ed had brought his team down there to talk to him.

Ryan's hunter soothed the dogs and looked over apologetically to where Ed and Bozo were sheltering from the rain that had just started to fall.

Ed returned his attention to the map. "Are you sure the South Bank's passable?"

"Yeah. It's the way to go," said Bozo. "No kids live in the ruins, so there's no oppoes around to prey on them. Unless they're still coming up from the south, it's usually pretty quiet over there. It wouldn't be too hard to get right the way along the river until you were opposite St. Paul's."

"I get it." Ed was now tracing the route himself. "Then we come back over one of the bridges down that way, but we'd still have to deal with the wall."

Bozo jabbed a finger at a line on the map. "Not if you use the Wobbly Bridge."

"Why the Wobbly Bridge?"

"It's one of their ways in and out. They've blocked it at the south end, but you can easily climb over the barricade. The cathedral kids go foraging over the river sometimes, for furniture and stuff, materials for the wall. There's still stuff there; it's not all completely burned out if you know where to look."

"So Matt's got the wall, what about other defenses?" Ed asked. "Does he have soldiers?"

"Doesn't everyone?"

"Yeah, I suppose. Are they any good?"

"Good enough. I mean, he's not big on fighting. With the Tree of Life, they hardly ever need to go outside the wall, but the cathedral *is* still surrounded by oppoes. That part of London is nuts."

"Yeah, don't I know it."

There were the stamp of boots and the rattle of metal on leather as Ryan brought his hunters out of the building. They'd been fed because they provided something useful. They were a combined security and messenger service for Nicola.

Ed stood up and slapped palms with Ryan. "You sure you don't want to come with us?" he asked.

"Nah, sorry, mate." Ryan hawked up a big gob of phlegm and spat it out onto the floor of the porch, then pulled down his mask. Ed realized with a jolt that it was made from a dried-out human face.

"I told you my dogs won't go in there," Ryan said. "And if my dogs won't go, I won't go."

"Fair enough."

Again Ed didn't blame him. It wasn't his fight.

"Can I ask you something, Ryan?"

"Yeah, what?"

"We saw a few grown-ups acting weird today. Standing really still with their arms stretched out, like choirboys who'd had their song sheets snatched away."

"Yeah, I know what you mean," said Ryan. "We seen some too lately. Remind me of the dogs. When a dog sees its prey, it goes all stiff and, like, raises one front leg, sticking its nose out." He mimed the action, tensed and alert. "Is called pointing. That's what they are, those frozen bastards, they're pointers."

Ed smiled. "Yeah, pointers. That does it for me." He looked over to where the rain was spattering the road. "You any idea what it's like out there now?"

"We just had a look from up top," said Ryan. "Seems pretty quiet. You going back into the badlands?"

"Looks like it."

"Good luck, soldier." Ryan gave a dark laugh. "I'll see you in hell."

50

"Okay, it's like this." Ed pulled his hood up to cover his head. "We've got to go back into the zone. But thanks to Bozo here we have a safer route. I won't pretend it's going to be any better than it was before, though. So if any of you want to duck out, I'll say it again, it's not a problem. I can't order any of you to do this."

"Can we just go?" said Adele, pushing past him. "You know, without thinking about it too much?"

"Yeah," said Macca. "We've come this far, we ain't gonna just abandon you now, are we, Ed? And on top of everything else we're going to get soaked. So the quicker we get this over with, the better."

Ryan's squad was out in the rain getting their dogs ready. The animals had gone into a frenzy of happy barking and tail wagging. Bozo opened the gates for them and watched as they trooped out.

"I wish they were coming with us," said Adele, standing in the rain. She wasn't dressed for bad weather, and her pink glittery clothes were already starting to look a bit sad.

"We'll be okay," said Will, and he walked out to join her. The rest of them followed. They said good-bye to Bozo at the gate, hunched their shoulders against the rain, and trudged out into the road.

As they rounded the end of the Houses of Parliament, Ed turned right, toward Westminster Bridge. Kyle fell in beside him.

"So, boss," he asked, "what do we do if Sam's there? Do we take him back to the Tower? Or we have to go all the way into town again?"

Ed adjusted his hood. "No more plans," he said. "We'll just take things as they come."

"Sounds good to me."

The bridge looked clear. There were no more sickos coming across for now.

"Hey," said Kyle, when they were about halfway to the other side. There were views both ways along the river and he had only just taken in where they were. "Does this make you feel all gooey inside?"

"What are you going on about?"

"This is close to where we first met, boyfriend." Kyle laughed and pointed upriver. "We got on the ferry over there. This could even be our anniversary."

It was true. The last time Ed had been up this way was a year ago, trying to escape the fire. They'd gotten bottled up at the next bridge along, Lambeth Bridge, and had been forced into a pitched battle with a horde of sickos who'd been driven there by the flames. Ed had found himself fighting alongside Kyle, who'd been armed with a garden fork. In the end they'd escaped downriver on a tourist boat, and he remembered with a stab of anger Matt causing it to crash into a bridge and sink.

He wondered how he was going to react when he saw Matt again. Wondered what he might be doing to Sam and the Kid. Ed had thought that the threat to Sam was from grown-ups, not children. He felt sick that he'd wasted half a day getting into town.

Matt. He'd been trouble ever since he got carbon-monoxide poisoning in Rowhurst. A big part of Ed wanted to just go in there and cut him down. Kill him on the spot.

He had to get there first, though, didn't he? It wasn't over yet.

They were exposed to all the weather could throw at them crossing the bridge. The others pulled on hats and caps and flipped up hoods to keep the rain off, but it trickled down their necks and slowly soaked their clothes.

"Beats washing them," said Kyle with a big happy grin. "We're using God's launderette."

Ed grunted and wiped water from his face. "Don't know how you can be so bloody cheerful."

"Hey," said Kyle, turning his own face up to catch more rain on it. "Life is good."

"Life is crap."

"This is the first shower I've had in over a year," said Kyle. "Washing don't seem so important now, does it?"

"Not if you don't mind stinking."

"Which I don't," said Kyle, and he gave a dirty laugh. "I don't have to worry about that no more, don't have to worry about nothing. Like using deodorant. And not just any deodorant. Oh no. You had to use the right deodorant, didn't you? If you didn't smell of the right deodorant, you'd be laughed at. Remember? Everything had to be right. You had to wear the right label jeans. I never knew which was the right label, did I? Changed all the time and I always seemed to get it wrong. 'Oh, Kyle, nobody wears Eckō jeans anymore, you loser.' Well, now I can wear whatever jeans I like and I can wear them every day if I want. 'Oh, Kyle, gross, you were wearing those jeans yesterday, you bum.' These days we got a better idea what's important. This is a much easier life."

"What d'you mean, life's easier? Are you nuts?"

"I never had days like this before," said Kyle. "This has been a fine day."

Ed made a dismissive noise, but Kyle ignored him and plowed on.

"Man, I was getting so bored at the Tower," he said. "This is good."

Ed couldn't hold it in. "It's been hell, Kyle," he spluttered. "We nearly all got killed, or didn't you notice?"

"Yeah, but we didn't get busted, did we?" said Kyle. "We knocked some heads. We *did* something. It was a blast."

"I don't see on what level you can count what happened today as fun," Ed protested.

"You see, that's where we're different, you and me," said Kyle. "Before all this I bet you was very happy."

Ed thought about this for a moment. "I suppose I was."

"Your life was well sorted, man. You had a nice family, a nice school, you was clever and good-looking, confident."

"I guess."

"Not me," said Kyle. "I was never happy. Felt like I was carrying a world of shit around on my back. That's why I say life's easier now. There's not so many decisions to make."

"It's like a bloody horror film, Kyle. What are you talking about?"

"No, hear me out, man. I weren't happy at all before all this. Life was confusing. I was a right miserable sod. Always in trouble, didn't get on at school, couldn't get my head around lessons, didn't see the point. Always behind. Trying to catch up. Well, not really trying that hard as it goes. Used to hang out with the losers, the troublemakers, the idiots. They didn't expect nothing of me. I felt like a zero. My mom always wanted me to do good at school. I let her down.

"I was okay at middle school, I guess. That wasn't so bad until eighth grade. We did tests, exams, you know? Then a lot of my friends, I realized they was cleverer than me, they was gonna do better at high school than me. I was okay at soccer and that, but never brilliant. I was good at art, used to like drawing battle scenes on giant sheets of paper with hundreds of little men, and tanks, and robots, and helicopters. It ain't easy drawing a helicopter. Teachers used to say why couldn't I draw something nice?

"The one other thing I was good at was fighting. That was what made things okay. I could batter someone and for a while I was the big man. Never lasted, though. Soon I was back to being a miserable loser. Then, when I went to high school, I couldn't get it on. Was behind in lessons even before they started. I was taken over by these black moods, man. Right down in the pit. Mom made me see a therapist.

"You're the first person I've ever told this to, Ed, and you were the sort of kid I hated at school, the sort I wanted to kill. And if you tell anyone else I saw a therapist, I will cut your head off and shove it up your ass. I mean it. Nobody at the time knew. But the thing was, Mom was right, I was depressed. I mentioned to a doctor once that I sometimes had really dark thoughts. You know. Of killing myself. A lot of kids do, I reckon. Or did. They don't really mean it, just want to, you know, like, DO SOMETHING. Shake things up. I used to have these dark fantasies of taking a samurai sword, or a machine gun, into school and mowing everyone down, all the clever kids, the smug bastards like you who never had to worry about nothing. I'd give them something to worry about. *Brap-brap-brap.* Then I'd blow myself up. Go out in glory. Be remembered forever. That'd show the world. Never did, of course, never would have, but I had these fantasies and they used to cheer me up.

"I couldn't ever settle, Ed. Felt uncomfortable in myself. Didn't know who I was. Struggled to read. Dyslexia. Well, that don't matter now, does it? The only books I could get into were war stories. True life stories. And I used to wish that there would be another war and I could be a soldier. I was jealous of the guys in the books, in World War Two, because their lives were simple. You're in the army. People tell you what to do. You go out there and do it. Simple. They feed you. They look after you. You're away from home. From all that *real life* crap. Your mom has a go at you, your girlfriend, you got an excuse—'Hey, I'm saving your ass here, leave me be.'

"War is easy. It's kill or be killed. You don't have to worry about all the annoying little things that go on in the world, back home—dealing with friendships, who likes who, who said what, putting up with my mom, who was depressed herself, to be fair, worried about money, and she took a lot of drugs. That whole boring, difficult, real life stuff, paying bills and buying the right clothes and learning crap. None of that matters in a war.

"I used to dream this was coming, a war or a big disaster, the zombie apocalypse, whatever. Then I could survive, be a hero, get a gun and hole up in a shack in the mountains, blasting away at anything that moved. I had a zombie survival plan all written up. Yeah. This was the simple life I dreamed of. I prayed that all this would happen someday. And you know what? My dream came true. Kill or be killed. Hunt for your food. Kill the enemy. Nothing else to worry about. Simple. I'm a fighter now, a good fighter, so people respect me. I got status, Ed, I got respect. And nothing to worry about. Let it all come down, I say. I don't want to go back to what them kids back there in Big Ben was doing—making life complicated. Boring. I just want to be able to go on doing what I'm good at—knocking sickos into the ground. I can make my mark. Show the world I'm a player."

"You really used to hate people like me?" Ed asked.

"Yeah," said Kyle. "And I bet you hated people like me."

Ed laughed. "Maybe."

"You were one of the clever, shiny ones that didn't have nothing to worry about. I was an ugly, spotty gonk. You've met me halfway, I guess, with that face you got on you now, but I bet, before, you had all the girls sniffing around you."

"Maybe."

"Maybe . . . yeah. Maybe, baby. But now everything's changed. You ain't so buff. I've got skills people need. I'm happy, you're depressed."

"You think so?" Ed asked, surprised.

"Takes one to know one," said Kyle. "I seen you, boss. You ain't always happy. You turn in on yourself. You got the darkness in there like me. Mine's shut away for now, but I know it could come crawling back up. But you, boss, you give in to it."

"Maybe." Ed wouldn't admit it to Kyle, but he did admit it to himself. There were bad memories inside him, and they poisoned his mood if he let his guard down. Too many nights he dreamed of setting fire to Jack's bed. Watching his best friend's dead body being eaten by the flames.

"Don't worry. I'm sticking by you, boss," said Kyle. "'Cause you're clever and because you accepted me. Didn't have to. From the start, though, you fought shoulder to shoulder with me and you fought well, best I ever seen, better than me even. You are a stone-cold killer, dude, and I respect that. We're brothers now, whether you like it or not. We've shared our secrets. I do wish you could be happy, though, man, like me. I sleep well at night. Never used to. Now—*bang*—the sun goes down and I'm in the land of nod till dawn. No interruptions.

"If all this hadn't happened what would I be doing now? I'd probably be locked up, or maybe I'd have finally done myself in. I'd be in trouble one way or another, though, that much I know. That much I *do* know for sure, brother."

"And this isn't trouble?" Ed asked. "What we've got now? A world of sickness and pain? Adults eating children? Children killing adults?"

"This? No way. This is fun!"

They were making good progress along the South Bank,

despite the destruction that lay all around them. The fire had ripped through the buildings, opening them up and tearing them down. Out of control, it had burned hot enough to crack concrete, to split brick and stone and bring everything tumbling down. In the worst-hit areas there were just the blackened skeletons of houses and offices, piles of rubble now thick with weeds and punctured by saplings, forcing their way up toward the sky as nature clawed back the city for itself.

Every now and then, though, they'd come to a street or a run of buildings that seemed hardly touched, little islands of order among the chaos. The big wheel of the London Eye was still standing, though it was smeared with black and spotted brown with rust. The main structure of the Southbank Centre—what had once been theaters, concert halls, restaurants, and galleries—was still there, a great dirty gray bulk, though the insides were gutted.

They saw a few sickos but hurried past them, eager to get on before it got dark. And night would come early today, as the sky was growing thick with storm clouds.

They came to Southwark Bridge and had to skirt around a big pile of fallen masonry. Will came over to Ed.

"Do you notice it?" he asked.

"What's that?"

"Up there." Will pointed out a sicko to Ed, one of the frozen ones, on top of the rubble. Ed had seen it, but it hadn't really registered. His brain had ceased to process them as a threat.

"What about it?" he asked.

"There's been one at every bridge," said Will.

"You sure?"

"Yeah." Will was smart, always looking, always thinking, spotting things others missed. Macca had better eyesight, but he never stopped to think about anything. Not like Will.

"I haven't seen them anywhere else, just at the bridges," he went on. "What are they doing, d'you think?"

"Ryan Aherne called them pointers. Like dogs."

"Dogs hear frequencies that humans can't," said Will.

"Yeah." Ed thought about this for a moment. "Ryan told me he couldn't bring his dogs this way," he said. "Something freaks them out. You think they can hear something we can't?"

"It's the same with girls, too," said Will.

"Is that right?" said Kyle.

"Yeah. Their hearing's better."

Ed remembered the strange noise that Adele and Hayden claimed they could hear coming out of the pointer that morning.

"Do you think the pointers are signaling or something?" he asked.

"Could be," said Will. "Something's attracting sickos from all over London. Could be the same thing that's scaring the dogs. A noise. Like a radio signal. Something that only sickos and dogs can hear."

"And girls," Kyle added.

"Only up close," said Will. "They're not getting the whole signal. I reckon it's like a network. And these pointers, they're like mobile-phone masts, boosting the signal, guiding the sickos in over the bridges."

"Sickos don't roll like that," said Kyle. "They're too dumb."

"Things are different in the zone," said Ed. "And we've seen something new today. Things are shifting. The sickos are getting organized."

51

It was carnage. Saif's war party didn't stand a chance. They were being engulfed by a greasy black tide of flailing, writhing flesh. From his lookout Shadowman couldn't hear anything, but he could see it all clearly enough through his binoculars. Once again he was watching a disaster play itself out in front of him, powerless to do anything to help.

When he'd first heard the cars in the distance, he'd gone out into the street and listened hard, not wanting to believe it. He'd clung on to the hope that he was wrong. He'd imagined it. It was something else. Not cars but distant thunder. This was too soon. Saif wasn't ready. *He* wasn't ready.

There was no doubt about it, though. What he was hearing was car engines. A sound that, until yesterday, he hadn't heard for over a year. How far away, though? They could have been miles away and the sound would have carried. They were the only thing making any noise in these silent, empty streets.

So Saif had stuck to his plan. Had put together a hastily organized revenge party, a posse, a lynch mob. Thinking they could charge in and sweep Saint George's army off the streets.

He hoped that Saif had put more soldiers into the attack than he'd first suggested. No way were twenty-five going to be enough, even with cars and weapons. How many troops did Saif have at IKEA, anyway? Shadowman had found it hard to get an accurate picture of the numbers as the place was so big, and the kids were spread out inside or had been working in the vegetable plots in the garage. He'd never seen them all together. Maybe twenty-five was all Saif had.

As he'd listened, the engine noise hadn't grown any louder. They weren't coming closer. Saif was probably searching the streets for the Fear. Shadowman could wait for the cars to find their way here or he could follow Saint George. One way or another, he had to try one last time to warn Saif of the danger he was in.

In the end he'd decided to stick with the Fear. Saif had to find them eventually, and he might never make it to the tire center at all.

Shadowman set off at a steady jog. He knew the way to find the strangers quickly.

Follow the sentinels.

He passed one. Another. A third one took him to the main road. And then he spotted Stumpy. He'd taken up a new spot at the junction where two roads met. Arms out, flies crawling all over him.

Shadowman had run on. It hadn't taken him long to catch up with the stragglers, still being herded along by Bluetooth and his little gang. They'd gotten separated from the main group, going too slow to keep up. Saint George was in a hurry today. Shadowman hadn't wanted to get into a fight, so he'd skirted around them and it had taken him a few minutes to get his bearings. Again it was the sentinels who'd helped him. He found another row of them strung out along a different side street, feeding into the main road. Shadowman sped up and finally got a glimpse of the Fear. A solid mass, completely blocking the way ahead.

From street level it was hard to get any real sense of their numbers, and Shadowman looked around for some kind of vantage point from where he could get a better idea of what they were up to and keep a lookout for Saif.

And then he'd spotted it: a tall crane standing over a long-deserted construction site. That would be perfect. As long as there weren't any strangers nearby.

He gave the main group a wide berth—easier said than done, as there were outliers all the way around and a network of sentinels. It had taken him twenty minutes of hard running, but he'd eventually made it to the construction site without getting into any trouble.

There was a solid wooden fence all the way around too, plastered with sunny, computer-generated pictures of the apartments, shops, and offices that had been planned for the site, plus the inevitable graffiti.

It was easy enough to climb over the fence and jump down into the muddy patch of ground on the other side. It had started to rain, and there were already soupy puddles forming.

Shadowman scooted over to the crane and looked up. It was a good ninety feet high, but there was a ladder at the back, built into the steel girder structure.

Hand over hand he'd climbed, thanking God that he'd never been scared of heights, because otherwise it would have been really scary up there. In no time at all the ground seemed a very long way away, and when he'd gotten to the top it felt like he was ninety miles high rather than ninety feet. He was God, up in the clouds. The rain fell down past him in long silver rods.

He easily broke into the crane's cab and was grateful to be out of the rain. He slipped off his backpack, pulled out his binoculars, and quickly took stock of the situation.

There were views right out across London from up here. To the north he could see the blue box of IKEA, to the left of it the high arching span of Wembley Stadium. Closer to hand he could see the tire center and the train tracks running behind it. Over to the northeast was the dark green expanse of Hampstead Heath. Then, turning south, he could see the labyrinth of roads and buildings that crowded their way right into the center of town. From here it looked so close. He could walk to Buckingham Palace in a couple of hours, maybe less.

Then he'd looked down and smiled.

He'd managed to get ahead of Saint George without realizing it and saw that they were advancing toward the construction site along a main road that ran roughly north to south. They would go right past him. He couldn't have chosen a better spot if he'd tried. Except that it struck him now that he was not in any position to warn Saif.

Sod it.

Saif wouldn't listen to him anyway.

Shadowman had done his best. He'd tried. Maybe Saif would see the Fear and realize his mistake. Back off. Shadowman looked at them; they filled the road like a vast herd of cattle. Even a jerk like Saif must see that you couldn't take on that crowd with only twenty-five kids.

Watching the Fear from up there in the sky was like studying some complex organism under a microscope. When you concentrated, you could see a rigid order. There, at the front, was the central core of grown-ups, moving steadily along, huddled together in a dense knot, Saint George at the heart of it. In a looser bunch around them were other strangers, and there, spreading out like tendrils along the side streets behind, and to the sides, were the sentinels. The whole thing was like a great dark star or a comet going past, trailing lines of dust. He could see that the sentinels were constantly shifting now that the Fear were on the move. Those at the ends of the tendrils would break away and walk along to the next sentinel in line, take their position, and bump them on, with a constant ripple effect. They were a zombie relay team. None of them was left behind.

Just as an octopus uses its sensitive tentacles to find out about its surroundings, Saint George was doing the same. It made him ten times deadlier.

And then Shadowman had noticed that there were still newcomers arriving, being drawn in down the long arms and making their way doggedly toward the central mass, so that the Fear were constantly growing. Saint George was sucking in every stranger in London.

The dark star had a satellite. There was Bluetooth's

group, dropping farther and farther behind the others. There were maybe thirty of them, including Bluetooth and his side-kicks, and they shambled in the middle of the road. Saint George's group was packed tighter, so it was still hard to judge how many of them there might be. Could be as many as two hundred of them, Shadowman thought, and growing all the time.

Finally, in the far distance, he'd spotted the cars. Five of them, crisscrossing the streets, going too fast to be methodi-cal, too fast to be careful. Which was why they hadn't caught up yet. He'd watched them stop to attack a sentinel. Then, after a while, they'd appeared to get the idea and had advanced down one of the tendrils directly toward Bluetooth's group. Shadowman had trained his binoculars on them and watched as they'd raced nearer.

Two pickup trucks, two big 4x4s like the Lexus, and there was Saif, standing up in the back of a yellow, open-topped sports car of some sort. He had a spear in his hand and a grin on his face, a barbarian chieftain in his chariot, a harpooner on the high seas.

They'd smashed into Bluetooth's group, except Bluetooth and his gang had quickly dispersed, leaving the sick and old unguarded. Saif made short work of them. The cars ran them down, the kids in the back of the pickups firing crossbows, jabbing with spears, and swinging clubs. Saif himself had speared two sick old fathers as his car passed them.

Then the motorcade stopped and the kids jumped out, laid into the surviving strangers with a wild, out-of-control frenzy.

It took them less than five minutes to kill all the strangers, and Shadowman had watched as they'd danced in the street, hugging and high-fiving. He could see them shouting in triumph, could imagine what they were saying—that Shadowman had been a twat, a coward, a noob. That these zombies were just like all the rest.

Only they hadn't killed a single one of Bluetooth's party, hadn't even noticed them slipping away. All they'd done was kill the weakest and feeblest of the Fear. Saved Saint George the trouble of doing it himself.

This wasn't good. It would give Saif a new and totally unfounded confidence. Shadowman's only hope was that Saif would think that he'd killed all the strangers and return to IKEA.

It soon became clear, however, that that wasn't going to happen. Saif's gang mounted up and set off south again, following the line of sentinels, cutting down a couple as they passed.

Shadowman had been distracted. He'd taken his attention off the main group and, as he swung his binoculars around, there was no sign of them. Impossible. How could two hundred adults simply disappear? But it was true. The incoming lines of sentinels all now met at a large roundabout where only about twenty strangers remained. Standing waiting in the center, among some shrubs and low trees.

What the hell had happened to the rest of them?

"Dammit, where are you, George?" he said, scouring the streets near the roundabout, but apart from the network of sentinels that clearly spread out from this point, and the handful in the center, there was absolutely no sign of the Fear.

And now Saif's cars were hammering down the main road.

Shadowman realized that Saint George had picked his spot well. There were crash barriers circling the roundabout, and as the cars arrived, they found that they couldn't run the strangers down. One of the 4x4s tried and got stuck on a barrier. The other cars uselessly circled the roundabout, taking potshots at the strangers sheltering among the trees, like Apaches around a wagon train in an old cowboy film. The kids from the crashed car got out and called to their friends, and the other cars parked alongside.

"No, you morons," said Shadowman, grinding his teeth. "Can't you see it's a trap? Stay in your cars. Drive away. Leave them."

The rest of the kids got out. Shadowman could see that they were laughing, jeering at the strangers in the center of the roundabout, who were cowering away from them. Saif took a crossbow from another boy and fired it, still laughing, still thinking it was all a big game.

And then Shadowman swallowed hard.

"Oh shit."

A great dark mass was suddenly rushing in from all sides, from every road that led to the roundabout, totally swamping Saif's gang.

It was as unstoppable as a tsunami.

Saint George's army was going in for the kill.

Soon all was confusion. Shadowman couldn't tell what was going on; the strangers completely covered the roundabout and the area around it. The kids had disappeared under a seething mass of bodies.

He could picture it down there, the heat of the grown-up bodies, the raw sewer stench of them, the bowel-emptying fear as the kids realized what was happening. Realized they were hemmed in, with no room to maneuver or swing their weapons. The agony as hands reached for them, teeth latched on to them . . .

"Get in the cars," Shadowman urged them. "It's your only hope. Get in the bloody cars and get out of there."

And then he saw one car moving, a silver 4x4 with blacked-out windows crawling hideously slowly through the forest of bodies. The sheer press of flesh was making it difficult to get up any speed. Shadowman could see strangers battering it with captured weapons.

"Come on, there must be more of you," said Shadowman, desperately raking his binoculars over the battleground. "Come on."

And then one of the pickups was moving. Again like a car driving slowly through floodwater.

"Go, go, go. . . . Get out of there! You can do it! Go on!"

The 4x4 was at the edge of the mob. The pickup suddenly accelerated and got in behind it. They were going to do it. They were going to get away.

The 4x4 broke free, went tearing up the road. Impossible to know who was in it or how many.

But what about the pickup truck? He saw a boy and a girl in the back of it, screaming. The girl was pulled over the edge and sank into the filthy press of bodies. The boy was clinging on. He looked okay.

No.

Shadowman gasped as the car was toppled over.

That was it. The rest of the kids had no chance. No chance at all. It was all over.

Shadowman was weeping with frustration. He couldn't believe that because of Saif's arrogance and stupidity he'd had to watch another massacre. Another hopelessly outnumbered and outgunned bunch of kids being overwhelmed and slaughtered like pigs. He swore at Saif for putting his people into this danger, for not listening. . . .

For losing.

Idiots. Beaten by strangers.

And then he felt a cold stab of guilt. For a second he had been proud of Saint George, proud of *his* strangers, how good they were.

The mob was feeding. He recognized the signs. Picked out Saint George holding a head in the air as if it were the World Cup.

They were getting better every day. This level of planning and order was terrifying. The way Saint George had seemed to know the cars were coming and had laid a trap. Had hidden all those mindless freaks in the nearby buildings. And he'd done it fast.

Like a swarm of ants. A million individuals forming one single unit with one single mind. That was what they looked like from up here. A swarm of ants. How could that be? Just days ago they'd been a disorganized rabble, with no way of communicating with each other. What had changed?

He couldn't answer any of these questions right now. The

thing was, Saint George was leading a proper army southward. Shadowman had been struck by how close to the center of town he was. If the Fear kept up this pace, they could be at Buckingham Palace before the morning.

All those kids in town. Grown lazy. Thinking they'd gotten rid of all the strangers. How would they cope if Saint George turned up on their doorstep? Oh, they could stay indoors, safe behind the palace walls, but how would they eat? And what would happen if they foolishly sent troops out to deal with the new threat?

Not just David and his kids, but the ones at the museum; at the Houses of Parliament. Even John and his pirates at the squatter camp. They were kids like him. They were all at risk.

No. Saint George had to be stopped somehow, before he became unstoppable.

It didn't take the strangers long to finish feeding. After only a few minutes they were on the move again, leaving behind a wash of blood across the road, littered with torn clothing and bones. Even the dead strangers had been eaten. Nothing was wasted.

Nothing.

Except . . .

There.

Could it be?

The pickup truck was on its side, smoke coming from the engine. The other pickup truck sat there with its doors open. The sports car was empty. The second 4x4 was untouched, though, and Shadowman was sure he could just make out the shape of someone sitting inside it. Was it possible that one of the kids had gotten in there and the strangers hadn't been able to get to them? In their drive to keep moving had they simply left them behind?

They could be wounded. They could need help.

Shadowman had to see. If he could save just one kid . . .

He packed up his gear and climbed back down the ladder. It was raining hard now and it made the rungs slippery and dangerous. His heart was pounding. His head ached. His injured ribs felt like they were digging into his lungs. Every cut and bruise on his body was complaining.

He tried to go too fast and was nearly at the bottom when he slipped, wrenching his right knee. He swore. That was all he needed. It sent shooting pains up his leg.

"You bloody moron," he cursed himself. "Go more carefully."

He slithered down the last few dripping rungs and winced as he jumped to the ground. He could walk okay, but it hurt like a bastard and would slow him down. Jesus, he was becoming just one big mess of wounds.

He limped across the construction site, the rain beating down on his head, and this time it was much harder climbing over the fence. What with the rain and his desperation and his throbbing knee.

He hobbled on toward the roundabout. The first flash of lightning lifted up the sky, and as he got to the car a few seconds later, it was followed by a rolling clap of thunder. He peered in the car window, wiping away the rain that poured down the glass. There was definitely someone there. A boy.

"Open up!" he shouted. The boy didn't move. Shadowman

tried the door. Locked. He looked around for something to smash the window with and saw a baseball bat lying under the sports car. He fished it out and swung it at the window, but it bounced off without doing any damage. So he tried the butt end, jabbing it at the window. After a couple of tries it shattered and a shower of glittering shards tinkled into the road.

"Are you all right?"

The boy was sitting bolt upright, face white, his fingers gripping the steering wheel. Terrified.

Shadowman recognized him as one of the gang who'd been shooting at the mother from the footbridge.

"Are you okay?" Shadowman leaned over and gave him a shake. The boy slowly toppled toward him, revealing that his neck on the other side had been torn out.

He'd made it into the car only to lock the doors on his friends and die.

What a waste of time. What a waste of a life. What a stupid, bloody waste.

Shadowman pulled his cloak around himself to keep the worst of the rain off and limped over the roundabout in the direction that Saint George had taken. It was back to this, following the Fear and watching them kill. How long was this going to go on?

He'd been walking for a couple of minutes, wondering if his knee was going to hold out, when he suddenly stopped and swore into the rain.

Moron.

The car.

He could drive it. Take the weight off his knee. He'd be

safer in a car, more mobile and, let's face it, drier. Okay, so he'd never driven one before, but how hard could it be with no other vehicles on the road?

He turned around, setting his face into the driving rain as a lightning flash ripped across the sky, turning the road brilliantly white, picking out a group of strangers coming toward him. Fast and purposeful. The father at their head was wearing a blue business suit, a mobile-phone earpiece sitting on the side of his warty head.

It was Bluetooth and his little gang. He'd forgotten all about them.

Moron, moron, stupid bloody moron . . .

He slipped his crossbow off his back and fired a bolt. Didn't wait to see if he'd hit anything. Just turned and started jogging, his knee exploding in pain with every footstep.

He couldn't get to the car now. All he could do was try to run.

Run for his life.

52

It was officially called the Millennium Footbridge, built to celebrate the start of another thousand years, for a city that was already nearly two thousand years old. A beautiful, architecturally daring new way to get across the river. A suspension bridge with the supporting cables out to the sides rather than over the top. It linked the City of London with the Tate Modern art gallery on the other side. Mr. Rosen, a teacher at Rowhurst, Ed's school, had been obsessed with modern architecture and was always bringing boys up to town to show them stuff: the Thames Barrier, the Lloyd's building, the Gherkin.

And this—the grandly named Millennium Footbridge.

Only everyone called it the Wobbly Bridge. When it had first opened, so many people had tried to cross it at the same time it had set up a rhythm that made the bridge vibrate and wobble. Mr. Rosen had loved telling the kids that story, had even taken them to see the Albert Bridge, farther up the Thames, where there was still an old sign that ordered soldiers from the nearby barracks to break step when crossing. They weren't allowed to march in time, because the vibrations could set up a shock wave, like an earthquake, that could bring the bridge tumbling into the Thames.

There weren't enough of them today to do any damage to the Wobbly Bridge. Only six of them were crossing it. Bozo had been right. It had been much easier getting here along the South Bank. Any sickos they'd seen along the way they'd easily avoided, and it was only when they'd gotten to the bridge that they'd needed to use their weapons.

There had been a small knot of sickos around the barricade at the southern end, staring dumbly at it. It had been no sweat getting rid of them. Ed hadn't even joined in the fight. He and Kyle had stood back and let Hayden take charge. Let her gain some experience. She'd led the attack well. She and Adele, Macca, and Will had dealt with the sickos quickly and efficiently, clearing the way so that they could climb over the barricade.

Ed was relieved that the journey back had been so much less stressful than the journey into town. It was going to be easy from here. There was a walkway from the north end of the bridge leading right up to St. Paul's. The cathedral looked impressive, with storm clouds overhead, its white stones under the great gray dome lit up every now and then by flashes of lightning.

The storm was right on top of them. Rain thrashed the surface of the river, which frothed and foamed beneath their feet.

Ed urged the kids on. They were so close and it had been a long day. Whatever else they could expect when they got to the cathedral, at least it would be dry inside.

"But there's one rule," he shouted above the noise of the wind whining in the metal struts of the bridge. "We don't kill kids. Whatever happens, we don't kill kids. That's not our way. If we start killing each other then we're the same as the grown-ups. We might as well try to catch the disease and become sickos ourselves."

He stopped shouting, remembering the girl he'd killed the other day. Tish's friend. That had been different, though, hadn't it? It was an accident. He hadn't seen her clearly in the dark and she was halfway dead anyway. . . .

At least that's what he told himself.

And Matt.

Well, his desire to kill him had gone away as quickly as it had arrived.

Matt wasn't worth it.

"My God!" Hayden, who had been leading them over the bridge, stopped in her tracks.

"What is it?" Ed shouted, his hand going to his sword.

"Look at that. . . ." She was pointing at something on the north bank. Ed squinted through the rain, not sure what he was looking for, and then realized with a jolt that he'd been looking at it all along without registering it. What he'd thought was a pile of wet rocks or rubble, part of Matt's defenses, was in fact sickos. A huge, tightly packed mob of them, their clothes black with grease and slick from the rain, their bald heads like pebbles on the shoreline. Ed was reminded of a herd of seals, packed together, too many to count. They were clustered around the end of the bridge, barely moving.

"Holy crap," said Kyle.

"Can they get onto the bridge?" asked Adele, coming close and standing right next to Ed, as if he might offer some protection from this army.

"If they could, they'd already be here," Ed answered her. "For now it looks like the defenses are holding. They're not clever enough to climb the barriers or pull them down. Remember when we were going along there this morning? How the bridges fly over the roads when they reach the riverbank? It looks like this bridge is the same. They can't get up to it."

The sky turned white and empty as lightning flared across it. It lit up the heaving mass of bodies. For a brief moment Ed caught sight of a blur of lumpy faces, staring eyes, wet mouths. At least the rain was damping their stink down. A deafening clap of thunder came hard on the lightning. Felt like it was right inside their heads.

"Let's hurry," he said, and the others didn't need to be told. They ran on to the end of the bridge and passed over the sickos. There was a familiar noise coming from them, a rhythmic rattling, clicking sound, and Ed saw that a lot of them, mainly those nearest the barricades, were hitting stones together or sticks or bits of metal they'd picked up.

"They're a right banging outfit," said Kyle.

"This is one weird day," said Macca, coming up fast behind Ed. "Keep moving, man."

Ed took one last look at the inhuman percussion orchestra and sprinted up the walkway toward . . .

Toward what?

53

Sam was still sitting on his throne. He was half asleep, drifting in and out of waking dreams. He'd lost all sense of time. He just wanted this to be over. The music had gotten inside him, so that he couldn't tell the difference between his own heartbeat and the thumping of the drums. His eyes were misty from the smoke. He was seeing things, shapes forming and re-forming. He had no idea what was real anymore.

And still Matt read from his book. . . .

". . . Then I looked, and there before me was the Lamb, seated on His throne, and with Him were those who had His name written on their foreheads. And I heard a sound from heaven like the roar of rushing waters and like a loud peal of thunder. The sound I heard was like that of harpists playing their harps. And they sang a new song before the throne and no one could hear the music of the song except those who had been redeemed from the earth. . . ."

At this, the musicians found fresh energy and played louder. How were they keeping it up? Hour after hour they clattered on. Sam had seen a couple get too tired to keep going, and their places had been taken by other kids, but most of them had been at it as long as he'd been sitting here.

Matt waved his hands, urging them to play louder still.

"Your music must drown out the storm!" he yelled as outside the thunder rolled across the sky. "Let the Lord know that Wormwood is doing his duty!" Matt wailed. Although he was trying to sound like an adult, he had the croaky, pinched, slightly squeaky voice of a teenager whose voice was breaking. "The Goat is being beaten; there is a great battle taking place; we must help the Lamb. I need more. Where are the trumpeters?"

Sam turned his head on his aching, stiff neck and saw even more musicians settling down in the choir stalls. It looked like all the kids in the cathedral who could play the trumpet were joining in, as well as two extra drummers.

Matt was raging again, like a kid in a bad school play.

"The smoke of the incense, together with the prayers of the chosen, went up before God from the angel's hand. Then the angel took the censer, filled it with fire from the altar, and hurled it on the earth; and there came peals of thunder, rumblings, flashes of lightning, and an earthquake. Then the seven angels who had the seven trumpets prepared to sound them. . . . *Sound them now!*"

The trumpeters blasted out a ragged fanfare, thunder boomed overhead, and then, almost as if it had been rehearsed, the big doors at the end of the cathedral burst open and a flash of lightning revealed six kids standing there in shining armor. In the center, his mortuary sword raised in his hand, his scar lit livid, was Ed.

The musicians were so surprised they all stopped playing at once, and there was silence in the cathedral for the first time since Sam had arrived.

He stood up from his throne and cheered.

"Sit back down," Matt hissed.

"Sod off," said Sam, throwing off his robes and running down the aisle.

"Stop him!" Matt yelled, but nobody seemed to know who this command was aimed at. Nathan and his guards were all gathered around Matt near the throne. The kids in chairs just sat there and watched the show.

"Ed!" Sam ran straight up to Ed and threw his arms around his waist. "I knew someone would come," he said, tears pouring down his face and mingling with the water that was dripping off Ed.

Ed gave Sam a quick reassuring hug, took the garland of leaves from his head, and tossed it away.

"Where's the Kid?" he asked, and the thunder crashed like an exploding bomb.

54

Shadowman was moving barely faster than a walk. His knee was on fire, and the muscles in his right leg were cramping. He wasn't sure he could go on for much longer.

But Bluetooth and his gang wouldn't give up.

They just kept coming.

Shadowman had kept well clear of Saint George and the main body of the Fear, avoiding any road where there were sentinels. He'd made so many switches and turns he wasn't even really sure where he was anymore, and the storm had made it black as night, even though he reckoned it couldn't be much later than about five o'clock. The rain was belting down on the road, which made it even harder to see anything. He hoped that he was heading roughly south, because the only thought he had in his head was to somehow make it back to the palace before Saint George got there.

Every few minutes the pain would get so bad he'd have to stop and check whether Bluetooth was still on his tail. And, every time, there he was with his pals, tramping through the rain. Shadowman would wait just long enough to get his breath back and for the pain to dim slightly—once he'd even risked grabbing some painkillers from his pack—and then he'd reload his crossbow, an agonizing process with his bad knee, and fire a bolt at his pursuers before setting off again, never sure if he was hitting anything. He thought there were perhaps fewer of the strangers on his tail than when he'd started, but it could just be wishful thinking. Whether he'd killed any or not, there were still at least ten of them and, in his weakened state, with his bruised ribs and his wrenched knee and his exhaustion, he couldn't risk those odds in a hand-to-hand fight, especially as Bluetooth still had the captured machete and a couple of the others also had weapons of some sort.

Old-school strangers, the dumb sort, the ones who wouldn't know one end of a sword from the other, even if it was sticking in their guts, would have been easy meat. He could have waited and then taken them on.

Not this group, though.

He stopped and turned, grunting with the effort.

One of the strangers was pulling ahead, younger and fitter than the others. Hungry. Desperate. Eager to catch up with Shadowman now that he'd stopped again. Shadowman slung the crossbow over his shoulder and slipped his own machete from its sheath.

Maybe this was the way to do it. If he could string them out, split them up, wait for the fastest ones to break ranks, he might be able to pick them off one by one. They might be cleverer than most strangers, but they weren't as clever as he was.

It was a tiny plan, but it was still a plan.

The danger, of course, was letting the rest of them get closer at the same time.

Oh well, at least, if nothing more, it gave him another few seconds to rest his knee. The young father came closer, leaving the rest of his gang farther behind.

"Yes, come on, here I am. . . ."

The father was unarmed but looked strong and determined, breathing through his mouth. The rain was making his pale, swollen face look mushy, as if the skin was dripping off.

Shadowman let him come right up until he was in reach of the machete and then ducked down and swiped the blade at his ankle. He didn't need to kill him, just put him out of the race. The father hissed and stumbled sideways, hitting the ground with a splash.

One down.

Shadowman turned and limped off. Jesus, his knee hurt. He wondered if he'd ever be able to walk again after this. The rest of the pack was frighteningly close. He would have to force himself to speed up a little if he wanted to try that trick again. He could hear their footsteps behind him. Bare soles as hard as leather slapping on the wet ground.

55

should have killed you a year ago, Matt." Ed's voice was
cold and flat. "On the boat, when I had the chance. And I
should kill you now, but I gave an order that no kids would
be hurt. You're bloody crazy, you know that? What are you
doing farting about in here with all your made-up religious
crap when all hell's breaking loose outside? I mean, have you
seen it? Have you seen what's out there? There's an army of
sickos surrounding this place."

"They can't get in," said Archie Bishop.

"They will eventually," Ed snapped. "There's too many
of them."

They were sitting at a round table in a little wood-
paneled room built into the wall of the cathedral behind the
choir stalls. It was one of Matt's private rooms.

"The Lord will protect us," said Archie.

"No, He won't, you jerk."

"The Lord protects those who protect themselves," said
Kyle.

Matt's security, completely taken by surprise, had done

nothing. Ed's crew had stormed down the aisle toward the throne with such an air of menace and pent-up violence that Nathan and his guards had hesitated, not wanting to risk a fight here in the cathedral that they had no sure chance of winning.

Ed had been so angry he'd been fully prepared to ignore the order he'd given and cut Matt down there and then. But Matt had ducked behind Nathan, who at last drew his own sword. Ed had glared at him, and Nathan had instantly lowered his sword, terrified.

Sometimes it helped having an ugly scar disfiguring your face, and when that scar was backed up by a genuine berserk fury, only a very brave or a very stupid kid would stand in his way.

Nathan was neither. These intruders were street-hard, dripping wet, and armed to the teeth. In the end Matt had been the one to tell his troops to stand down. The fact that Ed had put a sword point to his throat helped more than a little.

Everyone had then started shouting at once, until Matt had suggested that they go to his rooms to talk. So it was that Ed, Kyle, and Sam were sitting across a round table from Matt, Archie Bishop, and Nathan in something like peace and quiet, lit by several church candles that flickered and danced in the drafts.

They'd left Hayden in charge of the rest of Ed's team, who were drying themselves around a smoky grille while the cathedral kids talked excitedly among themselves, nudging each other and pointing toward the new kids.

"We're doing all right here," said Archie. "If you can believe that."

"I know." Ed was trying to hold his anger back. "I know all about your secret stash, your Tree of Life, or whatever the hell you bloody call it. You always were a little chunky, Archie, but just look at you now. You've grown fat while everyone else in London is starving."

"Yeah, all right," said Archie, blushing. "You don't have to get personal."

"I'll get bloody personal if I want to, Archie!" Ed shouted. "You bastards have been kidnapping little kids."

"We didn't kidnap Sam," said Matt. "He chose to come here."

Ed looked at Sam. "Well?"

"I didn't choose to come here," Sam said, wide-eyed at the cheek of it. "I mean, they rescued us, we were stuck in this tube station and they got us out, but I didn't know what was here; if I'd have known I'd never have come. Specially after what they said about the Kid."

"Okay." Ed stared Matt down. "Is anyone going to tell me where he is?"

"The Kid, as you call him, is important to us," said Matt. "You wouldn't understand."

"Try me."

"They killed him, Ed." Sam's voice was very small and quiet.

Ed jumped up from the table, knocking his chair over, and launched himself across the top, going for Matt's throat. Matt managed to scramble out of the way, and Nathan got up to help him. In a moment Kyle had come around the other side and was standing over Nathan with his ax.

"Stop," said Archie. "We don't need this."

Ed ignored him. "Is that true?" he snarled at Matt, climbing off the table. "Have you killed the Kid?"

"No," said Matt calmly. "I haven't killed him. None of us have."

"They're lying!" Sam shouted. "They did. They took him away; they said they were going to sacrifice him; they said he was this, like, demon thing, said he was the Goat, that he played tricks on us. Him there." He pointed a shaking finger at Nathan. "He took him away, to a place they called the Abyss, under the food place. They said he was going to be sacrificed there."

Ed advanced on Nathan, who backed away.

"Is this true?" he said.

"Sort of," said Nathan. Ed raised a hand to hit him.

"Stop it," Archie said again. "Look, Ed. Let me explain." He had a quick whispered conversation with Matt, who at first looked cross but eventually nodded. Archie then addressed the room. "Everyone except me and Ed should just leave, okay? Before there's a fight. I want to talk to him alone."

Ed thought about this. Archie had always been more sensible than Matt. He didn't hide behind twaddle and bullshit. He knew that if Matt and Nathan stayed in here, sooner or later he was going to attack one of them and do some real damage, if Kyle didn't beat him to it. The important thing was to find out exactly what had happened to the Kid.

"Okay," he said. "Everyone else out."

Kyle protested, but Ed convinced him that he'd be okay, and the others all filed out.

Now there were just the two of them left in the room. Ed and Archie. Outside, the storm was passing away. The thunder was just a distant rumble, but the rain was still hissing on the walls and the wind moaned at the windows.

"I know how this looks," said Archie.

"Yeah. It looks bad. Don't see how it can be any other way, Archie."

"Maybe Matt *is* mad," said Archie. "I can say that, now he's gone."

"Is that meant to be an excuse?" Ed shook his head. "Just tell me, Archie, what is going on?"

"A few months ago we found this sicko," said Archie. "He wasn't like the others. There's a strange energy around here. Matt says it's spiritual, the power of God. Maybe he's right. How do I know? But we're at the center of it here, or near the center anyway. Even if you don't believe in any religion, or stuff like that, you have to feel it—things are different."

"Yeah." Ed was cold, very aware of how damp he was, sitting there with his pants sticking to his ass. "I'll give you that, Archie. But what's this got to do with the Kid?"

"I'm getting to that. But you have to understand."

"Go on, then."

"We found the sicko living in some offices. We were going to kill him like all the others, but he was different."

"How?"

"He could talk, Ed. He still had his brains in his head."

"A talking sicko?" Ed leaned back in his chair, thinking this over. "After all this time?"

"We sometimes find them in the City, or we used to before the Wall went up and we shut them all out. There were ones who stayed in the dark, underground, and the sickness didn't seem to affect them so badly. Anyway, this one, he could talk, all right, but he wasn't exactly sane. Spouted a whole load of nonsense. Matt latched on to it, reckoned it was speaking in tongues, messages from God or something; he just had to understand it all. He was obsessed with him. Called him Wormwood, the fallen star. We caught him and locked him up out of the way in an old cellar underneath the warehouse. It wasn't easy. He's dangerous. Very strong and very quick when he wants to be. He sits there doing nothing and then—bang. He killed two of our kids early on. Begged us to let him have them. And we wanted to keep him alive, so in the end we had a ceremony. And Matt gave him the bodies of the two dead kids."

"You what?" Ed couldn't believe what he was hearing.

"Yeah. I know. Matt said it was God's plan. Everything that happens Matt explains as God's plan. I just thought—they were dead—what difference did it make? I mean, it was that or throw them in the river."

"He fed dead kids to this sicko?"

"Yeah. And it kept Wormwood happy. It was like he came alive. After eating them what he said made a lot more sense. And now we keep on feeding him."

"With children?"

"Most of the time we give him other stuff, from the warehouse, or dead animals."

"Oh, that's okay, then. You only feed him children *some* of the time."

Archie couldn't look at Ed. He stared at his hands on the table and spoke very quietly. "Sacrifices, Matt calls them. The next ones we gave him were some kids from outside. A gang of them turned up and tried to break into our supplies, tried to steal stuff. There was a fight. We killed one, badly wounded another. The rest of them ran off into the City. We never saw them again. Probably some sickos got them, but, whatever, they didn't come back."

"So you fed the dead one to this Wormwood?"

"Yes. Him and the wounded girl."

"She was still alive?"

"Barely. He liked that. Prefers them alive."

"Jesus, Archie, this is sick. I can't believe you're sitting here calmly telling me all this. Why'd you go along with it? How can you?"

"Because when I listened to Wormwood's babble, it didn't sound like the word of God, it sounded like something different. It began to sound a bit like the truth."

"What truth?" Ed asked. "I don't understand."

"I reckon that somewhere in all that noise there's clues to what's going on. He knows stuff, Ed. From what I can work out, before the sickness he was working for some kind of biological medical-research type place, not sure exactly what it was. And I think he knows something about the causes of the sickness. Matt's kept him down there for religious reasons. I go along with it, but what I really want to find out is what's going on. What it's all about. And he might know the answer. I mean, isn't that more important than . . . than anything?"

"No. No, it's not. I get it now. What's the phrase? The carrot and the stick? Matt bribes you all with food, and if you don't go along with it he throws you to his pet sicko. Who else has he killed?"

Archie sighed. "The next one was a kid from here who got killed in a fight with some sickos when we were building the Wall," he said. It seemed to Ed that he wanted to get all this stuff out, that it was bugging him more than he was letting on. "Then there was another live one. A boy called Nev had an accident, fell off one of the balconies in the cathedral. Broke his back. He was one of the most religious kids here. Even more fanatical than Matt, went along with everything Matt came out with. Begged Matt to sacrifice him. Said God had chosen him. Said it was an honor. Didn't stop him screaming when we put him in there."

"Nice."

"The last one that went down before today was a girl. She was always trouble, always getting into fights, never settled down or made friends. There was something wrong with her, if you ask me. One day she took it too far, killed this younger girl. Drowned her. Matt had to punish her in some way. . . ."

Ed was too numb to feel anything. Or say anything. He wondered if what Jordan had done to Brendan was really any better. He didn't know anymore.

"All right," he said at last. "So are you telling me that's where you took the Kid? That little boy? Nine years old? Fed him to a bloody monster?"

"I know," said Archie. "Today was different. It wasn't a punishment as such. We had to sacrifice the Goat. Matt wanted to make this big show. We've been waiting for the

Goat and the Lamb to show up since we got here. And there they were. Matt was so *sure*."

"And you let him do it?"

"The thing is, Ed," said Archie, leaning forward, "it's important what Matt's doing here."

"Killing kids?"

"No. Saving them."

"How does killing the Kid save him?"

"Not him. He was a sacrifice, for the others. For us. People need something to believe in. That's what Matt's given us, something outside ourselves. So that kids don't just sit around thinking about themselves and all their problems. Without it, there's nothing, no hope for any of us. If you stopped to think about what's happened, you'd go nuts. It's a nightmare. Matt offers something different, though. The way things are, we need crazy bastards like him to hold us all together."

Ed thought about Jordan Hordern at the Tower, with his rules and his training and his military obsessions. Nicola at the Houses of Parliament, with her voting system, her new government . . .

Something to believe in.

Did it make any difference whether it was the Lamb, democracy, or military order?

But that didn't excuse what they'd done to the Kid.

"How long ago?" he asked.

"What?" Archie finally looked up at Ed.

"How long ago did you take the Kid to Wormwood in the Abyss?"

"Well, I don't have a watch anymore, but I'd guess a couple of hours."

"How long would it take for, you know . . . ?"

"He's strong and fast and he's always hungry. The last time we took him a kid was a month ago. Since then he's only had scraps."

"How long, Archie?"

"It's usually over in about five minutes."

Ed stood up, started pacing the room. "Maybe I should just feed *Matt* to Wormwood," he said.

"Don't, Ed," Archie pleaded. "Leave him. The kids here need him. We're surrounded by sickos. Without Matt this whole place would fall apart. There'd be panic. Matt's convinced himself and everyone else here that the Kid was a demon, the dark twin of the Lamb, and that once he was sacrificed to Wormwood everything would be all right. Our war against the sickos would be won."

"Jesus!" Ed slammed his fist against the wall, cracking a wood panel. "This is all so messed up." He turned on Archie. "You almost had me thinking it was okay. But it's not. I keep coming back to that poor little boy, all alone with that freak. That's what this is. Nothing more."

"It's over, Ed. You can't do anything."

"Can't I? You're gonna take me there, Archie. Maybe he's still alive."

"He won't be. Leave it."

"I have to try!" Ed yelled. "You and me and Matt are gonna go there, and I'm gonna see for myself, and I'm gonna decide. Maybe I shut Matt in with Wormwood, maybe I just kill the sicko so that you screwed-up jerks can't feed any more children to him."

"He knows stuff," Archie protested.

"I don't care what he knows. As long as he's there, he's a threat to children. So get Matt and let's get this over with."

56

"Come on then, you bastards, here I am."

Shadowman had managed to put two more of the strangers out of the game, and now he was hoping for a fourth. A very tall father carrying a long crooked stick. Shadowman had figured that he was eager to get ahead of the others and close in for the kill. Hunger was making him reckless.

And Shadowman wanted that stick. His knee had locked and was now just a cold lump of agony.

There was a mother trying to keep up with Stickboy, only a few paces behind. Shadowman took careful aim and fired the crossbow directly at her chest. She walked a few more paces then slowly went down, turning around and around on the spot in her confusion. Stickboy was almost on Shadowman now, and he had to hurriedly put his crossbow back over his shoulder without reloading. He drew his machete and swung it all in one movement. Stickboy was ready for him, though. He held the stick up two-handed to ward off the blow, but Shadowman went in low, slashed him across the belly. Stickboy wasn't going to go quietly. He was tough, and as dark blood soaked his ragged pants, he came on, jerking the stick up and down in front of him. Shadowman didn't have time for this. He took aim at Stickboy's knee and let fly with the machete.

"Yeah," he said as the father fell over sideways. "Hurts, doesn't it?"

He grabbed hold of the stick and tried to wrestle it from Stickboy's hands. Stickboy held on with an iron grip. He wasn't letting go of his precious stick, and the rest of the pack was getting dangerously close.

"Look, just let go of it, will you?"

He hacked at the father's fingers with his blade, like a chef chopping vegetables, until Stickboy had nothing to hold on with anymore. Shadowman pulled the stick free and propped the curve of it under his shoulder. It wasn't the best crutch in the world, but it was better than nothing. He hobbled off, trying to keep the weight off his bad knee, the rain washing the blood from his machete.

The strangers weren't going to give up. They must have been miles from the rest of the Fear by now and still they came on.

That was Bluetooth's doing. He was a tough bastard, and Shadowman had noticed before that he never gave up. If he could only stop and shoot him or cut his bloody head off. Anything. Then the rest of them might stop chasing him.

Bluetooth was clever, though. He stayed back, hidden among the rest of the pack. Happy to let the others get ahead and take on the danger. He'd be first to feed, but he'd let the others do all the hard work of actually hunting and killing.

The only way to end this nightmare was to either kill him or kill them all.

In the end it might come down to the same thing.

57

It's a miracle." Matt's voice filled the dark, dusty cellar. "We have rolled away the stone and the cave is empty. The Goat and the fallen star are both gone. They have destroyed one another, just as it was told. We are rid of two evils. The Abyss is cleaned out. Wormwood can poison us no more, and the trickster Goat can fool us no more. The darkness will lift and all will be new and bright."

He went to Sam and held him by the shoulders. "The world is yours."

"I don't want it," said Sam. "You can keep it."

Matt was smiling at him, trying to show that he knew everything and Sam knew nothing.

What a loser.

Sam had a smile of his own, but he was keeping it inside.

The truth was that he knew everything and Matt knew nothing. If you looked at the world expecting to see miracles and magic and fantasy things, you were likely to miss what was really going on.

People didn't just vanish into thin air.

They'd come here through the rain, under umbrellas, big colorful ones with corporate logos on them for long-dead companies. Ed, hard-faced, with his five friends from the Tower, Matt trying to walk upright and uncovered, refusing the protection of an umbrella, the rain smashing down on his shaved head. Archie shivering under a bright blue umbrella advertising an insurance company. Nathan and three guards carrying spears.

The cathedral kids had been tense, frightened, as Nathan had unlocked the black door to the cellar. Sam had just felt cold and miserable.

And then they'd found . . .

Nothing.

Just a bad stink.

Ed had seemed pissed off. Matt had started one of his crazy rants, but Sam had realized there were no signs of any fresh blood anywhere and had looked a bit closer.

Now he was standing on a piece of wood. Looked like it might once have been the lid of one of the empty broken chests that littered the cellar. He'd spotted it straightaway. Tapped it quietly with his foot, heard the hollow sound underneath.

The Kid was the tunnel king, wasn't he? He'd promised he'd find a way out.

Sam was beginning to see the light, all right. These pesky mortals would marvel at his wisdom. He had to stop himself from snickering.

There was still hope.

Ed did one last final whirlwind search of the cellar, kicking stuff out of his way. Matt was quoting another passage from his book. No one was listening. The other kids were looking confused and starting to get bored. They'd hyped themselves up for an action scene and it had been a big letdown.

"Let's get out of here," Ed grumbled eventually, and they clumped back up the stairs to the warehouse, Ed laying into Archie Bishop all the way, telling him he hoped the whole thing hadn't been some kind of setup.

When they reached the warehouse, they found another surprise waiting for them.

A mob of cathedral kids, most of them armed. They looked determined. Ready to rescue their leader. When Matt saw them, he smiled.

"You can't beat me, Ed!" he called out. "Because I speak the word of God. We are an army. Put down your weapons, you unbelievers, and—"

"Oh, shut up," said Ed. And he turned to face the kids. Sam could see that most of them weren't fighters at all, and now that they had Ed and his crew in front of them again, they were looking just a bit nervous. He wondered how many of them would actually fight.

He knew Ed wouldn't be worried. He was a warrior.

"Listen to me!" Ed shouted. "You kids have a choice. You can go along with Matt here. I'm not going to stop you. If that's what you want, it's fine with me. If you're happy taking innocent little boys and feeding them to grown-ups. If that's what you think is a good way to live your lives, I'm not going to stop you. But I'll tell you one thing: *You* are not going to stop *me* from leaving this building. I made a promise to Sam and I'm going to keep it. Me and my friends are going to walk out of here and we're taking Sam with us. He's not what you think he is. He's just a boy trying to find his sister."

"The Lamb stays here with us!" Matt shouted.

"Come at us if you want, Matt, but I warn you, we've fought our way here today through an army of grown-ups, sickos, oppoes, Nephilim, whatever you want to call them. I can't tell you how many I killed, because I lost count. We're all fighters. Killers. I don't want to hurt any kids, it's not my way. But you all are different. You're quite happy to kill other children. So the rules have changed."

"It was a sacrifice," said Matt. "We were making an offering to—"

"I said shut up, Matt. I don't want to hear it. I'm going now. To the center of town. It's safe there. Normal. You don't need to be frightened of Matt anymore, his monster has gone. There's no sicko down there in the cellar. So if any of you want to come with us, I'll forget this ever happened. The rest of you, I spit on you."

Sam looked at the kids. Behind him were the shelves, row after row of food, stacked high to the ceiling. Nobody moved. There was a long, silent pause; no sounds from the outside world could penetrate through the thick concrete walls all the way down here.

And then the stillness was broken by a mad, high-pitched cackle, and Matt came strutting out in front of Ed.

"You're a fool, Ed," he said slowly and coldly. "Nobody wants to go with you. They're all true believers. See, they wear the green. In honor of Wormwood and the golden age when all was green. They don't stay here because they're scared or because of all this food. Look how many of them have the mark of the Lamb on their foreheads. They stay here because they want to enter God's kingdom with me. Nobody wants to go with you. You're a loser."

58

E d stood there, breathing heavily, his heart pounding. He was suddenly very, very tired. Washed out. He wondered if he really had the strength to make it back into town, to get Sam to the Natural History Museum. How much easier it would be just to stay here at the cathedral, wait, safe and dry, until the storm passed and the sun came up again. Eat some of Matt's food. Rest.

Matt's craziness had affected him. He couldn't think straight. He had to forget about Matt and think about what he had to do. He looked along his line of friends. At Adele, all in pink, Hayden, tall and determined, Macca and Will, Kyle . . .

He'd gotten them this far without any of them getting hurt. Moving on now was going to throw them all back into danger. Could he really ask them to do that again?

Could he really ask any of the cathedral kids to leave this place?

Or was he just making excuses for his own tiredness and fear?

Matt was grinning at him with a nasty, triumphant look on his face.

Maybe he was right. . . .

"Actually . . ." A voice rang out small and clear and high. "I'd like to come with you, if that's all right."

It was a young girl carrying a violin case. Looked about Sam's age.

Well, if *she* was brave enough . . .

Ed smiled, feeling his scarred cheek tighten. "Of course that's all right. What's your name, sweetheart?"

"Charlotte. I spoke to the other boy, Angus."

"Angus? Who's Angus?"

"The Goat boy."

"You spoke to the Kid?"

"Yes. I wasn't supposed to. I spoke to him and I quite liked him, and he called me Yo-Yo, which was funny, though I wasn't allowed to laugh. I liked him and I didn't think it was right to hurt him. It was a bad thing that happened. I believe in God and I don't think God would have wanted any of this to happen."

She walked over to Ed, and Adele took her hand, spoke quietly to her, reassuring her.

"Well!" Ed shouted. "It looks like Charlotte's braver than the rest of you."

"No." Another voice. Another girl. It was Tish. She pushed through the scrum of kids.

"I'm coming too. I know I did something shitty. I feel awful about the Kid. I tried to convince myself that he was evil, but I think he was just a boy. I can't stay here. I understand if you don't want to take me, but—"

"It's forgotten." Ed gave her a brief hug. "It was all Matt's doing. No one else."

"I ain't staying here." Now Brendan came forward. Ed had met him back at the cathedral, and Brendan had explained everything that had happened. "I never wanted to be here in the first place. This ain't nothing to do with me. If you'll get me into town and not back to the Tower, I'll come."

"Deal," said Ed.

It was decided, then. They were going. Ed was just starting to feel like everything was working out fine when a boy came running in through the open doors of the storeroom. He was soaking wet and clearly terrified.

"They're here!" he yelled. "The Nephilim are in the Temple. They've broken through the Wall!"

59

The open area in front of St. Paul's was filled with a boiling mass of bodies, slick from the rain, black in the darkness. The clatter from their makeshift instruments was filling the night with a noise that rattled Ed's teeth.

Kids were pouring out of the street that led to the warehouse and stopping, bunched up and confused. The way ahead was totally blocked. For the moment, the grown-ups didn't seem to be attacking anyone. They were just milling, aimless, like a crowd at an airport waiting for an announcement.

St. Paul's loomed above them, its white walls appearing to glow slightly, despite the rain.

"Why don't they attack?" Kyle asked, twisting his ax in his big hands.

"It's like there's something on their minds," said Will.

"They don't have minds," said Kyle.

"I don't know anymore," said Will. "These ones are organized."

Matt came striding past them. "Stay close to me!" he

shouted. "We'll find a way through. Nathan, get your best fighters together up front."

Matt stopped shouting and pushed his way back through the tangle of kids to Ed and his group. He fixed Sam with a wild stare.

"The Lamb must lead us," he said, rain running down his face, making it look like he was crying.

Ed had no time for this. "If you mean Sam," he said, "he stays with us."

"The Lamb will protect us," said Matt.

A sudden poisonous bubble of rage exploded inside Ed, and he lashed out, striking Matt in the face with the flat of his hand and making him stagger sideways.

"What did you do that for?" Matt said, dropping all his front. He didn't sound like some mad preacher anymore; he sounded like a sad kid on the playground.

Ed didn't answer his question. He simply swore at him and shoved him out of the way. Matt staggered back and tripped, falling in a puddle. One of his acolytes went to help him get up, but Matt snarled at him to leave him alone.

Ed left him there and started rounding up his crew. "We have to get back to the bridge," he said. "Stick together. I'll take point with Kyle and Adele."

They formed a wedge and went around behind the cathedral kids, who were hanging back, unsure of what to do. Still the sickos didn't seem to have noticed their arrival. They seemed as confused as the kids. Some were banging sticks and stones, bones, and pieces of metal together; some were wandering around as if they were looking for something. Whatever it was, they were distracted. If they'd all gone into the attack, none of the kids would have stood a chance. There had to be at least three hundred adults packed into the area below the steps, and Ed saw a steady flow of them plodding up toward the entrance. A small group of frightened kids was trying to close the doors on them and fight them off at the same time.

Matt had recovered and Ed could hear him shouting orders, gathering his troops around him. Luckily he seemed more interested in getting back into the cathedral and making it safe than in keeping Sam. Ed hoped he'd admitted defeat.

Nathan was with Matt, trying to get the kids into some sort of order. All the shouting was making the nearest sickos aware of them. They were stopping, turning, sniffing. . . .

Ed looked back as Matt's group finally set off. There were a lot of kids, and most were armed, but only a few of them looked like they'd be any use in a fight. The Wall had protected them. The Tree of Life had fed them. They hadn't needed to be out here, day after day, facing sickos. He reckoned only Nathan and a handful of his guards really knew what they were doing.

As they pushed their way into the crowd, a ripple passed through the sickos; more and more of them were becoming aware, becoming interested. They started to close in on Matt's group.

And then they began to attack.

Nathan and his team were at the front of the column. Behind them Matt and his acolytes, well protected. The kids at the back, though, the slower ones, the less brave ones, the younger ones, had no idea what to do. Ed heard screams as the sickos picked them off. Soon the tight order of Matt's group was falling apart; panicked kids were breaking away, running in all directions. And those who left the main group were instantly taken down and swallowed by the mob.

"Shit!" Ed barked, short and harsh. He stopped walking. Then he tensed and brought his sword up quickly as someone grabbed his shoulder.

It was only Kyle, though.

"I know what you're thinking," he said. "But it's not our fight, Ed. Leave it."

"They're kids like us."

"We can't do anything. We have to look after ourselves."

Ed checked the frightened faces of his gang. For the moment they were behind the mass of sickos, who were concentrating on Matt's kids. If Ed pressed on they might get right around the edge of the battle and down to the bridge without a fight.

He turned to Will. Trusted his judgment.

"Let's get out of here, Ed," Will said.

"Okay." Ed shut his mind down. Forgot all about Matt and his kids. He'd given them the chance, hadn't he? This was their choice.

"Come on. . . ."

They kept close to the curve of buildings around the edge of the churchyard, mostly cafés with offices above them. They could hear the sounds of the battle. Kids crying out, sickos moaning and hissing, others still clattering and banging.

Will turned occasionally to see what was going on.

"It's okay, Ed," he said. "Matt's kids are almost all through the doors now. Those that made it."

"Fine," Ed grunted. He was shutting down all the rooms in his mind, leaving only those animal parts functioning that would help him get out of this mess.

"The only problem is," said Will, "once Matt's kids are out of the way, the sickos are going to be more interested in us."

Ed took this in. So far they'd been left alone, but they were still only about halfway around to the walkway that led down to the bridge.

"They've closed the doors!" Adele shouted.

It was almost as if her voice acted like a signal. One moment the sickos were all facing the cathedral, trying to get in, the next they'd stopped and turned, and were coming toward Ed's crew.

Within seconds they were totally boxed in, the way forward jammed with sickos.

"Get off the street!" Ed yelled. "Now!"

60

Charlotte was more scared than she ever remembered being. Even when everything had started to go wrong, she'd never felt like this. Never seen so many sick grownups together in one go. They were everywhere. The smell of them was awful, like a whole pack of wet dogs mixed in with bad toilet smells and a moldy gas that stuck in the back of your nose. She wanted to close her eyes, block her ears. Instead she pinched her nose and clamped a hand over her mouth. The only thing that gave her any comfort was having the bigger kids around her. They'd made a human wall to protect her and Sam and were all chopping away with their weapons, pushing and shoving their way through the crowd, trying to find a way into one of the buildings.

They were going so slowly, though. Charlotte had seen children killed trying to get to the cathedral. She imagined herself being pulled away by one of the mothers or fathers, dragged into the crowd, pictured all those dirty fingernails clawing at her.

One of the bigger kids was making a special effort to look after her and Sam. A girl dressed all in pink and glitter, sparkling pins in her hair. Charlotte had heard one of the boys call her Adele. She stood over Charlotte and Sam when any grown-up got too close and bashed them away. Every now and then she'd look around to check on Charlotte and smile at her. Charlotte was glad of that smile. As long as Adele could keep smiling, it meant they were going to be all right.

This one time Charlotte had been on an airplane with her mom and dad, and they'd flown into a storm. The plane had rocked about and kept on suddenly dipping like a roller coaster. At first Charlotte had been terrified, but then she'd seen a flight attendant, just sitting there chatting to another attendant, and she'd smiled at Charlotte in the same way as Adele, letting her know there was nothing to fear.

There was a surge, and several grown-ups got very close. The bigger kids had to fight really hard. Sam took hold of Charlotte's hand, tried to smile the way Adele had done, but just looked sick and scared. He'd wanted to reassure her, but she ended up reassuring him.

"It's all right, Sam," she said. "Don't worry. It's all right."

Sam nodded, too frightened to speak.

"In here!" someone shouted. There was a broken-in doorway to an office; behind it a short passage led to a hallway. Charlotte was bundled inside with the other kids. Then Adele took her and Sam on through to the hallway while the others stayed to guard the door.

Charlotte and Sam flopped to the floor, getting their breath back, still holding hands.

"Are you okay?" Adele asked.

Sam nodded his head, gulped. Finally spoke, his voice just a whisper really. "I'm okay."

"We're going to get away. You'll be all right."

Charlotte hoped Adele was telling the truth.

"Where are we going to?" said Sam.

"The Wobbly Bridge," Adele explained. "It's how we got here. If we can just cross the river, we'll be fine."

"There's so many of them," said Sam. "We'll never make it to the bridge."

"We will. Somehow. Don't worry." Adele smiled.

"How can we?" Sam said. "There's millions of them. How can we even get out of here? They'll kill us. We're trapped here. We should have gone into the cathedral."

"Is that really what you wanted?" Charlotte asked.

"No," said Sam quietly. "I never want to see Matt again."

"Ed will think of something," said Adele. "He always does. You'll see."

She knelt by Sam and Charlotte. "I need to go and check how the others are doing. You be brave now, yeah?"

Charlotte nodded. Watched Adele hurry to the front of the building. She and Sam were alone in the darkness now. She could feel him shaking, hear him sniffing.

"Sam?"

"Yes?"

"Don't be sad."

"I'm sad for the Kid," said Sam. "He was my best friend and I don't know where he is. What happened to him? It was empty when we went down there. I hope he got out. I hope he's all right. But if he did get out, where is he? And what happened to the sicko man? All those grown-ups out there. The Kid's got no one to look after him. I was happy when I thought he'd escaped. But I'm never going to see him again, am I?"

"I liked him," said Charlotte. "That's why I'm here with you and not back there in the Temple with Matt. I don't like Matt. But it was safe and there was always food. The Kid was funny."

"Yeah," said Sam, and he gave a quiet little laugh.

"I think he was brave," Charlotte went on. "When Matt whipped him, he hardly cried at all. Matt was horrible to do that. I think the Kid was better than him, better than all of them."

Charlotte ran out of things to say and stopped. It was quiet back here. The floor was cold.

A voice came out of the darkness behind them, making Charlotte jump. A boy's voice.

"Don't stop now, Yo-Yo," it said. "You're only just getting going."

61

Sam turned to see a ragged figure in the murky depths of the hallway. Small and dark with wild hair. It could only be the Kid.

"I almost wish I *was* dead and daisies," he said. "If you'd make more pretty speeches like that."

Sam jumped up, ran to him, and threw his arms around him. Charlotte joined them, hugging the both of them.

"What are you doing?" Sam said. "Where did you come from? How did you get here?"

"I been hiding out here in these buildings," said the Kid. "Trying to figure out what to do. I eyeballed Ed and his soldier boys strolling up and going to church. Waited for them to come out. Only you've all come out. Couldn't risk getting into the clutches of Mad Matt and his Clickee Cult again, could I? Stayed put. Then along come the sickos and all hell breaks loose. Never thought to see the likes of it. Saw you fighting your brave and foolish way around here, battling like banshees against them buggers. Been scuttling from building to building trying to keep up. And at last you come in here and here I am and here we are."

"You got out through a tunnel, didn't you?" said Sam.

"Yeah," said the Kid, grinning.

"I knew it!"

"Told you I would, din't I? Nobody can hold Harry the Houdini Kid."

Sam slipped off the Kid's leather jacket and handed it back to him.

"I kept this for you," he said as the Kid wriggled into the jacket. "I knew you'd make it."

Ed came hurrying back from the doorway, his flashlight beam piercing the darkness. He gave a shout of happiness and also gave the Kid a big hug. "Where the hell did you come from?"

"The gutters and drains," said the Kid. "The wormholes beneath. Found a way back up and out in the underneathlings of a burger house down the way. Went up top for a better view."

"But what happened to the sicko?" Ed asked. "How did you get away from him?"

"I didn't," said the Kid.

"Don't talk in your crazy riddles." Ed gave him a little shake. "How did you get away from him?"

"Ain't no riddle, Scarface. I got him with me."

"You what?"

"Promised him I'd set him free. Only we been stuck here till you turned up. He's down below beneath the burger bar still, too frighted to come out and face the music."

"Well, for God's sake," said Ed. "Leave him there and let's try to get out of here."

"No can do, Mr. Boo." The Kid shook his head. "I made a promise and the Kid keeps his word. Keeps it in a box with a tight shut lid."

"Look, I'm sorry, Kid." Ed sounded like he was getting worked up. "It's going to be hard enough for us to get out—it's mad out there—but if we've got to drag some bloody sicko along with us . . ."

"Then I'll have to say good-bye." The Kid folded his arms. "The Kid stays in the picture."

Sam went and stood next to the Kid. From now on he was sticking close to him. He felt brave around him. The Kid might not be a fighter like Ed and the others, but he sure did keep bouncing back. He was a lucky charm. Maybe Matt had been right to think that there was something special about him. Sam wasn't special. He knew that much. Sam was just a boy. But the Kid? The Kid was . . .

Well, he was the *Kid*.

"If the Kid stays, I stay with him," he said. "I'm not losing him again."

"Bloody hell. Bloody hell." Ed was banging the wall with his fist.

"Ed!" Kyle shouted from the front. "It's getting hairy. We gotta do something. We're running out of time here."

"One minute," Ed shouted back angrily. "Just hold them off, Kyle. There's something I need to take care of first."

"Well, hurry, 'cause we are trapped, man. We are stuck here. We have run out of options. . . ."

62

Ed and Sam followed the Kid to the back of the building, through some offices. They'd left Charlotte behind with Adele. She hadn't wanted to come and meet the sicko. Ed couldn't really blame her. He wasn't sure about this himself. He remembered what Archie Bishop had told him about Wormwood. About how dangerous he was. He knew Sam would rather have stayed behind with Charlotte and Adele, but he obviously didn't want to get split up from his friend again.

A fire had partially destroyed the rear of the offices, and some of the walls at the back had collapsed, meaning you could easily go from one property to the next. They picked their way through the rubble until they reached the burger bar, where the Kid showed them to some stairs that led down from the kitchen.

Ed shone his flashlight down to make sure it was all clear.

"Careful with that beam, Eugene," said the Kid. "When we get down below, put your fingers over it, yeah? Wormy's like E.T. He don't like the bright light, bright light."

Ed pointed his flashlight at the floor and raised his sword. "This is stupid," he said, somehow feeling more scared of what waited below than he was of the army of sickos waiting outside. "What if he attacks us?"

"Yeah," said the Kid. "There is that. He's a sick Rick. A flesh-eater. A carnivore, a cannibal, and a carnival all in one."

"Great."

"But he's okay around me. You could say we're pals. We speak the same language."

"Gobbledygook," said Sam.

"Stow it, morsel," said the Kid.

"So you reckon we're safe?" Ed asked, taking an uncertain step down the stairs.

"Can't promise how he'll be with you two muffins."

"Look, Kid," Ed snapped. "For once tell it straight. Is it safe?"

"Don't worry," said the Kid. "This will all work out for the best in the long run, just you wait and see, brother. He'll be our ace in the hole. Our toad in the hole. Our hole in the road."

"That's enough, Kid. That's enough." Ed passed the flashlight to Sam. "You're in charge of the lighting," he said. "I need to concentrate."

Ed held his sword tight in both hands and went slowly and carefully down.

There was the unmistakable smell of sicko down here, and Ed's throat was very dry. They reached the bottom of the stairs and went past some staff restrooms and into a small utility room full of boxes and cleaning equipment. There was a steel door at the back that was closed. The Kid nodded to Sam and he shielded the light.

The Kid went over to the door. "Open Sesame Street," he said, pulling the handle. The door creaked as it swung out. The three of them went through.

Ed saw pipework, big tin cans, a boiler, and, sitting on a bench, a naked man.

His skin was covered in a fur of green mold. He had big pale eyes, a bald head, long stringy arms and legs, and a round, swollen belly. His nails had grown into horny claws that he was rattling together between his knees.

He turned away and hissed as Sam let the flashlight beam crawl over him.

"It's okay, Reverend Green," said the Kid. "They're on our side. We got ourselves a posse and we're gonna save your hairy green butt. Now let's get up and at 'em." The Kid clapped his hands.

"I don't want to go outside," the Green Man whined.

"You got no choice, Rasputin. Ra-ra-ra-ra wrecking ball. The devil is letting off out there. If you stay here I can't protect you."

"I'm a fallen star," said the father, sounding like a spoiled kid. "I deserve some respect."

Ed kept his distance. Archie had said the sicko could strike fast when he wanted.

"Just get up," said the Kid, as if he was talking to a naughty dog. "I got you this far, didn't I? Don't you trust me?"

"I'm so hungry."

The Green Man turned his wide, watery eyes on Sam,

licked his lips, his tongue bright pink. The Kid grabbed the flashlight and shone it straight in his eyes; the man hissed and cringed away from the light.

"No, you don't, Gobbo!" the Kid screamed at him. "We're your friends, not your dinner. Now get up and come with us or I'm locking the door on you."

"All right, I'm coming."

He got up slowly and stood there with shoulders hunched, arms hanging down straight at his sides.

"Just show me some respect."

"Chew it, clown," said the Kid. "You go ahead so we can keep our peepers on you."

The four of them picked their way upstairs and back to the office building, the Green Man groaning and muttering all the way, and when they got into the hallway, he froze and refused to walk any farther.

There was no sign of Adele and Charlotte. From outside came the sound of the sickos clattering and banging. The Green Man was rubbing his hands together, fingernails scraping.

"It's too noisy out there," he said. "They're all shouting at me; they won't leave me alone. My head is filled with the buzzing of bees."

"Shout back at them," said the Kid. "Tell them to button it."

"Maybe I will." The Green Man gave a sly smile.

"Try it," the Kid urged him.

The man closed his eyes, tilted his head back, held out his hands in front of him, and went very still. Ed held his breath. Wormwood was pointing. Like the others. Was it possible he could communicate with the sickos outside?

"What's he doing?" said Sam.

"He looks like a pointer," Ed replied.

"A what?"

"He's doing a Dr. Dolittle," said the Kid. "He can talk to the animals."

"Do we have to take him with us?" Sam asked. He was daring himself to properly look at the manky creature.

"I think we do." Ed was staring at the Green Man, his brain working hard.

"He ain't just a pretty face," said the Kid. "He just might be our ticket out of here."

There was a commotion from the doorway and Kyle came running in, his own flashlight beam swinging wildly. "I don't know what's going on, Ed," he blurted. "It's gone very quiet out there. I think we should go now. . . . Holy crap!"

He had spotted the Green Man. He made a disgusted face and swore.

"Want me to take him out?" he asked, but the Kid jumped in front of his sicko, arms spread wide.

"Leave him alone," he shouted. "He's with me."

Kyle looked to Ed, who shook his head.

"This is one freaky day," said Kyle.

The Kid prodded the Green Man. "Okay, Wormfood," he said. "Time to go."

The Green Man slowly opened his eyes and blinked, for a moment seeming not to know where he was. "They salute me," he said. "I can feel their insect love. They salute me. At last some respect."

63

As Ed and his crew emerged from the building, they were met by a strange sight. The sickos were all standing there, frozen, staring in their direction. The music had stopped. Everything had stopped, even the rain. Many of the sickos stood in the familiar pointer pose. Others just waited, mouths hanging open.

It was unnerving, so many faces turned toward them, so many eyes fixed on them. Was this really the Green Man's doing? Did he have a hold over them? Could he control them in some way?

This was no time to be asking questions. They had to take advantage of the situation. They held their weapons steady and started to walk.

They kept in a tight bundle, the Green Man and Adele in the middle with the three youngsters; Ed, Kyle, Hayden, Tish, Brendan, Macca, and Will on the outside.

The packed bodies of the silent sickos radiated heat. Steam rose off them. Ed stepped lightly, afraid to make any sound or do anything to startle them into action. He realized he was holding his breath, the blood throbbing in his skull, his throat painfully tight, his heart thumping in his chest. It seemed to him to be the loudest noise in the world. Would the sickos hear it? Would it disturb them? Break the spell? Cause them to wake up and come tearing at them? There were far too many to fight.

Slowly, slowly, the kids pushed through the crowd, nudging sickos out of the way, trying not to look at their worm-eaten faces, their boils and blisters and sores, their stupid, staring eyes, expecting at any moment that the mob would suddenly come alive. Bare their teeth. Go into a killing frenzy.

None of them moved, though.

Someone had pressed PAUSE on the DVD.

"Keep moving," Ed whispered. "Stay close together."

"My head aches," said the Green Man. "I can't keep them still much longer. There's such madness there. A hunger. They want to kill you all."

"Maybe it's you they want," said Kyle. "Maybe we should leave you here as bait."

"They don't want to harm me," said the Green Man. "They're my brothers and sisters. We came down from the stars together. They want me to tell them what to do. But I can't hold them."

"You have to," Ed hissed. "It's the only way we're going to get out of here."

He led his group to the end of the run of cafés and into an open space with a weird, angular metal building in the middle of it. He remembered that it stood at the top of the walkway that led down to the bridge.

"If we can get across to the South Bank, we can make a run for it," he said. "Get away from here. If we're fast they won't catch us."

"Why can't we run now?" Tish asked.

"I'm scared if we do that they'll come straight for us."

"I'm slipping," said the Green Man. "Can't focus."

"Hold 'em still, bogeyman, hold 'em still," said the Kid. "You can do it."

"I can't. I'm weak. I don't like it out here. I want to be back in my hole."

"No, you don't. You're a VIP, remember, not a POW."

"They're mad, they're all mad. And I'm hungry. I'm too weak. Let me go back."

Ed felt an awful tension in the air. The sickos were like fighting dogs being held back on leashes. All they wanted to do was attack, but this force was holding them. When it snapped, it would be like a cork released from a shaken-up bottle.

There was an equal tension in his group. They all wanted to break away, to run. The two forces were pulling against each other.

Which would break first?

Some of the kids were speeding up, walking faster, opening up their protective circle.

"Keep together," he said, trying not to raise his voice. "Don't go too fast."

But he could feel his hold on them slipping, just as the Green Man's hold on the sickos was slipping.

They'd reached the top of the walkway and could see right down it to the bridge. The walkway was narrow and gently sloping, with modern buildings on either side. There was a crossroads about halfway down. It looked like the sickos were thinner on the ground there, most of them having made their way to the cathedral.

There were still a lot of them, though. Still too many to fight.

Ed swallowed. Wishing for a drink of water.

It was an escape, but it was also a gauntlet. A rat maze.

They moved down it, the tension tightening with every step. Passing only inches away from the unmoving sickos.

Will came forward and fell in beside Ed.

"I used to come down here from the tube every day to get to school," he said. "That's it up there on the right. We go straight past it. I sometimes used to have little fantasies. What would happen if zombies attacked? Never thought it would come true."

"Does this make any sense to you?" Ed asked. "The sickos behaving like this?"

"Nothing that's happened today has made much sense," said Will. "And it looks like your Green Man has got something to do with it all."

"We couldn't have gotten this far without him."

"You trust him?"

"I have to."

There was a tall father with a big barrel chest standing right in the middle of the walkway just before the crossroads, glaring at them. A stone troll. An enchanted giant from a fairy tale. As the kids got nearer, he began to sway from side to side, letting out a low moan.

It was the first movement they'd seen since coming out of

the doorway. And it wasn't just him who was coming alive. Ed could sense a change in all the sickos. Some of the pointers were dropping their hands, like volunteers at a hypnotist's show waking up. There was more—shuffling, twitching, heads turning. Ed heard the rattling of breath in pus-filled throats. The shuffling and rustling of clothing. He raised his sword above his shoulder. Felt it shaking in his grip.

Hayden moved ahead. Macca sped up and overtook her.

"We're losing them," said Will, and Ed wasn't sure if he was talking about their own gang or the sickos.

And then Macca was running. And Hayden, Tish, and Brendan.

The world changed in an instant.

It was as if someone had thrown a switch. Pressed PLAY.

The sickos came alive.

64

Grown-ups were closing in from all sides now. More pouring in from the streets on either side of the cross-roads. The big father in the middle of the walkway lunged at the kids.

"Forget this," said Kyle, and he swung his ax. Charlotte watched, amazed, unable to look away, as the blade sliced clean through the father's neck and his head flew off.

"Run!" Ed yelled.

In a moment the kids were pounding down the walkway in a blind panic. The bridge was only about two hundred yards away, but to Charlotte it looked like miles. She was so tense her whole body ached, and having to suddenly go quickly was making her muscles burn. She hadn't run this fast in months.

The kids had split into two groups now. A few of them had run on ahead. Charlotte was holding hands with Sam and the Kid, not sure who was pulling who along. The bigger kids were in danger of breaking away from them, and the

Green Man was awfully slow. She had a stitch in her side. She could hardly breathe.

"Wait!" she cried out. "I can't keep up."

Ed stopped and the big boy, Kyle.

"Come on!" Ed shouted at her. "You can do it."

"I can't. I can't."

A knot of grown-ups came close, and the bigger kids could do nothing but hack at them. Up ahead the first group of kids was also in a fight. Ed and Kyle managed to force the grown-ups back, moving away from Charlotte as they did so. Adele went with them, like a charging rhino, smashing into the grown-ups. She was fierce when she had to be.

For a moment Charlotte, Sam, and the Kid were left unprotected. Charlotte wailed, clinging on to Sam, but Will came to their help, slashing grown-ups away until Ed's group returned.

As the sickos swarmed in all directions, with no sense of order, a gap opened up. The way to the bridge was suddenly clear. Ed spotted it.

"Move it!" he roared, and the kids were running again. Toward the crossroads, picking up the others on the way.

Charlotte's feet slapped down onto the ground. She looked up to see Adele at her side.

"You're doing all right. . . ."

It looked like they were going to make it. They were too fast for the grown-ups, but when they came to the junction, a thick mass of diseased bodies surged in from the side.

In an instant the mothers and fathers were among them. Charlotte couldn't tell where anyone else was. It was chaos. Bodies fell all around her, and she didn't have any idea if they were children or adults. She was so hemmed in by hot, stinking flesh that she couldn't see anything.

And then Adele was there again, cutting a path through the grown-ups. Charlotte knew that everything was going to be all right. Adele would look after her. Make sure nothing happened to her. The storm wouldn't knock her plane out of the sky. Adele was her flight attendant.

Adele leaned down to pick Charlotte up, and Charlotte gasped as hard, bony hands took hold of her and pulled her backward out of Adele's reach. The wind was sucked out of her and she could make no sound.

She threw up as she was spun around, no idea which way was up or down. She was being flung about like a piece of clothing in a washing machine.

"No, you don't!"

A thudding sound. A spray of hot blood over her face. Moonlight again. Broken clouds in the sky. She was lying on the ground and Adele was standing over her. Smiling. She held out a hand to Charlotte.

Charlotte smiled back at her.

And then Adele was gone.

Charlotte scrambled to her feet.

Three mothers had gotten hold of Adele and were dragging her away. In a second she was swallowed up by the mob, just as Charlotte had been moments before.

"Ed! Ed! They've got Adele! Ed!"

There was Ed, trying to get to her. He fought his way into the mob. He too disappeared from sight. And Charlotte felt sure that she would never see him again. Wouldn't see any of them. It was all over.

There was a terrible crunching sound, a thud, and a thump. The air was thick with blood. Bodies fell away. Kyle's ax came slicing down and Kyle was right behind it, cutting a wet passage with his ax. Moments later Ed emerged, Sam and the Kid behind him.

"Where's Adele?" Charlotte gasped.

"There's no sign of her," said Kyle. "What do we do?"

"Nothing," said Ed. "There's nothing we can do. She's gone."

"You have to do something," said Charlotte.

But before Ed could do anything there was another scream. Tish was being dragged away. Brendan was swiping at the grown-ups with his club, but there were too many of them for him to deal with alone. This time Will and Macca and Hayden came charging in and were more successful than Ed and Kyle had been trying to get to Adele. They freed Tish and she came staggering back, bleeding from cuts on her arms. She'd lost her sword, though, and a fat father with no teeth came wallowing out of the crowd, waving it around.

Ed swore and plunged his sword into the father's belly, ripping it sideways and spilling his guts. He tore the sword out of the father's hand and gave it back to Tish. He looked frightening, cold-faced, like a monster.

All the while the Green Man had been just standing there, a wide empty circle around him, clicking his long nails together. As if none of this was happening.

Charlotte tried to look for Adele. There was no sign of her. The sickos had been forced back, but they were returning, and it was still at least a hundred yards to the bridge.

"Brendan, Macca, Will, grab the youngers," Ed barked. "Kyle, with me. The rest of you make sure Wormwood doesn't get left behind. And Wormwood, if you can do anything to stop them . . ."

"No, no, no . . ." The weird goblin man shook his head.

The next thing Charlotte knew she was being swept up into the air by Brendan and he was running for the bridge, knocking grown-ups out of the way and yelling like a madman.

A hundred yards became fifty, fifty yards became twenty-five, fifteen . . . Charlotte looked back to see Hayden and Tish shoving the Green Man along. Too squeamish to grab hold of him, they prodded him like a cow. Ed and Kyle were bringing up the rear, holding off any grown-ups who got too close.

A tide of sickos followed them, swarming down the walkway.

"We've made it!" Brendan shouted, and at last they were on the bridge.

65

It wasn't over yet.

There were still loads of sickos down below on the embankment underneath the bridge. They obviously hadn't worked out how to get up yet. But there were other sickos on the bridge. They must have destroyed the barricades at the far end and come over from the South Bank. A group of them were bunched up directly ahead, blocking the way. Ed and Kyle saw the problem and ran past their friends to the front. It was vital that they kept moving. The bridge meant safety for all of them.

Ed didn't stop running. He was slipping into blankness. He saw a way ahead, like a red line drawn on a map, and he was going to go down that line no matter what. Nothing was going to stop him now. The sickos weren't humans, they weren't even animals; they were just obstacles he had to push out of the way. And push he did, using his sword, his elbows, his free hand, his sneakers, until a gap opened up.

He and Kyle held the rest of the sickos off while the kids

went past. They all looked exhausted and battered. Splashed with blood. Macca, Will, Sam, the Kid, Charlotte, Brendan, Tish, and Hayden. Then Wormwood, loping along. Adele was gone. Nothing he could do about that. They were lucky it hadn't been worse. They'd fought their way through God knows how many sickos to get here.

"Keep going," he croaked. "Once we get to the other side, we're away."

"That might be easier said than done," said Macca, and Ed turned to see what he was talking about.

There were sickos coming onto the bridge at the far end. It was too dark to see how many of them there were. More sickos were arriving at this end of the bridge as well. If Ed wasn't careful they'd be trapped and attacked from both sides. Kyle, Macca, and Will grouped together to try to stop the sickos advancing along the bridge from the St. Paul's end. How long could they keep them back, though?

"Wait. . . ." Ed tried to think what to do. He just wanted this to be over. Couldn't face losing any more friends tonight.

"I'm going to stay here with Kyle," he said at last. "We'll hold off the sickos until we're sure the rest of you are safely away. Hayden, you take command. Punch your way through as fast as you can. Look after the youngers and try to keep *him* alive." He threw a look at Wormwood, who was waiting there, his hands hanging limply at his sides.

"No." It was Tish. She stepped up to Ed. "I got you all into this," she said. "Let me hold the bridge."

"You can't hold it alone." Ed shook his head. "Kyle and I are the best fighters."

"That's why you have to lead the group," said Tish. "You're the only one who can get everyone to safety. Let me do it."

"She's right," said Brendan, and he walked over to stand at Tish's side.

"Bren . . . ?" Ed frowned at him.

"With two of us we stand a chance," said Brendan. "We can do it."

"Brendan, you don't have to. . . ."

"I'll show you I'm not a coward. I *do* care about other kids. You can tell Jordan bloody Hordern what I am. What a mistake he made."

"Bren . . . are you sure?"

"Me and Tish," said Brendan. "We'll hold them long enough, then follow on."

"He's right, Ed," Will shouted over. "We need you."

Ed didn't have long to make a decision. They needed to get moving again. What was more important? Him doing the right thing and taking a stand here? Or rescuing the kids he'd come for?

And there was Wormwood.

It felt wrong, to be balancing up a sicko's life against two kids, but . . .

Ed felt deep down that Wormwood was important. He had a power over the other sickos. He knew stuff.

What was most important?

"Get a move on," Macca shouted. "There's more coming."

Ed swore. He had to see this through or it would all have been a waste of time. A waste of Adele's life.

"Okay," he said. "You got it, Bren. Hold the bridge with

Tish. Just for a few minutes. No longer than you have to. We'll try and kill as many of the sickos on the way as we can."

"Come on!" It was Macca again. Ed glanced back at the walkway. It was solid with bodies, flowing down from St. Paul's. He swore again. What the hell must Brendan and Tish be thinking?

"Spread out," he said, marching to the head of his group. "Me, Hayden, Kyle, and Macca first. Will, you come behind with the goblin and the little ones; keep eyes in the back of your head. If any sickos get past Bren and Tish, I want to know about it."

"Okay, Ed."

"Let's go!"

66

Tish's hands seemed to be working on their own. Chopping at the Nephilim who came close. Why had she said it? Why had she volunteered for this suicidal job? There were so many sickos. Had she really thought she could survive this? Or had she been hoping to get to heaven? To wash herself in the blood of the Nephilim. To wash away the sin of bringing Sam and the Kid to the Temple?

What she had done was wrong.

She felt like being sick.

There was a limit to what she and Brendan could do. It was a losing battle. If there had been ten of them, side by side, they could have blocked the bridge and kept the Nephilim back all night.

But there were only two of them. The Neph could get around the sides, and if Tish turned to stop them, more pressed in at the front.

How had she ended up here, with this boy she hardly knew? Was she going to die here with him? It seemed like months ago that she'd set out for the Tower of London with her friends, but it was only really a few days.

They'd had such high hopes. Matt had fired them up, inspired them with dreams of glory. They were doing God's work.

So this was God's work, then, was it? Cutting down these diseased pus-bags?

She remembered leaving the cathedral, with all the musicians playing them down the steps. Dawn breaking over the buildings to the east, turning the sky a brilliant pinky-gray. How proud she'd felt . . .

And how quickly it had all gone wrong once they were over the Wall, chased by the Neph, running, getting split up. Half the group had gone back to St. Paul's, but Tish had pressed on with Louise and the others. And one by one they'd been picked off until, hoarse from shouting for help, they'd managed to get into the office building near the Tower, where Louise had been wounded.

Ed had killed Louise and saved Tish. He couldn't save her now, though. He was gone. Why go through with this pain anymore? She could lie down here, go to sleep, and wake in heaven. Maybe all that Matt had told her would come true. Maybe everything he had filled her head with was true.

She'd always had a strong faith. Since she was tiny she'd felt that there was a God up there watching over her. Smiling down. It was what had kept her going through the really bad times.

But Matt. He'd twisted everything. What he'd filled her head with was poison. If she really believed in what he said, then why was she here? Why wasn't she in the Temple with him and the other believers? Why had she deserted him?

Why was she here?

To show Matt. To show him he was wrong.

She prayed to God now. Not for herself. It was too late for that. But for Sam and the Kid.

For them to get safely away.

67

Ed's team had made it. Just. Fighting their way across the bridge. Couldn't have done it without Tish and Brendan holding the sickos off behind them. And now they were on the South Bank, looking back.

"Look at that," said Will, his voice full of wonder. In their desperation to get to the kids and follow the Green Man, the sickos were surging down to the embankment and were pouring over the side like a herd of wildebeest trying to cross a stream. They tumbled into the river, which was foaming white around the falling bodies.

"Yes!" Ed screeched. "Keep calling them, Wormwood. Bring them all on! Wipe them out. Drown the bastards."

The Green Man closed his eyes and concentrated.

The kids cheered, watched as the horde got washed away. They weren't home safe yet, though. Ed tore his eyes away from the spectacle, put a hand on Hayden's shoulder.

"We're going to split up," he said. "You head east. Make for the Tower. Go as fast as you can. Don't stop for anything.

You were always the fastest runner. You can do it. It's not far. Tell Jordan what went down tonight."

"What do you want me to tell him to do?" Hayden asked.

"Nobody tells Jordan Hordern what to do. He'll decide for himself. Just make sure he understands that if he wants to come over this way, he'll need to bring an army. And tell him once I've got Sam to his sister I'll rest up and head back."

"We need to get out of here," said Macca. "The green bastard's attracting every sicko in south London."

It was true. Sickos were advancing through the charred ruins of the South Bank, creeping out of the streets. Ed cursed.

"Go, Hayden. Run," he said.

"All right." Hayden gave Ed a quick hug, then set off, sprinting east along the riverside. Ed was amazed to think that the Tower was only about ten minutes away. A big part of him wanted to go with her, back to the safety of those high stone walls.

But he wasn't going to let Sam down again. He squatted next to the youngers. "Are you okay to run?"

They all nodded, glassy-eyed.

"Then let's go."

"What about Tish and Brendan?" said Will. Ed had forgotten about them. He looked up at the bridge. It was impossible to see what was happening at the far end.

"They'll just have to do the best they can," he said. "We'll draw the sickos away from here at least."

"Will they make it?" Macca asked.

"I hope so," Ed replied, and shut them out of his mind.

68

Tish was so tired she actually thought she might pass out. She felt like she'd been on this bridge for days. She could picture stopping and just switching off, letting everything roll over her. Not having to deal with this anymore.

In the darkness of the night her exhaustion was playing tricks on her mind, so that she couldn't tell what was real and what she was imagining. She kept seeing the faces of her friends, kept flinching as she thought she'd killed one of them.

Her mom, her sister, friends from the cathedral.

And then there was Louise, her guts hanging out of her belly, reaching to her and pleading for help. . . .

Except it wasn't her, was it? It was a Neph that she'd gutted.

Gutted . . .

How often had she used that word before?

I was, like, totally gutted when he didn't show up. . . .

But this is what *gutted* really meant. To spill your guts.

Don't lose your head now, Tish, she said to herself, her

mind dancing about. She and Brendan were backing slowly over the bridge, stumbling over fallen bodies. In front of them an endless press of Nephilim. As fast as they chopped one down, another took its place. She could see more of them below, scrambling over the embankment like rats and splashing into the Thames, washing away downriver.

So many.

She and Brendan were forced steadily back by the sheer weight of the oncoming sickos. They were already halfway across the bridge. She couldn't risk looking behind her, to see if the rest of the way was clear, to see if Ed's group had gotten away. She had to keep concentrating as her hands rose and fell, rose and fell, her sword cutting into the crowd of Neph.

There was Louise again, crawling toward her, her arm reaching out, although her hand was missing, her wrist a bloody stump.

Not Louise! Not Louise.

Think straight, Tish. She screamed and hacked away at the Neph.

"We should make a run for it," said Brendan. His voice sounded cracked and dry. "We've done what we had to."

"Okay," said Tish. "We just turn and run, okay?"

They gave it one more go, laying into the wall of Nephilim with a final ferocious onslaught, then Brendan yelled, "Go!" and they turned, and they ran. . . .

Straight into a group of Neph who had gotten onto the bridge at the other end.

In the confusion, unsure of which way to turn, teetering off balance, Brendan slipped in a mess of blood and spilled innards. He crashed into the side of the bridge, cried out in pain. The Neph were on him in an instant and Tish tried to haul him up, lowering her sword for a moment.

Only a moment, but long enough for both sets of Nephilim to close on the two of them, to pile on top of them. She could feel their warmth, their dampness, their grasping hands. And she felt a kind of peace.

Another pair of hands came down to gently wrap themselves around her.

God's hands.

She closed her eyes and let sleep take her as the moonlight was blotted out by the bodies of the grown-ups, mothers, fathers, teenagers. . . .

And out of the utter darkness came a light.

She had made her sacrifice.

69

Ed's crew was tramping down the Strand, past the Savoy Hotel, dragging their aching feet along, starting to really feel all their injuries. They hadn't come a great distance from St. Paul's, but the battle had seriously taken it out of them. Getting along the South Bank hadn't been nearly as easy as before. In calling to the sickos on the north bank, the Green Man had attracted every wandering grown-up in this part of London. The kids had had to fight their way along and had been forced back over to the north side of the river at Waterloo Bridge.

It had been a little easier after that. They'd managed to outrun the few sickos who tried to follow them across, and thankfully the streets were quieter over here. The Strand was wide and open. If they stuck to the middle, there was less chance of a surprise attack. All of Ed's senses were on the alert, all the survival skills he'd learned in the last year were being used. He couldn't allow himself to relax yet. They were making good progress, but it was still a fair way to the museum. They had to keep pushing on, even though he felt like he was dragging some huge dead weight behind him. The buildings on either side were incredibly tempting. The thought of lying down and going to sleep . . .

He didn't know this area, though. Didn't know where the dangers might be. Breaking into anywhere was a risk. The last thing he wanted right now was to disturb a nest of sickos.

Keep going. The museum meant safety. Rest. A bed.

They came to a building with a grand archway at the front held up by pink marble columns, and as they passed it Ed sensed a movement. His head snapped around. There was a courtyard beyond the archway and a mob of sickos was spilling out of it onto the pavement. They were getting bunched up in the entrance way and jostling each other, so that they came out in a confused pack, arms pinned to their bodies, swaying from side to side.

They reminded Ed of something.

And then it hit him. He laughed—a wild, crazy cackle that startled the other kids.

"What is it, boss?" Kyle turned to see what Ed was looking at.

"I'll take care of them," he said, slipping his red-stained ax off his shoulder.

"Leave them." Ed giggled. Kyle hesitated and the sickos came waddling into the road.

"What are you laughing at?" Kyle asked. "You finally lost it?"

"Probably. This has been one long day."

"But what's so funny?"

Kyle wasn't taking his eyes off the advancing sickos, although they were a sorry bunch and didn't look much of a threat.

"Look at them!" Ed waved a hand toward the sickos. "They look like bloody penguins. Off some nature program."

By now all the kids were watching the sickos who were packed together, bumping and bumbling about in the road. They really *did* look like penguins, and soon all the kids were laughing and jeering, and the sickos stopped, confused.

Then the Green Man stepped out of the ranks and walked over to them.

"Go back, brothers and sisters," he said. "Go back."

The sickos shuffled away, over the pavement, between the pillars, back into the courtyard. Ed stopped laughing. His sides were aching too much. He took a deep breath. He was shaking and light-headed.

He looked at the green furry shape of Wormwood, his sagging bony ass. He was glad the Kid had persuaded him to bring the weird sicko along. He'd had to argue twice with the others on the way here from the Wobbly Bridge. Kyle in particular had wanted to ditch the Green Man when it had become clear just what a magnet he was to other sickos. Ed had had to point out that without Wormwood they'd never have escaped from St. Paul's. He was useful, and Ed had a strong feeling that the Kid was right—Archie was right—he might become even more useful.

The Kid took hold of Wormwood's arm and pulled him along the road. "Come on, Wormy," he said. "Got to keep moving."

They all set off again, not running anymore but keeping up a fast walk. Ed fell in beside the Kid.

"You all right?" he asked.

"Been better, been worse, bean stew," said the Kid.

"If you say so."

"I do, I do, I do."

"What about him?" Ed nodded at the Green Man, who was mumbling and muttering to himself.

"Why don't you ask him yourself?"

"Wormwood?" Ed felt strange talking to a sicko. "You all right to keep going?"

"My head's buzzing," Wormwood moaned. "I can hear the fallen calling to me, their angel voices. Are they angels or are they insects? Hmm? Chirruping. It was quiet in my hole, but out here it's like being back in the big green; oh, you don't know how loud the jungle orchestra can be. *Click, click, bang, bang, zzzzip, zzzzzip.* The green is coming to the city. My fallen brothers are coming and I can hear them down the long pipeline; spreading out, they are, all around, like a spider's web. You know what I mean? And there's a great brother far away. He's strong, stronger maybe than me, and he wants to come closer. But that won't be tonight. He wants his swarm around him first. There are others, though, coming closer, running, chasing; they're so hungry and they've spoken to me through the pipeline; they've sent their love. Listen. They come closer."

"What d'you mean?" Ed was trying to make sense of the jumble of words that came tumbling out of the man. He turned to the Kid. "Do you understand what he's saying?"

"Not a clue."

"They're coming," said Wormwood. "My brothers."

"D'you mean there are more like you?" Ed asked. "Coming this way? Should we be careful?"

"We could find them. They're very hungry. They are chasing a fly. Fresh meat. God, I can almost smell it. They need it bad."

"A fly?"

"Meat on the move. Moving fast."

"You mean a child?"

"I mean dinner."

"There's sickos chasing someone, yeah?" Ed wished Wormwood would just talk straight. "How many? How many adults?"

"I don't know," said Wormwood, sounding very sorry for himself. "Leave me alone. Don't bug me."

"How many? Too many for us? I need to know."

Kyle had been listening to their bizarre conversation. Now he spoke up. "We're not doing any more good deeds tonight, boss."

"There's a kid, maybe more than one. Imagine if it was you, Kyle."

"I can look after myself, Ed," said Kyle. "Wouldn't expect anyone to help."

Ed ignored him, pressed Wormwood for more info. "How close?" he said.

"As close as the bug flies. The flapping of a butterfly's wing in Australia."

"What's that supposed to mean?"

"So long since I've seen the night," said Wormwood, looking up at the clearing sky, where the stars were beginning to show. "The clouds and all the houses and the life," he went on. "Too long. I'd love to go back to the big green. I had space there, all right. I had the whole world, the whole green world. I was king of the jungle."

"Tell me where these sickos are!" Ed was getting angry. "This kid they're chasing."

"We don't stop," said Kyle. "You can't risk any more of us getting hurt."

"No one else will get hurt," Ed snapped. "I promise."

"It's not really up to you, though, is it? If a thousand hungry sickos come around the corner, there ain't much you can do about it."

Ed stopped walking, took hold of the Green Man, and shook him by the shoulders. "How many adults?" he spat in his face. "How far?"

"Not many. Close."

"And how many kids?"

"One square meal."

"It's one kid," Kyle shouted. "Just one. Leave it, Ed. You can't save everyone. You can't rescue them all. You can't save the whole world."

"We have to do what we can."

"I know what this is about," said Kyle quietly, so that the others wouldn't hear.

"What?"

"Matt's kids, at the cathedral. You couldn't help them."

"It's not that. . . ."

"Adele. Gone."

"Kyle . . ."

"Tish and Bren. Leaving them on the bridge. Tish's

friend, Louise. Killing her that day. You're trying to make up for it. A life for a life. One kid lost, another one saved. But what if you lead us into a fight we can't win? Do you want to lose everything we won today?"

Ed said nothing. Kyle was smarter than he acted most of the time. Knew Ed better than anyone else. It wasn't just about the kids today, though. It was all of them. Everyone he'd lost. Malik, Aleisha, Bam . . .

And Jack.

This was mainly about Jack. It always was. He was always there, in the back of his mind. Ed knew he'd never see Greg again, the father who had killed his best friend, so any sicko would have to do.

And if it meant saving every kid in London to make him forget Jack, then he would.

"You don't have to come with me if you don't want to," he said to Kyle. "Stay with the others. Get them to the museum. I'll do it alone. But I'm going to help this kid— whoever it is."

Kyle sighed. Wiped his gory ax on his pants leg, then raised it and blew it a kiss before propping it back on his shoulder again. "No sleep for you tonight, Brain-biter," he said. "Lead on, boss."

Ed prodded the Green Man.

"Show us," he said.

70

They were coming down Regent Street toward Piccadilly Circus. At their head was a single boy, limping along, head drooping, eyes fixed on the road at his feet. He was dressed in gray camouflage, with some kind of cloak flapping around him. If Ed felt tired, this boy looked a hundred times worse. He could barely stand and was propping himself up with a long stick. He had a crossbow strapped to his back and a machete dangled from his free hand. Heavy as a packed suitcase. He didn't look like he'd have the strength to use either of his weapons. There were about ten sickos on his tail, barely twenty paces behind him, like a pack of wolves trailing a wounded deer. The alpha male appeared to be a father wearing a filthy business suit, a Bluetooth phone device stuck in his ear.

He was also carrying a machete.

Ed's crew took up position in the middle of the pedestrian area, with the statue of Eros to their left and a row of protective railings to their right.

Macca hadn't had the chance to use his own crossbow yet

today. The fighting had all been close up, hand to hand, and to use bolts would have been to waste them.

This was different. They had time. The numbers were right.

"Do it," Ed instructed him, and Macca loaded a bolt.

"He don't look like much," said Kyle. "He'd better be worth it."

Ed grunted. Where had he heard that before?

"Last one tonight," he said. "I promise."

Macca waited until the sickos were in range and fired off his bolt. One of the sickos went down. The limping boy looked up, amazed to see other kids. Life seemed to flow back into him. He scooted forward with fresh energy.

Ed called out to him. "This way! Get over here."

Macca had already fitted another bolt, and it whizzed past the boy as he hopped toward them. Another sicko went down.

"You're all right now, mate," said Kyle as the boy arrived, almost fell. Will caught him.

"Thank you," he croaked.

The rest of the sickos came on, too intent on their pursuit to stop. Too crazed with blood fever and hunger.

"Take it to them." Ed was already striding forward, mortuary sword at the ready. Kyle was right behind him. Macca let off a third shot and then dropped the bow and drew his own sword, went charging out with a cry. Will stayed behind, holding the boy up and keeping an eye on Wormwood and the three smaller kids.

It took less than a minute to deal with the sickos. Four of them were chopped down in the first assault, joining the three that Macca had already shot. A brief flurry of action and the only sicko left standing was the father with the Bluetooth, his pack lying dead around him.

He was holding his machete up, ready to take the kids on, and they held back, wary of the blade in his hand. Ed wondered again at how the sickos were relearning all their human skills. The father looked dangerous. None of the kids wanted to risk getting too close.

"That one's mine." With Will's help, the boy had come over. He limped up to the father, who raised the machete in readiness, but the boy was in no mood for a sword fight. He swatted the blade to the side with his stick, then swiped his own machete cleanly across the father's throat. The father made an obscene sucking, gurgling noise, like a bath empty-ing, and fell backward.

"Nicely done," said Kyle, and he whistled.

But the boy hadn't finished. He stood over the father's body and began chopping at his neck until his head came off.

"That's for Jaz," he said. Then he knelt down in the road and wept.

71

The last ragged tatters of the storm were flickering in the sky, way off to the east, out over the Thames estuary. Above the Tower of London the clouds were breaking up and the stars were bright behind them.

Jordan Hordern was standing on the top of Byward Tower, leaning on the battlements and looking out over the rain-soaked buildings toward St. Paul's. Before the storm had gotten too fierce he'd been up here, watching the sickos as they streamed past, heading west. The streets had been full of them. From this distance, with his failing eyesight, they'd just been dark shapes. Now that the rain had stopped, he'd come back up here. He liked to be alone in the night.

And it was here that Tomoki had found him when Hayden returned. She'd told Jordan and Tomoki everything that had happened, and Jordan had listened with interest. He was glad that Ed hadn't been killed. He needed soldiers like Ed.

Now she'd finished speaking and Tomoki had gone. He was aware that Hayden was waiting for him to say something.

She was shuffling uncomfortably. He did that to people—made them uncomfortable. Always had. Didn't really know what he could do about it.

The stars were simple. They were always the same. You always knew where they'd be, could track them across the sky. He liked the stars. People were complicated, though. It would have been much easier if they were all toy soldiers with painted-on expressions—the same every time.

"We'll do nothing tonight," he said.

"You sure?" said Hayden.

"Too dangerous."

"Yeah."

Jordan didn't look at Hayden. He found it easier not to look at people when he was talking to them. He could concentrate on what they were saying. The way his eyes were now he couldn't see much anyway.

"D'you think Matt will survive until the morning?" he asked.

"Depends," said Hayden. "I think they got the cathedral doors shut, but who knows how many sickos were already inside. And there was a million of them outside."

"A million?" Jordan needed facts to be exact.

"No, not a million, but you know what I mean."

"No."

"There were a lot," said Hayden. "Too many to count. The kids'll be under siege in the cathedral. I mean, they've got fighters. . . ." Hayden tailed off. She was covered in blood. Needed to clean up and sleep. Jordan would let her go soon.

Not yet, though.

"This sicko you rescued?" he asked.

"Yeah?"

"Tell me about him."

"I can't tell you much. It was all really weird. Matt's kids called him Wormwood or the Green Man. He seemed to have some sort of control over the other sickos."

"You think that's where they were all going earlier? To this Wormwood?"

"Could be," said Hayden. "As I say, the ones on the streets, the pointers, looked like they were signaling to each other somehow."

"Things are changing."

"D'you know what you'll do in the morning?" Hayden sounded very tired.

"I'll get together an army and we'll march over there and sort it out. Crush any sickos that might be left. Drive the rest of them into the river."

"And what about Matt?"

"He's not my business. My business is to get rid of the no-go zone. We make all the streets safe between here and the cathedral and then keep on, into town, right up to the Houses of Parliament. I've got no beef with Matt. He can stay in charge for all I care."

"What about all the food he's got? All the stuff in that warehouse?"

"It's his. I ain't no thief. I ain't gonna go in and jack his stash. That being said, I might just tax him a little for my hard work. I'll do a deal with him. We protect him, he gives us a few groceries. If he don't want to play ball, then we'll see about slapping him down. But he's more use to us keeping a lid on things. We need kids there, Hayden. We need safe places all through London. Like that girl Nicola you was telling me about. Things is opening up. We got to go with it."

"He's got so much stuff in there, Jordan. You should've seen it."

"I will see it," said Jordan. "Thing is, though, we start in on that, we might go soft. We got to keep on scavenging, keep on trying to grow stuff, training to fight. We got to build for the future, not live on the scraps that the grownups left us."

"But he's got some good stuff there," said Hayden.

Jordan straightened up. "Don't worry, Hayden," he said, making ready to go back down. "We gonna taste some of that sweet stuff, no doubt about it. Now get some sleep. We gonna be busy in the morning."

72

Nicola was getting ready for bed. She had her own room in the Palace of Westminster. It wasn't like they were short of space, after all. The place was huge. There were loads of rooms here she'd never even been in.

Her room wasn't all that big. She didn't need much. There was a closet for her clothes, a bookcase for her books, a bed beside a low table where a candle burned. It was dry in here. Safe. It got freezing cold in the depths of winter, as they had no heating, but that was the same everywhere.

Wasn't too bad tonight.

She was standing at her mirror, brushing her long red hair and thinking of the boy who had come earlier. Ed, with his armor and his scar. She wondered if she'd ever see him again. It had been an unusual day, to say the least, what with all the oppoes out on the streets. Even Ryan and his hunters had been freaked out by it all, and normally nothing fazed them. She'd stayed up late, talking to some of her Cabinet about it. Going over the day's events.

Things were changing, that was for sure. She couldn't

fight it and she knew they couldn't live in this false bubble they'd created forever. Playing at adults, taking votes, passing laws, and hardly ever leaving the grounds. Sooner or later the kids had to stop hiding from the grown-ups. Take London back. Start to live normal lives.

And if they were going to survive they'd have to start having children of their own. One of the girls here was pregnant. And she was terrified. Everyone was. How were they going to deliver a baby, for God's sake? Would the girl survive? Would the baby survive?

Nicola laughed. It was crazy. People had been having babies for thousands of years, hadn't they? It couldn't be that hard. Mice did it. Flies did it. Monkeys did it. But she'd read enough books to know that in the past having children was dangerous. There were a lot of things that could go wrong. Without doctors. Without medicine. Without somebody who knew what they were doing.

Sooner or later Nicola would have to find a boyfriend, settle down with him, decide to have children, take that scary plunge.

In a way, life after the disease had been a big game. You didn't have to worry about all the old problems anymore. But she knew they couldn't go on like this forever.

Change was coming.

Real life was returning.

And she was thinking of Ed. He'd seemed intelligent and decent, certainly knew how to look after himself.

She laughed again. No point in having silly schoolgirl fantasies about him. He might be dead now for all she knew. Hadn't he gone back into the badlands?

There was always David, over at Buckingham Palace. She knew full well that he was obsessed by her. David was a catch, as her mom used to say. He was powerful, in charge of all those kids. But she didn't have the slightest interest in him on that level. Couldn't force herself to fancy him. Had no desire to link up and be like a queen from the Middle Ages, marrying some king just to make a strong alliance.

The thought of kissing David . . .

She made a face in the mirror. Pretended to gag.

But Ed . . .

Well, Ed had a weird face with that scar; somehow, though, it didn't bother her. She'd never gone for the boring pretty boys, had always been attracted to the outsiders, the ones who were different. The ones her mother didn't like.

She got into bed, flinching at the coldness of the sheets, and kicked her legs to warm them up. She blew out her candle. Lay there in the dark.

Wondered once more if she would ever see Ed again.

73

Ryan cursed as his dog shifted in her sleep and her legs twitched, scrabbling at the floor.

"Be still," he growled, and slapped her. He was having trouble sleeping tonight. He had trouble sleeping most nights.

He and his hunters and their dogs were all piled on top of each other on the floor of a big old house near Victoria station. The hunters lived alongside their dogs. The dogs kept them warm and safe.

They never stayed anywhere long. Didn't want any wandering grown-ups to get their scent. Plus, the buildings got pretty filthy. They never did any cleaning and just left garbage where it dropped. The dogs always picked a room to use as a toilet, and in a few days the place would be stinking worse than a grown-ups' nest. So they'd move on, break into somewhere else.

Why not? There was no shortage of empty buildings, was there?

On the whole they had a good life. Getting food and anything else they needed off the more settled kids in exchange for helping them out. Plus, there was always stuff to be found on the streets.

And Ryan was king of the streets around here. He could walk proud and free wherever he wanted.

He was respected.

But at night, when it was dark, with them all huddled together, mixed up with the dogs, living like animals, he felt very lonely. He could never tell anyone. He was Ryan Aherne, the meanest bastard in London, with a mask made out of a dead father's face and a string of trophy ears hanging from his belt.

He missed his mom and his dad, though.

He lay there on his back and pictured how it had once been. Sitting at his computer, using Facebook, drinking Coke, watching horror DVDs with his dad, eating his mom's food, and chatting about stuff.

He'd sometimes pretend that he was back in his old bed. In his old room with all his things. If he closed his eyes tight, he could remember exactly where everything had been, how it looked. His TV, his posters, his DVDs and computer games, his weights, his soccer trophies.

His mom and dad sleeping next door.

Sometimes, like tonight, he let himself cry.

And it helped a little bit.

74

"What are they doing?"

"I don't know."

"Are they all right?"

"I don't know, David. How am I supposed to know? I mean, they've never done this before, yeah?"

"I'll say it again. Are they all right, Pod?"

"Well, er, no, they're not all right, are they? They're grown-ups. They're sick. They've never been all right."

"You know what I mean, Pod."

David was with his head of security in the royal bedroom at Buckingham Palace. They called the room that, not because it had been where the queen had slept, but because it was where they now kept what was left of the royal family. The six men and women were in various stages of decay. They smelled awful. David had tried to house-train them, but they still went to the toilet whenever and wherever they wanted.

"They're still alive," said Pod. "They just stand there, though, not moving."

David raised his candle and let its light fall on the strangers' faces. Normally they would have backed away, shielding their eyes. Tonight they didn't react at all. Just stood there with their heads tilted back, their arms held stiffly in front of them. Still as a bunch of royal waxworks at Madame Tussaud's.

"How long have they been like this?"

"Not too sure, mate. One of the guards looked in on them sometime late this afternoon. Saw them like this, yeah? And when he came back an hour later, they hadn't moved. They haven't moved for ages now."

"Get someone to stay in here with them," said David. "Let me know if anything changes. They are important to my plans. I really don't want them to die on me."

"I'll put two of my best guys on it."

"I'm going to bed," said David. "I just hope tomorrow's a better day."

"God, yeah, it's been, like, *well* weird today," said Pod. "With all those strangers mooching about. One stood over the road by the statue of Queen Victoria in exactly the same position as this all day. Even right through the thunderstorm, yeah? She's still out there now, I think. Something's going on, all right."

"Yeah." David pinched the bridge of his nose. He felt a headache coming on. "Listen, Pod," he said, "if there's still a stranger doing a clothes-shop-dummy impersonation outside the gates in the morning, do me a favor, will you? Go out there and kill it for me, will you? Yeah? I mean *you* personally. See to it for me."

"Okay, yeah, sure, no problemo."

"I just want everything to be back to normal," David said angrily.

"Normal. Yeah. No worries."

David yawned and gave a final cold look at the bloody royal family. Why did things have to change? Why couldn't everyone just do what he told them?

Why couldn't things be normal?

75

Shadowman had never brought anyone here before. It was his secret place. His safe house.

"I only use it in emergencies," he explained to the kids who had rescued him.

"It's really cool, Dylan." The big bony-headed boy with the vicious ax was nodding appreciatively. When they'd asked him, Shadowman had told them his real name, Dylan Peake, too tired to lie anymore. He'd let all his defenses down and now here they were. In his base.

"Is this where you were headed when we found you?" asked Ed, their leader, who was horribly disfigured with a scar down one side of his face. He'd been stained black from head to foot with blood when they'd met. But now they'd washed and changed into some clean clothes that Shadowman had dug out for them. Mostly stuff he'd found there when he'd broken in.

"I wasn't really headed *to* anywhere," said Shadowman. "I was headed *from*. Just trying to, you know, get away. Too knackered to think straight. Those bastards had been chasing me for miles. All the way from Kilburn."

"Kilburn?" said the bony-headed boy.

"Yeah," said Shadowman. "It's crazy, I know. They wouldn't give up. Wouldn't stop. As many as I killed, more joined them. I couldn't risk trying to get in anywhere to hide. At night. In the dark. Could have been strangers hiding in any of the buildings."

"Strangers?" Ed asked.

"Grown-ups."

"Sickos."

"Sickos?" Shadowman smiled. "Yeah, sickos. I like that." He felt the smile dying on his face. "They've changed," he said. "They're acting . . ."

"I know, we've seen it," said Ed. "They're acting more intelligent."

"They're not acting, though, are they?" said Shadowman. "They *are* more intelligent." And he started to tell Ed all about Saint George and his army. Their organization, their purpose. They swapped notes on the sentinels, or pointers, as Ed called them. And Ed told him a little about the green stranger they had in tow. Shadowman felt like he was on the verge of understanding something. Like this was all going to make sense to him. If only he wasn't so tired. Aching all over.

"Sickos . . ." Ed settled back in his chair and wriggled his toes. "We're going to have to deal with them one day. But right here, right now, let's forget all about them for a time, yeah?"

"Yeah." Shadowman closed his eyes for a moment and enjoyed the feeling of peace.

Forget about the strangers.

Forget. Everything.

76

Ed's socks had holes in them and they stank, but it felt good to have his shoes off and his feet warming by a fire. He'd smash into a shop tomorrow and get a fresh pair.

Dylan had this place nicely set up. It was an upstairs private members' club in a narrow backstreet near Trafalgar Square, all leather sofas, carved wood, bearskin rugs, and oil paintings. A fire burning in the fireplace. It had more security than the Bank of England and was well stocked with food, water, and weapons. Dylan was sharing. Ed understood how hard that must be for him. This was his crib. A hideout like this could mean the difference between surviving and dying. He must have been very happy the day he found it. It hadn't been wrecked or looted. It was a fortress.

It was safe.

They were safe. Ed's strange little gang had made it here in one piece.

Kyle was drinking warm beer, warming his ass by the fire, a bright green bowler hat perched on his head. Must have belonged to a doorman at the club or something. Macca and Will were playing cards. Small Sam, Charlotte, and the Kid were chatting away madly by themselves on a huge sofa. Catching up.

And then there was Wormwood, the Green Man, wrapped in an old tartan blanket, sitting stiff-backed in an armchair, his hands in his lap, his eyes glinting in the candlelight.

His smell battled with the smell of Ed's socks.

It was mad. To be sitting this close to a grown-up. Especially one covered in fungus. A mad end to a mad day. Ed had explained to Dylan who Wormwood was—what he was—and Dylan had gone along with it. Had seemed to get it. Seemed to understand sickos. Wasn't too uncomfortable about having one sitting in his chair.

"So you reckon he might be useful?" Dylan asked him.

"Reckon so. He knows stuff, if we can only make sense of it. Plus, like I said, he's got this power over the other sickos. Some kind of mind-control thing. Telepathy."

"You really think so?" asked Dylan. "You really think they're communicating just with their minds somehow?"

"What d'you think?"

"I don't know." Dylan shrugged, and shook his head.

Ed leaned closer to him. "Seems to me," he said quietly, "that the disease has given them a whole new sense."

"That's not possible." Will got up from the sofa and came over to the fire.

"We all saw it," Ed protested. "You said yourself that the pointers looked like they were acting like antennae or something, spreading the word. And the way Wormwood made them hold back, and—"

"I know," said Will, cutting him off. "That's not what I meant. What I meant was it's not possible for humans to suddenly develop superpowers like in a comic. We can't change. We're what we are. We couldn't suddenly start flying or walking through walls. It doesn't work like that."

"Then how come they all seem to know what to do without talking to each other?" said Dylan.

"I don't know," said Will. "All I know is that people can't change what they are. It's not scientifically possible. But if something got into them . . ."

"Something like what?"

"As I say, I don't know. Something from outside. Something else that could communicate like that."

"Like a parasite?"

"Yeah, maybe."

Ed sighed. "Man, that's too much to think about right now," he said. "When my brain doesn't hurt so much, we're going to have to have a proper talk with Wormwood. See what he can tell us."

"It's going to be difficult dragging him around with you, though," said Dylan.

"Yeah. I don't suppose every other kid in London's going to be as understanding as you."

"No. I don't suppose they are."

"Ed?"

Ed looked up to see Sam and the Kid standing by his chair. Sam looked anxious.

"You all right, small stuff?"

"Are we staying here tonight?"

"If that's okay with Dylan. I don't think I could walk

another step, and *you* look like one of the walking dead, if you really want to know."

It was true. Sam's eyes were sunk in black pools, his lips cracked and dry. "It's just that I want to find my sister."

Ed pulled Sam close. "We'll find her, mate. We will. We've come this far, haven't we? The hard part's over. But I'm not wandering around out there anymore tonight. I'll go with Kyle in the morning. We'll see how safe it is. When we're sure it's okay, we'll head over to the Natural History Museum. That's where we reckon Ella is."

"We can't go out in the midday sun," said the Kid. "Not with all the mad dogs and Englishmen."

"What do you mean?"

The Kid nodded at Wormwood. "He don't like the bright light and the big city. We can only move him under cover of darkness."

"Jesus, Kid, everything's ten times more dangerous at night."

"I know."

"And besides, we can't just show up somewhere with a great green sicko. 'Hiya, guys, meet Shrek.' We've got to be careful about this."

"That's why we need to spend tomorrow planning," said Kyle, and he let rip with a beery belch. He went over to Wormwood. He'd only downed two bottles, but he looked drunk. "Hey, sickbag," he said. "You gonna play the game?"

Wormwood just stared at him. Hadn't said a word since they'd arrived.

"Or are you gonna be trouble?"

"He won't give you any trouble," said the Kid.

"He better not. But listen to me, Green Man. If we have to move you in daylight, we will, you get me? No argument. You can keep that blanket over your head if you want, but you do as we say."

"I'm not a fan of the sunlight," said Wormwood. "But I will behave."

Kyle leaned close to him. "You ain't gonna try and eat any of us in the night?"

"We'll take turns keeping watch," Ed said. "Two of us at a time."

"Ed—"

Ed cut Sam off, trying not to get angry. "Listen, Sam. We've gone out on a limb for you, okay? All this is for you. We'll find your sister. Don't fret. We'll find her. One more night won't make any difference."

Sam's face crumpled and he began to cry. "What if she's dead?"

Ed held him. "Everything's going to be all right, little man," he said. "This is all going to be over soon."

Dylan stood up. Ed could see the pain in his face as he put weight on his bad leg.

"You know what?" he said. "I think I've got some candy somewhere. Let me see if I can find it."

"Yeah," said Kyle, shoving his beer bottle into Wormwood's hands and his bowler hat onto his head. "Let's have a party!"

Sam began to laugh. Wormwood looked so ridiculous and surprised.

The Kid joined in, then Ed and Dylan, and soon they were all laughing. And, just for that moment, everything did seem to be all right.

77

Saint George finished the piece of meat he'd been chewing on. Seemed like he'd been chewing on it all his life. He swallowed the lump. Felt it struggle down his throat into his burning stomach. The meat had tasted good. Always did. Filled him up with light.

All around was his army. They'd come to him. So many now, their strength flowed into him. They were one beating heart. And each thump shook the darkness from his brain. Let more light in.

They were all him and he was all them. One single mind, spreading out all around. He was spreading, eating the world. It was all his. He was making some sense of it. Chewing it over, like the meat.

It was like this.

There was him. There were two of him and there were thousands of him, millions. . . .

Did that make sense?

He'd been here a long time. He understood that now. He was a sort of god, wasn't he? Fallen from the stars. Fallen into all that green. He'd lived for all time in the jungle. Why had he forgotten that? The memories were all there inside him.

He'd been king of that world and now he would be king of this one. All he had to do was destroy the last of them. The young ones. They were the only thing that could stop him. With them gone, the world would be his.

Oh, but they tasted good. Nothing tasted better. When he'd been a butcher . . .

When was that, then? Was that before or after he'd lived in the jungle? It was confusing. He remembered his boy. His Liam. Some other boys had done something to him. Taken him away.

Something like that.

Something.

It was confusing, all right.

He'd been a butcher and he'd loved his Liam. Liam had been different. Wouldn't never have done anything to hurt Liam. The other ones, they were just . . . meat. And he knew all about meat. He was a butcher.

He snarled and pressed his hands tightly on either side of his head. Felt an itch. His eye throbbed. He rubbed it. Something came out. He felt with his fat fingertips. There was a tiny lump, trapped under his lower eyelid. He picked at it. Looked at his finger, at the thing wriggling there, gray and shiny, like a maggot. He squeezed his eye and more wrigglers came out from the corner. He licked his fingers.

Where was he?

He wanted to get this straight.

Take it slowly. It was painful. All these thoughts and

memories coming back to him after so long. Like bubbles rising in a pint of beer. He had to get strong, and clever, so that he could do what had to be done. He could sense them there, the young ones, warm and soft. He would march on them when he was ready.

Far, far away he could hear his brothers singing. A great many of them. They were getting closer. At times in the night he'd hear it very strong. One voice louder than all the others. One clear voice. Calling out.

Wasn't sure about that one. Might need to have words.

Because he was the boss, wasn't he? And his people . . . they were a swarm of flies. That was it. Insects. With angel wings. They were locusts. And they would swarm. Like before.

When they were ready.

When all was ready.

When he was too strong to be beaten.

He smiled, and in the darkness three hundred other grown-ups smiled with him.

ABOUT THE AUTHOR

Charlie Higson is an acclaimed writer of screenplays and novels, and is also a performer and the co-creator of the British television programs *The Fast Show* and *Bellamy's People*. He is the author of the internationally best-selling Young Bond series: *SilverFin*, *Blood Fever*, *Double or Die*, *Hurricane Gold*, and *By Royal Command*, and *SilverFin: The Graphic Novel*; and four books in the Enemy series. Charlie, a big fan of horror movies, is hoping to give readers many sleepless nights with this series.